"This is such a powerful narrative of a compelling journey. Kristy Shelton artistically writes this piece, inviting the reader into an exploration of faith within the context of immense challenge. Prepare to read a book, yet live a story."

—Dr. Orpheus J Heyward, Pastor of the Renaissance Church

"*Blind Faith* is the result of masterful storytelling. Kristy expertly weaves the tragedies and triumphs of characters—who you will want to jump through the page to meet—through a story that begs you to turn the page. This is so much more than a tale that takes place on a plantation. Several times I laughed, teared up, or shared anger with the characters. I couldn't wait to get to the next chapter. With great accuracy, this is historical fiction at its finest."

—Darya Crockett, Editor, Coastal Editing

"*Blind Faith* is a compelling story of two generations that draws the reader into an intricate view of the early lives of Franklin and Rachel Hawkins, whom we met in *Blinders*. Each line kept me eager to see what would happen next—from tears, to laughter, to anguish, and to celebration. Kristy's storyline and character views immerse the reader into the family—of which I thought I was a part."

—Dr. Linda Byrd, Teacher, Greater Atlanta Christian School

3
THE BLINDERS TRILOGY

KRISTY SHELTON

innovo
PUBLISHING

Published by Innovo Publishing, LLC
www.innovopublishing.com
1-888-546-2111

Providing Full-Service Publishing Services for Christian Authors, Artists & Ministries: Books, eBooks, Audiobooks, Music, Screenplays, Film & Curricula

BLIND FAITH
The Prequel to *Blinders*

The Blinders Trilogy
Volume 3

Library of Congress Control Number: 2022935835
ISBN: 978-1-61314-820-4

Cover Design & Interior Layout: Innovo Publishing, LLC

Printed in the United States of America
U.S. Printing History
First Edition: 2022

Has God called you to create a Christian book, eBook, audiobook, music album, screenplay, film, or curricula? If so, visit the ChristianPublishingPortal.com to learn how to accomplish your calling with excellence. Learn to do everything yourself, or hire trusted Christian Experts from our Marketplace to help.

This book is lovingly dedicated to my parents, Kent and Norma Rollmann.
Thank you for always believing in me!

Kentucky 1855

R uth gasped and pressed trembling hands to her chest. She willed her heart to stay within its dwelling place. One more step could mean the death of her precious son. She stood stock-still, trusting his fate to the One above.

"Lawd," she breathed. "Still your mighty creature."

Three-year-old Franklin walked fearlessly beneath the massive stallion, his tiny hand trailing above his head along the beast's black belly. Ruth watched in horror as he moved forward and stood between the horse's powerful forelegs.

Franklin paused between the two legs, placing one hand on each limb as if he were Sampson standing between the two pillars in the Philistine temple.

Ruth held her breath and her ground. She couldn't bear to lose yet another child. Four of her offspring lay in the earth not a hundred yards to the south of where she stood. *Please, Lawd. O, please.*

She heard her son giggle as he stroked the powerful legs of the stallion. For precious long seconds, Ruth watched from her position in the stable doorway, and when the beast's head dropped toward Franklin's, a scream came forth before she could yank it back.

With wild eyes, the stallion threw his head and stomped his front hoof, narrowly missing Franklin's tiny bare foot. The boy's eyes, however, remained placid as he reached both arms around the foreleg that had just been perilously raised above his head.

The stallion craned his neck to get a better look at the woman standing nearby. Ruth could see the white of his eye. She had frightened him, but not as much as he was frightening her.

"Franklin," she whispered. "Come to me right now."

Franklin didn't move until the stallion's muzzle connected with the top of his head. Another soft chuckle reached Ruth's ears, and the boy curved his face directly upward and into the horse's lips. The beast's lower lip dropped open, and Franklin slowly turned to face him, placing both of his hands inside the sagging lip.

Ruth couldn't take it any longer. She closed her eyes, forcing the warm tears down her brown cheeks. *O, Lawd, have mercy.* She would not watch any more of—

Something brushed past her skirt, and Ruth opened her eyes. Franklin was walking down the dirt road that led home. With one malevolent gaze toward the stallion, she turned on her heels and ran to her son. Ruth snatched him by the arm and tugged him to a weeping willow tree on the banks of a nearby creek. Fear turning to ire, she yanked the nearest branch from the tree, applying the stinging whip to the back of Franklin's little legs. He yelped like a dog being kicked, and a little stream of tears leaked from his eyes.

"You will never…ever do that again," she hissed vehemently. "Ever. You hear me, baby child?"

Little Franklin squirmed, trying to release himself from his mother's firm grasp. But he was no match for Ruth, especially when she was angry and scared.

It wasn't until little welts began to form on the boy's bare legs that she threw the switch into the weeds and dragged him back onto the road.

"Did you hear me, little man? You is not to go back in that barn without your pappy. *EVER!*"

The boy looked up at his mama, moisture glistening in his eyes, and meekly nodded. His little legs were working as fast as they could to keep up with her anxious strides.

"I mean it," she said, turning her eyes toward their cabin now within sight.

By the time mother and son reached their porch, Ruth led him up the two steps and finally let go of his hand. Her heart had slowed down from its storming pace, and the pounding thrum on her temples had tapered off a bit. Still, she paced back and forth for a moment in the late August sun until she knew she could speak to him in a calm voice.

Franklin stood still, never once touching the backs of his legs. Ruth knew they must be stinging something fierce. She hoped it would be a lesson he wouldn't soon forget. But anger had now given way to shame. Never had her hands been used to harm one of her children.

Moving into the shade of the porch, Ruth sat down in her corn-shucking chair. "Come 'ere, baby," she breathed, opening her arms wide.

Without hesitation, Franklin moved into his mama's tender arms. She enfolded him close to her breast, then gently pulled him into her lap.

Bending her mouth to his ear, she whispered, "You's so important to me and yer pappy. We don't wanna lose you." Her lips caressed his cheek before resting her head on top of his. Finally, she reached around him for an ear of corn and went back to work.

When Isaiah returned home an hour later, Ruth was still in the chair, humming and shucking one golden ear after another. Four baskets were full to the brim, and Franklin was sound asleep in her arms.

"Here now," Isaiah whispered, "let me take 'em from ya."

Her husband bent low, brushing a light kiss onto her lips while lifting their only son out of her arms. A squeal rose up from Franklin's throat as Isaiah straightened to his full height.

"Wus a matter, little un?" he asked. "You gots a pain or somethin'?"

Ruth bent her head in utter shame. She didn't even want to make eye contact with her man.

Sitting down on the top step, Isaiah set Franklin on his thigh, then turned to lean against one of the rough beams of their front porch. "Ruthie, is he taken sickly?"

All she could do was shake her head, but by doing so, a stream of tears rushed from her soft brown eyes.

"Tell me, gal," he whispered.

When Isaiah reached out and tugged lightly on his wife's skirt, Ruth turned her gaze upward. "Look at the back of his legs."

Isaiah held his son high, facing him toward his mammy. For a long, breathless moment, he stared at the welts on Franklin's legs. "Who done such a thing, Ruth?"

Isaiah was suddenly on his feet, pulling their son tight to his chest. "Who done it?"

It was rare to see such a wild look in her husband's eyes. He was a man not easily riled. That's why he was so successful in their master's stables. He trained all of Samuel Hawkins' thoroughbreds with a gentle hand and quiet voice. But there was nothing gentle about the fiery glint in his accusing stare.

"Sit back down, Izzy…please."

"I ain't sittin' down till you tell me who done this!"

Ruth looked away from his gaze, feeling the heat creep up her neck and into her face. "It was me."

Her voice was so quiet, Isaiah leaned in. "Who?"

In an anguished voice, she cried out, "I done it."

Isaiah's eyes grew wide, shifting from rage to disbelief. For several heartbeats, he stared into Ruth's eyes, his lips parting, but no words coming forth. She watched him turn away and walk a wide circle in front of their cabin. A dust cloud formed around his boots while Isaiah hugged his son close, mumbling words of comfort with every stride. She had never felt so helpless to explain herself in all her days—there simply was no excuse for what she'd done.

After what seemed like an eternity, Isaiah paced slowly back to the shade of their porch. His voice was low and full of emotion. "Gal, you know how I feel about puttin' a beatin' on one o' our own. We's been blessed by a kind massa—t'ain't ever had him lay a hand on a single one o' us. So by the name of the Lawd in heaven above, we ain't gonna be doin' it ourselfs."

While Ruth had acted out of sheer panic, she knew what she'd done was wrong. She'd broken the promise that the two of them had made on the day their first child, Sarah, was born seventeen years ago.

Ruth herself had been raised on a separate plantation where unspeakable acts of violence and horror had been committed against her and her fellow slaves. Her papa had not only borne the scars on his back and arms to prove it but had been cruelly hanged for reasons she had never known. Ruth thanked the Lord every single day that Joseph Hawkins, the current master's father, had purchased her from her previous owner in South Georgia on the very day she'd turned fourteen. While she'd been appallingly humiliated on the auction block and separated from her brothers and sisters, coming to the Hawkins Plantation had brought Isaiah into her life. While they dreamed of sweet freedom with every breath, at least they served under a more benevolent master than most. How could she have laid a hand on her own son when she had been shown such extraordinary mercy?

One sob after another wracked Ruth's body. She dropped roughly to her knees on the splintery wood, doubling over in grief. "I's so sorry, Izzy," she bawled, over and over again.

Isaiah set his son down on the porch and knelt beside his wife, lines of agony creasing his forehead. "It's all right, gal, come on," he whispered, pulling her to her feet. Noticing Eula gawking from her cabin porch next door, he added, "Les go inside and talk 'bout it, you and me."

When he finally got her inside their one-room cabin, Isaiah lowered her to the side of the bed, where she continued weeping into her hands. Little Franklin stood in the open doorway, taking in the scene.

"Come 'ere, Son," Isaiah beckoned. Taking a clean cloth, he dipped it in the water bucket on the table and sat down in the straight-back chair. He gently touched it to the switch marks on the boy's little legs. Franklin fidgeted between his daddy's knees until the task was done and he was released. Instantly, he went to his mama, crawling up on the bed beside her.

For the next several minutes, Ruth found a way to describe what she'd seen in the stables earlier that afternoon. Shaking her head slowly, she told her husband, "I can't watch another one o' our chillins die—I just can't. My heart can't take it no more."

Isaiah dropped the wet cloth on the table and rested his strong hands on his knees. Eyes full of compassion, he said, "Ruthie, gal, ain't none of us knows what's gonna happen t'morrow—why, we don't even know whether we's gonna be breathin' in the next hour. But we's not the ones in charge, sweet gal. Not even Massa Hawkins be in charge, even if he thinks he is. Our true Massa, the maker of heaven an' earth, is the only one that knows. He's got our sweet babes in the most gentlest arms—jus lovin' and kissin' on 'em, and tellin' 'em how special they is. Why, they's as happy as can be, and you and me is gonna see 'em again someday."

He reached out and patted his son's little head. "We's gonna trust the Lawd either way, Ruthie. This world ain't our home—never wuz."

Fresh tears sprang to Ruth's eyes as her husband's tender words pierced her heart. She'd been in desperate need of encouragement ever since her thoughtless deed.

"Now, Ruthie, get yer face washed up. You been called to the big house by the missus."

Wiping the last remnant of tears from her cheeks, Ruth leapt to her feet. "For heaven's sake, what do the missus want?"

Slapping his hands on the top of his thighs, Isaiah stood up and reached for Franklin's hand. "Not fer me to know. Alls I was told was to fetch my perty wife. Come on, little man, we's goin' to the stables."

Ruth had to swallow the sudden fear that wrenched her heart. She didn't want her son going anywhere near those stables—not after what she'd witnessed this afternoon. But deep down, she knew why that powerful animal had not trampled her boy. The Lord had seen fit to give him the same talent as he had given Isaiah. There was an otherworldly connection between Isaiah and horses that couldn't be taught. It was a gift that had been passed on to their son through the generations.

Still, she couldn't help herself. "You keep an eye on him, Izzy. You hear me?"

Isaiah chuckled as the two headed out the door and down the road.

Chapter 2

With determined focus, Ruth propelled herself down the path to the back porch of the massive white plantation house. Just outside the steps, three washerwomen were mournfully singing, "Sometimes I feel like a motherless child—sometimes I feel like a motherless child—sometimes I feel like a motherless child—Lawd, Lawd, I know my time ain't long."

Acknowledging the hard-working women with a wave, she climbed up the stairs to the indoor section of the spacious kitchen. The brick cookhouse was through the back door of the pantry and down a short flight of stairs.

"Whatchu in such a hurry fer?" one of the kitchen maids called as Ruth sped through. "There a fire somewheres?"

All the women giggled as Ruth waved off their questions. "I been called to see Missus Elizabeth, that's what fer."

"Well, get yerself over here. You can't go lookin' like that, girl."

Ruth didn't bother to slow her harried pace. She didn't want to keep the mistress waiting, especially since so much time had gone by while she'd cried over little Franklin. Just the thought of what she'd done this afternoon made her face flush with shame. Even so, she smoothed her skirt and blouse while heading down the broad hallway to the front of the house.

Little Ella was just coming down the stairs with an armload of laundry to take to her mama out back. She smiled a toothy grin at Ruth. "Da Missus be waitin' in her sittin' room upstairs."

Ruth touched the top of the girl's head as they passed. "Thank you, child."

"But mammy—"

Ruth cut the girl off, ignoring her wide-eyed stare. "Not now, young'un. Not now."

Before knocking on the door to the sitting room, Ruth prayed her eyes had lost their puffiness. Pressing her skirt one more time, she rapped her knuckles lightly on the rich mahogany door.

Surprisingly, Naomi, the plantation's talented seamstress, opened the door to what appeared to have been a fitting session. Draped across Naomi's arm was one of the most beautiful emerald satin gowns she'd ever seen.

Ruth had never known a more gifted seamstress than Naomi. Her handiwork was simply gorgeous, mirroring the young woman herself. Naomi turned heads wherever she went on the plantation. Every man in slave town wanted to be *with* her and every woman wanted to be *like* her. But no matter how many admirers she collected, all of Naomi's passion was expended on her exquisite creations.

Mistress Elizabeth's back was to the door as she was being helped into her day gown by old Berthy. Ruth could read the pain written all over the elderly woman's face as she worked the hooks on the back of her mistresses' bodice.

Naomi announced Ruth's entrance into the sitting room.

"Wonderful," Mistress Hawkins replied. "Please have a seat in the chair by my desk. I won't be but a moment."

Before Ruth could take one step toward the chair, Naomi grabbed hold of her arm and gently pulled her in front of the tall swivel mirror. Ruth followed the direction of Naomi's gaze and almost laughed out loud. There on the top of her head was a corn shuck, sitting just as pretty as a bonnet. Ruth immediately pulled it out of her hair and laid it in Naomi's open hand. Both women shared a knowing smile while Ruth patted her hair down and took a seat in the chair.

"Mistress," Naomi said in a smooth voice. "I'll hem your gown for our fitting tomorrow. You're going to be the most stunning woman at the Fall Gala."

Elizabeth Hawkins beamed with joy—a rosy pink coloring her smooth cheeks. "Well, I don't know about that, but I do know I'll have the most gorgeous gown. Thank you, Naomi," she said, turning her head slightly toward her seamstress.

"My pleasure, Mistress." Naomi stepped toward the door to the hallway. Holding up the corn shuck and winking at Ruth, she softly closed the door.

"There now, Berthy, that'll do." Elizabeth turned around and smiled at her dear lady's maid. "I want you to go to your room and rest a while. You've been on your feet all day."

Surprisingly, old Berthy didn't ask if she could do anything else for the mistress. She merely dipped her chin and said, "Yes'm," exiting the room with a slow, lopsided gait.

"Now then," the mistress crooned, taking a seat in the plush chair opposite of Ruth's. "I have something important I'd like to discuss with you."

Ruth felt uncomfortable sitting in a chair while her mistress was speaking. It almost put her on level ground with her owner. She knew her place, and this most certainly was not it. Her hands wrung in her lap like a sopping dishrag.

Elizabeth's gaze trailed to Ruth's nervous hands, then back to her slave's eyes. "Ruth, please be at ease. I want us to get to know one another."

Without thinking, Ruth blurted, "Whatever for, missus?"

The moment it left her mouth, she wanted to take it back. "Oh, missus, I's so sorry—"

Elizabeth held up her hand, stopping Ruth from a long apology. "I understand your wariness—we've never spent much time together. I know this must seem very strange. But as you can see, Berthy has been struggling for quite some time now. Her hands have become painfully arthritic, and her eyesight is waning. She's been with me for over thirty years—since I was a young girl, so she is very dear to me."

Ruth nodded her head, not knowing whether to look her beautiful mistress directly in the face or keep her gaze lowered. She finally decided if Missus Elizabeth really wanted to get to know her, she'd better be courteous enough to look her in the eyes.

"I'm going to allow Berthy to keep her room in the house, but from now on, she will be my companion when I'm reading and resting, nothing more. So you see," she said, leaning slightly forward in her chair, "I am in need of a new companion. You come highly recommended," she said with a smile.

"I can't imagine by whom," Ruth said softly, shaking her head.

Elizabeth's smile grew wider. "Why, your daughter, of course. Sarah has been telling me all about her mother's fine qualities. And I've seen how wonderful Sarah is with my own daughter, Isabella. If Sarah is even half of what her mother is, then you are my obvious choice."

Ruth felt flames licking at her face. All she could think about was the incident with little Franklin not two hours earlier. If this woman only knew who she was asking to be her companion, she would probably send her packing immediately.

"Oh, missus, are you sure?"

"Very much so. I've been watching you when you come to the house. You treat everyone with such respect, and your friendliness is infectious. Besides, your husband is a very important man to my husband, and your daughter to my daughter, so why don't we keep it all in the family?"

For the next several minutes, Mistress Hawkins spoke about her daily schedule and gave Ruth most of the specifics about her new position. Ruth began to feel an excitement welling up inside, knowing that she was about to be given such an important role in the household.

"Now, do you have any questions for me?" the mistress asked.

"Well, yes'm. Am I expected to leave my young'un and live at the house like Berthy and Sarah?"

"That's a fine question," Elizabeth replied. "I'm very aware of your little one and realize you'll want to be with him and your husband. So Berthy will tend to me in the evenings before bed, and you can go home to your family. If I need any extra help, Sarah is here. Will that be acceptable?"

Who was she to be answering such a question? Ruth only expected to do what she was told, not to be extended such a courtesy. But she knew this was a position too good to be true, no matter what the circumstances required.

"Missus, that would be a wonderful thing."

"Then it's settled," Mistress Hawkins responded, rising to her feet. "Right now, I want you to go see Naomi. Tell her there's plenty of time for her to hem my gown later. She needs to make you a set of clothes befitting your new position."

Ruth was on her feet in an instant, smiling broadly and thanking her mistress for such an amazing opportunity. "I'll do everything in my power to make you happy, missus. I won't let you down."

Mistress Hawkins laid a gentle hand on Ruth's shoulder, guiding her toward the door. "I'm counting on that, Ruth. Now, don't forget to stop by the sewing room, and I'll see you in the morning."

"Yes'm. I'll be here bright and early."

Ruth's eyes were as shiny as two marbles when she opened the door to Naomi's sewing room. She could barely contain her excitement. Naomi glanced up from her hemming and laughed softly. "Have you come for your corn bonnet?"

Ruth slapped both hands to her cheeks. "If you hadn't been there to save me, I would've died of embarrassment right there on the spot."

"Do you mind me asking what that was all about with Mistress Hawkins?" Naomi inquired, pausing once again before her next stitch.

"I's been given Berthy's job! I'll be companion to the missus."

"Oh, dear one, how wonderful for you." Naomi set the gown aside and went to Ruth, pulling her into a tight hug. "I can't think of anyone more deserving."

Ruth's throat constricted once again, knowing she needed to confess her shameful deed to God. She felt so unworthy of anyone's praise at the moment. Telling her husband what she had done to Franklin was one thing, but more urgently, she needed to give it to the Lord as soon as possible. The weight of it was getting hard to bear. But for now, there was a more pressing matter.

"The missus told me you's to stop working on her gown. She wants you to make me somethin' worthy of bein' her companion."

Without a moment's hesitation, Naomi went to an armoire in the corner of the room. "You can borrow some of my clothes for now, although after all of those babies you've produced, your bosom is…well, let's say a bit more ample than mine. But this blouse never quite fit properly on me, and I'm sure I know why."

Both women giggled as Ruth slipped out of her well-worn cotton blouse, yellowed and stained by its many years of use. Trying on the blouse that Naomi offered almost seemed like a dream of sorts. It had been a long time since she'd worn something so neat and clean.

Taking hold of the blouse at Ruth's shoulders, Naomi exclaimed, "Perfect fit!" Then, pulling out a cream-colored skirt, she added, "Try this on too."

Beaming from ear to ear, Ruth looked at her reflection in the tall mirror mounted to the wall of the sewing room. She felt pretty—maybe for the first time in her life.

"Well, I do see something that *won't* do," Naomi said.

Ruth looked quizzically at her friend's reflection.

"Those boots will have to go."

Many miles had been trodden on this old pair of brown, leather boots. Most days, Ruth would lead a mule into the field to pick up large sacks of corn that needed shucking. When her baskets were full, she would bag the corn again, load them on the mule, and walk him to the agriculture barn, over a mile round trip. Looking at them now, she felt certain these boots weren't going to last her through the coming winter. The slaves were always given a new set of clothes at Christmastime by the master, but there was never a guarantee that she'd get new boots. However, her life and work was just about to change drastically.

"Here," Naomi said. "Try this pair on."

Ruth's mouth dropped open as she looked in the bottom of the armoire. "How many pair do you have?"

Naomi's smile was almost apologetic. "More than I need. Now sit down and get those old things off your feet."

Ruth gladly complied and was grateful for the comfortable fit of her new pair of shiny black boots. "How's I gonna keep all this clean? I don't have anywheres to put 'em."

"Not a problem, my friend. This will become your dressing room every morning. There's plenty of space for my clothes and yours in here." Naomi pointed to the enormous armoire. "Now, get out of your new outfit and let me take your measurements. I'll whip up a few more blouses and skirts for you to impress our mistress."

A fresh batch of tears formed in Ruth's eyes. "What did I ever do to deserve this?" she whispered.

Picking up her tape measure, Naomi humbly replied, "Only our Jesus makes us deserving, dear one. None of us merit special treatment after the way we've treated him. Just be thankful for our Lord's sweet grace and tender mercy."

"Every mornin'," Ruth replied, shedding her new clothes and allowing Naomi to get all of her measurements. Dressing back into her shabby, timeworn outfit, she recognized that Jesus made her feel every bit as clean as her new blouse and skirt. For that, she was grateful.

"How can I ever thank you, Naomi? This be more than I ever dreamt of."

Naomi was already busy clearing a space on the large table beneath the window for her next project. "You can thank me by being the companion our mistress desires. That way we'll get to spend a lot more time together."

"Oh, I plan on it. Won't that be wonderful?"

"Yes, it will. Now go tell your husband the good news while I get started on your new wardrobe."

Leaving the house, Ruth felt lighter than the frothy white clouds in the afternoon sky. Yet there was one more important task to take care of before hauling her shucked corn to the barn. She desperately needed to make a stop at her prayer log near the cabin.

When she spotted the opening just off the side of the road, Ruth turned onto the path through the woods. It was only a short walk to a small clearing where a log rested beneath a massive elm. Instead of sitting on the log, as usual, Ruth went to her knees, resting her elbows on the smooth surface. It was there that she spent the next several minutes lamenting over her actions of the day and asking the Lord to forgive her.

"And Lawd, please help me never to lay a hand on my baby child again. But Lawd, would you please help Franklin to never, ever do what he done today? Thank you, sweet Jesus. I trust you, and amen."

As she rose from the ground, dusting off her skirt, Ruth suddenly plunged back to her knees. "Oh, I's so sorry, Lawd, I nearly forgot. And thank you for the missus takin' notice of me. Help me never to let her down."

A violent shudder ran all the way through Ruth's body, causing her to feel nauseous and weak. For a moment, she couldn't even pull herself off the ground. When the feeling began to pass, she dragged herself onto the log, trying to take in slower and deeper breaths. It took a few minutes for her heart to return to a normal rhythm.

Finally, feeling her legs return to full strength, Ruth stood and wiped the sweat from her brow with the back of her hand. Whatever that had been could not be explained, at least by anything she'd ever known. Nevertheless, it now seemed to be completely gone, and Ruth hurried home, convincing herself it had not even happened.

Chapter 3

Isaiah couldn't help but grin when he glanced down at his son. Franklin held a tight grip on his pappy's leg just like he'd been told. Isaiah had always believed his son to be safe in the stables, but this afternoon, the boy had learned a mighty tough lesson with his mammy. Maybe it had been a lesson worth the learning. After all, a little extra caution wouldn't hurt, especially since Franklin was such a wee thing. He didn't want one of the horses to accidentally trample on the boy. If Franklin took to the horses the way he had, Isaiah knew his son's feet would get tread upon more times than he'd ever be able to count. That's why a good, sturdy pair of boots was of utmost importance. At the moment, Franklin's little bare feet would be no match for a thousand-pound animal.

"So, you think he's a winner?" Master Hawkins asked Isaiah as he eyed the long-legged beast before him. "I don't plan on losing to the Braddocks again this year."

Isaiah held the halter close to the stallion's chin, keeping his potent energy in check. "Yessir. He be the one to win it all this year. I know it in my bones."

Samuel Hawkins had long trusted Isaiah where his thoroughbreds were concerned. Isaiah had learned unique training methods from his own papa, who had served Master Joseph Hawkins well. He had already started teaching Franklin those very same skills and techniques.

When Master Hawkins laid his hand on the animal's sleek neck, the stallion let out a shrill whinny, throwing his head and stomping one of his powerful forelegs. Before he could be stopped, Franklin stepped away from his daddy and rested both hands on the stallion's leg. Immediately the horse settled, and Isaiah could literally feel an aura of peace emanating from the beast. It was almost eerie.

Master Hawkins must have felt it too. He locked a quizzical gaze on his trainer. "How long have you known about the boy?" Samuel asked in a hushed tone.

"Fer 'bout a year now, sir," he replied quietly.

Holding a deep breath, Master Hawkins watched in amazement as Franklin reached up beneath the stallion's chest and traced his hand along the horse's black belly. The beast remained placid, almost trance-like. Neither man moved a muscle until the boy stepped out from under the horse and took hold of his pappy's leg again.

"Amazing," Master Hawkins breathed. "I've never seen anything like it. Did you teach him how to do that?"

Sheepishly, Isaiah shook his head. "He been given a pure gift from above, massa."

Master Hawkins whistled out another deep breath. He took off his hat, running a hand through his dark brown hair. "That was nothing short of miraculous. Is it just this one, or can he do that with any horse?"

"Well, sir, I seen him do that once or twiced before. But he do seem to have some sort o' connection with Prince that can't be explained."

The master eyed the little boy for a long moment, then settled back into a business frame of mind. "We've got three weeks to the Fall race. Is everything working out with young Jehu?"

"Oh, yessir. They's got a good understandin' of each other. They's gonna win you that race—you jus wait 'n see."

"Good! That's what I want to hear. Keep up the fine work, Isaiah."

"I will, sir."

"All right," the master said, shoving his hat back down on his head. "Come by my study in the morning first thing. We'll go over the mule plan for the rest of this year."

"Yessir. Have a good evenin', sir."

Samuel waved as he turned to leave, but just before reaching the stable door, he called, "And bring your boy with you in the morning."

"Will do, massa."

Isaiah rested his hand on top of Franklin's head for a moment. There was a presence inside this child that felt unearthly. It was a supernatural power that made Isaiah feel small in the hands of a mighty Creator. Even the warmth of Franklin's head sent a pulse through his hand that soothed the very core of his being. *He be all yours, Lawd. Don't let me get in the way o' yer plans for 'im.*

"C'mon, little man. Les get Prince back to his palace and feed him supper. What do ya say?"

Franklin looked up at his pappy with a lopsided grin, then walked beside the beast all the way to his stall.

⇜⚛⚛⇝

Ruth thought she'd be later than usual getting back from the agriculture barn, but she'd been so excited about her new position with the missus, she nearly ran all the way home. Even the mule had a hard time keeping up with her.

Isaiah and Franklin were already washing up at the well when she arrived. The old green water bucket served a dozen cabins, all built around their water source. There were at least another ten wells just like it in slave town—twelve cabins built around each one. The occupants of each group of twelve families called themselves *kinfolk*, and most of them were related by blood. Isaiah had been born in the very cabin he and Ruth lived in, but none of their kinfolk were his actual blood kin. He didn't have a single relative still alive except his wife and son and daughter.

Ruth and Isaiah loved their kinfolk as if they really were family. They shared noon meals together, helped birth each other's babies, laughed, cried, prayed, and worshipped together. There wasn't much of anything they didn't know about each other. Even though they felt a connection with most of the slaves on the plantation, there was a fierce bond with the ones they called *kinfolk*.

Phibe and Ceceilia came running out of their cabins and cut Ruth off before she could even get to her husband. "We hear-ed all abouts yer new position!" they squealed.

Ruth immediately glanced at Isaiah, disappointed that he didn't get to hear the news from her first. She noticed his look of bewilderment.

"I ain't even had a chance to talk to Izzy yet," she hissed. "Now you two go on," she said, shooing them away as if they were chickens at her feet.

Phibe covered her mouth while Ceceilia lamented, "We's so sorry. Just pretend we didn't say nothin'." Locking elbows, the pair quickly headed back to their cabins to prepare the evening meal.

Isaiah sauntered over to his wife and put his hands on her hips, holding her firmly in place. "What's this I's hearin' 'bout my woman?" His simmering smile melted away Ruth's irritation like ice in the summer sun. "You gots somethin' to tell me?" he asked.

"I surely do," she said, excitement pumping through her veins. "Let's get inside, and I'll tell ya all about it."

Isaiah didn't readily let go. As a matter of fact, he bent his head and kissed his wife long and hard. When the other women started crooning from their cabins, Ruth pushed herself out of his arms and slapped him on the chest. "You is a scoundrel, Izzy…a scoundrel through and through."

Gazing toward the other cabins, Isaiah let out a deep laugh and waved to the women who were watching from their doorways. But his arm was quickly yanked down as Ruth dragged him across the yard.

While Ruth put together a supper of rice, peas, and cornbread, she showered Isaiah with details of her conversation with the mistress. She told him all about her new wardrobe and how she'd get to spend more time with Sarah at the big house. Chattering nonstop, Ruth could hardly get the details out fast enough.

But when they sat down at the supper table, Isaiah grew quiet and pensive. He didn't seem to share in her excitement quite like she'd anticipated. "What's a matter, Izzy? Ain't you happy for me?"

A pained look crossed his face. "How's I gonna get along without ya, sweet gal? I wants you right there in my bed at night. I's gonna be awful lonely—"

"Oh, no, no, no, Izzy. I ain't leavin' ya," Ruth said quickly. She reached across the table for his hand. "The missus told me I could come home every night to be with you and Franklin. I'm gonna be here for supper with my two men just like always. Don't you worry 'bout nothin'."

Anxiety immediately slid right off of Isaiah's shoulders. He sat a little straighter and gave her a relieved smile. "And in my bed too?"

"Yes, Izzy," she said good-naturedly. "In yer bed too."

Bouncing his eyebrows at her, he looked as if he'd proposition her that very minute, but Ruth would have none of it. She withdrew her hand from his, giving it a good slap. "You just bow yer head right now and say grace. Get yer mind on more important things, mister."

"Yes'm," he said with a wily grin. "Whatever you say."

❧ ❧ ❧

Ruth was up the next morning long before the sun. Isaiah turned over in bed, watching his wife hurriedly put breakfast together. She already had a fire going, and he could smell eggs frying in the iron skillet. Grabbing a thick cloth, she pulled the skillet from the fire grate and slid the eggs onto three plates.

"Come on, boys, breakfast be ready."

Isaiah sat up and nudged Franklin who was lying sideways on the foot of their bed. It wouldn't be long before he'd need to make the boy a bed of his own. But for now, Franklin was happy as could be to sleep at their feet.

Still rubbing his eyes, Isaiah sat down in his chair at the table. "Is we havin' breakfast at midnight?" he asked.

"Hush yer teasin' and eat. Sun'll be up soon."

Ruth was a little nervous about going to the missus for more reasons than one. Even though Ceceilia and Phibe had been all afire over her new position last evening, she'd seen fighting amongst kinfolk when someone got called to the big house. Naomi was one of their kinfolk too and had been one of the Hawkins' maids since childhood. But when she got called to move into the plantation house three years ago, the women had shown definite signs of jealousy and disdain. Hurt beyond words, Naomi quit coming to slave town altogether.

Certainly Eula, in the cabin next door, wouldn't be a problem—she was too old and feeble to go to the fields anymore. She and old Solomon stayed at the cabins, preparing a noon meal for the rest of the kinfolk when they came in from the fields for a midday rest. Ruth would now be eating her noon meal at the big house. She would miss that special time with her kinfolk every day.

Isaiah captured his wife's anxious gaze. "So is you a bit spooked 'bout yer new work?"

"Oh, Izzy, I'm not so worried about the missus as I am our kinfolk. I don't want the others to be jealous or make more o' this than they should."

"They won't if you won't," he responded matter-of-factly.

Thinking on that a moment, Ruth realized the truth in that statement. She would have to remind herself not to talk about her job unless someone asked. Humility would be her best bet. She would ask the Savior every day to pass on his humble nature to her.

Finishing her last bite, Ruth leapt up from the table, dipped her breakfast plate in the water bucket, scrubbed it clean, and laid it out to dry. "I be seein' you two this evenin'," she said as she headed for the door.

"Now hold on a minute, gal. Ain't you forgettin' somethin'?"

"What?" she asked breathlessly.

"Us boys needs a little lovin' afore you go. Surely you gots time for that." He reached out and captured her wrist, not giving her a choice in the matter.

With a giggle, Ruth shook her head. "Sorry, Izzy. I's just so anxious—this bein' the first day and all."

"I know, I know," Isaiah said softly, standing to take her in his arms. "I's so proud o' you, Ruthie. The missus don't have no idea how good things is about to get for her."

Ruth turned her mouth to his, then bent to kiss Franklin. "You hang onto your pappy's leg in the stables, little man. You hear me?"

"Yes'm," Franklin said with a mouthful of eggs.

When Ruth stepped out of their cabin, daybreak was barely stirring. And by the time the sun began making its glorious appearance, she was already walking silently through the clearing. Her prayer log brought comfort that no other place on earth could—this is where she would start each day before heading to the big house. It was here in these quiet moments with the Lord that her soul found peace.

After several minutes had passed, Ruth stood to go. She noticed how the dew had completely soaked the hem of her skirt and boots. A half-smile crossed her lips—there would be a new set of clothes waiting for her at the house. Ruth was quite aware that her position with the missus would not only require a new wardrobe but a whole new set of skills. Fortunately, she had always been a quick learner. She trusted that the Lord would help her be up to the task at hand.

But as she left the clearing on that first morning, she had to forcibly pat down the feeling in her gut that she would not be in this position for long.

Chapter 4

M ama!" Sarah called as Ruth stepped through the door of the house kitchen. Ruth hadn't seen her daughter since Sunday, and she eagerly wrapped the girl in a loving hug. "Oh, baby gal, it's so good to hold ya."

The two embraced for a long moment, savoring the fact that they would be seeing each other every day from now on.

"Have you eaten breakfast?" Sarah asked, gesturing toward the table where the house slaves were eating.

"Yes, I done ate with your pappy and brother. I'll be havin' breakfast and supper with them two as usual."

"Come sit with me while I finish. I can tell you everything you need to know."

Ruth looked down at her ragged clothes. "But I ain't changed into my new outfit yet. Won't I need to do that first?"

Naomi was spreading peach jam on her biscuit and nodded toward an empty chair. "You have plenty of time to get dressed, Ruth. Have a seat."

Learning how things worked inside the house was one of Ruth's top priorities. She would trust her daughter and Naomi to give her all the information she needed. Apparently, they weren't in a big hurry to get their day started, so Ruth did their bidding.

"One thing you need to learn from the start is the mistress and Isabella are not early risers," Naomi began.

"Especially Miss Isabella," Sarah chimed in. "Why, sometimes she doesn't get up till I pull open her curtains just before noon."

"Do she not eat breakfast?" Ruth gasped.

"Skips it altogether. She don't want me rousin' her from bed till the noon meal's almost ready. The missus gets up earlier 'cause she's got baby Catherine comin' to her bed at nine."

"You mean I gots till nine before I see the missus? She told me yesterday to come to her at eight this mornin'."

"Today she probably wants you to come early to learn what she requires in the mornings," Naomi responded. "As soon as I'm finished, we'll go get you dressed for the day. Relax, dear one, you've plenty of time."

Ruth was finding it difficult to be at ease. "So what am I to do every mornin' when I get here?"

Her daughter answered that query. "Unless the missus tells you different, you'll help me clean up from breakfast so everyone else can get on with their work."

Ruth's eyes grew wide. "You mean you and me'll have all this time together?"

"Yes, ma'am," Sarah said with a sparkling smile. "Won't that be nice?"

"Indeed, child, it will."

Before leaving the breakfast table, Naomi made sure Ruth was acquainted with all of the women sitting there. Ruth had known most of them for years but had rarely seen the ones who lived at the big house. They all welcomed her, and Tabitha, the chamber maid, added a little warning to her greeting.

"You best be careful goin' back to yer kinfolk every night. Somes will wanna know everythin' that goes on in the house. But the missus don't like gossip, so's you best keep what you do here to yourself."

Ruth glanced at Naomi, who confirmed Tabitha's statement. "You must be trusted beyond measure with Mistress Elizabeth." Rising to leave the table, Naomi added, "Fortunately, our mistress has chosen well."

At eight o'clock on the dot, Ruth entered the mistress's sitting room. The bedroom door was slightly ajar, so she knocked lightly. "Missus," she called, "may I come in?"

"Yes, yes, please come in, Ruth."

Pushing the door wider, Ruth walked into the spacious bedroom where heavy blue draperies prohibited all but a tiny sliver of light from shining through. "May I open the drapes, ma'am?"

"Yes, but start with the ones at the back corner of the room. I like to get used to the light slowly. And be sure to raise the windows to get a breeze coming through."

"Yes'm," Ruth replied, making her way to the other side of the room. The drapes were made of heavy velvet, reaching from the high ceiling all the way to the floor. She took hold of one and slowly walked it as far as possible, then did the same with its mate.

"Is this fine, ma'am?"

"Yes," Elizabeth said, covering her eyes with one hand. "There's a sash to hold each curtain back."

Ruth found the sash and realized the hook on the end fit into an anchor on the wall. After raising the heavy window and performing the same task two more times, she turned to her mistress. "Would you like me to help you get ready for the day?"

Elizabeth waved her off. "Oh, no, it's far too early. Would you please put the pillows behind my back so I can sit up?"

"Yes'm," Ruth said, pulling the extra pillows from the other side of the bed.

"There, now," Elizabeth said, covering a yawn, "that's perfect."

"What else you be needin', ma'am?"

"Please go ahead and pick up my husband's dirty clothes. That's Tabitha's job, but she doesn't know to come in early today." Elizabeth gestured toward the pile on the other side of the bed. "He leaves them on the floor since he doesn't want anyone helping him get dressed or undressed. There's a basket by the door in my sitting room. One of the laundry girls will pick it up."

Ruth quickly gathered the master's trousers, shirt, and various clothing items he'd worn the previous day and took them to their proper place. She felt certain little Ella would be the one to pick them up for her mama to wash.

"I think I'd like hot tea and a biscuit this morning before Catherine arrives. Would you let them know in the kitchen?"

"Yes'm, right away."

"Bring it yourself, and I'll have more instructions for you when you get back."

When Ruth returned from the kitchen, Tabitha was on her hands and knees beside the bed. Very slowly the girl pulled out the chamber pot from underneath. Fortunately, there was a lid on it. Tabitha didn't look up as she passed Ruth, concentrating on every step.

Ruth laid the tray of food on Mistress Elizabeth's lap and backed away with a pleasant smile, awaiting further instructions.

"While I eat, you can lay out my clothing. If you'll open the armoire, I'll tell you what I want to wear."

There were two giant armoires in the room—one in the back corner and the other facing the mistress's bed. From Elizabeth's hand motions, Ruth knew exactly which one to open. She realized it had been strategically placed for the missus to pick out her clothing for the day from the comfort of her own bed.

An explosion of colors and patterns met Ruth's wide-eyed gaze. She had never seen so many beautiful garments in one space. She had to willfully stop herself from touching each one.

"I'll wear the light-yellow skirt and the white blouse with yellow trim today. We'll dispense with the matching jacket since the weather has been so hot lately."

"Yes'm," Ruth responded and proceeded to pick out Elizabeth's outfit.

Fortunately, Naomi had told her exactly how to dress the mistress. She would start with the chemise and then help her into her drawers or bloomers, which had an open crotch. Naomi had instructed her on how to lace the corset in the back and how to use the whalebone busk to close the corset in the front. Since it was summer, she would then dress the mistress in a light-weight petticoat before helping her with the blouse and skirt. This was what the mistress usually wore from day to day. However, if she planned on visiting or receiving guests, she would wear a *Toilette de Viste,* or a visiting dress. There were carriage dresses, riding dresses, evening dresses—enough clothing to make Ruth's head spin. But thanks to Naomi's information, she knew that her mistress generally dressed only once for the entire day, except for the occasional scheduled events. There were very few reasons to change clothes in the course of a day.

As Ruth laid out her clothing, the mistress talked about her plans, and before long, Violet appeared in the doorway with a fair-haired babe in her arms. Tabitha quickly followed the pair inside the bedchamber to remove Elizabeth's breakfast tray.

"Good mornin', missus," Violet beamed. "I's got a sugar plum wantin' to see her momma."

Elizabeth gladly received five-month-old Catherine into her arms, kissing both cheeks before settling the child into her lap.

Violet had been with the family for many years, having raised fifteen-year-old Isabella and sons, Joseph and William, to ages thirteen and ten, respectively. Little Catherine had come along unexpectedly, long after Mistress Elizabeth had given up on bearing any more children. While another child had been a complete surprise, Catherine was loved and doted on by everyone in the household.

"Missus, she gots herself a little tooth comin' in." Catherine didn't seem to mind when Violet used both thumbs to raise her upper lip. "Looky here. Right on top."

Elizabeth smiled proudly, as if Catherine had won first place at the Kentucky fair. "Thank you, Violet," she said to the nursemaid, who was nearly as round as she was short. "Ruth will let you know when to come take her."

Violet glanced at Ruth a bit warily, obviously used to seeing old Berthy in the mornings. But she didn't say anything. She merely dipped her head and murmured, "Yes'm," before heading to the door.

After playing with Catherine for several minutes, Elizabeth turned her gaze toward Ruth. "Would you like to hold her?"

"Oh, may I, missus?" Ruth asked reverently.

"Of course," she said, holding the child up to her new companion.

Ruth crooned over the plump little bundle in her arms, enjoying the feel of an infant again.

Surprisingly, the mistress asked, "Do you only have the two children—Sarah and your little boy?"

"Yes'm," Ruth answered quietly. "I do miss havin' a babe to cradle, though. My Franklin is soon to be four."

"Seems as though you have a bigger age difference between your children than I have," Elizabeth mused as she rearranged one of the pillows behind her back.

Feeling her heart pinch, Ruth quietly answered, "Yes'm."

Ruth's emotional response did not go unnoticed by her mistress. "Here, come sit down and put Catherine between us." Elizabeth patted the side of the bed, causing Ruth a bit of angst. Was she really supposed to sit down on her mistress's bed?

"It's all right," Elizabeth soothed. "If you're to be my companion, then I need to know everything about you."

Trembling inside, Ruth took a seat on the bed and laid the baby beside her mother.

"Were there others?" Elizabeth prompted.

"Yes'm, there be four others in heaven," she said as calmly as possible, trying desperately to hold her emotions in check.

Elizabeth took Catherine back into her lap, caressing the soft golden curls at the base of the baby's neck. Her eyes grew soft and tender. "Please tell me about them."

Ruth tugged in a deep breath, praying she could even say their sweet names without weeping.

"First there was Sarah," she began slowly. "I birthed her when I was the very same age that Sarah be right now—seventeen. Then there was Jonathon, the sweetest little 'un you ever saw, but too small to make it through the winter. We couldn't get no weight on his bones. After that come Isaac and Malachi, twin babes. Only Isaac took a few breaths, and Malachi be stillborn."

Ruth thought by giving few details, she could make it all the way through. But by the time she got to little Lucy, she felt the warmth creep up behind her eyes. "I had one more before Franklin—a little gal—Lucy. Lost her the day after she turned five," she said with a catch in her throat. Ruth felt she couldn't go any further without crying, and that was the last thing she wanted to do on her first day with the missus. She quickly brushed her eyes with the back of her hand and tried to focus on little Catherine.

But Elizabeth pressed her for details she didn't want to give. "Tell me what happened to Lucy…please," she pleaded softly.

Swallowing hard, Ruth painstakingly told her how little Lucy had gone missing for most of the day. She was supposed to be with Mammy Lou, who cared for the children while their parents worked the fields. But at the end of the day, the horrible truth had been discovered. Somehow, Lucy had fallen into the well across from their cabin. Isaiah wouldn't let anyone be lowered into that well but himself. They'd tied a harness from the stables around him, and he cradled his precious girl to his chest as the kinfolk pulled him up with ropes.

When Ruth finished her story, she took a deep cleansing breath, working hard to hold a rush of tears at bay. Even though Mistress Elizabeth's eyes held a look of genuine sympathy, she quickly said, "Please go tell Violet I'm ready for Catherine to go to the nursery."

"Yes'm," Ruth said submissively, moving hastily toward the door. Once inside the sitting room, Ruth leaned against the wall to take several deep breaths. Then, with one final intake, she released the air from her lungs and went in search of Violet, praying her mistress would ask no more questions about her young'uns.

Ruth found Violet sitting in old Berthy's small room across the hall. It was clear the two women were close friends as she heard them quietly laughing together. However, their jovial demeanor dissipated as soon as Ruth walked in the room.

"The missus wants you to take Catherine back to the nursery," Ruth told Violet cautiously. It was clear by the look on their faces she would need to tread lightly around these two. Maybe it would take them a while to get used to seeing her with the mistress. Ruth had no intention of taking Berthy's place of honor—surely the elderly woman knew how important she'd always been to Missus Elizabeth.

Violet leaned close to her friend and whispered something only meant for Berthy's ears. Then, without a glance, she pushed past Ruth while Berthy snickered.

On a whim, Ruth decided to stay behind for a moment. Offering the old woman a gracious smile, she said, "The missus told me how much you mean to her. I'm so glad you's still here with her."

Berthy's cloudy eyes slowly took on a look of satisfaction. Ruth's statement seemed to have melted away a bit of frostiness. Ruth didn't press any further for fear she might ruin the moment. Nodding her head to the old woman, she respectfully left the room.

A full hour later, the mistress stood ready for the day in front of her mirror while Ruth finished tying a black ribbon behind her neck. The choker necklace exhibited a sizeable pearl that dangled elegantly at Elizabeth's throat.

The Mistress eyed herself in the mirror with a look of approval. There had been almost no conversation between the two women as Ruth assisted her through the routine of dressing and grooming. Elizabeth only spoke to give Ruth instructions on how to sweep her flaxen hair into a loose bun at the nape of her neck. Being this woman's slave meant Ruth would only engage in conversation when the mistress wished her to. Even so, the silence had been a bit unsettling.

Ruth stepped to the side of her mistress and smoothed out a wrinkle on the front of her skirt. But before she could pull her hand away, Elizabeth reached for it and held it tenderly in both of her own.

"I want you to know how sorry I am about your four precious children. My heart has been so heavy for you this morning." Moisture glistened in her eyes as she turned to face Ruth, still holding her hand.

"I have never lost a child of my own, but I can only imagine the agony you've gone through." Then, unexpectedly, the mistress declared, "I would like for you to take me to your children's graves."

Ruth's eyes grew wide. "Oh, missus, why would you want to see such a place?"

"Because, dear Ruth, I imagine that's an important place to you. I would like to take flowers to lay on their places of rest." With a tender smile, she added, "Would you like that?"

"Oh, yes'm—if you's sure."

"Quite sure," Elizabeth declared. "Go tell Sarah to get Isabella out of bed. The two girls can join us. I'll be with Berthy until she's ready."

"Thank you kindly, missus."

It had taken a while for Sarah to rouse Isabella from sleep and ready her for the day. But with a little good-natured coaxing, Sarah had brought her around. Soon the four women headed out a side door to a lovely walking garden at the side of the house.

"Choose whichever flowers you would like," the mistress said, nodding to both Ruth and Sarah. "Isabella and I will do the same."

Ruth had never dreamed that such a lovely place existed—much less on the Hawkins Plantation. She had never had the opportunity to venture behind the walls of the flower garden. She imagined this was what the Garden of Eden must have looked like.

After gathering four roses, one pink and three red, Ruth waited for the others to make their selections. Sarah had done the same, only gathering four flowers—two purple irises and two yellow peonies. But the mistress and her daughter had wandered to the far corners of the garden, returning with an armload. One of the gardeners hastened to their side with a basket.

"Thank you, Moses," the mistress said, laying her bouquet of flowers inside. The other women also placed their flowers in the basket, and Sarah took it from the gardener.

The foursome walked at a leisurely pace, staying in the shade of the trees as much as possible. Ruth felt her face flush with shame as they approached her cabin, the first one on the corner nearest the stables. She knew she shouldn't be embarrassed; surely Mistress Elizabeth knew what slave town was like. Still, it didn't seem right bringing her here.

"They's right back here, missus." Ruth gestured toward a worn path behind their cabin.

Isabella didn't wait. She headed onto the path with Sarah close on her heels. The short walk brought the women beneath several sycamore trees.

"Right here," Sarah said, noticing Isabella's blank look.

"Where?" the girl responded, turning all the way around.

Ruth quietly knelt and laid a gentle hand on the ground. "This be Jonathon," she whispered.

Sarah knelt between two other graves. "And this is Isaac and Malachi."

Isabella shook her head in confusion. "How do you know?"

Both slave women reached out and touched the rocks at the head of the tiny graves. If strangers were to walk through this area, they would have no idea that it was a family burial plot. Only the most observant would notice the rocks protruding from the ground.

Ruth rose to her feet and walked to an area beside the twins. There was a much larger rock marking this grave.

"Lucy?" the mistress inquired softly.

"Yes'm, this be my Lucy gal."

The four women stayed for a long time, exchanging few words and arranging the beautiful flowers on top of the graves. And when it was time to leave, Elizabeth and Isabella held their slaves' hands the entire walk back to the house.

Chapter 5

With the fall race quickly approaching, Isaiah spent most of his time with Prince and the stallion's young rider. Jehu was fifteen, but he was small and wiry and had an outstanding command of Prince at top speed.

Isaiah had raised The Prince of Madagascar from birth. The two-year-old stallion was of outstanding stock and had been admired by many throughout central Kentucky. His reputation even extended into southern Indiana and Ohio. When Prince's racing days were over, he would end up making Master Hawkins a pretty penny as a stud horse.

"Les get him cooled down, Jehu," Isaiah called. "Hop down, I'll walk him."

Jehu swung his right leg over Prince's neck and leapt to the ground. The horse's back end pranced sideways in the opposite direction, and Isaiah held the reigns a bit tighter while whispering soothing words to the powerful beast.

"You want on?" Isaiah asked his son, who had spent the last couple of weeks right beside his pappy's legs whenever he was in the stables.

It was a rhetorical question. Isaiah already knew what the answer would be. Truthfully, he wanted Franklin sitting atop Prince after a hard workout. It brought the animal an extra measure of calm after an adrenaline-charged run.

Franklin's arms were held high, waiting for his pappy to lift him up. As soon as he was sitting astride the mighty stallion, Prince became a submissive beast. Isaiah could've handed Franklin the reigns and the horse would've done his bidding. But he would never do such a thing.

"You holds on tight, little man, 'n case Prince here gets spooked."

Instead of grabbing the front of the leather pommel, Franklin filled his hands with Prince's wiry black mane. Isaiah liked that better since it kept a more intimate connection between the boy and the beast.

After a good twenty-minute cool-down, Isaiah led Prince into the stables, removed his bridle, and tethered him to the outside of his stall. Franklin scooted his little body onto the stallion's neck, and Prince immediately dipped his head while the boy hung from his mane and slid to the floor. When all of the horse tack was removed, Isaiah dropped Prince's body temperature further by dousing him with buckets of cold water.

"Jehu," he called, "come brush him down whilst I head to the mule barn."

"Yessa, boss," Jehu replied, throwing his pitchfork in the hay where he'd been mucking an empty stall.

"Feed 'im well, and don't forget his minerals," Isaiah added. "We wants his bones to be good an' strong fer next week."

"Yessa, boss," Jehu echoed again.

Isaiah took off his hat and hung it on a nearby post. Then, in one swift motion, he scooped Franklin off the ground, lifting him atop his shoulders.

"Grab my hat, young'un," he told Franklin, bending at the waist so the boy could reach it. "You wears it while ridin' yer pappy."

Little Franklin reached for the floppy-brimmed hat, then let out a giggle as it nearly swallowed him alive.

❧❦❧

The energy level in the big house thrummed at an all-time high. This year the Hawkins Plantation would be hosting the fall gala, which meant more hands than usual were needed in the house and around the grounds. Many slaves were pulled from the fields to work on the lawn and in the gardens. Several more slave women were brought in to decorate, cook, and serve.

Naomi gathered all the best seamstresses on the plantation to outfit each of the men and women who would be serving during the all-night gala. She remembered when Samuel and Elizabeth hosted once before. It had been a dozen or more years ago when she was but a girl. Her only recollection from that night was the pouring rain, which kept the party almost exclusively inside the house. She also recalled getting soaked to the skin, as she was a runner between the cookhouse and the kitchen. Thankfully, a large cooking kitchen had been added right onto the house after that difficult night. Now the old cookhouse was used as a storeroom.

One fitting session after another had taken up most of Naomi's time. Being blessed with six other talented assistants had kept her from having to go without sleep. While the other women worked on outfitting their fellow slaves, Naomi had concentrated exclusively on Mistress Elizabeth and Isabella. Samuel and young Masters Joseph and William had bought fine, tailored suits in Lexington.

Holding Isabella's sky-blue gown over her arm, Naomi headed upstairs. Laughter drifted down the upper hallway from the girls' room. She couldn't help but smile just thinking about Isabella and Sarah's relationship. She didn't believe two girls of the same color could be any closer than these two.

"Miss Isabella?" Naomi called from outside the half-open door. "Time for your last fitting."

Isabella groaned and rolled over on top of her bed where she and Sarah had been playing "The Mansion of Happiness" board game. "We're just getting to the good part, Naomi. I'm going to be married!" she squealed with delight.

Sarah threw her hand over her mouth, trying not to laugh too loudly. The girls had already been scolded for waking up the mistress from her nap.

"Up you go, Miss Isabella. This is the last time—I promise."

Hopping down from the four-poster canopy bed, Isabella started disrobing. Sarah ran around the bed to catch her summer dress before it fell to the floor.

Once in the new dress, Isabella good-naturedly complained about not having a gown that fell off the shoulders. "I don't understand why mother won't allow it."

Naomi smoothed the gown to Isabella's hips and laughed softly. "For the tenth time—or is it the eleventh? Until your coming out ball next year, you will be dressed like a proper girl."

"But when I turn sixteen, I'm going to have a scoop neck and bare shoulders," she said with delight. "And I'll get to dance with all of the eligible men!"

Suddenly, Isabella took Sarah into her arms and began whirling her around the room. "I'll get to dance all night long with one partner after another." She sent Sarah twirling away and took Naomi as her next dance partner. But Naomi would have none of it.

"Stop your nonsense right now, little miss, and get that gown off before you rip it to shreds."

"Oh, all right," Isabella groused. "You're not a very good dance partner, Naomi."

"Whatever you say, missy. Now stand still and let me get you out of this gown."

Isabella turned toward Sarah and rolled her eyes, causing both girls to giggle.

Once Naomi had the gown safely back on her arm, she glanced at the playing board on the bed. "Take your time where marriage is concerned, Miss Isabella. Make sure you find a good man like your daddy."

"No worries, Naomi. I plan to find someone even better."

As Naomi left the girls to finish their game, she thought what a difficult proposition that would be. She'd known very few men in her life as good as Master Hawkins.

⋘⋙

The morning before the fall race, Isaiah said goodbye to Ruth and Franklin and headed for the stables. He and Jehu would be taking Prince to the Sheffield plantation. They loaded a mule wagon full of supplies for the race and tied the thoroughbred to the wagon. It would be a slow and steady twelve-mile walk during the cool of the day. Prince would need to get acclimated to his new surroundings. Plus, they planned a light workout on the two-mile race track this afternoon.

When they arrived at the Sheffield stables, a young slave boy met them outside and led them to the stall reserved for the Hawkins' racehorse. There would be seven horses in the race this year, and each one would have their own stall away from their competitors.

Master Hawkins and his sons, Joseph and William, would arrive this evening to spend the night at Maple Hill, the Sheffield's sprawling brick mansion. There would be no women at the race tomorrow morning. Only men and their sons from the surrounding plantations would be present, although many other male spectators would come from miles around. All of the owners provided a small purse, and the winner would take all. A silver cup was also awarded to the champion and passed around from year to year.

"Ain't no way that scrawny *boy* is gonna win a *man's* race tomorrow," a voice jeered from somewhere in the stables.

Isaiah spun around, but in the shadows, he couldn't see the man who had spit out those words.

Jehu gave his boss a wary glance, but Isaiah tried to put him at ease. "It's all right," he whispered. "Just some gamesmanship, that's all. You's just the *man* to win, and this be the horse to take you 'cross that finish line."

They worked to get Prince settled in, making sure he had plenty of water and oats. Then Isaiah told the boy to get their food from the wagon. "Les sit under the trees and eats."

Just as the two exited the stall and closed the gate, a man came sauntering toward them down the long row of stalls. Isaiah recognized him immediately. He was the young, upstart trainer from the Braddock Plantation—last year's race champion.

Even though there was nothing in the man's character to recommend him, Isaiah tipped his hat. "I's wonderin' if that was you, Terrance."

"Whatchu talkin' 'bout, mista?" he said with a snarl. "You talkin' 'bout me?" He pointed both thumbs at his chest and thrust his chin toward Jehu. "This yer boy?"

"Yessir, he's a fine rider."

"Humph. We'll just see 'bout that, won't we?" he hissed, shoving his left shoulder into Jehu and knocking him against the stall as he passed.

"Hey now," Isaiah responded. "T'ain't no cause for that."

"Fer *what?*" Terrance shouted over his shoulder before walking out into the sunlight.

That evening, Master Hawkins and his sons came into the stables, looking for Isaiah. Finding him inside Prince's stall, Samuel peered over the gate. "How's our champ doing?" he asked in a low voice.

"Real fine, sir. He be nice and relaxed. He done been out for a lap on the track and took to it like it belong to 'im."

"That's good to hear." Samuel looked around guardedly before opening the gate and stepping inside. "We just came from dinner at the house, and there was quite a bit of talk."

"What kinds o' talk, sir?"

Joseph and William stepped in behind their father and closed the gate. William gave a little wave to Jehu sitting in the corner.

"The kind of talk that has me a bit concerned about Prince's welfare," Master Hawkins responded.

"How's that, massa?"

Samuel's eyes narrowed, and he shook his head slightly. "I don't really know. It's just a gut feeling I got from Charles Braddock. He spouted off a few things that made me think either Prince or the boy might not be safe here."

Jehu came to his feet, brushing the hay off his backside. "Massa, I can sits here all night and make sure Prince stays safe."

"No, that won't do. You need to get plenty of rest before the race. But Isaiah, I'm afraid you're going to have to keep an eye open all night and protect these two."

Isaiah let out a long breath. "I understands. Don't you worry none, massa. I'll watch out for both of 'em. Won't nothin' happen whilst I's around."

Master Hawkins nodded approvingly toward his well-muscled trainer. "You're a good man, Isaiah. I trust all will be well in your hands."

"Yessir, massa. T'ain't no cause for worry."

Samuel put a hand on William's shoulder and gestured for him to open the gate. "We'll see you in the morning."

Isaiah turned to Jehu after the master left and noticed his anxious stare. "Here's what we gonna do," he said, leading the boy outside the stall. "You's gonna sleep in the empty stall next to Prince here, and I's gonna stay right out here wheres I can keep a close watch on the both of ya. I won't sleep none."

"You sure?" Jehu pleaded.

"I's sure as I ever been. Now go gets yer bedroll and lay it out in the hay. I be right here all night long. Right here," he said soothingly.

In the wee hours of the morning, Isaiah sat with his back against the wooden railing between Jehu and Prince's stalls. The stables were far from quiet during the night. Occasionally, one of the horses would snort or stomp the floor. Even some of the riders sleeping in other stalls let out a loud snore occasionally . . . or coughed. But Isaiah was vigilant on watch. Sometimes his mind would get to wandering, and sometimes he talked to God, but mostly he kept reminding himself that he would not let his master down.

It was close to dawn when Isaiah knew he needed to get to the woods. He'd been pacing back and forth between the stalls, and he couldn't wait any longer. Knowing the boy had gotten plenty of sleep, he stepped inside his stall.

"Jehu, wake up. You needs to watch Prince for a while," he said, gently shaking his shoulder. "You awake?"

Jehu rolled over, rubbing his eyes. "Yes, boss, I's awake."

"I won't be gone too long. You gots to keep a watchful eye."

"I will," Jehu said sleepily.

But when Isaiah returned from the woods, something had gone horribly wrong. Prince was in a state of panic, and Jehu looked much the same way.

Isaiah quickly swung open Prince's gate and tried to figure out what was going on in the gloomy light. Both horse and rider were agitated to the point of hysteria.

"Whoa, whoa, whoa. Settle down now, both o' ya." He reached up and laid a gentle hand on Prince's muzzle, but the horse let out a shrill whinny that sent terror through Isaiah's heart. There was no calming the stallion.

Isaiah took hold of Jehu's shirt and shoved him toward the gate. "Get outta here right now. You's scarin' 'im."

Jehu scrambled for the gate and closed it behind him.

"Come on now, boy. Come on," Isaiah crooned. "All's well. Come on, now."

Over and over Isaiah spoke soothing words while rubbing gentle hands down his neck and chest. Everything that had usually worked to calm Prince was suddenly having the opposite effect. What could've happened in the short time that Isaiah had been away?

After several long minutes, Prince began to calm a bit, but Isaiah could still see the white around his eyes. He was troubled like never before.

Isaiah quickly stepped out of the stall to talk to Jehu. "What happened here, Son?"

Jehu looked like he was close to tears. He wrung his hands and bit his bottom lip nervously. "I don't know, boss. I don't know."

"What do ya mean, you don't know? Did ya see anyone come near the horse?"

"No boss," Jehu said, dropping his chin to his chest.

"Jehu, I's not mad at ya. Just tell me what ya saw."

"I saw nothin', boss. Nothin'!" All of a sudden Jehu started sobbing uncontrollably. Rocking back and forth on his heels, he could barely get out his next words. "I fell . . . back . . . asleep, boss."

Isaiah closed his eyes and dragged in a deep breath through his nose. Someone had been waiting for an opportunity to get to Prince all night long, and unwittingly he had given it to them. Trouble was, he couldn't figure out what had happened.

Leaving Jehu, Isaiah went back into the stall. He cupped his hand and dipped it into Prince's water bucket, bringing it close to his face. There was a funny smell when there should've been no smell at all. Surely Prince hadn't already taken a drink from the bucket.

"Here," Isaiah said, passing the bucket over the gate to Jehu. "Go dumps this on the ground and find a new bucket. Fill it straight from the well."

Jehu sniffled and wiped his face, then reached for the water bucket. Isaiah watched him run out of sight into the grayish light of dawn.

Chapter 6

It must've been around six in the morning, Isaiah guessed, when sunlight began streaming through the windows of the stables. All the animals were rousing from sleep, along with the slaves, who had spent the night in the hay. In a couple of hours, the trainers would be walking their horses and warming them up for the big race at ten o'clock. Master Hawkins would be here at eight. Surely Prince would be calm by then.

But when the master strolled into the stables and peered over the gate, his face paled. "Isaiah, what's happened to him?"

"I dunno, sir. Someone gots to 'im. We didn't see nothin', but somethin's got 'im all riled up."

Master Hawkins cursed under his breath. "Did you stay awake all night?" he demanded.

"Yessir, all night long."

"And you didn't see anything?"

"No, massa. But I think someone poisoned his water. It didn't smell right."

Another curse rolled off the master's tongue. "Have you walked him?"

"Yessir. It didn't do no good."

Samuel removed his hat and slapped it on his thigh. "All year, Isaiah. All year we've trained Prince for this very day. He may be the best I've ever seen. And now . . . look at him!"

"I know, sir. I's awful sorry."

Master Hawkins took several deep breaths and began pacing the stable floor. After a while he came back to the stall, having calmed down a bit. "What if it wasn't the water? What if it's just a case of the nerves or something? I've seen racehorses do this before a race when they're put in a strange environment. It can't always be explained."

Isaiah put his fist to his forehead, thinking hard about what the master had said. What if it was just a horrible case of crippling anxiety before a race? If so, there would be only one cure.

"Franklin!" Both men practically yelled his name at the same time.

"Yessir, massa. That be it. We needs Franklin right now!"

"I'll be right back," Master Hawkins called over his shoulder as he ran for the stable door.

In less than a minute, he was back with his eldest son. "We can send Joseph to get Franklin. If he takes his horse with all speed, he can be home in less than an hour."

Isaiah was already nodding his head vigorously. "Franklin be with Mammy Lou today whilst Ruth's at the house. You needs help findin' her cabin."

"Find Micah," Samuel told his son. "Go straight to our overseer. He'll go get Franklin and meet you at the stables. Choose a fresh mount when you get there, and be ready to go when Micah brings the boy back to you."

Joseph's expression held a combination of excitement and tension. At thirteen, he'd been expected to spend more time with his father lately, learning the ways of the plantation. This summer he'd learned more about cotton, corn, tobacco, and mules than ever before. Samuel Hawkins wanted to give him a more hands-on education before his tutor returned in September.

Samuel grabbed his son by both shoulders. "Ride hard, but be safe. We need the boy before this race starts at ten. You don't have much time."

The boy's eyes took on a steely edge. "I won't let you down, Papa."

"I know you won't," Samuel nodded.

Jehu was already busy at work saddling Master Joseph's horse, Gallant. Seconds later, he was running down the corridor with Gallant trotting dutifully beside him.

Samuel boosted his son into the saddle, trying to save precious seconds, and before Joseph's feet had found the stirrups, he was already at a gallop. Master Hawkins ran out the stable door, watching his son speed down the plantation road until he was out of sight. Then he headed back to the house for a stiff drink.

❧❧❧

It took nearly thirty-five minutes for Joseph to make it home, but unfortunately, at least a quarter of an hour was wasted just trying to find Micah. Every slave Joseph met on his way to the stables was instructed to find the overseer.

Joseph handed off his horse to the first stable boy in sight and instructed another boy to bring him Boaz, saddled and ready to go. He'd thought long and hard about the best mount for his return trip. He was certain that Boaz would get him back to the Sheffield's faster than Gallant had brought him home. But where was Micah?

Pacing nervously outside the stables, Joseph thought his head would explode. Blowing off some of the steam, he yelled out Micah's name as loud as he could.

"I'm comin'!" a harried voice echoed through the trees. In a few seconds, Micah came into view, running hard with perspiration dripping off his face and neck. "What's happened, massa Joseph?" he croaked, shoving air in and out of his lungs.

"I need little Franklin right now! He's with Mammy Lou."

Micah's brow wrinkled. "Isaiah's son?"

"Yes, I need him now. Hurry up—go get him!"

"Yessir. On my way, sir."

Micah wasn't an old man by any means, but he wasn't exactly in his youth. Joseph knew he could probably outrun him even with a young boy in his arms. He decided to follow the overseer to Mammy Lou's cabin. When they got there, Micah barreled inside, but it was empty. "Not here," he said, gasping for air.

Slave town was nearly deserted—anyone not working at the big house getting ready for tonight's gala was out in the fields doing double work. Micah threw caution to the wind. "MAMMY LOU!" he yelled with all the force of his lungs. "Where you be?"

Relief washed over Micah and Master Joseph alike when they heard the crackling voice of the beloved Mammy. "We's at the stream," she called.

Sprinting down a short path, the men found Mammy Lou and her passel of young'uns splashing around in the shallows near the bank.

Not wasting time for explanations, Joseph told her, "I need Franklin. He has to come with me right now."

The old Mammy instinctively moved into a protective stance. She was well aware that the master's son was standing before her, but by the looks of her, she would not be giving up the boy without good reason.

Micah took over. "Mammy Lou, we need the boy right now. He'll be fine. We just need to get 'im to his pappy."

"Well why didn't you say so in the beginnin'," she cackled, dropping her hands from her hips. "Come 'ere, Franklin. You gots somewheres to be."

Franklin came wading out of the cool stream, barefooted, only wearing a long shirt that barely passed his little knees. When Joseph saw the boy coming, he scooped him up in his arms. Looking the child right in the eyes, he said, "Franklin?"

The boy merely nodded his head, not showing one ounce of fear.

Without another word, Joseph took off like a shot out of a canon, through the woods, and down the road to the stables. Micah followed, breathing hard, but no longer able to run. He made it to the stables just in time to see Joseph gallop away with little Franklin holding tight to Boaz' copper mane.

With Jehu's help, Isaiah managed to get the racing saddle on Prince's back and cinched up tight. It took both men holding the halter rope to keep the stallion from rearing up. They could no longer keep him tied to the post—in his attempts to pull free, he had rolled to the ground more than once. Fearful the stallion would break his neck, the men had to hold him the best they could.

Over and over Prince rose up on his hind legs and punched the air with his hooves like a bare-knuckle boxer. He had already broken two of the boards in his stall, for which Master Hawkins would have to make reparations.

Isaiah didn't see how Jehu would ever be able to mount the horse. He would be thrown instantly and maybe even trampled in doing so. But Master Hawkins had entered the stables only thirty minutes before race time, demanding the horse be readied. It was clear the master had been drinking, which was perplexing since his reputation was one of temperance.

Without hope of a true warm-up before the race, Isaiah managed to slip the bit into Prince's mouth, getting his thumb mashed in the process. He ignored the pain and deftly slipped the bridle behind his ears before ducking away from the stallion's next punch.

"Open the gate," Isaiah told Jehu, "and get out o' the way."

The poor boy was sweating with fright, but he obediently did as he was told. He had already dressed in the Hawkins' green and gold racing outfit but looked as if he might run in the opposite direction at any minute.

It soon became clear that Isaiah couldn't handle the roiling beast alone. "Grab me the rope," he yelled. "We gotta get it 'round his neck. I don't wanna tear up his mouth."

Together the pair slipped the rope over his head, and Isaiah held it firmly in both hands. "You take the reins," he said, "I gots to put all my weight on this rope."

The struggle was so grotesque, Isaiah knew the stallion would have almost no energy left for the race. Even if Joseph somehow made it back with Franklin, Prince had already wasted all of his needed strength during his tirade.

The other six horses were already on the track, trotting on the freshly plowed dirt, loosening their muscles in anticipation of a race. The thing about racehorses was, the most successful ones were the horses that couldn't stand for another one to be in the lead. They would give every ounce of strength just to keep a nose in front of the one next to them. That's how Prince was. He had a formidable instinct to be the lead horse. Dominance was bred into his bones.

The crowd around the two-mile course was larger than Isaiah had anticipated. A rumble filled the air as Isaiah and Jehu led the frantic beast through the gate. Everyone standing nearby took several steps back, hoping to avoid a hoof to the face.

The race master, dressed in a long-tailed coat, climbed the stand next to the chalked starting line. "Riders, take your mark," he bellowed through a voice-amplifying megaphone.

"Take the outside," one of the starting officials yelled at Isaiah. "And get your boy on that horse or get off the track."

Isaiah looked around, searching for Master Hawkins, but he was nowhere in sight. He knew the decision to pull Prince out of the race was not his to make.

Gradually, each of the horses danced to the line, their riders holding back an onslaught of power and energy. Hooves pawed at the earth with unbridled eagerness.

Jehu finally cried out, "What do we do, boss? I can't ride 'im."

The race master seemed amused by the scene and called out, "You gonna run with that horse, boy, or ride him?"

The crowd guffawed and began heckling the two.

"Take your mark."

Isaiah didn't hear the race master at all. He was suddenly throwing his arms wildly in the air at the sight of Joseph galloping in fast, holding Franklin tight up against his abdomen.

Isaiah sprinted to the railing as Boaz skidded to an abrupt halt, scattering more spectators from their viewing spots. Joseph scooted Franklin off the saddle right into his pappy's outstretched arms. As Isaiah ran back toward Prince, he vaguely noticed one of the other horses jump the line, buying them just a few more seconds.

Little Franklin grinned when his pappy held him up to the crazed stallion. At the child's gentle touch, Prince utterly relaxed.

"Get on, Jehu," Isaiah pressed urgently. But the stallion was too tall and the stirrups too high for the boy to climb up.

Not wanting to break his son's connection to Prince, Isaiah set Franklin atop the placid beast, giving Jehu a boost into the saddle.

At that very instant, the race master pointed his pistol toward the sky. And pulled the trigger.

Isaiah reached for the rope around Prince's neck, but it was too late. Even more significant than the rope was Franklin, now lying flat against the stallion's neck, holding tightly to his mane. Isaiah ran several frantic yards behind them in vain—Prince's instincts had kicked in, and he was running helter-skelter behind the pack.

When Isaiah realized his efforts were for naught, he dropped to his knees on the track in utter disbelief. He didn't want to watch what was about to happen to the threesome he cared so much about. The rope twisted and flailed precariously, trailing its tail along the dirt only inches from Prince's powerful strides. One step. Just one step on that rope would flip the horse violently onto its back, crushing the two riders beneath his weight.

"Oh, Lawd, no," Isaiah lamented, grabbing handfuls of rich black dirt. He leaned back on his heels, turning his face toward heaven. "Lawd, no!"

A collective gasp from the crowd snapped Isaiah's eyes back to Prince and his two riders. Franklin had moved out a little further onto Prince's neck and now held the mane in one hand and the rope in the other. Jehu's body, too, was prone as he held the reins in his left hand and Franklin's shirt all bunched up in his right. There would be no stopping Prince now—their only hope was to pull the rope off the ground.

What seemed like hours in reality took only a few seconds. Franklin was able to tug just enough rope up for Jehu to grab and drape it across his legs. The crowd gasped again the moment Jehu let go of the little boy to clutch the rope. The scene was harrowing.

Someone called Isaiah's name loudly from the fence. He glanced over his shoulder to see Master Hawkins fervidly beckoning him. Isaiah came to his feet and ran to his master, taking his eye off of the trio.

"I saw what happened, Isaiah. I'm sorry," he said, red-faced and sweating profusely.

Isaiah could smell the alcohol seeping through his pours and felt utterly helpless. There was nothing he could do or say to fix the situation—he couldn't even make sense of it at the moment. He simply turned back to watch this horrible race play out to the bitter end.

"One mile," the race master called.

Squinting his eyes, Isaiah searched for the Hawkins' green and gold, but he couldn't find it at the back of the pack. He began frantically scanning along the first mile of the track for his boys. It was empty. What could've happened to them?

An air of enthusiasm began to ripple and surge through the crowd. Some of the spectators bobbed up and down on their tiptoes to get a better view. Several began running toward the final turn a half mile away.

It wasn't until the horses made the turn—four abreast with two behind and one in the lead—that Isaiah realized what all the excitement was about. Prince was barreling down the track toward the finish line, creating distance between him and the pack with every stride. His sleek, powerful muscles gleamed in the sunlight as they ate up ground like a locomotive with a full head of steam.

When Prince flew across the finish line, far ahead of the other six horses, the crowd cheered loudly for the champ and his two valiant riders. The roaring applause continued until Prince slowed to a canter, then a trot, and finally a spirited walk back toward the finish line.

Isaiah pushed away from the fence and sprinted toward the victorious trio. Tears of relief streamed down his dark cheeks as he grasped his son and pulled him into a smothering embrace. The Prince of Madagascar pranced proudly by their side as they made their way to the winner's circle just outside the gate.

The crowd circled around in awe, allowing Isaiah to guide the champions to a designated spot.

"Put the boy back on the horse," someone called from the crowd.

"Yeah, put him on the horse!"

With a satisfied grin, Isaiah set his son astride Prince once more. And when Jehu held Franklin's arms above his head, the crowd whistled and cheered like never before.

Chapter 7

Elizabeth sat before the vanity mirror while Ruth swept her mistress' hair into an elegant swirl at the nape of her neck. She was still wearing her dressing gown, waiting for Naomi to bring her latest creation for the fall gala. A worried expression filled Elizabeth's eyes.

"It's not like Samuel to ever be sick. I do hope he's feeling better before guests start arriving."

"So do I, missus," Ruth agreed.

"Maybe he got overly excited about winning the race this morning. He's been talking of little else since Charles Braddock beat him last year. He thinks Braddock somehow cheated him out of victory," she sighed.

Ruth couldn't wait for Isaiah to give her all the details. Oh, how she wished she could've been there to see Prince run across the finish line. It must've been a glorious moment. Ruth pressed her lips tight. One thing was for sure, she never wanted Franklin around that horrible black beast ever again. She was thankful he was safe with Mammy Lou back at the cabins. Isaiah had wanted to take him to the race, but Ruth had been adamant about leaving the child behind.

A soft knock sounded on the bedroom door, and Elizabeth called, "Come in."

Naomi entered the bedchamber with the gorgeous gown draped carefully over her arm. "Mistress, I'm here to help you dress for the gala," she said.

Elizabeth's face beamed with delight. She caught Ruth's eye in the mirror. "Are we ready?"

"One last touch, missus. There," she said, making sure the last comb would hold.

Naomi smiled at her mistress. "You're already the most beautiful woman at the gala, and you have yet to put on your gown."

"Naomi," Elizabeth crooned, "you do know the way to my heart."

Ruth helped her mistress out of the dressing gown and allowed Naomi to take over. She would be at the ready should they need her.

As soon as the mistress was dressed, Naomi stood in front of her, puffing the cap sleeves just off her shoulders. The emerald green brought out the golden streaks throughout Elizabeth's hair and gave her eyes a deep turquoise hue. She was simply stunning.

"It's absolutely lovely," she told Naomi. "I am in awe of your talent."

Naomi blushed at the compliment. "Thank you, Mistress."

"Ruth?" Elizabeth said.

"Yes'm?"

"Would you please find out if Samuel is dressed? He was so kind to give me the bedroom this afternoon and said he would dress in the guest room at the far end of the hall."

"Yes'm. Right away."

Ruth left the room and headed down to the other end of the hall. She couldn't help but peek into Isabella's room to see how the girls were getting along. Just like her mother, Isabella looked exquisite in her new dress. No doubt, she was going to turn a lot of heads tonight, even though she would only be allowed to attend the supper portion.

Leaving the girls, Ruth headed further down the hall to the last room. When she knocked lightly on the door, she was taken aback by the one who opened it.

"Izzy, whatchu doin' here?" she exclaimed.

Isaiah had only opened the door a few inches and immediately looked back over his shoulder before sliding out of the room. Quietly closing the door, he took Ruth's elbow and led her back up the hallway to a small alcove out of sight.

Ruth didn't give him a chance to speak. "Look at you, mister. You is so handsome." Her hands ran up and down his arms, a look of admiration in her eyes. "Where'd you get that fine suit, Izzy?" She was clearly in awe of her man.

"Aw, Ruthie, I's thinkin' the sames about you." He let out a low whistle. "You is the most perty woman I ever did see. I could eat you up right here on the spot," he said in a husky voice, moving in close.

Ruth took a step back, peering down the hallway. She didn't want anyone to see them exchange such intimacy in the big house. Thankfully, all was quiet.

"Whatchu doin' in the guest room with the massa?" she pressed.

"I's helpin' the massa gets ready for the gala, that's all."

"The missus wants to know how he's doin'. She said he might be feelin' poorly after the race this mornin'." She stepped closer to her husband, laying a hand on his chest. "For which I heard your Prince be the champ." Her eyes shone with esteem for Isaiah's accomplishment.

But instead of his usual rascally grin, a cloud passed over her husband's face. There was something he wasn't telling her. She didn't have time for details about the race right now, so she pressed him again on the master.

"Is he gonna be fine, Izzy? I gots to tell the missus."

Isaiah nodded his head confidently. "He be just fine. Matter o' fact, he be joinin' the missus in a few minutes. Tell her it won't be long."

"All right, Izzy, I'll tell her. But you men need to hurry it up—guests are comin' soon."

Looking down at his wife, Isaiah's demeanor turned playful again. "How 'bout I gets a kiss from my perty gal first?"

"No, sir, mister. Don't you be playin' like that in this house," she said good-humoredly. "But mmm, mmm, I do like that suit."

"The massa give it to me fer winnin' the race today. 'Sides, he wants me out front with the carriages when guests arrive."

"I can see why," she said, running her hand down his arm one more time. "Now, go get the man."

"Yes'm," Isaiah said dutifully and headed back down the hall.

Ruth joined the women again, and as soon as she walked into the bedroom, Naomi bowed her head to the mistress, taking her leave. Though Abigail held a special position as head of the Hawkins' household, Naomi herself was a power of a person. Many of the house slaves looked to her first for a multitude of reasons. She carried herself with such an air of quiet confidence, and it rubbed off on anyone within her sphere. She would be indispensable tonight during the gala. If everything ran according to plan, Naomi would deserve much of the credit.

Within a few minutes, Isaiah delivered the master as promised before heading outside. When Samuel walked into the bedroom, Ruth noticed immediately the pallor of his skin. His normally tanned and vibrant face seemed a bit pasty, his eyes not as bright.

"Are you under the weather?" Elizabeth immediately asked. "You don't look well."

Samuel waved off her concern. "I'm fine, Elizabeth, just fine. I feel much better after a long nap this afternoon."

"I can only imagine how nervous you must've been last night before the race. You look like you didn't sleep a wink."

Walking over to the mirror, Samuel jutted out his strong chin and straightened his tie. "Is it that noticeable?" he queried.

Elizabeth put a hand on his arm and turned him toward her. "I'm not talking about the way *you* look," she said, demanding his full attention. "You didn't say a word about the way your *wife* looks when you entered the room."

"Oh, darling, I'm so sorry. Truly. You look absolutely gorgeous. Not one woman will compare to you tonight."

"You mean it?" she asked coyly.

Reaching around her slender waist, he splayed his hand on the small of her back and drew her in. "I'll have to keep my guard up tonight. I don't want you stolen away from me."

Visibly satisfied with her husband's answer, Elizabeth smiled into his dark brown eyes. "Thank you," she said, accepting an admiring kiss.

"Shall we?" Samuel asked, turning to offer his elbow.

"We shall," she responded. Then, as they left the room, she discreetly remarked that his cologne was a bit stronger than usual.

❧✦❧

With dinner complete and tables removed, the guests now felt free to roam about the house and grounds at their leisure. Many strolled through the gardens, where dozens of lanterns had been lit at dusk. Others had played croquet on the front lawn until the evening shades shrouded the wickets in darkness.

The weather couldn't have been any more perfect. All of the doors and windows were flung wide, allowing a light September breeze to meander through the house. Guests could move from inside to outside with abundant ease. The orchestra was seated on the large patio beside the French doors, increasing the size of the dance floor by more than double. Couples whirled about to the music indoors or out, depending on their mood.

Dessert platters and drinks were continuously replenished by dozens of slaves working in the kitchens. The serving-men had been outfitted in black suits tailored to perfection, and the women wore spotless, well-made black dresses with crisp white aprons at their waist. No expense had been spared to ensure that those who had traveled a long distance would be given a night to remember.

Isabella, Joseph, and William bade their parents and guests good-night right on cue as the orchestra began to warm up. Joseph and William dutifully went to their rooms, yanking off their ties as they went, and Isabella straggled into her room, throwing her body across the bed.

"Umph," she complained. "I'm almost sixteen. What on earth do three months matter?" She plopped over like a fish on dry land and stared at the canopy of her bed.

Sarah had been awaiting Isabella's return and laid down on her back beside her mistress. "That doesn't mean you can't watch," she quipped.

Isabella released a loud sigh. "You can't see the dance floor from the landing. Mother would be upset if she saw us sitting on the stairs."

"Yes, but you can see the patio dance floor from the outdoor balcony," Sarah said conspiratorially.

Rising to her elbows, Isabella practically yelled, "You're right! No one would ever see us up there." Then turning onto her side, she added, "We can even see the gardens from there." She gave Sarah a peck on the cheek. "You're a genius."

"Do you want me to help you get out of that dress?" Sarah asked.

"No, you and I will dance on the roof. Let's put this dress to good use."

Both girls giggled and sprinted the length of the hall. While the house had been built with large windows at both ends of the hallway for lighting purposes, they were actually hiding a secret. By releasing a latch and raising the window, a second latch could be tripped to open the wall as if it were a miniature door. They were rarely ever opened but were practically made for this occasion, according to Isabella.

The girls moved to the railing at the end of the porch, peering down into the whirling crowd. It would be impossible for any of the guests to see them, even if they looked up. Lanterns had been strung across the patio, keeping the dance floor well-lit and effectively hiding the curious duo upstairs.

It was the perfect solution as far as Isabella was concerned. "We won't go to bed all night," she exclaimed. "As long as they stay up, we will too."

For a while the two girls twirled around their private dance floor, but it wasn't long before Isabella lost interest. "I have another idea."

Sarah looked at her eagerly, ready for their next adventure.

"Let's go to the balcony on the other end. That's where we can see what *your* people are doing."

Sarah knew that if she weren't companion to Miss Isabella, she would certainly be down in the kitchens with the rest of the slaves. Or even worse, she would be doing back-breaking work, constantly washing and cleaning up after all of the Hawkins' guests. She much preferred sharing the evening with Isabella.

Sneaking out onto the opposite balcony was like stepping into another world. The girls crouched low so as not to be seen. The only light shining in this area was from a fire pit with a whole pig roasting on the spit, a couple of strategically placed torches, and light escaping from the windows inside.

Isabella was instantly mesmerized. Some of the Hawkins' slaves and slaves from the other plantations were mingling together—laughing, singing, animatedly conversing. Some had come out from the cooking kitchen to take a short break and catch a bit of the breeze. Isabella pointed to two women who had just recognized each other from separate plantations. Four of the men got into an argument about the morning's horse race. One of the men grabbed a girl around the waist and whirled her around before they disappeared into the trees. Some of the men were smoking while others were passing around a flask.

"This is amazing," Isabella whispered. "I had no idea." She glanced over at Sarah. "Did you?"

Sarah hated to admit it, but she had never witnessed such a gathering either. It almost seemed as though she didn't belong there, but deep down inside, she knew she did.

"This is a lot better than the other end of the house," Isabella declared.

Eventually, Isabella decided to part with her dress and went inside to put on something more comfortable. A few minutes later she came out with an old quilt, so the girls would be able to sit down and watch the scene below.

Isabella leaned against Sarah's shoulder. "Let's pick out someone just for you."

Sarah felt her face grow warm. "No, missy, there's no need for that."

"Oh yes, there is. Just for fun, let's choose someone."

"All right," Sarah grudgingly agreed.

The girls searched the crowd, pointing out one man after another. Some were too old, others too skinny or short. Finally, Sarah pointed out a young man sitting on a stump just at the edge of the flickering firelight. "That one, right there," she declared.

Isabella wholeheartedly agreed. He had a fine face and well-muscled arms. Every now and then he would stand up and stretch, check on the roasting pig, then sit back down. He seemed to keep to himself, not interacting much with the others.

Hours went by, and the girls had yet to weary of the scene. But when it came time to cut the roasted pig, Sarah's young man was called over. He checked out the beast, rolling it over and over, then declared it was ready for consumption. When he began to cut off slabs of ham, both girls' mouths began to water.

"Mmm, what I wouldn't give to have a bite," Isabella crooned.

"Me too," Sarah agreed.

Isabella's mouth suddenly gaped wide. "We *can* have a bite!"

Sarah's brow furrowed. "How?"

"Those are your people, Sarah. You can go right down there and get a plate."

"My mama would have a fit if she caught me down there."

"Then don't get caught. Come on, I want some ham and so do you. Besides, you'll get a chance to meet your man."

Sarah's heart picked up speed. It really would be nice to meet him. She rarely even got the opportunity to be with the young people on her own plantation. What could it hurt just to talk to someone from another one?

Her head began bobbing up and down. "All right, I'll do it."

Isabella nearly jumped out of her shoes with glee. "I'll be right here watching everything. Don't you dare just get some ham and not talk to him."

"I won't," Sarah said with a bravado that Isabella's excitement was fueling.

"Take the back stairs to the kitchen, and make sure your mama is nowhere in sight."

Sarah nervously walked to the open window and stepped through, but stopped in the hallway. Should she be doing this?

"Go on," Isabella waved to her. "We don't have all night . . . well, actually we do," she giggled.

Making the excuse that her mistress was commanding it, Sarah turned and hurriedly headed for the back stairs before she had the chance to change her mind.

Chapter 8

Sarah inched to the bottom step of the back staircase and peeked around the corner to the inside kitchen. It was a frenzied scene yet somehow functioning with measured precision. Just then, her mother stepped into the room, and Sarah quickly ducked back around the corner. She could hear Abigail giving orders over the hubbub. Thankfully, Abigail's directions were for Ruth to take a platter of tea cakes to the parlor.

Waiting patiently for the perfect time, Sarah came out of her hiding place and walked nonchalantly across the large room, carefully avoiding eye contact. It wouldn't have mattered. No one was paying her a bit of attention.

Once out the back door, Sarah slowly made her way around the house and to the side where the slaves had gathered. She immediately felt out of place and skirted around the backside of the gathering. Standing outside the scope of the dim light, she stared once more at the scene from ground level. She couldn't believe she was actually doing this. But then again, why shouldn't she? She was seventeen, for goodness sakes. Her own mama had already been married with a child by now.

Moving a little closer to the fire pit, Sarah ventured a glance up at the balcony. She couldn't see Isabella in the inky night, but she could literally feel her presence. She knew her eyes would be on her like a hawk.

Drawing in a deep breath, Sarah stepped forward, picking up a tin plate by the firepit. "May I?" she asked the young man quietly.

He turned and looked her fully in the face. She thought she might faint—he was more handsome up close than what she had thought from her perch above. His eyes, however, didn't remain on her face. He looked her up and down, making Sarah feel naked.

"Yes, you may," he said eagerly.

He searched around the roasted pig, trying to find the best possible slice, and laid it on her plate.

"Umm . . ." she swallowed hard. "I have a friend who would like some too."

A smile touched his lips. "That be a female or a male friend?"

"Female," she replied a little too quickly.

"In that case, let me finds another good portion for your *female* friend."

Once again, he took his time and found the best portion from the rump. But this time, when he put it on her plate, he took hold of the other side of it so she couldn't walk away. "Come eat with me," he said smoothly.

Sarah knew she should make an excuse and get away, but something in the timbre of his voice drew her in. Wrestling with her conscience, she finally said, "My friend is waiting."

With a gentle tug on her plate, he said, "Your friend can wait. You can eat with me first."

Leading her to his stump, he motioned for her to have a seat. He took the other piece of ham right off her plate and started eating. Noticing her surprise, he said, "Don't worry none. I'll cut your friend another slice."

She smiled shyly and picked up her piece of ham. It may have been one of the best things she'd ever put in her mouth. She couldn't help but tell him. "This is . . . wonderful." She hadn't realized how hungry she was nor how good a roasted pig would taste. "Are you the one who did this?"

His grin made him even more attractive, if that were possible. "Yes, ma'am. I learned it from my pappy."

Sarah nodded, not knowing what else to say. She ate the rest of her slice in silence.

When she was done, he set her plate on the ground and asked her to scoot over. "There's room for two."

She slid as close to the edge of the stump as she could without falling to the ground. He sat beside her, smelling of wood fire and outdoors. It was virtually impossible for them not to touch each other sitting side by side. He turned slightly to face her.

"My name's Josiah—most calls me Josey," he added.

"Which do you like?"

"Depends on who's sayin' it, I guess. What about you?"

"What about me?" Sarah asked shyly.

"You gots a name?"

"Sarah," she said softly.

"Sarah," he repeated admiringly.

It took a while for them to warm up to one another, but soon the two were talking a blue streak. Sarah wanted to know everything about him, and it seemed he wanted to know all about her. Comfortable was how it felt being with Josey—she could feel the spark in her heart turning into a low-burning flame.

They must've talked for an hour when Sarah was startled by the sound of her mother's voice. There were only a handful of times she'd heard her name spoken in such a tone. Jumping up off the stump, she turned to see her mama standing near the fire, hands planted firmly on her hips.

"Mama," Sarah said in a tight voice. "What are you doing out here?"

"That's the very same question I has for you, gal."

Sarah thought she had no choice but to introduce her to Josey, who had come to his feet with a look of confusion.

"Mama, this is Josiah."

"Josiah," Ruth said in a motherly tone. "Where are you from?"

"The Stafford Plantation, ma'am . . . just past Frankfort."

"Well, I reckon that means you'll be headin' back there come daylight." Ruth stepped forward and clasped her daughter's arm. "Nice to meet you, Josiah. Good night."

Ruth didn't give the pair a chance to say another word. Her grip tightened as she pulled Sarah toward the house.

"Mama, you're hurting my arm," Sarah complained.

"Not as much as you're hurtin' my heart, child. Come on, now." Ruth didn't stop yanking her along until they made it all the way to the back porch behind the kitchen. That's when she turned and took hold of Sarah's shoulders, piercing her with a hard gaze.

"Child, you can't be makin' affections with some man from another plantation."

Sarah instantly started crying. "Why, Mama? Why can't I love someone like everybody else?"

"Do you think I don't want you lovin' nobody? That's not it at all," Ruth declared harshly.

"Well that's sure what it do seem like," Sarah wailed, breaking free from her mother's grip and sitting down on the porch steps. She folded her arms tight against her body.

Ruth let out a languid sigh and sat down beside her daughter. "Sarah, gal," she said, a bit more gently, "you're becoming a fine-lookin' woman. There be lots o' men who'll want you, but you gotta find 'im on the Hawkins Plantation. Nobody's as kind and good to his slaves than Massa Hawkins. Why he's so kind and good, he might even let you marry and go somewheres else to be with your man."

Sarah suddenly sat straighter. "That's right, Mama. So why can't I do that with Josey if I want to?"

"Josey? Is that what you call him?" Ruth said in consternation. "Girl, you don't even know him."

"Oh, yes I do, Mama. And I love him!"

Ruth let out a humorless laugh. "You only thinks you do," she said, looking away.

After a long silence, she turned toward her daughter again. "Gal," she said softly, "I know what it's like—it was just that quick with me and your pappy. So don't think I don't understand. But here's what *you're* not understandin'. What if you was to go with this Josey to the Stafford Plantation, and gets married, and have babies, and all of a sudden Massa Stafford say, 'I gots too many slaves. I think I'll sell Josey and one o' his chillins'.' Whatchu gonna do then, gal? Hmm?"

"That would never happen," Sarah declared in disbelief.

"Oh child," Ruth said with deep emotion. "You got no idea what happens on other plantations. No idea at all."

Another extended silence fell between them. Ruth noticed Naomi heading outside of the cooking kitchen for a break. That poor young woman was working herself to death.

Finally, Ruth wrenched open her wounded heart. She told Sarah numerous horrors she had tried to forget from the plantation where she'd been raised. How all the slaves lived in fear of making a mistake—how the white overseer would take any woman he wanted, whenever he wanted her—how the mistress slapped the very women who served her and had them beaten if anything were to break in the house or be done in a way displeasing to her—how her pappy was whipped on a regular basis just to make sure he knew who was in charge—how she never even knew who her own mammy was—and worst of all, how she'd seen her pappy hanging by the neck from a tree, just swaying in the breeze like a flag on a pole.

"As long as I live, I can never get that picture out o' my head. Never," she whispered.

Sarah's eyes were full of grief. Tears flowed down her cheeks unrestrained. "How come you never told me all this, Mama? I didn't know."

Ruth reached out and pulled her daughter close. "I guess I wanted to keep you from havin' to know how bad this world can be. We's still not free, but at least we ain't treated like animals here." She bent her face close to Sarah's. "You ever been slapped by your missy?"

"No, ma'am," Sarah said quietly.

"That's right—and you never will be. So don't go wishin' for someone else's massa. You hear me, child?"

Sarah sat up, wiping the tears from her face. Her mama's earlier rebuke didn't seem quite so cruel after all. "Yes, ma'am, I—"

Her next words froze inside her throat when she saw Miss Isabella running frantically out of the cooking kitchen. When the girl caught a glimpse of Sarah and her mother sitting on the porch steps, she started running toward them, waving her arms wildly.

"Missy!" Ruth chastised, coming to her feet. "You get yourself back in that house before I tell your—"

"It's Naomi!" Isabella yelled. "She's in trouble!"

Ruth caught the girl by her shoulders to keep from being knocked to the ground. "Whatchu talkin' about, missy?"

Isabella could barely catch her breath. "I was on . . . the balcony, and . . . I saw some man drag . . . Naomi behind the . . . storehouse. We have to help her."

"Not *we*, missy. You get in that house right now. Go straight to your room. You hear me?"

Isabella's eyes were wild, but Ruth pressed the girl to do exactly as she was told—for everyone's sake. "Don't tell nobody in the house—we're not spoilin' your mama's party." Shaking her shoulders hard, she gave the girl another strict command. "You mind me right now, missy."

Isabella gave her a wide-eyed stare but thankfully submitted to her slave's command.

৺৶৻

Ruth felt her emotions swirling like a hurricane. "Go get your pappy right now, child. He's out front."

Sarah's compliance was immediate. She took off at a sprint, skirting around the outside of the negro gathering.

Josey bounded to his feet from the stump. He'd seen the frenetic scene with Isabella unfold. Without a word, he ran at top speed to catch up with Ruth, who had hiked up her skirt as she ran. Together they rounded the back of the storehouse on the edge of a large, freshly plowed field, but it was black as pitch—they couldn't see a thing.

Ruth grabbed Josey's arm and forced him to come to a halt. She shushed him with a finger to her lips. The pair did their best to quiet their breathing. Without a moon in the sky, the stars did very little to illuminate the landscape.

"There!" Ruth hissed. "You hear that?"

Josey nodded vigorously. "I heard somethin' over there."

The duo took off running again toward the sound of the muffled cry. When Ruth tripped in one of the furrows, Josey reached down and pulled her to her feet. He held onto her for a few steps, then let go and picked up speed. They could now detect a terrible struggle taking place nearby. A vague form lying prone on the ground came into fuzzy view.

Josey landed in on the man like a mountain lion pouncing on its prey. He balled up handfuls of the man's shirt in both fists and yanked his whole body into the air. With surprising strength, Josey threw him off of Naomi onto his side with a loud thud. The horrible struggle that ensued reminded Ruth of two wild animals fighting for their lives.

Ruth dropped to her knees at Naomi's side, quickly sliding her skirt back over her legs, and helping her to a sitting position. Her blouse had been ripped open to her waist, and Ruth gently pulled it back together, while surrounding her with a protective arm.

"I'm so sorry, Naomi. Can you stand?" she asked, still worried about the outcome of the nearby struggle. The men were yelling and punching and flailing about on the ground. She desperately wanted to help Josey but didn't know how.

46

"I think so." Naomi's words were strained, her breathing shallow.

But when Ruth got her up, Naomi's knees buckled, so she helped her sit back down in the dirt.

Ruth was afraid Josey would be killed. She had to do something. But just as she made up her mind to help, Isaiah came flying in with full force, taking both men down to the ground with a thundering crash. Sarah was right there with him. "That one, Pappy!" she yelled, pointing out the man she didn't know.

Isaiah landed a punishing blow to the man's face and knocked him out cold. Sarah fell to the ground beside Josey, her hands grasping his arms, her eyes searching every inch of him for signs of serious injury. Even in the dark, it was obvious he would need tending.

In just a few seconds, Overseer Micah showed up on the scene, breathing hard. "I brought a rope," he said, holding it out to Isaiah.

Isaiah shook his head. "You gots to tie 'im up. I broke my hand."

"Oh, Izzy," Ruth moaned. "Are you sure?"

"Perty sure," he said. "But that's no matter." He squatted down beside his wife. "Is Naomi gonna be all right?"

Naomi instinctively reached for her blouse, helping Ruth keep her covered.

"Yes," Naomi said softly.

"We need a doctor for that hand," Ruth told him.

"And for Josey," Sarah added.

But Josey wouldn't hear of it. He pulled himself to his feet, albeit with Sarah's help, and declared that he would be fine, even though his body swayed from side to side.

Isaiah went back over to the man he'd hit. Micah had hogtied his hands and ankles behind his back. Isaiah bent to turn the man's face upward. "I knows him," he said in disbelief. "That be Terrance from the Braddock place. He may be the onliest person on earth I'm happy to 've broke my hand on."

Ruth leaned into Naomi and whispered, "Did you know him?"

All Naomi did was shake her head, releasing a stream of tears down her cheeks.

"Come on, sweet friend. Let me get you back to the house." Ruth said.

This time Naomi was able to remain upright, and slowly the two walked across the field. Sarah and Josey followed closely behind, but when they came to the back of the storehouse, they stopped to discuss how to proceed.

Josey sat down with his back against the rough stones of the building. He was weak and bleeding and needed a moment to rest.

Ruth took over with instructions for her daughter. "Go to Naomi's room and bring a new blouse. I'll take care of getting her to her room, but you're going to have to sneak Josey into your room through the back door. We need to look at his injuries in the light."

Sarah started to hurry away, but Ruth caught her arm. "Slowly, gal. We don't wanna cause no ruckus."

"Yes, ma'am," Sarah said and disappeared out of sight.

Chapter 9

Activity was beginning to slow to a crawl in the cooking kitchen as the night wound down to its final hour. While food baskets were being prepared for the guests' travels, Naomi and Ruth walked unhurriedly through the kitchen as if they were inspecting the progress. When they entered the back hallway, Ruth encircled Naomi's waist and led her to her room.

Taking her by the shoulders, she sat Naomi down on the side of the bed. "I'll be right back." Leaning down, she brushed a tender kiss on her friend's cheek, then headed across the hall to unlock the back door. All of the women who lived in the big house had rooms along this back corridor but rarely used the door at the end of the hallway.

Sliding the bolt, Ruth opened the door wide. Sarah and Josey were already there on the landing—her arm around his waist, his arm across her shoulder. He was leaning heavily upon her to walk.

Ruth opened the door to Sarah's room and helped get Josey on the bed. The other bed in the room belonged to Tabitha, but none of the girls would be using their rooms until all of the guests had departed. Several of the slaves around the plantation would then come in and take over the task of cleaning and cooking until the house slaves had been given a full day and night of rest.

Ruth quickly poured a pitcher of water into the basin and grabbed a clean cloth from a drawer. "Get 'im cleaned up, child, and come get me if he's needin' the doctor."

"I will," Sarah said.

As Ruth headed for the door, she glanced back at the pair. Sarah had already started unbuttoning Josey's shirt. *Oh, Lawd*, Ruth prayed silently, *you's in charge*.

When Ruth entered Naomi's room, she found her dressed in a fresh skirt and working on her hair.

"What are you doin'?" Ruth asked in dismay.

Naomi raised an apologetic hand. "It's all right. The night is about over. I can see this through."

"No, ma'am. Ain't no way that's happenin'. You'll have to get past me to go back out there." Ruth planted her feet firmly by the door.

For a moment it appeared Naomi would put up an argument. If anyone could go about business as usual, it would probably be her. But a resigned expression fell across her face. She slowly laid down her comb. "You're right," she said with a quiver in her voice. Then, leaning back against the dresser, she began to quietly weep.

Ruth went to her, pulling her friend into a tender embrace. "Shh, now. I gots you. He can't harm you no more."

The two clung together for a long time, Naomi releasing the horror of the night and Ruth taking it upon herself.

"There now," Ruth said as Naomi began to calm. "Let's get you cleaned up and in the bed."

Naomi nodded and allowed Ruth to help her wash and dress in her nightgown. Ruth was dismayed by the bruises on her friend's throat and arms and thighs. When she thought about the man who did this, she wished she'd had the chance to punch him once or twice herself.

When Naomi laid down, Ruth pulled the sheet up to her shoulders and held it there securely.

Gazing into her eyes with deep concern, Ruth gently asked the question that still hung between them. "Did he?"

Naomi's eyelids fell, and she squeezed them tightly shut. A tear slid down her cheek. "No," she said softly.

Ruth let out the breath she'd been holding, relieved to hear that one small word. Even though Terrance had been stopped short, he had still assaulted Naomi mercilessly. Just the terror of her abduction and having to fight for her very life would leave a scar to be reckoned with.

A soft knock on the door drew the women's attention. Ruth opened it only a crack, and there was Isabella. Her face was splotchy from crying. "How is Naomi?" she whispered tearfully.

"Oh, child," Ruth said with a great deal of emotion. She opened the door, letting the girl inside the room, and enveloped her in a loving hug. "You saved her life."

Naomi slowly sat up in bed. "What do you mean?"

Ruth kept her arm around Isabella's shoulders and walked her to the bedside. "If it hadn't been for Missy here, we would o' never know'd you was in trouble."

Naomi took hold of Isabella's wrist and drew her down on the bed. "How did you know?" she asked curiously.

Isabella explained how she and Sarah had watched the negro gathering on the other side of the house for hours. She admitted to falling asleep while Sarah talked to the young man on the stump. But when she woke up, Sarah was gone, so she went to the far end of the balcony, searching the area behind the house.

"That's when I saw you trying to push some man away. When he put his hand over your mouth and started dragging you . . ." her words got caught in her throat. Fresh tears filled her eyes, and she practically dove into Naomi's arms.

"It's all right, Isabella," Naomi assured. "If it hadn't been for you, things would've been much worse." She cupped Isabella's face in both hands and kissed her forehead. "Thank you, dear one."

Ruth softly touched the girl's back. "Come with me, missy. We need to get you in the bed, and I need to prepare your mama and papa's bedchamber."

Reluctantly, Isabella released her hold on Naomi and stood. Ruth turned down the oil lamp, then touched her friend lightly on the arm. "You sleep now, and I'll be back to stay with you soon."

"Thank you," Naomi said in an exhausted voice.

When the pair stepped out in the hallway, Isabella asked, "Where's Sarah?"

"She's in her room, missy. You two can see each other tomorrow."

"But I just want to ask her something. I won't be long."

Ruth shook her head vehemently. The last thing she wanted to do was involve Isabella in the mess that was still going on. "No, Miss Isabella. Sarah needs her rest, and so do you. You'll see her tomorrow, if not sooner."

That seemed to satisfy the girl, and she acquiesced to Ruth's instructions for a second time tonight. Keeping steady pressure on her back, Ruth led her up the back staircase and straight into bed.

❦❦❦

Isaiah squatted in the dirt, holding his throbbing hand while he and Micah discussed what to do with their prisoner. This was not going to be a matter for the plantation owners—the overseers had ways of dealing with their own.

Micah reached over and checked the pulse in Terrance's neck again. "Still beatin' like a hammer," he commented. "You all right to sit here with him, whilst I go fetch Cecil?"

"Uh, huh. He ain't goin' nowheres."

Micah laughed and plucked the rope like a fiddle. "That's for sure."

Isaiah sat all the way down in the dirt, resting his hand on his thigh. He couldn't even squeeze it shut; it was so swollen. He wondered what it was going to look like when he saw it in the light of day.

While he waited in the predawn hour for Micah to bring the Braddock's overseer, Isaiah thought he better pray for a wise decision concerning this situation. He'd heard stories of what it was like on the Braddock Plantation and knew young Terrance's life could very well be hanging in the balance. If he had raped Naomi, Master Braddock would be informed. Terrance would likely be hanged before they ever made it back home.

⋦⋰⋙

Sarah finished with her tender ministrations and helped Josey back into his shirt. She had ripped up one of her petticoats, making a bandage to wrap tightly around his ribs. When she finished with the last button, they sat facing each other on the bed. While Josey had taken a hard blow to the jaw, most of the damage had been done to his body.

He smiled, then moaned, and cupped his chin with his hand. "I don't guess there's anything to be done about this," he said wryly, fingering the large bruise on his jaw.

A soft smile turned Sarah's lips. "Maybe this will help." She leaned in and lightly kissed his cheek near the injury.

He drew a long breath, capturing her eyes with a steady gaze. Not allowing her to withdraw, he held her by the shoulders and carefully pulled her close, pressing his lips to hers.

Sarah had never been kissed before, but she knew one thing, she liked it. Her lack of experience along with her shyness quickly evaporated.

After a long, passionate moment, Josey withdrew. His breathing came in ragged spurts. The two sat gazing at one another—passion building between them.

That's when a knock sounded on the door.

Sarah startled from her yearning and practically leapt from the bed. She smoothed her blouse before saying, "Who is it?" grimacing at the sound of her voice.

The door swung open, and Ruth sped into the room. Thankfully, she didn't look at Sarah's face or she would've known immediately what had happened.

Instead, she went straight to Josey. "We have to get you out o' here right now. Sun's about to come up, and there's somethin' you gotta do before we get you back to your massa's people."

Josey swung his legs off the bed with a cry of pain. Sarah couldn't help herself—she went to him. But he sat up on his own, holding a hand to his ribs. He gladly accepted her help getting to his feet, however.

"I gotta take care of the pig," Josey said urgently.

"No need. It's already been done," Ruth explained. "Micah's waitin' outside. He'll take you where you need to be."

Josey merely nodded and allowed the women to help him to the end of the hallway. Micah spun about when the door opened, and he reached up to take hold of Josey's arm. "Come on. Not much time."

Sarah fought to draw a breath. It felt as if her heart was being severed in two. "Wait!" she cried, but no words followed. All she could do was stare at Josey in disbelief. She didn't know how to ask if he loved her. Would they ever be together again? Was this the beginning or the end?

They merely stared into each other's eyes, helpless to the situation at hand.

Ruth broke the awkward silence. "Josey, I wanna thank you for saving Naomi. If it hadn't been for you, something awful would've happened." She slipped her hand behind his neck and kissed his cheek. "God bless you, young man."

Josey's eyes moistened. "And you," he said quietly.

With one last powerless gaze at Sarah, he dipped his head and walked briskly away with Micah's aid.

⋖⋗⋖⋗

"Go to bed," Ruth said roughly to her daughter. "There's nothin' more you can do."

"Where are you going?" Sarah cried, tears gushing down her cheeks.

"To find your pappy. This ain't over yet."

Ruth needed to hurry if she was going to be able to get cleaned up and help get the missus undressed and ready for bed. It would be a good hour or more before all the guests were away, but there were still loose ends needing to be sewn together.

Sarah ran after her. "I'm coming with you."

"No," Ruth commanded, taking a firm hold of her daughter's shoulders. "Go back inside right now."

Sarah's mouth dropped open—excruciating pain written on her face. Ruth felt awful—like her heart was being ripped out of her chest. Here stood her precious girl in need of tender care, but if she gave in to the pressing desire to comfort her, she would surely not be able to perform her next task. She had no choice but to push her away and make up for it later.

But as she spun around to leave, it suddenly hit her. Sarah, too, would be needed for what was about to take place. She was no longer a little girl, Ruth realized. She had become a woman who knew her own mind.

Turning back, she grabbed her daughter's hand. "Never mind, gal. You're comin' with me."

Chapter 10

Ruth broke into a run, still holding Sarah's hand. They made it around the backside of the storehouse just as the first rays of sun glimmered across the field. One glance at the furrowed ground turned Ruth's stomach sour. She quickly averted her eyes.

A small group had gathered close to the back wall. This tribunal of sorts needed to ensue with all haste before the Braddocks took their leave from the all-night gala. Terrance was expected to drive their carriage.

Cecil, the Braddocks' overseer, had a firm grasp on Terrance's arm—the ropes had been removed so he could walk across the very field that he had dragged his victim. The young man's chin sagged down to his chest. Ruth didn't know if it was because he was ashamed or if he was still reeling from the beating he'd taken.

Besides Cecil, Isaiah was there, gingerly holding his broken hand, along with Micah and Josey. In addition, three more overseers had been summoned from the Curry, Greene, and Thornton plantations. Only the negro overseers had been asked to join. Each one of them had chosen a young slave to let them know when their masters were about to leave for home.

Micah stepped forward to start the proceedings. "Terrance, here, is bein' tried for the rape of Naomi, slave to the Hawkins family. We got witnesses to prove it." He nodded around the circle. "Make yourselves known."

Isaiah, Ruth, Sarah, and Josey slowly raised their hands.

Immediately, Terrance dropped to his knees, crying bitterly, begging for mercy.

Cecil jerked hard on the collar of his shirt. "Get up, you sorry scoundrel."

Terrance clambered back to his feet, sobbing profusely. "Please don't kill me," he pleaded. "Please!"

"Do any of the overseers see any reason why he shouldn't be hanged by the neck?" Micah asked.

Ruth couldn't let this go any further. She stepped forward unsteadily. "I has somethin' to say."

Everyone turned their eyes on her, and Isaiah gave his wife a quizzical gaze. He nodded to her respectfully. "Go on, Ruth. Whatchu know?"

As disgusted as she was with this man standing before her, she couldn't let them think that the charges against him were completely true. "He didn't rape her," she said. "But he took her against her will and dragged her across that field and *tried* to rape her." Ruth took one more step forward, ire rising inside of her with every passing second. Pointing her finger directly at Terrance, she cried, "Your vile hands put bruises all over her body—you tore her clothes—and worst of all," she said fervidly, "you stole her dignity."

Ruth's face grew flush. She thought she was about to pass out. Sarah came to her side, taking her arm and helping her back away from Terrance.

"Well, that do change things a bit," Cecil admitted. "But I think we all know what he was intendin' to do. So it's still up to our vote. Are you'ins ready?"

Terrance once again fell to his knees. "Please have mercy—I'm beggin'. I've learnt my lesson," he wailed.

Cecil gave him a rapid kick to the ribs. "Shut up. We don't wanna hear none of your whinin'." He leveled his gaze at the overseers. "Let's put it to the vote."

Isaiah slowly shook his head. "I ain't got no right sayin' this, but I's thinkin' a vote ain't necessary." He stepped in front of Terrance and faced the gathering. "What he done was bad . . . real bad, and maybe Terrance even deserves to be whipped or worse. But I knows hangin' him ain't gonna give 'im a chance to change his ways. Only livin' can do that. You'ins could whip him till he bleeds, but all a whippin' does is makes you angrier than you already was. Seems to me the best thing you can do for Terrance is shows 'im mercy."

Terrance put his face clear down on the ground, crying like a baby.

Isaiah wasn't done yet. "I's perty sure Naomi would be votin' for mercy, but I knows for a fact our Massa Jesus would, so that's what I's proposin'. But Cecil," he warned, turning a hard gaze on the Braddock's overseer, "if I sees Terrance step one foot on this here ground belongin' to Massa Hawkins again, I swears, I'll kill 'im myself."

Terrance grasped Isaiah's feet with both hands, pressing his forehead onto the top of Isaiah's boots. His body quaked with one sob after another. "You's never gonna see me again—I swear. Thank you, Isaiah. Thank you."

Isaiah didn't move, letting the man grovel at his feet. Then he said, "Is we done here?"

For a suspended moment everyone stood still, stunned by what had just happened. Cecil glanced around the circle at the other overseers. They were all nodding their heads. Then, reaching down, he yanked Terrance to his feet, giving him a shove. "You's a lucky man, Terrance. Now go on, get outta here."

Terrance started around the storehouse, limping and battered. But he glanced back over his shoulder at Isaiah, eyes no longer full of malice—they were filled with sincere gratitude. Isaiah nodded, then turned away. Ruth went to him, and he held her with his one good arm and hand.

"I hope I didn't speak out o' turn for Naomi," he said softly. "I don't wanna hurt her none."

Ruth shook her head against his chest. "No, you did exactly what our Lawd would do. I'm proud of you, Izzy."

He smiled, resting his chin on top of her head. Then he looked over at Sarah. "Come 'ere, gal. Gets yourself in here with us."

All three stood behind the storehouse for a moment, basking in the love of family and the feel of each other's arms. But Sarah didn't stay there long. She slipped out of their embrace and went straight to Josey.

"What are we gonna do, Josey?" she lamented.

The two clung to one another, and Josey pressed his face close to hers, whispering in her ear. "I don't know, sweet gal." He kissed her ear and hair and cheek, then looked her in the eyes. "I wants to be with you."

Isaiah stepped away from Ruth, obviously ready to protect his daughter, but Ruth clasped his arm and kept him grounded where he stood. "Nuh, uh," she whispered. "I'll tell you 'bout this later."

For a minute Ruth was afraid she wouldn't be able to restrain him. She could literally feel the tension rippling through his muscles. But she was not about to let Isaiah ruin a tender moment for these two.

Josey had proven himself to be unselfish and brave tonight. Ruth's heart had altered toward him, as well as her opinion about Sarah's obvious love for him. She now wanted to give Sarah and Josey one last moment of peace together. She knew they were about to be ripped apart, most likely never to see each other again. First love cut so deep.

"Come on, Izzy, let's you and me talk in front of the storehouse." She tugged on his sleeve, dragging him around the corner in the half-light of morning.

Isaiah's voice was laced with uneasiness. "What is that, Ruthie?" He pointed back toward the direction they'd come. "I can still use this fist if I needs to." He brought his broken hand up in front of his chest.

She laughed softly, taking hold of his wrist with both hands, pressing a light kiss to the swollen fist. "Those two are fine. You needs to think o' more important things right now."

"What's more important than my girl makin' lovin' with that boy?" he asked fervently.

"Well for one thing, that hand o' yours. You need to go find Henry right now. He'll fix you up."

Henry was the so-called doctor for slave town, even though he had no credentials to speak of. Everyone knew that he had a way of fixing anything that had breath in its body. People or animals, it made no difference. Henry simply had a special gift for healing.

Isaiah shook his head wearily. "I needs to get back out front 'fore I can do anythin' else. We gots to get all them people in their carriages and send 'em home."

"Not lookin' like *that*, you're not." She pointed to the blotches of dirt all over his fine-looking suit. "Come on to the kitchen with me. I'll get a wet rag and fix you right up."

He looked as if he might go back around the storehouse first, but Ruth grabbed his good hand. "Don't make me drag you, mister."

Resigned to obey his wife, Isaiah followed her reluctantly to the kitchen.

⊰⊱⊱

Josey leaned up against the storehouse wall and pulled Sarah to him. She tried not to press in too close, fearing she would hurt him. But he would have none of it.

"Don't you worry none, gal. I can handle it." His bravado was admirable if not reckless as far as his ribs were concerned. He pulled her body up to his, and she reveled in the strength of his arms.

His mouth found hers, and Sarah felt the warmth rush all the way through her. Her mind now swirled with thoughts. Dangerous thoughts. Running away together thoughts. The kind of thoughts that could get them both killed.

Their mouths separated, but only an inch or so. Josey breathed tender words to her, telling her how beautiful she was, then kissing her lips softly. Telling her he loved her, kissing her neck. Telling her he couldn't live without her, kissing her mouth again.

All of a sudden Micah came striding around the backside of the storehouse, interrupting their passionate embrace.

Clearing his throat loudly, he barked, "Come on, boy. You gotta get with your massa's people before they know you're missin'."

Sarah felt her heart crumble. Leaning her forehead against Josey's, she whispered, "No."

"That won't do, girl," Micah growled. He grasped Josey's arm, wrenching him away from her. Josey let out a cry of pain, making Sarah want to hold onto him all the more.

But Micah shoved her shoulder. "Let him be, girl, before you get 'im killed. Is that what you want?"

Her breath now came in great gasps, and she reached for Josey's hand, clinging with all her might. But Micah was a man on a mission. He sliced right through their grip with his hand, then put his body in between the two lovers. "This boy's only seconds away from gettin' the life beat out o' him. Now go on, girl," he yelled.

Sarah followed behind them, crying, and this time Micah showed no pity. He planted his hand right in the middle of her chest, shoving her hard to the ground, knocking the air right out of her.

Sarah's mouth dropped open, trying to pull in precious air, but her lungs wouldn't fill. She gulped, trying to find life-giving oxygen. It wouldn't come.

From across the yard, Micah yelled, "Lawd, girl, put your arms above your head." Then he and Josey disappeared around the house.

Ruth was waiting in the upstairs hall when Samuel and Elizabeth climbed the stairs, arm in arm. She remained silent, awaiting instructions from the missus.

"Oh, Ruth, I'm so glad you're here. I don't have one ounce of energy left in my body."

Samuel opened the door to their bedroom, ushering his wife in ahead of him. Ruth didn't know what to do. Was she expected to go in there with the massa too?

"Come on, Ruth," Elizabeth beckoned. "My husband has no clue how to get me out of this gown."

Samuel laughed heartily. "I could try."

"Go," Elizabeth commanded, pointing toward the door of her sitting room.

He laughed again and disappeared into the other room.

Assisting Elizabeth out of her gown, Ruth couldn't help but ask, "Was it everythin' you'd hoped for, missus?"

"And more," she beamed. "Everyone went on and on about the food, the orchestra, the gardens. It was all so perfect."

"Oh, I'm so glad to hear it."

Ruth helped her wash and put on her nightgown, then released her luxurious hair from its combs. As she brushed through the long tendrils, Elizabeth called to her husband.

He opened the door of the sitting room, having taken off his boots and socks and jacket. He'd pulled his shirttail out, and the top few buttons were undone. He sat down on the end of the bed, watching the two women.

"I saw Isaiah this morning out front. What did he do to his hand?"

Heat filled Ruth's body. How could she respond to that? She knew if she lied and the massa found out, she would be sent back to the fields. She suddenly thought of the premonition she'd had at her prayer log. Was this the moment she had feared?

Ruth hoped her momentary hesitation hadn't been noticed. "I saw that too, massa," she said. "Maybe he'll tell you and me all about that," she said casually.

Samuel let out a low chuckle and flopped back on the bed. "Yes, there must be a story there. I hope it's not serious."

"Me too, massa," she murmured. "Me too."

❧❧❧

Before heading back downstairs, Ruth cracked the door to Isabella's room, making sure the girl was asleep. To her surprise, she wasn't alone in the bed. Sarah had crawled in beside her.

In the meager light seeping through the heavy curtains, it was obvious that Isabella was sound asleep. But not so for Sarah. She lay awake on her back, staring up into the canopy of the bed. Ruth's heart broke for the girl.

Sliding around to Sarah's side of the bed, she sat down gently, hoping not to wake up the missy. Sarah's eyes were red and puffy. Evidence of dried tears still on her cheeks.

Ruth bent and kissed her tenderly, and Sarah's arms reached up around her mama's neck. They held each other tight for a long time. No words were spoken. No tears were shed. They simply found solace in each other's arms.

❧❧❧

"Finally," Isaiah moaned, as Ruth walked out the back door. "Come on, Ruthie. Let's get in bed and sleep all day and all night."

"Aww, Izzy, I can't. I'm gonna lay down with Naomi."

Isaiah stroked the stubble on his chin with his good hand. "That be a fine idea," he agreed, covering a big yawn. "You's a good friend."

"But you can't go to bed till you see Henry about that hand, Izzy. I mean it."

Isaiah shook his head. "I'll wraps it up real tight and see 'bout it later. I ain't seen a bed in two straight nights. There's nowhere else I'm goin' but there."

Ruth shook her head. "Well, go on then. I'll see ya when I see ya." She feared he wouldn't make it back to their cabin, he looked so worn out. But he kissed her and assured her that's where she'd find him tonight.

Feeling as if she'd been trampled by a herd of wild horses, Ruth dragged her weary frame down the hall to Naomi's corner room. It was the biggest room on the corridor, providing large windows on two separate walls. It was normally a bright and cheerful room, perfect for the Hawkins' clever seamstress. But even with the morning sun penetrating the white cotton curtains, this room was now filled with a spiritual darkness from the devil himself.

When Ruth slipped through the door, she found her dear friend in much the same state as she'd found Sarah. Naomi was lying on her back, staring at the ceiling. She turned her head to meet Ruth's gaze.

"Is it over?" she asked quietly.

Ruth nodded. "It is."

Naomi scooted over next to the wall in her small bed and pulled back a corner of the sheet. Ruth quickly removed her boots and skirt, then slid in beside her. A long, silent moment passed. Ruth was struggling to find the right way to tell her what they'd done. When she finally spoke, her voice was tight with emotion.

"We showed 'im mercy," she breathed. "He's gone home."

Naomi drew in a gasping breath, and Ruth turned on her side to face her, panic spreading like wildfire. What if they'd hurt Naomi with their decision as much as Terrance had with his heinous act? How could she live with herself if Terrance's soul had been released from prison, but Naomi's was convicted to a life of torment?

"Oh, Naomi," Ruth cried. "I'm so sorry for—"

Her words were suddenly cut off when Naomi gasped out a mournful sob. "No!" she cried. "I was so. . . ." Another sob wracked her body while Ruth's spirit was shredded to the core.

Naomi started again. "I was so worried . . . they . . . would kill him," she finally got out. "I could never live with myself," Naomi sobbed, "if a man was dead because of me—no matter what he'd done."

Ruth felt like there'd been an earthquake inside of her. She blew out a breath of relief. "Come 'ere, sweet thing," she said, opening her arms wide.

Naomi turned into the arms of her friend, laying her head on Ruth's chest, close to her heart. Together they lamented the terrors of the night with emotional weeping and moaning.

Finally, Naomi took a shuddering breath and raised her head. "Thank you, dear one," she said in a soft tone.

Ruth eagerly accepted her gratitude and finally felt the peace of God fill her anguished soul. It had been a long and terrible night, but the will of the Lord had prevailed. "You are so much like our Savior," Ruth spoke admiringly. "If I'd been allowed to vote, I would've. . . ."

"Shh," Naomi whispered, moving back to her slender space on the bed. "The Lord knows all our weaknesses, including the many I carry." She lightly brushed Ruth's cheek with the back of her hand. "Thank you for being my anchor in the storm."

Ruth covered her hand and whispered, "Always," just before falling asleep.

Chapter 11

R uth startled awake, confused by unfamiliar surroundings. When her eyes acclimated to the dim light, she remembered she was still in Naomi's room. She guessed it must be close to evening. Her stomach growled noisily, and she placed her hands over her abdomen, trying to muffle the sound. Peering over at Naomi, it was obvious she was still sleeping soundly. It was good to see her friend's face devoid of the fear and misery of last night's ordeal.

For several minutes Ruth lay there, replaying the dreadful events. But soon a question occurred to her—what if Miss Isabella were to share the incident with her parents? That might set off another uncontrollable chain of events. Not that she felt anything was ever under her control as long as she belonged to another human being. But for now, she was convinced that talking to Isabella and Sarah was of utmost importance.

Carefully casting the sheet aside, she stepped out of bed and dressed. Slipping out into the hallway, Ruth noticed the household was still abuzz with the cleaning efforts. But when she walked upstairs, all was quiet. Everyone must still be asleep.

Ruth peeked into Isabella's room and could just make out two shapes still in the bed. She knew it was quite possible they wouldn't wake until morning. Closing the door softly, she decided to stop by Berthy's room. Elizabeth's dear old companion was expected to be available throughout today and tonight in case the mistress needed anything.

The door to Berthy's room stood wide, and Ruth softly knocked as she stepped inside. Berthy sat, rocking and peering out the window overlooking the back of the house.

"Berthy," she called softly. "Can I talk to ya a minute?"

By her unguarded glare, it appeared Berthy had returned to her jealous ways. Ruth hesitated near the doorway, not sure this was the best course of action. But the old woman's face abruptly softened, as if she had just remembered their earlier conversation. "Set yerself down a spell," she rasped.

Ruth had no desire to sit, but she also didn't want to hurt Berthy's feelings, so she took the straight back chair across from her.

"Has the missus been awake yet?" Ruth asked.

"Naw," Berthy answered. "I specs she may not wake till mornin'. But if'n she needs me, I'll be right here to take care of her."

"Thank you kindly for that, Berthy," Ruth offered.

Berthy kept rocking—a look of satisfaction crossing her weathered features. "The missus and me has a special bond, ya know."

"Yes, I know. I'm so glad for that." Leaning forward, Ruth needed to get to the point. "I was hopin' you'd do me a favor. If Sarah should wake up later this evenin', would you tell her to come straight to me?"

Berthy's chair stilled. "To yer cabin?"

"Yes, I'll be there all night. Tell her she can wake me up."

Starting the rocker again, the old woman nodded. "I'll tell her."

"Thank you," Ruth said as she came to her feet and headed for the door. But just as she was about to step into the hallway, Berthy's next remark stopped her short.

"This be 'bout Naomi?"

Ruth captured a deep breath and turned to face the old woman whose gaze was still fixed on the backyard. Not wanting to deceive her, but also not wanting to talk about Naomi's private matter, she simply said, "Yes," then quietly slipped away.

As Ruth headed through the front kitchen, she grabbed a couple of biscuits and two boiled eggs from the baskets that had been prepared for the house workers. Evening was just turning to twilight as she started her walk home. Though her prayer log was a mighty temptation, she didn't relish being there after dark, so she continued her trek to the cabin.

Rounding the curve in the road, she was delighted to see Isaiah sitting on the porch. When he caught sight of her, a wide grin turned his lips.

"There's my Ruthie gal," he said warmly. "I been waitin' for ya." He quickly stepped inside and brought out another chair.

"How long you been up?" she asked, joining him on the porch.

"I been up a while. I been checkin' on the horses and all."

Ruth looked at him in consternation. "Them horses are not as important as your hand."

"Now hold on, gal, I knows that. I already seen Henry. Looky here." He held up his broken hand for her to see. "I gots it wrapped good 'n tight. There even be a piece o' wood in there to keep it straight."

"Good," she said, visibly relaxing. "But you gotta be extra careful till that heals."

"Yes'm, I knows that," he said, taking the biscuit and egg that Ruth held out to him.

For a minute they ate their food in silence. Finally, Ruth said, "Izzy, we got a problem. What are you gonna tell the massa 'bout that?" She pointed to his wrapped hand.

"I been thinkin' long and hard on that," he answered, rubbing the back of his neck. "If he asks, I gotta tell him the truth. I won't be lyin' to Massa Hawkins—I won't be lyin' to nobody."

"But do you have to tell him who it was and what he did?" Ruth asked. She was worried that Master Hawkins would feel obliged to tell the Braddocks about the incident. If that happened, Terrance's life could possibly take a turn for the worse. He might reap what he'd sewn after all.

"Well," Isaiah said, then paused while he consumed the egg all in one bite. "I can try to tell him what happened and how we took care o' things. Maybe I can do that without tellin' him it be Terrance. But if'n he wants to know, I has to tell him."

Ruth nodded solemnly. "It's just so hard knowin' what to do for Naomi's sake. I know she don't want everyone hearin' all about this. You know how word gets around. She won't like bein' talked about, especially for somethin' so awful."

Isaiah agreed. "I don't wanna hurt Naomi no more, neither."

For a long time, they sat on the porch talking. Isaiah wanted to know all about Naomi's reaction to their merciful decision, but most of all, he wanted to hear about Sarah and the young man who was showing her far too much affection. Isaiah seemed to find a bit of relief when Ruth told him the whole story.

"Still," he said with uneasiness. "I don't want our gal lovin' some man from another plantation. She gots no idea who that man be and what he's like."

Ruth released a deep sigh. "I know, Izzy. But I don't think they'll ever see each other again. That boy lives clear on the other side of Frankfort somewhere. She'll forget 'bout him soon enough." Ruth looked away toward Mammy Lou's cabin and abruptly changed the subject. "Did you check on Franklin?"

"Yes'm. He be happy as a fly on honey."

"I'm glad you left 'im here for that race yesterday, Izzy. Maybe in a few years he can tag along with ya, but he's way too young for such things."

All of a sudden Isaiah stood up and stretched his arms above his head. "Ya know, I think I's ready to get back ta bed. What 'bout you, Ruthie?"

"Hold on a minute—I still wanna hear all about that race."

"Ain't ya tired, Ruthie? Why, I can hardly hold my eyes open," he said, then proceeded to cover a wide yawn.

Ruth's eyes narrowed. She still felt certain there was something Isaiah wasn't telling her about that race. But she had to admit, her body and mind were still weary. Maybe it was better to hold onto that story for just one more night.

⊰⊱⊱

When Ruth woke up the next morning, she found her son beside her in bed instead of her husband. "Oh, Lawd," she whispered aloud. "What time is it?" She feared she'd slept passed time to be with the missus. But when she looked over toward the grayish light outside the window, her heart slowed its harried pace.

A more leisurely smile tickled her lips. What a precious face lying so close by on her pillow. She couldn't help but kiss his cheeks and forehead and chin as he began to rouse from sleep.

"Mornin', little man," she said.

Franklin rubbed his eyes with two small fists, then scooted over onto his mama's chest. Ruth wrapped him in a loving hug, relishing their rare moment together.

Realizing she hadn't seen him in two full days, she asked, "Did you enjoy bein' with Mammy Lou and the chillins?"

"Uh, huh," the little voice answered.

"Did you play in the creek?"

"Uh, huh."

"What else did you do?"

"Horse race."

For the space of several heartbeats, Ruth lay completely still. What on earth was he talking about? Mammy Lou would never take all those young'uns to the stables. Maybe they had pretended to have a horse race of their own.

"You mean with sticks?"

She felt his head shaking against her chest.

Her eyebrows dipped. "Real, live horses?"

This time his little head bobbed up and down. "Yes'm."

She sat up, nearly toppling the boy onto the floor. Holding him by the shoulders she said, "What are you talkin' about, young'un?"

Franklin gave her an adorable smile, as if he felt no hint of his mama's rancor.

"I rode Prince," he said matter-of-factly.

A rush of air escaped Ruth's lungs. "When?" she nearly yelled.

His little shoulders hunched into a shrug. "In a race."

For a moment she gave her son a wide-eyed stare, then she suddenly breathed out a sigh of relief and slapped her thigh. "I'm gonna get that pappy of yours. Puttin' you up to a tale when your mama is so tired." She got out of bed laughing. "Yessir, I'm gonna get your pappy good."

‹›‹›‹›

Ruth made it to the big house before eight o'clock, hoping to check in on Naomi before heading upstairs. Surprisingly, Naomi was standing on the gravel path outside of the kitchen. Ruth noticed the worry in her friend's eyes.

"What is it?" she quickly asked.

Naomi's voice was strained. "The mistress asked to see me early this morning in her sitting room."

Ruth drew in a sharp breath. "What for?"

"She asked outright if something happened to me during the night of the gala."

Ruth felt a remnant of fear forcing its way back to the surface. "Who told her? Was it Isabella?"

"No," Naomi sighed. "It was Berthy. Apparently, she had gotten up in the night and heard Isabella running down the hallway to the back stairs. She must've watched out her window most of the night. She had no idea what went on, but it was the first thing she told the mistress when she awoke this morning."

Ruth folded her arms against her body. Why couldn't Berthy mind her own business? "I should've given that old woman a stern warning when I had the chance."

"What are you talking about?" Naomi asked in a puzzled voice.

Ruth proceeded to tell her about the conversation she'd had last evening with Berthy. She should've known that Elizabeth's former companion would do anything to stay within her good graces, even if it meant giving her some tidbits of gossip.

Naomi laid a weary hand on Ruth's arm. "There's nothing to be done now. If Berthy told the mistress, I'm sure she told Violet. Between the two of them, well. . . ." Her words trailed away, as did her gaze toward the storehouse.

Ruth felt her heart breaking for Naomi all over again. While their age difference was less than ten years, she felt protective toward her—almost maternal. She opened her arms and drew the young woman into a tender embrace. Then, kissing her on the cheek, she said, "I'll talk to the missus. Try not to worry yourself."

Naomi stepped back, looking defeated. "The mistress saw the bruises on my neck—I had no choice but to tell her what happened."

"I've got to get up there right now," Ruth said hastily. She didn't like the thought of the missus being awake in her sitting room without her being there. "Will you be all right?" she asked.

Naomi nodded solemnly. "Go."

Taking the back stairs to save time, Ruth hurriedly made her way to Elizabeth's sitting room. The door stood ajar, so Ruth pushed it a little wider. "Missus, can I come in?"

To Ruth's tremendous relief, Berthy was nowhere in sight, but to her dismay, Isabella was sitting on the sofa with her mother. Both women were in their dressing gowns. It appeared she had interrupted an important conversation.

"Oh, good, you're here," Elizabeth said to her. "Close the door. It seems we have a great deal to discuss."

Chapter 12

Worried beyond measure, Ruth sat down in the chair her mistress indicated. Every second that passed felt like an hour. She could feel her palms beginning to sweat.

Finally, Elizabeth said, "I don't even know where to begin with you, Ruth. I've been told some shocking and . . . intriguing stories this morning."

Oh, Lawd, Ruth thought. *This is how it ends.* Her mouth felt so dry she could hardly swallow.

"I think we should just start at the beginning," Elizabeth offered. "I've heard three separate stories as to what happened during the night of the gala—one of which is from my own daughter. She's told me about the girls watching the gatherings from both balconies."

Isabella's eyes were down-cast, making Ruth wonder if the girl might be in a bit of trouble herself.

"Yes'm," Ruth said. She eased into the story as best she could. "It was late in the night, and I went out back to get some supplies from the storehouse. That's when I seen Sarah at the negro gatherin'. Right away I went to fetch her. That's when Missy Isabella come runnin' with news about Naomi bein' attacked by a man from another plantation."

Ruth gathered all of her courage to tell how Josey and Isaiah had saved Naomi at the last possible moment. She explained how a tribunal among the negro overseers had taken place and how Isaiah had led them to a merciful conclusion. It was a brief, yet truthful telling of the events of that night.

Elizabeth sat very straight and still during Ruth's discourse. As uncomfortable as it was to tell her mistress some of the sordid details, she was relieved to see her eyes soften. It was no secret that Mistress Elizabeth had a fondness for Naomi.

Taking in a deep breath, Elizabeth said, "I will of course need to tell Samuel about the events that took place on our property. As much as I would like to think this is over, I'm not sure he will see it as such. I want to assure you we will be doing everything to guarantee that Naomi is well taken care of."

"Thank you, missus," Ruth replied softly.

"But there's another matter that Isabella has brought to my attention for you and me to discuss." She turned her gaze toward her daughter. "Privately."

Isabella dipped her head and scrambled off the sofa. She quickly left the room without a word.

"Ruth," Elizabeth began, "Isabella has told me about Sarah and this young man named Josey."

"Oh, yes'm." Ruth squirmed in her chair, not knowing where this conversation would lead.

"She tells me that there may be a spark of romance budding between the two."

Ruth immediately chimed in. "Missus, there's no need for concern 'bout Sarah. She'll forget all about—"

"No, Ruth, you misunderstand me," Elizabeth interrupted. "Isabella has asked me, and rightly so, if there is some way we can allow the two to be together. That is, if you and Isaiah approve."

"Oh, ma'am, Josey lives clear over on the Stafford Plantation."

"Yes," Elizabeth said, "near Frankfort. Sally Stafford is a very good friend of mine, and with a little correspondence, I can check on Josey. Would you like that?"

"Well, missus, I know Sarah would be grateful, and I surely wouldn't mind, but. . . ." She hesitated. "I'm not so sure 'bout Isaiah. He didn't take too kindly to the affection he seen between the two."

Elizabeth half smiled, highlighting the dimple on her left cheek. "I can only imagine that Samuel will have the same response next year when we begin receiving suitors for Isabella."

Both women shared a soft laugh.

"I will leave it to you to work on Isaiah. But from what I understand, Sarah is utterly smitten. I'll work discreetly behind the scenes for now and let you know what I find out," Elizabeth offered.

"Oh, missus, you are too kind."

"It's totally my pleasure. Isabella couldn't stop talking about it this morning. She has all sorts of romantic notions in that head of hers." Elizabeth sighed. "Oh, to be young again."

With that said, there was a knock on the door. Violet entered on Elizabeth's command, bringing little Catherine.

"Oh, my precious," Elizabeth crooned, holding out her arms. "Come to your mother, sweet darling."

Ruth couldn't help but smile. Seeing Elizabeth and Catherine together seemed to wash away the difficulties of the last two days—even with Violet hovering close by.

❧❧❧

That evening, when Ruth turned the corner to her cabin, Phibe and Ceceilia were standing about with four other women of their kinfolk. They were huddled in a tight circle near the well, and as soon as Phibe saw Ruth, she cleared her throat. Conversation immediately came to a halt.

Ruth had no patience for gossip. She didn't mince her words as she joined the group. "What are you'ins talkin' about that you need to stop when I get here?"

An awkward silence commenced, for which Ruth was decidedly not about to fill. If her kinfolk were talking about her, then they would have to confess or stay silent. She folded her arms across her chest and waited.

Ceceilia could never hold her tongue for long. "Sister, we ain't talkin' about you, so don't go gettin' yer hackles up."

"You may not be talkin' about *me*," Ruth responded, "but dependin' on who it is, you might as well be."

The women's eyes darted about the circle for a moment, finally coming back to roost on Ceceilia. "Oh, all right," the older woman said. "I done heard stories about Naomi bein' with one of the Hawkins' guests during the gala. We heard she went with him behind the storehouse, and he had his way with her. Some says Missy Isabella set the whole thing up."

"Oh, Lawd," Ruth moaned loudly. "Ain't none o' you know what you're talkin' about."

Lyde, a stout field slave, chimed in. "Well, why don't you tell us what you knows?"

"Because it's none o' your business," Ruth replied sharply. She felt such loyalty to Naomi—she would protect her at all costs. But these stories were absolutely ridiculous. Gossip constantly swirled around Naomi because of her pleasing appearance. Some of the slaves thought she was more beautiful than the mistress herself. Many could see how preferred Naomi was in the house, and unfortunately, jealousy tends to bring out the worst in even the best people.

Ruth was going to have to set them straight without telling them every detail. But at the moment, her patience felt as thin as a razor, and she was afraid of what she might say. She took several deep breaths, conceding how much she loved the women standing before her. She knew each one of them would gladly take a beating for any of the others, if that were the way of things. How could she blame them for what others were saying? But how could she not? They were unashamedly passing on rumors they had no way of knowing were true.

"All right," Ruth finally relented. "I'm gonna give you the honest story, and if you hear anything different than this, yer gonna say, 'No, that ain't the truth!' Do you hear me?"

All six heads nodded in unison.

"Naomi did *not* give herself to one o' the Hawkins' guests," she said fervidly. "She was attacked by a negro from another plantation, against her will. But we was able to stop the attack before it went too far." She leveled her gaze at the women. "So, you see, none of what you heard is the truth. Naomi would never willingly do such a thing. Never!"

"What 'bout the missy?" Phibe asked.

Ruth shook her head vehemently. "It weren't Missy Isabella who set somethin' up—it was the missy who saved her! She saw it happenin' and got help."

All of the women visibly relaxed in that moment, as did Ruth. She knew by telling the truth, Naomi would be less hurt than by the absurd tale now being spread far and wide.

"We can't be listenin' to such awful things and then passin' 'em on," Ruth told them. "Can't you see how hurtful that is?"

Phibe trained her eyes on Ruth. "Well, we ain't the ones at the big house. You's the only one to tells us what's goin' on."

Ruth felt her heart pinch. Jealousy could be so sneaky. "I tell ya what, if you'ins hear anything about what's goin' on at the big house, you come to me first. Don't go spreadin' things you don't know nothin' about. Can we make a pact on that?"

Ceceilia nodded earnestly. "Yes, we can, and *we will*," she practically commanded. The other women immediately fell in line with their gossip gatherer. "I'm sorry, Ruth. Will ya forgive us?"

Ruth didn't hesitate. "I will."

The women eventually said their good-nights and wandered off to their cabins. Ruth quickly turned her sights on her own place, ready to hear all about the big race.

❧❦❧

Seeing the door wide open, Ruth called out from the steps, "Izzy, you in there?"

"Yes'm," was all she heard from inside the cabin.

When she stepped up on the porch, she could see Isaiah sitting at the table inside, but he wasn't alone. Sarah was also sitting there with her back to the door.

"Well, gal, I ain't seen you all day. Whatchu doin' here this time o' the evenin'?"

Sarah sat motionless and silent, causing Ruth's nerves to quiver. Searching Isaiah's face, she realized they'd been discussing something serious. He didn't acknowledge Ruth with his normal jollity.

Rounding the table, Ruth could see why. Sarah's face was splotchy from crying—her eyes were pools of liquid.

Ruth immediately sat down at the table and took both of her daughter's hands. "What's happened?"

Instead of looking at her mama, Sarah turned an obstinate gaze toward Isaiah. There was definitely a battle of the wills going on at this table. But neither Sarah nor Isaiah seemed inclined to share.

"Well, I'm not gonna sit here and watch you two stare at each other. One o' you speak up." Ruth sat looking from one to the other.

Finally, Isaiah said, "Sarah, here, done overstepped her place with the missus. Come to find out, she be tellin' Missy alls about her love for that stranger—"

"He's not a stranger!" Sarah bellowed.

Ruth squeezed her hands. "Hush, child. We don't want all the kinfolk knowin' our business."

Sarah lowered her voice. "He's not a stranger," she reiterated. "We know everything about each other."

All Isaiah could do was shake his head back and forth, a low moan rumbling from deep in his chest.

For the life of her, Ruth couldn't figure out why Isaiah was so provoked by the situation. It wasn't as if Josey lived on the Hawkins Plantation. Even with the missus sending correspondence to the Stafford place, the likelihood that anything would come of it was almost nil.

"Izzy, whatchu all a feared for? Josey done went back to his own plantation two days ago."

Suddenly, Isaiah's chair scraped loudly on the old wooden floor, and he came to his feet. "I think you knows what I's a feared for, Ruthie." Then he turned an uncharacteristic gaze toward his daughter. "And you knows 'specially what I'm talkin' 'bout, girl."

With that, he went over to the corner of the room and pulled Franklin into his arms. "Come on, young'un. Les you and me go to the stables."

"Izzy, hold on now. It's gettin' late, and I'm makin' supper."

"Save us some," was all he said.

Ruth sat staring at her daughter for the space of several heartbeats. "What'd you say to get your pappy so riled up?"

Sarah stubbornly shook her head.

"Girl, you already done disrespected your pappy. You ain't gonna treat me that way too." Ruth felt like jerking a knot in her tail. "You tell me right now."

"Fine," Sarah said, pulling her hands away from Ruth's. "Pappy thinks we . . . you know."

"I'm listenin'."

"Oh, Mama, don't you get it? Pappy thinks me and Josey was up to no good. He just came right out and said he saw blood on my skirt and he knew what we'd done."

Ruth's chest rose and fell at the pace of Isaiah's racehorse. Thinking back on that night, Sarah and Josey had definitely been alone together for a lot longer than she felt comfortable with. She had always trusted her daughter, but Sarah had now become a woman, capable of making her own decisions. Still, the truth remained: how much could they really trust Josey? He truly was a stranger to all of them, whether Sarah wanted to admit it or not.

She swallowed hard and captured her daughter's gaze. "Well . . . did you?"

Sarah's chair scraped the floor every bit as loud as Isaiah's. "Not you, too!" she yelled.

Ruth jumped to her feet and took Sarah by the shoulders. It seemed like everything had been turned upside down these past two days. "I'm sorry, sweet gal. I shouldn't have asked. I know you as well as I know myself. Forgive me."

Sarah's shoulders drooped down, and all the fire seemed to go out of her. She leaned her head onto her mama's shoulder. "How can I make Pappy understand that nothing like that happened?" she sighed.

"Oh, Sarah gal," Ruth breathed, gathering her daughter in tighter. "I'll make him understand. He's just rememberin' what it was like to be a young man in love. That makes him want to protect you even more."

Sarah pulled back and looked into her mama's face with a sly grin. "Well . . . did *you?*"

Ruth playfully pushed her daughter away. "Nuh, uh, gal. You ain't got no right to ask your mama that question. Now help me get some supper on," she said, quickly changing the subject.

Chapter 13

Lying beside Isaiah with Franklin softly snoring at their feet, Ruth carefully turned over in bed. "Izzy, you awake?"

"Uh, huh," he replied softly.

Placing her hand lightly on his chest, she whispered, "Thank you for listenin' to me and Sarah t'night. I know you want to protect yer baby girl, but she became a woman when we wasn't even lookin'."

"I knows that, Ruthie, but I's gonna say it one more time—there's somethin' 'bout that boy that can't be trusted. I don't even knows what it is. It be somethin' deep down in my gut tellin' me that. I don't wants her havin' anythin' to do with him. That's all."

Ruth thought for a long time about Isaiah's misgivings. She had felt the same way earlier during that night, until Josey gallantly came to Naomi's aid. That had changed her perception of him completely. Maybe tomorrow morning she should ask the missus to forget about it. Sarah would never have to know. But then again, she had no right to ask anything of her mistress.

"There's somethin' I need to tell ya, Izzy." Ruth continued. "The missus is gonna send a letter to the Stafford's askin' about Josey."

Isaiah lay completely still. Even his chest stopped moving up and down. Ruth rose up on one elbow. "It weren't my idea, and Sarah don't even know about it. The missus is tryin' to please her daughter, that's all. There won't be nothin' come from it, I'm sure."

Ruth felt her husband's heart beating strong, and he released a long, slow breath. "We's gonna have to trust the Lawd on that one, Ruthie." He rose up and gave her a quick kiss before turning over. Then, he quietly added, "I's gonna make it up to Sarah somehow. We can't go worryin' 'bout somethin' out o' our control. But I ain't gonna upset our girl 'bout it no more."

"Woman," Ruth corrected.

"Yes'm . . . woman."

For a long stretch, Ruth contemplated their daughter and wondered if there was a young man on the Hawkins' place that could capture her heart. Then, as thoughts are prone to do, she suddenly started thinking of something else entirely.

"Izzy, tell me 'bout that horse race."

Instantly, Isaiah began to snore softly, just like their son. Ruth let out a long sigh. She was going to have to wait yet another night before hearing all the exciting details. But if Ruth had bothered to look over at her husband, she would've noticed that his eyes were wide open.

⟐

The next morning, while Ruth prepared breakfast, Isaiah got up and hurriedly dressed. He even put a pair of britches and a short-tailed shirt on his son.

"Whatchu doin', Izzy? Franklin don't need all them clothes at Mammy Lou's. Just put his shirt on 'em."

"We ain't goin' to Mammy Lou right now," he replied. "The massa done asked fer me to come to his study this mornin'."

"With Franklin?" she asked curiously.

"Yes'm."

"What for?"

"Aw, Ruthie, sometime the massa just wants me to bring 'em, that's all," he said quickly. "Matter o' fact, we's not gonna have time to eat breakfast probly."

"Now hold on a minute, you two. There's always time to sit and eat somethin'. Yer not takin' Franklin anywhere until he's fed. Besides, massa Hawkins is probably still in bed."

"Massa gets up *real* early. Can't keep 'im waitin', you know."

Ruth would have none of it. "I mean it, Izzy. You set yourself down and feed your son."

Isaiah gave her a look of resignation but didn't sit down at the table. Instead, he grabbed two fresh biscuits and a couple of chicken gizzards left over from last night. "Sorry, gal, we's gonna have to eat on the way," he said. "Come on, Son. Les go."

Ruth stood with her hands on her hips. "Well, ain't you forgettin' somethin', mister?"

Stopping with one foot already out the door, Isaiah gave his wife a blank stare.

"You best be givin' me a proper good-bye."

Isaiah immediately stepped back inside and kissed his wife firmly on the mouth, then turned and disappeared through the door, Franklin right on his heels.

⤜❧⤛

Rounding the corner in the road, Isaiah slowed his pace and glanced over his shoulder. Ruth was nowhere in sight, so he and Franklin stopped to finish their meager breakfast. He would've much preferred to sit down to eat the ham gravy she'd prepared for the biscuits, but all her curiosity about that horserace was bound to come up again. Isaiah still wasn't sure how to break the news to her that Franklin had been riding Prince across that finish line.

"Come on, Son," he said, wiping his mouth with the back of his hand. "Let me give ya a ride."

Isaiah reached down and picked up his boy, setting him down on top of one shoulder. Franklin giggled, causing Isaiah's heart to relinquish its oppressive burden, if only for a moment.

Holding Franklin's little legs with one arm, Isaiah meandered down the road, in no hurry to get to the big house. Feeling the cool morning breeze on his face and carrying his boy atop his shoulder somehow made him feel like a whole man. Almost like he was free. A feeling like that didn't come along very often. Considering the troubles of the last few days, it felt glorious.

"Someday, Franklin," he said, glancing up at his son, "you's gonna be a free man. I feels it in my bones."

Franklin's tranquil brown eyes held his pappy's. They were so innocent—so pure. They had yet to witness the cruelties life had to offer. They had yet to weep over harassment and domination and possession . . . and death.

Leaving the road, Isaiah took the gravel path to the side door leading to the master's study. Abruptly, the lighthearted feeling escaped, and Isaiah knew when he stepped inside that house, he would once again feel like half a man.

How long, Lawd? How long? he lamented.

Isaiah set Franklin down on the covered porch and knocked on the door. This was the entrance used by Master Hawkins' business guests and his overseer, keeping them from having to walk through the main house. Micah opened the door and stepped aside for Isaiah and his son to enter.

"Good morning," the master said from behind his rich mahogany desk.

"G'mornin', massa," Isaiah responded.

"And there's our little champion," Samuel exclaimed, as he strode around the desk. "Come over here for a minute, Franklin. I've got something for you."

Master Hawkins walked across the room and sat down on the sofa beneath a large window. Isaiah gave his son a little nudge, nodding for him to follow his massa.

Surprisingly, Master Hawkins pulled Franklin right up onto his lap. "I think it's time you earned your boots," he said while reaching inside a box on the sofa. Pulling out a shiny pair of black boots, the master held them out in front of the boy. "These belonged to my son Joseph when he was about your age. He didn't get to wear them for long, but I want you to have them. What do you think of that, Franklin?"

Little Franklin bobbed his head up and down and allowed the master to pull on the knee-high boots.

"Well," Samuel said, "I think you'll have to grow into them a bit. Stand up and see if you can walk in them."

When Franklin was set down on the floor, he took a few awkward steps. Isaiah knew it would take some getting used to. His son rarely wore anything on his feet except in the cold of winter. And even then, he'd never worn anything as fancy as these riding boots.

Samuel let out a good-natured laugh and rose from the sofa. "It may take a while for those to fit right. Here," he said, "let's put those back in the box, and you can take them with you."

"Massa, thank ya kindly," Isaiah said. Then, turning his gaze toward Franklin, he said, "What do ya tell the Massa?"

Franklin echoed his pappy in a small voice. "Thank ya, massa."

Samuel smiled broadly. "You are most welcome, Franklin. But I'm the one who should be thanking you. If it hadn't been for you, we wouldn't have won that race." He reached down and rubbed the top of Franklin's head.

"Now, Isaiah, we have some business to take care of. Is your wife at the house?"

"Yes, sir, I specs she is by now."

Turning to his overseer, he said, "Go find her, and have her come get the boy."

Micah nodded respectfully and left the room.

Isaiah felt his heart beating an uneven rhythm. What was Ruthie going to say about such an overgenerous gift to Franklin from Master Hawkins? She would have a hundred questions.

In less than a minute, Micah reentered the study, Ruth following behind. She dipped her head. "Good mornin', massa."

"Good morning, Ruth. Would you take Franklin now? I have some business to discuss with Isaiah and Micah."

"Yessir," she said, moving across the room to take Franklin's hand. She would need to take him home and change his clothes before walking him to Mammy Lou.

"And don't forget his boots over there on the sofa. Just take the box."

Isaiah noticed Ruth's curious glance, as she followed the master's order. He could literally feel her inquisitiveness as she and Franklin walked past him and out the door. That pretty much settled it—he would have to tell her everything at supper tonight.

"Sit down," Master Hawkins told the two men as he took his chair behind the desk. A more serious look flattened his smile. "My wife and daughter shared a disturbing story with me last night at dinner, and two things now come to mind. Number one," he said, directing his gaze at Micah, "why did my overseer not inform me immediately about the terrible incident that took place with one of my slaves? And number two, why was I not told right away that my head trainer's hand was broken in that incident?"

While Master Hawkins, like his father before him, had never stooped so low as to beat the negroes on his plantation, he certainly made it clear who was in charge. While his kindheartedness made him a beloved master, his authoritative manner and commanding presence just as easily kept his slaves in line with his wishes. Real or perceived, there was always an underlying concern of being sold to another master.

Micah had come a long way in his lifetime. Starting out as a slave in Mississippi, then an indentured servant in Tennessee, and now the Hawkins Plantation overseer for the last six years all before the age of thirty. He was a proud man who worked hard to stay in the master's good graces. He sat forward in his chair, nervously sliding the brim of his hat between his thumb and forefinger. "I'm sorry, massa. We took care of the situation so you wouldn't be disturbed with it." He swallowed hard. "We didn't want to ruin the night for you and the missus."

Master Hawkins' eyes narrowed. "I'll give you that. But I should've been told everything before the Braddocks left our property that morning. Did you not believe I should make the final decision on this matter? You've put me in bad standing with Charles Braddock."

Lowering his eyes, Micah reiterated his earlier apology. Isaiah sat completely still, wondering when his time was coming, but he didn't have to wonder for long.

"You know, I noticed your swollen hand that morning, Isaiah. I even said something to your wife about that. She didn't out-right lie to me, but she certainly wasn't forthcoming about it, either."

Everything inside Isaiah cringed at the thought of Ruth being sent back to the fields for a decision he'd made. Isaiah sat up straighter and cautiously met his master's gaze. He would gladly face harsh consequences for his wife's sake. "Massa, I's so sorry for what happened that night—sorry most of all for Naomi's terrible troubles. But I give you my word that we wasn't tryin' to hide nothin' from ya, we was tryin' to save a man's life."

Samuel Hawkins put both elbows on his desk, keeping a hard gaze on Isaiah. "Go on."

"Do ya knows what kind o' man Massa Braddock be?"

A short silence fell between them while Samuel contemplated Isaiah's question. Then, relaxing his shoulders, the master sat back in his chair. "I do," he said thoughtfully. "I know exactly what evils that man is capable of."

"You's right, sir," Isaiah continued. "We know'd beyond a shadow of a doubt that Terrance was gonna be hanged 'fore he gots a mile down the road. We showed 'im mercy, massa. We knew if'n we was to tell ya what happened, massa Braddock would have to be told too. Fer keepin' it from ya, I humbly apologize . . . but fer savin' Terrance's life. . . ." He shook his head determinedly. "I can't say that I's sorry."

Letting out a deep breath, Master Hawkins stroked his neatly trimmed beard with one hand and tapped the top of his desk with the other. For a long moment, all three men sat in silence. Isaiah could feel his heart thundering in his ears.

Master Hawkins finally seemed to come to terms with the difficult situation. "I see your point, Isaiah. And while I don't like being left in the dark on something so important, I'm not so sure I wouldn't have made the same decision under those circumstances. I've heard stories about the way Braddock treats his people."

Isaiah glanced sideways at Micah, remembering stories the Braddocks' overseer had told them that night. Cecil relayed how slaves on the Braddock Plantation would sometimes be stripped and tied to a wooden stake all day long for the smallest of grievances. How children would be torn from their families and sold or used as pawns in their master's game of power. How beatings were just a regular way of life. Even though the overseer had laid those brutalities at his master's feet, Isaiah knew that Cecil was just as guilty. If they'd voted that night, Cecil would've undoubtedly found pleasure in hanging Terrance himself.

"Isaiah, you can go," the master abruptly declared. "Micah, you stay."

Immediately, Isaiah rose to his feet and bowed his head respectfully to Master Hawkins. "Thank ya, sir," he breathed, then took his leave.

I saiah couldn't help it. He stayed in the stables longer than necessary. Truth was, he needed to pray a little more about the upcoming conversation with Ruth. While the race had happened over three days ago, their son's part in it would no doubt tear open a fresh wound, especially where Prince was concerned. Even with Franklin making it through the race safe and sound, Isaiah was preparing for his wife's inevitable wrath.

Walking slowly down the road from the stables, Isaiah held his hat to his chest. Amos, the plantation's blacksmith, called out a greeting from his workshop that went utterly unnoticed. He must've thought Isaiah was losing his mind.

"Ruthie, I gots somethin' to tell ya," he said out loud, then kicked up the dirt at his feet.

He tried again.

"Ruthie, Franklin and I have some excitin' news. . . ."

Isaiah shook his head. "Naw, that ain't it."

With an upward tilt of his chin, he said, "Ruthie, I's the man and you's the woman, and. . . ."

Shaking his head vigorously, he decided to leave that one alone too.

Finally, making it to the cabin, he stepped up on the porch and drew in a nervous breath. The Spirit would just have to take over. He could hear Ruth inside talking to Franklin while she cooked supper.

"Ruthie," he said quietly in greeting.

"I was wonderin' 'bout you, Izzy. Come on now, supper's ready. Franklin, sit down at the table with your pappy." As soon as they were all seated, she said, "Yer gonna get the ham gravy left over from breakfast. I know it's not as good with corn cakes and peas, but you two didn't stick around this mornin'."

Isaiah was fine with whatever she put on the table, and he told her so. He would do anything to make her happy at this moment.

Bowing their heads, he led them in a short blessing, and they began to eat. Just as Isaiah was getting up enough nerve to speak, Ruth interrupted his anxious thoughts.

"Izzy, I can't tell ya how excited I am 'bout Franklin ridin' Prince in that big horse race! Yessir, I bet that was somethin' special to see."

Isaiah nearly choked on his corn cake. Maybe he wasn't hearing her right. "Whatchu talkin' 'bout?" he asked carefully.

Ruth cast her husband a playful grin, then went on and on about Franklin winning that race. A couple of times she looked at their son and winked, like it had been her idea for him to ride Prince in the first place. She went on so long, Isaiah finally decided someone else must've already told her about it.

With a feeling of pride, he jumped right into the story with her. "Ruthie, you shoulda seen 'im, ridin' up there on top o' Prince like he'd been born for it. He didn't fear nothin'!"

"Oh, I bet that was a sight for sore eyes," Ruth said lightheartedly. "I'm thinkin' Franklin should be the massa's rider every year in that race from now on. Don't you?"

"Well, I wouldn't goes that far." Isaiah reached over and rubbed Franklin's head. "But he done saved the day for Massa, that's fer sure."

Isaiah puffed his chest out a little more, now feeling confident to give his wife all the details. "I thought you's probly wonderin' 'bout them boots the massa give him this mornin'. That be a nice gift to say thank you to the little man, for winnin' him that championship. Now, I don't wants you thinkin' I wasn't worried none. Ruthie, I be cryin' like a baby for the first part o' that race, but when. . . ."

Isaiah's words trailed into midair when he saw the look on Ruth's face. It was almost like a whole different woman was sitting there in front of him.

"What's a matter, Ruthie?" he asked warily.

Ruth slumped back in her chair—her hand pressed tight against her chest. For a moment her mouth dropped open, but no words were coming out. Isaiah didn't move a muscle.

When Ruth attempted to speak, her voice came out in little squeaks. Clearing her throat, she finally said, "Mister, you better be spinnin' a tale right now, 'cause if you ain't. . . ." Her eyes turned to little slits. "If you ain't," she repeated, "you might be sleepin' in the stables from now till the Lawd comes."

Isaiah glanced over at Franklin, who was staring right at him. Poor boy didn't know what was going on. Looking back at his wife, he softly said, "Ruthie, I think we gots a misunderstandin' here. Why don't ya tell me what ya knows."

"Two mornin's ago," Ruth said flatly, "our son told me that he'd ridden Prince in that race. Course, I knew you'd put 'im up to tellin' me a wild tale, so I thought I'd play along. But come to find out, it's not a wild tale after all, is it?"

"No, ma'am," Isaiah said humbly. "But it weren't planned, Ruthie. I swears, we didn't mean for Franklin to be atop that horse when the gun went off."

Ruth's glare didn't let up, and her voice rose another notch. "Well I expect if he hadn't been at that track, he wouldn't o' been on top o' that beast in the first place."

Nodding his head, Isaiah agreed. "You be right on that account, Ruthie. But the massa and me know'd we needed somethin' to calm Prince down. He be out o' control. We knew Franklin were our only hope." He realized how weak that sounded, but it was the truth, and he didn't know what else to say.

"So let me get this straight, mister. You decided to make that horse race more important than our son. Is that about it?"

"Oh, no, Ruthie, that ain't it at all. No, ma'am, not at all. It's just so hard to explain."

At that moment, Franklin slipped out of his chair and climbed right up into his mama's lap. Taking her face in both of his hands, he kissed her, then cuddled up close to her breast. A lone tear rolled down Ruth's cheek as her arms surrounded him.

Kissing the top of his head, she turned her gaze back to Isaiah. Silence sat between them like a brick wall. For a long time, Isaiah watched his wife and son in their affectionate embrace. *Oh, Lawd, forgive me for what I done.* He now wondered how he could've made such a choice. Even sending young Joseph after the boy had been a dangerous proposition.

Convicted to his core, Isaiah slid his chair back and dropped to his knees beside Ruth. He took one of her hands and drew it to his lips for a lingering moment. When he looked up, their eyes met, and he could read the pain there. He suddenly felt the full weight of those four little bodies out back in their graves, and the hurt wound a deep path through him. While he had been at the mercy of the man who owned him, he too had made that thoughtless decision to use his boy.

"I's sorry," he said passionately, tears escaping his eyes. He kissed her hand again, then kissed Franklin. "I loves ya both more than my own life."

Ruth sat rigid for only a moment, then, releasing a deep sigh, she lowered her forehead into Isaiah's. After a while, she leaned back and nodded toward her husband's plate.

"Finish yer supper, Izzy," she said quietly, still holding the boy.

Even though he wasn't feeling hungry anymore, Isaiah did exactly as he was told. And his wife's next words weren't entirely unexpected.

"And take a warm blanket with ya to the stables."

⋘⋙

The next week slipped by uneventfully, although Micah had shared with Isaiah that Master Hawkins had nearly sent him packing. Naomi had thankfully come to his defense with the mistress, who convinced her husband to give the young overseer another chance.

Ruth had also relented from banishing Isaiah to the stables until the end of time. With the cool October winds rising at night, she had told her husband that she would allow him back in her bed to keep her warm. She didn't have to say it twice. Isaiah promised Ruth that three nights with the horses had caused him to see the error of his ways.

This morning, a gray sky threatened to release its storehouse of rain at any moment, so Ruth pulled her shawl a little closer and headed straight for the big house. She would pray as she walked today instead of stopping by the prayer log. Sarah was already washing breakfast dishes when Ruth came into the kitchen.

"Mornin', child," she said, pulling off her shawl. "I'll be right back to help ya soon as I get dressed."

Sarah didn't respond. Her gaze remained on the task at hand.

Naomi greeted Ruth from her sewing table. Two lamps glowed brightly, giving her extra light on such a gloomy day. "Did you talk to Sarah when you came in?" she asked.

"Well," Ruth said, opening the armoire to retrieve her outfit, "I spoke to her, but she didn't have nothin' to say back." She started unbuttoning her blouse. "Is there somethin' I should know?"

Pressing her lips together, Naomi shrugged. "I'm not sure. She's been pining over her young man for several days now, but she seemed extra quiet this morning. When I asked her about it, she said she was fine. But I'm not sure that's the case."

"Maybe it's just this dreary day," Ruth supposed.

Naomi agreed and went back to her sewing. The mistress had wanted a new gown for Isabella for the Christmas party at the Simpson's in Lexington. Even though her coming out ball wouldn't be until next July, Isabella would be turning sixteen three days before the Christmas party. She was finally getting her chance to be with the adults.

When Ruth was dressed, she moved the quilting pieces Naomi had collected and sat down in the chair to put on her boots. "That's a beautiful color," she commented, reaching out to touch the red velvet material. "I can just see our little missy in that now."

"Not so little anymore," Naomi responded.

Ruth agreed before changing the subject. "How are you doin', sister?"

"Oh, I've had better days, but I'm fine."

"Are you sleepin'?"

Naomi let out a languid sigh. "On and off. Sometimes I wake up in a sweat—I can feel my heart about to beat out of my chest." She shook her head. "I don't want to live in fear, but at night. . . ."

"Do ya want me to sleep with ya for a while?"

"Oh, no, that won't be necessary. I'll be fine," she said valiantly.

Ruth sat for a bit, watching her friend work. Then she delicately asked, "Have ya ever wanted a man next to ya at night, Naomi?"

A soft smile played on her lips. "Of course. I'd like to know what tender hands feel like, instead of. . . ." Naomi blushed. "I think you know what I mean. But then, it would have to be the right hands."

"I know what ya mean. Is there anyone at all?"

For a moment, Ruth had the distinct impression that Naomi was about to say yes, but the look quickly faded. "None that I know of."

Ruth put her hand on Naomi's arm and smiled. "Well, I'm gonna start lookin'."

"Oh, no you're not. It'll happen when it happens." Naomi gave her a wry smile. "Go on and talk to your daughter. I think she needs you more than I do right now."

Giving Naomi's arm a little squeeze, Ruth rose from her chair and headed back to the kitchen, but Sarah was already gone.

At nine o'clock, Ruth knocked on her mistress' door. To her chagrin, Elizabeth was already up and starting to dress.

"Oh, I'm so sorry, missus. You should o' sent for me."

"It's all right, Ruth. I've been awake for quite some time. I had Violet bring Catherine to me earlier than usual."

"Here, missus, let me help ya." Ruth set the hooks on her corset and noticed the dress she'd laid out. "Are you goin' visitin' today, missus?"

"Yes. Isabella and I are going to see Clarissa Blackstock and her daughter over in Richmond for the day. We'll be leaving by eleven."

"I surely hope we has good weather for travels," Ruth responded.

Elizabeth said, "As do I. But you and Sarah won't be needed. Richmond isn't far."

Ruth nodded agreeably. "Is there somethin' you'd like me to do for ya whilst yer away, missus?"

"As a matter of fact, there is," Elizabeth replied softly. "And it has to do with Sarah. Help me finish dressing, and we'll go to my sitting room."

There was something unsettling in the mistress' tone. Ruth chewed on her bottom lip, wondering what had happened. Whatever it was surely explained Sarah's mood this morning. Ruth's thoughts were suddenly plagued by doubt and worry. What had her daughter done?

Chapter 15

F orcing her hands not to shake, Ruth put the finishing touches on her mistress' hair. "Thank you, Ruth, that will do," Elizabeth told her.

The mistress rose and immediately walked into her sitting room. Taking her place on the sofa, she reached for a letter on the side table. "I have something to read to you. Please sit down."

Ruth could feel her emotions rising unchecked. *Oh, please, Lawd, give me strength.*

For a moment, Elizabeth stared at the contents of the letter, as if she were contemplating a decision. Finally, she rested her gaze upon Ruth. "This is a letter from Sally Stafford. I received it last evening. I'm afraid it holds some difficult news as far as Sarah is concerned."

Ruth nodded anxiously.

"There's quite a bit to the letter of no concern to you, but this paragraph here," she pointed to the second page, "is about the young man, Josey or Josiah, which is his given name. I think you need to hear it."

"Yes'm," Ruth breathed.

"This is what Mrs. Stafford wrote: *As to the negro Josiah, you inquired about on our plantation, he works with our livestock. Jack says we have owned him and his family for three years now. When the McClintocks of Springfield went into decline at about that time, Jack was able to get a very good price for the man, his wife, and two children. His wife is a very capable cook, as is Josiah himself. You did not make yourself clear as to the purpose of your inquiry, but in speaking with my husband, we would not be inclined to sell him nor his wife at this time.*"

Elizabeth lowered the letter to her lap. Her eyes were filled with concern. "I'm afraid Josey was not very forthcoming in his dealings with Sarah."

Was it possible to be heartsick and outraged at the same time? Ruth felt like crying and cursing all in the same breath. Heat immediately rose to her cheeks.

Noticing Ruth's reaction, Elizabeth went on. "I know this is hard to hear, particularly after all of the things this man told Sarah that night. Isabella shared most of it with me." Leaning forward, she briefly touched Ruth's hand. "It seems he led Sarah to believe that he loved her and wanted them to be together."

Sitting back, the mistress continued to carry the conversation. "Sarah knows nothing of this letter, but I'm afraid Isabella, in her youthful immaturity, told Sarah last night that it was time for her to forget all about Josey. In fact, I think she scolded her a bit on her feelings toward him."

That explained Sarah's demeanor this morning. It must've caused a rift between the two girls. Sarah would need to overcome her mood quickly. She must learn to keep her feelings to herself at all times around her mistress.

With that thought, Ruth declared, "I'll be havin' a talk with her today, missus. I'm so sorry 'bout the way she's acted."

"As am I about Bella," Elizabeth interjected, using her daughter's name from childhood. "But I'm so thankful we found out what kind of man this Josey really is.

Take heart, Ruth. I don't want you to think that we blame Sarah for this young man's blatant dishonesty."

"Thank you, missus," Ruth humbly replied.

Mistress Elizabeth folded the letter and returned it to its envelope. Then she said something that caught Ruth completely off guard. "Considering Sarah's age, if you like, we could make a match for her on our plantation. How do you feel about that?"

Ruth didn't know what to say, although she could certainly imagine Isaiah's thoughts on the matter. After a momentary pause, she responded to her mistress. "That is so kind of you, missus. I'll talk to Sarah and let you know."

"That's fine, Ruth. Take your time. I hope you'll be able to help Sarah work through her difficulties today. I've told Abigail that the two of you are to be left undisturbed in Isabella's room when we leave."

Ruth lowered her head, expressing her gratitude and assuring the mistress that she would do all within her power to help Sarah overcome this unfortunate situation.

⤬⤬⤬

Sarah turned away from Isabella's window, a sullen look on her face. She'd been watching her mistress' carriage roll down the long plantation drive. In that moment, Ruth felt more irritated with her daughter than sorry for her.

"Gal, you best be wipin' that look off your face. You got no right to act like you's been actin' 'round your mistress."

Sarah's brow wrinkled. "Well what am I supposed to do? Isabella told me I was acting like a fool over Josey. She practically told me I wasn't allowed to have feelings for him anymore."

"Then gal, you ain't allowed to have feelin's for him no more—least wise 'round your mistress. You better wise up, girl, or you'll be sent packin'. You wanna work in the kitchen or scrub clothes out back? How 'bout pickin' cotton all day in the fields?"

"Mama, stop it! You don't—"

"No, girl, you listen to me right now." Ruth knew Sarah was sailing on dangerous waters. If she wasn't careful, she'd be sinking to the bottom in no time. "Yer not your own—you don't belong to me nor your pappy nor even yourself. We be *slaves* to two people in this world—our Savior and Massa Hawkins. That's it! You ain't got the right to tell your missy nothin'."

Sarah's mouth dropped open, but she didn't speak, for which Ruth was glad, because she wasn't done yet. She stood toe to toe with her daughter.

"Lately, you been actin' like you's privileged. You know what that means?"

Sarah nodded her head.

"No, you don't!" she hissed. "You were born on this plantation, and you been livin' in the big house since you's nine. You think life's all 'bout eatin' good food and wearin' nice clothes and restin' when yer tired. But it's not!" she shouted.

Ruth took several more breaths, trying to calm herself down. She didn't want Berthy shuffling down the hall and eavesdropping outside Isabella's door. She lowered her voice but not her level of passion.

"How many slaves you think our massa owns?"

Sarah didn't answer.

"How many, girl? Take a guess."

"I don't know," Sarah replied sourly.

"Two hundred and nineteen souls on this one place. That's two hundred and nineteen souls that ain't got no rights at all. If we's told to sit down, we sit down. If we's told to stand up, we stand up."

"What if we're told to drown ourselves?" Sarah cried. "Are we gonna do that too, Mama? I can't even love who I want to love!"

Ruth's expression went from one of irritation to utter bewilderment. "What on earth you talkin' 'bout, gal? You know we ain't gonna be asked to drown ourselfs. And even if we was, well, we don't got much of a choice in the matter, now do we?" Ruth felt like shaking her. This was getting out of control in a hurry. She needed to put a little space between them.

Turning away, she walked over to the loveseat by the wall and sat down. Ruth couldn't help but shake her head at Sarah. Living in the big house for eight years had spoiled her. It was time to bring her back down to the way things really worked.

"I'm gonna tell you somethin' that I ain't even told your pappy. Now, I know your pappy's seen a lot, but he ain't never seen what I seen. He ain't never endured the humiliation that I have. I told ya some of it that night of the gala, but I didn't give you no details. The only reason I'm tellin' you this now, is 'cause you got to get your head out of them clouds and back to real life."

Ruth tugged in a deep breath, cringing at the thought of what she was about to share. "When my massa in Georgia decided to take me and some of his other slaves to auction, we was chained together by our necks and rode for miles in the back of a wagon. We had to stay sittin' right there, from early mornin' in the dark till late at night in the dark—we was left on that wagon. Do you think they fed us or gave us water? Do you think they stopped to let us do our business? By the time we got to the market, we was sittin' in our own mess."

Sarah's eyes were as round as twenty-five-cent pieces. She sat down on the edge of the bed, facing her mama.

"That night we was taken inside a big room at the market. It was damp and cold and smelled like vomit. Torches burnin' everywhere. Course, we smelled like worse than vomit too. So the first thing we had to do was take off all our clothes. Men, women, it didn't matter none. We was all still chained around our necks, standin' there tryin' not to look at each other. They threw buckets and buckets of cold water on us and made us scrub ourselves down with our hands. We was so thirsty, we opened our mouths to just get a tiny bit o' water."

"Mama, stop," Sarah said softly. "You don't have to tell me anymore of this."

"Oh, yes, I do," she said fervidly. "Yer gonna hear every bit of what I went through. You need your eyes opened right now." Without flinching, Ruth went on.

"After that, they unchained the men from the women and sent us to separate cages. There were empty feed bags on the floor, and we were told to sit down on 'em. By the time the sun came up the next mornin', we were shiverin' cold and all huddled together in a corner."

Ruth turned her gaze toward Isabella's window and noticed it had started to rain outside . . . so unlike the day she had been led onto the auction block. Yanked by the chain around her neck, Ruth had been brought out of the cell into bright sunshine. The air was cool, and she remembered not a cloud in the Georgia sky. Her dark, smooth skin glowed in the sunlight.

"When it was my turn, I was pulled up the stairs of the auction block. My chain was hooked to a post, and I stood there all alone and naked. I tried not to look at all them white men and boys standin' around gawkin'. Even some women standin' there too. I remember thinkin' to myself, *Hows come you women ain't botherin' to help me none?* But they weren't. They had the very same look in their eyes as them men. I was nothin' but a piece o' meat to 'em—some kind o' animal."

Sarah quietly left the bed and sat down beside her mother. She looked like she was going to be sick.

"I remember someone yellin', 'Show us her teeth.' So the man come up and stuck his thumbs between my lips and twisted my head all around for everyone to see. Then he made me turn around so they could see my backside. That's when they started yellin' out numbers. And them numbers were low, 'cause they didn't think much o' me. You know how much I cost?"

"Please, Mama, I don't wanna know."

"Ninety-five dollars. That's all I'm worth, Sarah. Ninety. Five. Dollars. Why, you can't even buy a mule for that."

Sarah's chin fell toward her chest, and she closed her eyes. Ruth was certain her daughter was finally getting a true picture of what it meant to be owned.

"I'll never get over what they done to me. I was just bloomin' into womanhood, and they stole it away from me out there in that bright Georgia sun." Ruth reached over and cupped Sarah's chin in her hand. "Look at me, child," she said. "I hope you never live to see a terrible day like that. But as long as this country allows a white man to own a black man, we'll not be free till the day Jesus comes again."

Sarah leaned into her mama, and Ruth held her for a long time. It had been twenty years since the day she went to auction, and the wound still felt as fresh as the day it was inflicted. She shuddered to think that it was still happening to her people today.

"I wanted you to hear my story, 'cause I wanted you to understand how blessed our family is to be sheltered by the Hawkins. But we ain't their equals. They *own* us, gal. You gots to remember that. And if somethin' ever happened to Massa Samuel, I shudder to think what'd become of us."

Sarah leaned back out of her mama's arms. "I understand, Mama," she said softly. "And I'm awful sorry for what was done to you."

"Thank you, child. I pray you never have to endure such a thing."

"I'm sorry, too, for the way I've been acting. I'll keep my feelings about Josey to myself from now on. But I'm not going to stop loving him, no matter what the missy says. I just won't talk about him anymore."

Ruth felt her heart do a flip flop in her chest. She was now wondering if she had the nerve to tell Sarah the truth about the man she thought she loved. But there was no way she could let her go on longing for a lover who already belonged to someone else. Besides, the girl needed to know what kind of man Josey really was.

"I gots some more hard news for ya, gal, and I'm sorry it's gotta be now. It's about Josey."

Sarah's chin came up. "What about him?"

"The missus sent a letter to the Staffords askin' about him. Seems Isabella wanted to see if there was somethin' she could do for the both of you."

"Why would she do that, then tell me to forget all about him?" Sarah moaned.

"'Cause, the missus got an answer to that letter, and it weren't a good one." She took both of Sarah's hands into hers. "Seems Josey is already married. He's got hisself a wife and two young'uns on the Stafford Plantation."

Sarah withdrew her hands. "I don't believe you," she breathed. "Are you sure?"

Nodding sympathetically, Ruth said, "It's the truth. Missus Stafford said they bought Josey and his wife and two children from a plantation in Springfield three years ago."

Sarah covered her face with both hands and leaned back on the loveseat. Ruth could literally feel the shock running through her daughter. She was sure her mind was trying to make sense of it all.

Sarah spoke through her hands in an agonizing voice. "How could he have said all of those things to me? He made me think we belonged together. He told me I was beautiful and that he loved me."

She suddenly dropped her hands to her lap and sat straight up. "How could he have done that to me, Mama?"

"Oh, gal, Josey is nothin' but a liar. Although he told the truth about one thing—you *are* beautiful. But he was wantin' to get somethin' from ya whilst he was away from his wife. He was just playin' with ya, knowin' all along that he'd never see ya again."

"Well, he sure took a beating for it," Sarah scoffed.

"And for that, I'm glad," Ruth responded. "Serves him right."

For the first time Sarah allowed the hint of a smile to touch her lips.

"I know it stings, gal, but there's lots better men out there than that one."

"Oh, Mama, I hope so. But how can I ever trust anyone again?"

Ruth softly laughed. "You ever look in your pappy's eyes?"

Sarah nodded.

"Did you happen to see goodness and kindness and steadfastness in Josey's eyes like you see in your pappy's?"

Sarah shook her head. "No, ma'am, I didn't. I think there was something deep down inside of me that was a little scared of him. He seemed to know a lot more about love than he was letting on."

"Girl, that weren't love," Ruth said with a grin. "That were somethin' else altogether."

For a while, both women sat in contemplative silence until Ruth took both of her daughter's hands again and laid them in her lap. "I sure wish it weren't rainin' outside, so I could take ya to my prayer log. But I guess this place be as good as any."

Sarah wholeheartedly agreed, and for the next several minutes, both women poured their hearts out to their heavenly Master, begging for wisdom and peace, while daring to plead for the chance to be free someday.

"Someday, Lawd," Ruth fervently breathed. "Someday soon."

Little did they know, *someday* would come sooner than either one could've ever imagined.

Chapter 16

As the year came to a close, many changes began taking place on the Hawkins Plantation. At the persuasion of the mistress, all of the wells in slave town had been replaced with water pumps. She had declared that not one more child on their land would be lost to a gaping hole in the ground. Mistress Elizabeth had even gone to slave town in order to inspect the project herself.

Master Hawkins had given all of his slaves a new set of clothes for Christmas. Naomi and her assistants had been commissioned to make a new skirt for all of the women and girls. The rest of the clothing and shoes had been purchased at the market in Lexington.

While Sarah had respectfully declined the search for a match on the plantation, as fate would have it, she met Jon at a Sunday worship service in slave town. He was a tall, lanky field hand, who asked if she would like to join him on a walk after services. At first, Sarah had only accepted the invitation to be polite, but as each Sunday approached, she found herself looking forward to a walk with Jon. While he wasn't as handsome as Josey, there was something about Jon's eyes that had fostered great trust and affection. His family was large, and Sarah was drawn to their fondness for dancing and singing on Sunday afternoons.

Not to be left behind, Isabella was now entertaining a young beau, whom she had met at the Simpsons' Christmas party. Master Steven Hardy of Lexington had apparently been smitten with Isabella at first sight. While Isabella declared him to be a good friend, Sarah knew her missy was equally besotted. Steven would be away at college in Virginia all spring but had declared his intentions to come for a visit at his first break in March.

The field hands were now busy rotating the crops on Master Hawkins' extensive property. Cotton crops were moved every two years, allowing one field to lie fallow for the following season. Tobacco and corn fields were rotated on a three-year cycle. Micah had worked his way back into the master's good graces with his keen agricultural skills and his ability to get the most out of his slaves.

Isaiah had also made quite a name for himself in the horse trade, but it was the mule business that was bringing in the most profit for his master. Mules were a necessity on any plantation. Isaiah could sell a broke mule for $125. Last year alone, he and his team of trainers had sold nearly a hundred mules that had been broke and another two hundred that hadn't. He could still fetch $100 for an unbroke mule at auction. Master Hawkins had given Isaiah a brand new pair of boots and a matching belt for Christmas to reward him for his work.

Ruth had likewise been given a special gift by the mistress. On Christmas eve, Elizabeth gave her companion a delicate gold necklace holding four tiny pearls, one for each of her babies in heaven. While Ruth had accepted the present with deep, heartfelt emotion, she would only wear it while at the big house. It was such an extravagant gift she didn't want it to cause hard feelings among her kinfolk. Every evening while walking home, Ruth would put it back inside its velvet case, wrap it in a cloth, and hide it inside her prayer log for safe keeping. But, oh, how she looked forward to putting on the lavish gift each morning while saying her children's names out loud: *Jonathon. Malachi. Isaac. Lucy.*

❧❦❧

JUNE 1856

Filling a carpet bag with her best clothes, Ruth prattled on about her upcoming trip. "I've never been away from my two for such a long time. I hope Izzy won't be too lonely."

Naomi walked over to the bed where Ruth was packing. "Well, I don't know about Isaiah, but I'm sure going to miss you for the next four days."

"Oh, sweet friend, I do wish you were comin' with us."

Naomi smiled serenely. "I have plenty here to keep me busy. I hope to make great progress with Missy's gown for her coming out ball. I can't believe it's less than a month away."

Ruth continued to pack with fervor. Her hands trembled.

"Dear one, calm down," Naomi soothed. "You're quite ready for this undertaking."

"I hope yer right. I just don't wanna let the missus down." Ruth had never travelled so far with her mistress, nor had she ever accompanied her on an extended visit. They would soon be leaving for the Hardys' plantation in Lexington where Isabella could spend time with Master Steven and his younger sister, Edith. It gave Ruth great comfort knowing Sarah would also be coming along.

Naomi continued to encourage her friend, as well as give her advice for the trip. "Just remember to stay out of sight as much as possible, but make yourself easily accessible to the mistress. You needn't worry yourself. Mistress Elizabeth will instruct you on everything you need to know." Naomi sat down on the bed as Ruth finished folding her last blouse. "I do envy the fact that you'll be with them when they shop for the jewelry to match Isabella's gown."

Ruth gave her a timid smile. "I'm a little nervous 'bout that too."

"You'll be fine, dear one." Naomi took Ruth's hand and kissed it. "Just be yourself. That's all the mistress expects."

A few hours later, two large trunks and several bags had been loaded on top of the plantation's most luxurious carriage. Ruth was surprised to see Isaiah standing out front with Ezekiel, who would be driving the four women to Lexington. Both men were checking the harnesses attached to the two fine horses chosen for the trip.

Isaiah's face beamed when Ruth and Sarah descended the stairs. "Mm, mm. Now there be two o' the pertiest women on this plantation."

Ruth shushed him. "Don't you be lettin' our missus hear you say that."

He winked at his wife. "That be our secret."

It would be a few minutes before the mistress and Isabella would be coming down. They were saying their good-byes to all the other children in the house. Ruth took the opportunity to speak with Isaiah one more time. "You and Franklin better behave yourselfs."

"Oh, yes'm. We's gonna make sure all the women be gone from our cabin 'fore you get back."

Ruth playfully slapped his arm. "Good. And can ya have 'em clean up the place for me?"

He slipped his hands around her waist and pulled her in close. "It'll be clean and tidy, just waitin' for ya." He kissed her quickly then released her. "I's gonna miss ya more than I can say."

"I'm gonna miss you too, Izzy. But four days ain't long. I'll be back 'fore you know it."

Isaiah walked over to Sarah and gave her a tight hug. "You and your mammy be safe."

Sarah smiled and kissed him on the cheek. "We will."

Soon, Mistress Elizabeth descended the stairs, holding to Master Samuel's arm. He kissed her on the cheek and helped her into the carriage. Then he kissed his daughter and offered his hand as she joined her mother. Ruth was next, taking her place beside her mistress with Sarah sitting beside Isabella.

Ezekiel, dressed in finery befitting his master's position, waited patiently, holding the reins taut. Master Hawkins looked up at his driver. "You take care of our women, Ezekiel."

"Oh, yessir. All will be well," he responded, tipping his top hat.

Samuel slapped his hand on the side of the carriage. "Safe travels," he said, and the carriage jerked forward as the horses quickly found their pace.

❧❧❧

The spacious mansion in Lexington was only one of two homes owned by the Hardy family. Their extensive property outside of the city held another large plantation house with a sizeable stable of horses. Master Stanton Hardy was not only a horse breeder but was one of Kentucky's leading rice growers. He was considered a powerful and respectable man. Young Master Steven would not only inherit the family business someday but he also had his sights set on the political arena. This coming fall, he would be entering law school at the University of Virginia.

On the second day of their visit, Steven gained permission for Isabella to accompany him on an open carriage ride to their plantation in the country. Sarah would be riding along as their chaperone. When arriving midmorning at Oak Hall, a picnic lunch was already waiting for Sarah to retrieve from the kitchens. When she returned to the carriage with the basket of food, Master Steven told her she would no longer be needed.

"You can stay with the slaves in the kitchen," he told her. "We'll be back to pick you up in a few hours."

Sarah's heart picked up speed. She held tightly to the basket. "I was told specifically by Mistress Hawkins that I was to stay with Miss Isabella," she replied respectfully.

Master Steven gave Isabella a most captivating smile. "And what do you say, fair lady?"

Casting her handsome companion a wary gaze, she replied, "Well, I wouldn't want to upset my mother."

"How would she know?" he quipped. "Your negro will do what you tell her."

Glancing at Sarah, Isabella shrugged her shoulders. "It will be fine, Sarah." She reached for the basket. But Sarah wouldn't let go.

"Missy," she said softly, "my orders come straight from your mother. I'm to go with you."

Steven reached for his horse whip on the floor of the buggy, but Isabella instantly put her hand on his arm. "No," she said firmly. "I won't go against my mother's wishes. Sarah, get in the back."

Sarah quickly climbed into the back of the carriage and was thrown hard into the seat as Steven cracked the whip on the rump of his horse.

Following a shaded road through the woods, Master Steven pulled the horse to a stop in view of a beautiful lake. "This is what my family calls Eagle Lake. If we're lucky, we'll see several bald eagles today." He set the brake and wrapped the reins tightly around the shaft before jumping down and walking to the other side.

Isabella closed her parasol and stood to accept Steven's hand, but instead, he surrounded her waist, lifting her easily to the ground. Isabella giggled, leaving her hands on the top of his shoulders for a prolonged moment.

Without looking in Sarah's direction, Master Hardy gave her a strict command. "Set up our lunch under that tree." He pointed to a spreading oak not far from their location.

Sarah stepped down from the carriage and obediently took the basket to the oak. It was a beautiful spot for a picnic lunch. She quickly spread the quilt and set out the food trays covered in monogrammed cloths. When she was done, she moved away to give the couple their privacy, but they were nowhere in sight.

Sarah's eyes darted about the landscape, hoping the two were nearby, but there was no sign of them. She hurriedly took the path to the lake, thinking they would surely be standing near the water's edge. But they weren't there, either. Nerves on end, she scanned left, then right, and back to the left again. Where had they gone?

"Lord, have mercy," she breathed aloud. "What am I gonna do with you, Miss Isabella?"

Finally deciding on a course of action, she walked down the path to her left, but before long, the trail came to an end. They hadn't come this way at all. Hurrying back the other direction, she decided to take the opposite trail. That's when her attention was drawn to a movement on the lake. Shading her eyes, Sarah's heart skipped more than one beat. There in the middle of the lake, she spotted Master Steven rowing Isabella in a small boat toward the other shore.

Sarah watched until they were out of view, then despondently returned to the picnic site. She had no choice but to wait for the couple to return. For the first hour, all she could do was pace back and forth in front of the quilt, occasionally looking out over the water. But eventually, her feet started developing blisters, so she decided to check on the horse. He was straining to reach the grass at his feet.

"Poor boy," she crooned, rubbing his neck. "Let me help you out." Sarah released the reins and tied them to a nearby branch. "Now, at least *you* can eat lunch."

By now, Sarah's stomach was rumbling, but she didn't dare eat any of Master Steven and Isabella's lunch. All she could do was resign herself to waiting in hunger.

Nearly two hours passed before the couple walked up from the lake hand-in-hand. Sarah quickly came to her feet, where she'd been leaning against the oak tree, guarding the picnic lunch from unwelcome varmints. She immediately walked over to the carriage to give them privacy.

Isabella merely gave her a fleeting glance, then allowed the young man to seat her on the quilt. It was obvious how familiar they had become with one another.

Sarah walked around to the other side of the carriage so she wouldn't have to watch. Her mind wandered to Master Steven's visit to the Hawkins Plantation back in March. He had seemed like an entirely different man, but then, he had been their guest. Now he was on his own property, poised on the brink of becoming the master in his own right. He had already made it clear what kind of master he would be.

Taking in a tremulous breath, she worried about what the future would now hold. If Isabella were to marry the young Master Hardy, Sarah would most likely go with her. She would be at the mercy of her new master. The recent conversation with her mama promptly came into sharp focus, and it scared her.

Sarah discreetly peered over the carriage at the scene beneath the oak. Steven leaned on one elbow—his long legs stretching out across the quilt. He was tracing an index finger lightly down Isabella's arm, then raised up to kiss her. It was obvious by Isabella's response that this was not their first kiss.

Suddenly, Sarah's heart was torn back to her own reality. What about the affections she and Jon held for one another? Would she be allowed to have a life and love of her own? How would it even be possible if Jon remained on the Hawkins Plantation while she was sent to the Hardys'?

"Oh, Lord," she sighed. "How can this be happening?"

Chapter 17

During the carriage ride home, Isabella and her mother sat side by side, chattering nonstop about the excitement of the past four days. It was now very clear that the young Master Hardy and Isabella would make a fine match for both families.

"Steven told me he would wear a cummerbund to match my dress at the ball next month. I won't want to dance with anyone but him." Isabella's joy was abundant.

Elizabeth gave her daughter an affectionate smile. "You'll need to be gracious toward all of your guests, Bella. That means you can't be exclusive to Steven."

Isabella's eyebrows rose. "What if this ball were to be for another reason . . . other than my coming of age?"

"It's too soon for that, young lady," Elizabeth chided, patting her daughter's hand. "Let's not try to rush things."

Snatching off one of her gloves, Isabella held her left hand out for all to see. "Too late," she declared, displaying a thin gold band with a diamond surrounded by two pearls on either side.

Elizabeth took her daughter's hand and pulled it closer. "What is this?" she asked in obvious dismay. "Surely you didn't get engaged without telling us."

Laughing gleefully, Isabella answered her mother. "Not exactly. Steven wants me to be promised to him. After two years of law school, we plan to be married . . . if not sooner," she trilled.

Sarah thought she was going to be ill. She sought her mama's hand and held it tightly. If only she could be afforded the same opportunity to talk to her mother so freely. Ruth gave her daughter a curious gaze and lovingly squeezed her hand.

❧❦❧

Three hours into the trip, raindrops began to spatter the road. Ezekiel brought the carriage to a halt beneath a thick covering of trees and quickly stepped down. Opening the passenger door, he held the black top hat to his chest. "Missus, we needs to stop so I can cover the bags. Won't be but a minute," he said.

"That's fine, Ezekiel, do what you need to. We're not far from home now."

"No, ma'am, we ain't. I'll have ya home within the hour."

Immediately he closed the door, and the women felt the carriage rock back and forth as Ezekiel fulfilled his task. Soon the door reopened. "All done, missus. We be on our way, but there's some mighty dark clouds ahead."

Elizabeth craned her neck to peer out the window. "Oh, my," she said. "I hope we're not about to go through a bad storm." Right on cue, a loud crash of thunder ripped through the heavens, causing all four women to startle.

The carriage suddenly lurched forward, leaving the shelter of trees behind. Rain began falling in sheets, drenching poor Ezekiel to the bone.

"Should we close the windows, missus?" Ruth asked.

Elizabeth immediately approved while leaning away from the spray of water starting to blow inside. Ruth and Sarah each closed a set of glass windows. It wasn't long before the compartment grew overly warm. Elizabeth and Isabella removed their gloves and pulled out handkerchiefs to blot their brows.

It was almost impossible to carry on a conversation with the heavy rain and nearly constant booming thunder. Frequent streaks of lightning lit up the cabin, and Ruth was frightened for Ezekiel's safety. Occasionally the carriage would lean in one direction or the other, as their driver avoided large pools of water in the roadway. Every strong gust of wind threatened to topple the carriage over.

Despite the oppressive heat, Isabella clung to her mother's arm. Ruth could see the fear in her eyes—and not just the missy's. All four women were distressed to say the least.

Mistress Elizabeth spoke above the din of the storm. "Ruth," she said in a strained voice. "Would you pray for us?"

Without hesitation, Ruth leaned forward. "Oh, yes'm. I been prayin' without ceasin' already."

Ruth took Sarah's hand into her lap but was grateful for Elizabeth's extended hand as well. Isabella and Sarah completed the small prayer circle. All four women clung tightly to each other while Ruth poured her heart out to God on their behalf. She prayed for the Lord to have his hand on Ezekiel in this struggle and prayed for protection from the terrible storm.

"Lawd," she spoke loudly, "we beg for ya to hold us in your mighty grip. Send your sweet angels to keep us safe. And we plead with ya in the most powerful name of our Lawd and Savior, Jesus Christ, who calmed the storm of old. And all your womenfolk cried. . . ."

"Amen," the four proclaimed in unison.

Even when the prayer ended, the women continued to hold their bond securely. They might be battered and bruised by the time they reached home, but they much preferred to cling to one another than hold onto the sides of the compartment.

The carriage came to another sudden halt, and Ezekiel soon appeared at the door. He opened it only a crack, but Isabella screamed when it was ripped wide by a strong gust of wind, smashing it against the side of the carriage. Ruth covered her mistress's skirt with her own, trying to protect her from the deluge while Ezekiel hauled the door back to a smaller opening. Ruth noticed his hat had been lost, probably long ago.

"Missus," he yelled, water pouring over his face, "I's not sure we should be crossin' the Rock Creek bridge. The water be nearly to the top."

Elizabeth peered through the small crevice of the door, trying to see what was ahead. "Is the bridge underwater yet?"

"Almost, missus. You want me to try an' turn us 'round?"

"Is it possible? The ditches are practically running like rivers."

"I know, missus. I's 'fraid we might get stuck."

The mistress raised her chin. "Take the bridge, Ezekiel. Quickly! We're almost home."

"Yes'm," he shouted, then slammed the door tight.

A violent shudder ran all the way through Ruth's body, causing her to feel nauseous and weak. She had experienced this feeling on one other occasion—the first day Mistress Hawkins had called her to the big house.

"No, missus!" Ruth cried in panic. Her body trembled so violently Sarah surrounded her mama with both arms. But Ruth was inconsolable. Tears poured down her cheeks. "We have to stop—"

At that very moment the carriage shot forward, throwing the women back in their seats. Ruth grasped for the door handle, but the carriage had already moved onto the bridge.

⋰⋱⋰⋱

Isaiah paced in front of his cabin while keeping an eye on Franklin. The boy was dragging a long stick through the mud left behind from the fierce afternoon squall. All the kinfolk had finished supper and were sitting on their porches or conversing in small groups. Old Solomon kept a beat on his snakeskin drum while some of the young'uns frolicked to the rhythm or chased one another around the pump.

Isaiah was worried. The womenfolk should've been home by now. He tried to console himself with all sorts of scenarios. Maybe they decided to stay an extra day in Lexington. Perhaps they'd gotten a late start. It was possible they'd stopped to ride out the storm at a neighbor's place. Whatever the reason, nothing seemed to ease the tension in his gut.

Unable to wait any longer, Isaiah took Franklin by the hand. "Come on, little man. I's takin' you to Mammy Lou for a bit."

Franklin walked along with his pappy, dragging the stick all the way to Mammy's cabin. After dropping off his son, Isaiah made a beeline to the carriage house, hoping to find Ezekiel polishing the tack. But the carriage house stood silent and empty. He quickly decided to head over to Micah's place.

Micah occupied a log house out back from the mansion. Master Hawkins preferred to keep his overseer close at hand should he be needed.

Knocking furiously on the door, Isaiah was met with another silence. He hastily looked around the property, debating a more troublesome decision. Should he go to the massa's study? It wasn't his place to do so without being summoned. He stood on the overseer's porch, staring at the big house.

At that moment, he caught sight of Micah leading two saddled horses toward the house. Isaiah leapt from the porch and cut him off before he could get to the door of the master's study.

"Where you goin?" Isaiah asked.

Micah gave Isaiah an uneasy glance. "The massa and me is gonna ride the road whilst there's enough light. He's worried 'bout the women."

The door to the master's study immediately opened and slammed shut, drawing Isaiah's attention. "Massa," he called breathlessly. "Has ya heard from our womenfolk?"

Samuel's face looked anxious and drawn. He shook his head, then pulled his hat on with both hands. "I'm afraid something might have happened during the storm. I hope they're not stuck in the mud somewhere. They're probably at one of the neighbor's, but I can't wait around any longer."

The master pierced Micah with his worried gaze. "Give Isaiah your horse. He's going with me."

Micah dutifully handed over the reins. "Do you want me to saddle another horse and catch up with ya?"

"No," Samuel said, swinging his leg over the saddle. "Stay here and carry on. We'll try to be back by dark."

Isaiah was in the saddle before the master could finish his sentence, anxiety plaguing his every thought.

The two men rode hard, covering a couple of miles in silence. The mud was deep in several places, and they had to slow their mounts to get through it.

When they came upon a long fencerow, the master called over his shoulder, "Let's check in with the Jenkins." He turned his horse down the road to their farm. Isaiah followed close behind, praying the women would be there. But a few minutes later, they were back in the saddle, galloping along the main road.

As they approached Rock Creek at dusk, the men slowed their horses to cross the bridge. But something had Master Hawkins' horse spooked. He half-reared, then backed away, refusing to step onto the wooden runners.

"Massa," Isaiah said, "the railing be off the bridge. Might not be safe to cross."

Both men dismounted and dropped their reins to the ground.

Samuel tested the wood with a tentative step. Tree limbs and debris were scattered all across the bridge. "Looks like the water must've covered the bridge this afternoon. I bet Ezekiel had to turn around."

"Yessir, I specs so."

The bridge creaked and moaned, but it seemed sturdy enough to bear the weight of the horses. Quickly returning to their mounts, they grabbed up the reins to walk them across. But once again, Master Hawkins' horse refused to step onto the bridge. This time he reared all the way up, causing Samuel to take a quick step backwards. "See what you can do with him," he told Isaiah in an irritated voice.

After several attempts, Isaiah apologized profusely. "I's so sorry, massa. If ya think the stream be low enough, we can cross down below."

Not wasting any more precious time, the master agreed and began leading his horse down the steep, muddy bank. Shoving the reins back over his horse's head, Samuel mounted up and started across a fairly shallow section. The water was still rushing higher than normal, but it had receded a long way since covering the bridge earlier in the day.

Isaiah clicked his tongue, urging his horse into the stream, then sharply pulled the reins back. "Massa!" he yelled loudly just before jumping with both feet into the water.

Chapter 18

Isaiah struggled and slashed his way through waist-deep water. At one point, his feet were swept out from under him, and he went beneath the water, dashing his body against the rocks below the surface. Gaining a tenuous foothold, he came back out of the stream, coughing water out of his lungs. But nothing could keep him from getting to the lifeless form, caught against a fallen tree.

Clasping hold with both hands, he pulled the body closer, turning it face up. Ezekiel's eyes were still open, his body cold and stiff. "Oh, Lawd, no. No, no, no," Isaiah moaned.

Master Hawkins waded back through the stream, reaching out to grab Isaiah's arm to keep his balance. His face was white as a sheet peering down at Ezekiel. Turning away, he scanned the stream and banks in desperation. "Elizabeth!" he yelled. "Isabella!" But only his echo returned to him.

Isaiah pulled Ezekiel's body across the stream and laid him on the rocky shore, gently closing his eyes. Resting a hand on his friend's chest, he whispered, "You be free now, Ezekiel," then turned back to look for the others.

By now, Samuel Hawkins was feverishly splashing about in the stream, yelling for his wife and daughter. Isaiah knew he had to get to him before he was swept downstream.

"Massa," he called, "come outta the water. Les look 'long the banks."

But Samuel was frantic.

Isaiah waded out to him. "Come on, now. Les get outta this water." He took his master by the arm and led him to the nearest bank, but on his way, Isaiah spotted something else in the stream.

"You sits down here, massa. I be right back." Isaiah waded out past the tree where he'd found Ezekiel. The water came all the way up to his chest, causing him to take quick, shallow breaths. Unable to swim, Isaiah took tentative steps, trying to keep his head above water at all costs.

Reaching out, he took hold of the object he'd seen earlier—it was a wheel from the carriage. A powerful emotion rose up from his very core, and Isaiah quietly breathed, "Ruthie. Where you be, gal? Please don't leave me, Ruthie." He squeezed his eyes shut, praying to the Lord with every breath that his wife and daughter would be found alive.

"What is it?" the master called from the bank. He'd now come to his feet, a little color returning to his face.

"It be a wheel, massa. Les keep lookin'."

Isaiah waded out of the water, and the two men began walking along the muddy bank. But in a few short minutes, the woods grew impossibly dark—there was no way to even see what was in front of them.

"We've got to get help," Samuel finally conceded. "You ride back and tell Micah to bring forty men with torches. If the flood waters reached as high as the bridge, they could be anywhere in these woods."

Isaiah stood stock still. He didn't believe his master was thinking straight. "Massa," he said respectfully. "If'n I gets caught, I won't be makin' it to the plantation."

Slave patrols and white militias often travelled this road at night. Isaiah could be imprisoned or hanged if they caught him without a pass from his master.

Samuel sighed heavily. "I can't leave you here either. Come on, we'll go together."

Making their way back to the horses, they quickly mounted and rode as fast as they dared back home.

Within an hour, a long line of slaves walked the road, all carrying torches and following behind Master Hawkins and Micah on horseback. Isaiah drove one of the four mule wagons, joining in the procession to the Rock Creek bridge. When they arrived, Micah led half the men down one bank while Samuel and Isaiah led a group down the opposite side. Some of the men carried coils of rope and others long sickles to cut out the undergrowth along the banks and in the woods. One group had been instructed to take Ezekiel's body back to the plantation on a mule wagon.

All throughout the night, the men painstakingly searched along the stream and through the woods. Oftentimes, a voice could be heard through the trees: "Got somethin'," or "There's somethin' in the water." Every now and then, Master Hawkins would yell out for his wife and daughter, but nothing was found other than bags and clothes and parts of the carriage.

Just before sunup, a voice resounded with a heart-wrenching call. "I gots one of 'em, massa. Oh, Lawd, I gots one of 'em."

Samuel and Isaiah turned back, hurriedly following the sound of the mournful cry. Their steps slowed as they came upon a solemn circle of slaves, torches casting light on one man in the center, holding a precious body in his arms. When the man looked up, tears shimmered on his dark cheeks. "I's so sorry, Isaiah. . . ."

Isaiah's breath caught in his throat. He handed his torch to a fellow slave and slowly moved inside the circle. His lips quivered, and he dropped to his knees. "Ruthie," he gasped. He felt like the air had been forced from his lungs. Tears streamed from his eyes as the other man laid Isaiah's beloved wife in his arms. He pulled her close to his chest and rocked back on his heels, turning his tortured face to the heavens. One sob after another tore through his body. Every slave dropped down to their knees, tearfully watching their brother mourn.

Master Hawkins stepped inside the circle, laying a shaky hand on his trainer's shoulder. "I'm so sorry, Isaiah," he said in a trembling voice. "Take her home."

Isaiah held Ruthie in one arm and wiped his face with his free hand. "I gots to find my Sarah gal too."

"We'll find her," the master said in a hollow voice. "Take Ruth home."

Rising unsteadily to his feet, Isaiah cradled Ruth tenderly, talking to her in a soothing voice, telling her how much she meant to him. Someone came running with a blanket to cover her, but Isaiah refused. "No. I needs to see my gal a while longer."

When he struggled up to the road, Isaiah took Ruth to one of the mule wagons. A quilt had been spread out in the back, and he laid her on top. Then, kissing her brow, he wrapped her in a cocoon and slid up into the bed of the wagon. He would hold his gal as long as he could.

As the mule plodded into slave town at dawn, a crowd of women surrounded the wagon. At the sight of Isaiah holding Ruth's body, his kinfolk began to wail. The cacophony of grief continued while Isaiah carried his lover into Eula's cabin. He laid her gently on the table and walked outside, leaving the women to care for her.

Naomi had stayed awake all night in prayer, walking through the garden, beseeching the Father to bring her dear ones home. At dawn, she heard the mournful cries echoing through the woods, and she ran with all her might toward the terrible sound. When she made it to Ruth and Isaiah's cabin, she stopped to take in the scene. The wailing had intensified as more and more women joined in the throng.

Not wishing to be a part of it, she went inside Ruth's cabin, but it was empty. Coming back out on the porch, she could hear the distinct sound of a shovel at work. Naomi's heart was instantly struck with anguish. She anxiously walked the short path behind the cabin and found Isaiah digging a grave.

"Isaiah," she cried. He immediately dropped his shovel to take her into his arms, but she held him off, shaking her head.

"Who is this for?" she asked in a quivering voice.

Isaiah's grief-stricken face threatened to destroy her. "It be our Ruthie," he sobbed.

"Oh, Lord. No," she cried, giving in to Isaiah's embrace. His head dropped over her shoulder, and they wept inconsolably in each other's arms.

After several minutes, Naomi put her hands upon Isaiah's chest, looking into his eyes. "Where is she now?"

Isaiah nodded his head toward the cabin next door. "She be with Eula and the kinfolk. They's takin' care of her for now."

Tears started all over again, and Naomi went back into his arms. It seemed the light of their lives had been extinguished. "What about Sarah?" she asked.

At Isaiah's silence, Naomi stepped back for the second time. "They still be lookin'," he said. "Ain't found the mistress or Isabella neither."

Naomi thought she wouldn't be able to breathe. How could any of them stand to lose all four of their beloved women in one day? Never had she felt so mired by heartache.

"Go to her," Isaiah said quietly.

Naomi searched his despondent eyes for a moment, then silently nodded and left him to dig the awful grave.

Ceceilia caught sight of Naomi from Eula's porch and told the grieving women to let her through. She reached for Naomi's arm, leading her inside. The kinfolk had already washed Ruth's body and dressed her. She lay peacefully on the table with her hands folded on her chest.

Naomi went to her, placing a hand gently on top of Ruth's. "Oh, dear one, I love you so." She bent and lovingly kissed her forehead, then whispered with deep emotion, "Be at peace until we meet again."

Unable to stay a moment longer, Naomi turned and left her kinfolk to mourn together. She would have to grieve alone. Ruth had once shown her the prayer log, and that's where she needed to go. It was there that Naomi allowed her spirit to release its agony in loud cries and moans.

As the morning dragged on, the wailing continued. Naomi went back to the big house to continue her vigil. Her grief would be a private matter between her and her heavenly Father. She decided to watch and wait from the front porch of the plantation house.

Before the noon hour arrived, a solemn company of slaves, along with two mule wagons, turned down the plantation road. All of the house slaves silently made their way to the front walkway. Master Hawkins followed the procession on horseback, not taking his gaze from the two wagons.

Naomi's heart shattered into a million pieces. "Oh, God in heaven, how will we survive this?"

One breath at a time was the answer she heard in her soul. *One breath at a time.*

Chapter 19

Three days after Elizabeth and Isabella's bodies were recovered, a large service was held at the Presbyterian church in Richmond. The two were brought home and buried in the family cemetery on the hill behind the house. Every soul on the plantation attended the service on the hill. There was no doubt how beloved the mistress and her daughter were to their slaves.

Day after day, the Hawkins' friends and family came to pay their respects. For two full weeks, the house staff received one guest after another. Young Joseph and William tried to bravely endure the loss of their mother and sister, but most nights, they could be heard crying themselves to sleep. Little Catherine was far too young to understand what had happened, but she constantly whimpered and begged for her dear mother.

Samuel Hawkins was but a shell of a man. It was obvious to everyone in the house that he wasn't eating or sleeping. There was even talk that he might take his own life. Micah took it upon himself to be his constant companion when no guests were around, but he couldn't entice the master to think about the day-to-day work around the plantation. Everything had become meaningless.

When the mourners stopped coming by, Isaiah felt he had given the master all the time he could afford. He could no longer wait to seek permission for his important task. He decided it best to start with the overseer before taking it to Master Hawkins.

Knowing Micah's mornings usually started in the mule barn, Isaiah took his son to Mammy's and headed there first thing. Spotting him as he was going into the barn, Isaiah called his name.

"Mornin', Isaiah. How're you gettin' along today?"

Isaiah swallowed hard, still finding it difficult to answer that question, especially when he missed his wife and daughter with every beat of his heart. "I's gettin' by," he simply said.

"What can I do for ya?"

Not wasting time, he told Micah, "I needs to see the Massa on important business."

Micah was already shaking his head. "Massa ain't seein' nobody these days. He's still mournin' somethin' awful. He sometimes goes a whole day without even talkin' to his own children."

Isaiah took off his hat and scratched his head. "I still gots to ask him somethin'. Can ya just talk to him for me?"

"Is it about the thoroughbreds?" Micah enquired.

"No, sir. It's more important than that."

Micah scrunched his brow. "How 'bout you tell me first."

Isaiah nodded and proceeded to pour out his heart to the overseer. When he was finished, Micah told him, "Come on. Let's go see the massa right now."

Within minutes, Micah was knocking on Master Hawkins' side door, Isaiah standing behind him, hat in hand. When there was no answer, Micah tried the door—it was locked. "We'll have to go inside," he said.

When the men came through the kitchen entrance, Naomi happened to be standing near the door. Isaiah felt a strong emotion squeeze his chest. "Naomi," he said quietly. "Are ya doin' all right?"

She looked as though she might cry. He hadn't wanted to cause her any angst. But after drawing in a deep breath, she simply said, "Yes." Then with a curious gaze, she asked, "Where are you two going?"

"We can't get in the massa's study," Micah responded. "We're goin' to the door in the hall." He didn't wait around for more conversation.

Before Isaiah could follow, Naomi touched his arm. "Master Hawkins isn't doing well at all. I want to talk to you when you get done in there."

Isaiah nodded. "I'll find ya."

Micah rapped his knuckles on the door but didn't wait for an answer. Isaiah was surprised that he opened the door and walked right in. Master Hawkins wasn't behind his fine desk as usual but was lying on the sofa, one arm hanging over the side. He looked as though he'd spent the night there—maybe several.

Micah cleared his throat. "Massa?"

Samuel stirred, then covered his eyes against the morning light. "What is it?" he asked in a scratchy voice.

"We got some business to discuss this mornin'. Can I get ya some breakfast first?"

"No," he replied gruffly. "What do you want?"

"Isaiah is needin' to ask you somethin' really important. Can you talk with him, sir?"

"Not now, Micah. Tell him some other time."

"Uh, massa, he's standin' right here."

Samuel slowly raised his body into a sitting position. His normally tidy beard was growing long and scraggily—his thick, dark hair hanging down over his eyes. He leaned forward, planting his elbows on top of his thighs, then looked up at the two men. "What do you want?"

Isaiah stood speechless. He didn't see how he would be able to make this man in front of him understand what he was needing.

Micah tilted his head toward the master, urging Isaiah to speak.

Clearing his throat, he said, "Massa, I knows this be a hard time and all. But I gots to talk to ya 'bout my gal, Sarah."

Samuel leaned back on the sofa, giving his trainer a blank stare.

Isaiah tried to swallow, but his mouth was too dry. "I'm thinkin' my gal can't rest till she be found. I's needin' your permission to keep lookin' for her. It won't interfere none with my work—I give ya my word. But I gots to have a pass from ya so's I'll be safe on the road." He wiped his sweaty hands on his trousers and waited for his master's reply.

Samuel's lids covered his brown eyes, and Isaiah glanced over at Micah. But at that moment, a tear rolled down the master's cheek, and he reached up to wipe it away.

"Isaiah," he said, without opening his eyes. "I'm sorry for your great loss too."

"Thank ya, sir," Isaiah said quietly.

For a long moment, nothing else was said. Micah and Isaiah didn't move from their position. Finally, Master Hawkins hauled himself up off the sofa and walked around his desk. Opening and closing a couple of drawers, he ended up slamming the third one shut. "Micah, where are my passes?"

Micah slid around the desk. "Right here, sir." He pulled open the first drawer the master had tried and took out a small stack of papers. "Just fill in Isaiah's name here and your signature here, massa."

Samuel glared at his overseer. "I think I know how to fill in my own pass, Micah."

"Yessir. Sorry, sir." Micah backed away from the desk.

When it was complete, Master Hawkins handed the paper to Isaiah. "You be sure to carry this on you at all times. I don't want to lose you too," he said.

Isaiah held back another wave of emotion. "Thank ya, kindly, massa. You have no idea how much this means to me."

Samuel merely nodded, then leaned back in his chair as if that small task had worn him out. "See yourselves to the door," he said curtly.

Both men headed back to the hall door. Micah opened it and motioned for Isaiah to proceed, then he told his master, "I'm sending someone in with your breakfast." Without giving him time to respond, Micah closed the door.

Naomi was the only one still in the kitchen when they left the study. Breakfast was long over, but she had waited around for Isaiah. Micah quickly took his leave and headed back to the mule barn.

"Do you have time to sit down, Isaiah?"

He had a lot to do this morning, but for Naomi, everything could wait. He simply nodded and sat down, laying his hat on the table.

"Can I get you something to eat or drink?" she asked.

"Thank ya, no. But the massa be needin' breakfast. Can ya take him some?"

"I will," she nodded. "That's what I want to talk to you about. What did you think about him?"

Isaiah shook his head warily. "He ain't doin' well. Not at all."

"Everyone in the house is worried sick," she went on. "But there's no one who can help him, not even young Master Joseph."

"I knows Micah be tryin' as hard as he can, but the massa seemed irritated with him when we was in there. You think there be someone else who can help him?"

Naomi's gaze held a great deal of compassion. "I was hoping it could be you," she said.

Isaiah's brow wrinkled. "Whatchu think I can do? I can barely help myself right now."

She reached over and touched his arm. "I know, but since you share the same experience, I thought maybe you would be able to help each other through it."

"I don't know how. I can't be goin' to the massa unlessen he asks me first."

Naomi conceded the point. "It was just a thought." Then, changing the subject, she asked about the paper in his hand.

"Oh, this here's a pass for me to be on the road. I's gonna start lookin' for Sarah again." Noticing the worry in her eyes, he quickly went on. "I'll be fine. I ain't goin' in the evenin' when it's so dangerous. I's gonna get out there 'fore the sun comes up every mornin' till I find my baby girl."

Tears welled up in Naomi's eyes, and she quickly blinked them away. "Be careful, Isaiah."

"I will. Don't you worry 'bout me."

Naomi came to her feet. "I guess I should go get the master's breakfast."

Isaiah stood as well and gave her a loving hug before heading out the door with his hat and the pass from his master.

❧❧❧

Setting the breakfast tray on the hall table, Naomi knocked lightly on the study door.

"What?"

Closing her eyes, she took in a nervous breath. "It's Naomi. I have something for you to eat." Not waiting for another harsh response, she opened the door, then reached for the tray. "Where would you like it, sir?" she asked calmly.

Samuel was still sitting behind his desk, which was completely devoid of papers. He hadn't been working on anything before she walked in. "Not on my desk," he responded.

There was only one other choice, so Naomi set the tray on the table in front of the sofa.

"You can go," he told her in a slightly more courteous tone.

Naomi didn't move nor flinch in the long moment they stared at one another.

Finally, he said, "You're not going, are you?"

"No, sir. Not until you eat."

Master Hawkins exhaled loudly and stood up. Naomi was shocked by his disheveled appearance. Never in all her days of service to this family had she seen the master in such a state. He looked down at himself and must've realized how he appeared. After tucking in the front of his shirt, he ran a hand through his hair.

"Please," he said, pointing to the sofa.

Naomi's eyes grew wide. "You want me to sit down, sir?"

"Yes. If I have to eat, then you have to stay." He sat down on the sofa and reached for a blueberry muffin and mug of coffee. "Would you like something?" he asked, pointing to the tray.

"No, thank you. I've eaten."

"So, you're the spy sent in to watch me eat, huh?"

She raised one eyebrow. "Perhaps."

While he didn't outright smile, Naomi could feel his mood lift. She needed to keep him talking but had no clue what to talk about. Fortunately, Master Hawkins led the way. However, his next words set her nerves on end.

"Tell me what's being said about me in the house."

It was his turn now to stare at her until she responded. When she looked at him, he was peering at her over his coffee mug, both eyebrows raised.

"Sir, I don't listen to nor engage in gossip."

This time she thought he smiled as he took a sip from his mug. "Smart answer," he responded. He put his coffee and half-eaten muffin back on the tray before dropping his elbows to his knees. Without looking at her, he told her in a flat voice, "I can't get past this. I don't think I'm strong enough."

"Oh, but you are," Naomi responded vehemently. "You're just not giving yourself a chance." All of a sudden, she felt brave enough to tell him what she was thinking. "You can't move forward by sitting in this room all day and depriving yourself of food and ignoring your. . . ."

He suddenly sat up when she went silent. "Ignoring my what?"

Naomi froze.

"Say it!" he practically yelled.

"Your children need you," she said softly. "We hear your sons crying at night. They need their father to hold them and assure them that they will be all right . . . that *you* will be all right."

"But I'm not," he said bluntly.

"Not yet. You need to give yourself a chance. You don't have to get back to work right away, but you can start small, like a simple evening walk in the garden with your children. Tuck them in bed tonight. Play with little Catherine. Eat dinner together or breakfast. Anything to start healing."

He leaned forward again, and long seconds ticked by. She was about to speak when she noticed his shoulders start to shake. He was weeping.

Naomi desperately glanced over to the open door. She felt like running away before she herself fell apart. The master wasn't the only one dealing with a heavy heart. Looking back, she asked him, "Is there someone I can get for you, Master?"

He leaned back on the sofa, running both hands through his hair. His face was red—tears on his cheeks. A heart-wrenching moan came up from his chest. "Help me," he cried.

A profound emotion suddenly overwhelmed her. He needed to be held, but she had no right to reach out to him in that way—she was his slave. Naomi immediately rose to her feet, fearful of losing her composure.

"I'm sorry," she breathed, before running from the room.

Chapter 20

Naomi's hands were shaking so badly she had to put the quilt aside. She'd worked on it all day, hoping to take her mind off of the morning incident in the master's study. Oh, how she longed for her dear one. Ruth would've been the only soul who could help her amidst such tragedy and grief. Naomi's heart was completely decimated by the loss of the four most important women in her life. She hadn't found a moment's peace from the constant ache to her spirit. Was it any wonder why the master was struggling so?

For a while, Naomi toyed with the thought of going to see Isaiah and Franklin. They would be done with supper by now. She could sit with them on the porch. But envisioning the gossip that would ensue from that simple visit forced her to search for another way to find relief.

Prayer seemed to be her only answer, but she found it a nearly impossible task inside this house of gloom. The garden had become her place of respite. The fact that it was totally inappropriate for her to go there continually troubled her conscience. After all, the only slaves allowed in the garden were the ones who tended to it. It was strictly meant for the family's pleasure. She had decided many days ago to start looking for another place to pray—but not this evening.

Opening a wooden gate on the back wall of the garden, Naomi marveled at the beautiful summer evening landscape. It never disappointed. The chestnut trees rustled overhead as she walked along the shaded paths, stopping occasionally to admire a delicate rose or combinations of brightly-colored peonies. The fragrance of honeysuckle overwhelmed her senses, and on a whim, she plucked one, tasting its sweet nectar.

Her feet wandered aimlessly along the garden paths, merely following the fragrant floral scents. There were no words to describe the peaceful feeling—she simply communed with her Lord through his lovely creation.

A smile touched Naomi's lips as a chipmunk scurried across her path, quickly hiding away in the colorful ground cover. Noticing the gray lamb's ears, she knelt to touch their softness. They beckoned her to lean close, letting them gently caress her face.

Unexpectedly, Naomi felt self-conscious. She had the distinct feeling that she wasn't alone. Remaining on her knees, she glanced about, hoping not to be caught in the family's private space. But there was no one in the area nearby. Maybe it would be best to leave.

When she came to her feet, Naomi was disturbed by how close she had wandered to the house. That had not been her intention. A small sound from above caught her attention, and she glanced upward. The windows at the end of the upper hallway had been opened, the miniature doors thrust outward. There on the balcony stood the master, holding little Catherine in his arms.

Their eyes met for a prolonged moment—master and slave. His dark hair had been combed and beard neatly trimmed. He wore fresh clothing and was cradling his daughter to his chest. The two had been over-looking the garden together. Something about the scene affected Naomi's heart.

Dipping her head, she turned and slipped back into the garden. No words were spoken.

∾❧∾

Isaiah roused himself from bed in the early morning hours. He dressed quietly in the dark, then leaned down over the bed to make sure Franklin was still asleep. The boy now occupied the space where Ruth had lain. Slipping out the door, he quickly made his way around back to talk to her.

When he came to her grave next to Lucy's, he went down on one knee. "I's gonna find our gal today, Ruthie. I knows yer waitin' for her." He kissed his palm and laid it gently on the rock marking her grave, then quickly headed to the mule barn.

As soon as he had a mule saddled, he grabbed a torch from the tool shed and dropped some matches under the flap of his shirt pocket. He patted his other shirt pocket for reassurance that the pass from his master was there. Tying a short rope around the butt of the torch, he hung it over the saddle horn and mounted up.

On his first day of the lonely search, Isaiah had decided to take an old farm road that ran the length of the stream. It was outside the wooded area, but the waters had risen so high the day of the squall, Sarah's body could've been carried anywhere. He planned to search until the first stars started to disappear from the sky.

When he found the farm road, he turned the mule and travelled a bit. "Whoa," he said quietly, pulling back on the reins. Hopping down, he took the torch and lit it, then mounted up again. He held the torch wide, scouring the area along the road and outside the trees.

After a long hour, the light of the torch flickered across a lump partially lying inside the woods. His heart sank. He was certain of what he'd found.

Dismounting slowly, he walked toward the motionless object on the ground, disfigured from being slammed violently against the trees in the raging waters. It was the body of one of his master's fine horses that had been pulling the carriage.

Although the smell of death was pungent, Isaiah knelt to touch the horse's muzzle. "I's so sorry, boy. I knows how frightened you was."

Twisting the butt of the torch into the ground, Isaiah picked up long branches and dragged them over the horse's body. He wasn't going to leave him uncovered. Gently placing one last branch on top, Isaiah said, "I knows you tried. You rest now."

Isaiah went on until a tiny band of gray light rimmed the horizon. He dismounted once more, rubbing the torch in the dirt to extinguish the flame. The trip back would be much quicker, and he wanted to be home before Franklin awoke. He'd told the boy if he ever woke up in the dark without his pappy, to trust that he'd be home by sunup. He knew Franklin wouldn't be afraid. Besides, his kinfolk would always be glad to take care of the boy in his absence.

After seeing to the mule, Isaiah walked back home by way of Ruth's grave. Kneeling down once more, he shook his head. "Maybe tomorrow, sweet gal. I love ya."

When he walked inside the cabin, Franklin was sitting on the side of the bed in his little nightshirt, rubbing his eyes. Isaiah was overwhelmed by his love for the boy. He went to him and lifted him into his arms, kissing him tenderly. "I loves ya so much, young'un."

Franklin threw his arms around Isaiah's neck and snuggled in close. "I love ya, Pappy."

Isaiah set his son down and wiped the moisture from his eyes. "All right, little man, what's we gonna eat fer breakfast?"

∽ৎৎৎ৯

Naomi rose early, knowing that Isaiah would be out there somewhere, looking for Sarah. She sat in the chair by her window, praying silently for the Lord to protect him. She knew how troubled he was by the fact that Sarah's body hadn't been found.

Letting out a deep sigh, Naomi tried to rid her mind of the sight of her mistress and Isabella. Their bodies had been horribly battered in the violent waters. Ruth's body had also borne terrible trauma, but Naomi had been spared from seeing it all. Not so with her mistress's.

With such morose thoughts threatening her sanity, Naomi poured water into a basin and splashed it on her face. Then, washing herself, she dressed for the day. She decided to go to the lower kitchen and make herself useful. Staying busy would help keep her mind off of her sadness.

Abigail met her in the kitchen. "I heard you got the massa to eat breakfast yesterday. You can take it to him again this mornin'."

Naomi suddenly felt her heart pounding. She had already decided to stay as far away from the master today as possible. Not only had she run out of his study without being dismissed, she had been caught in the family gardens that evening. The last thing she wanted to do was take him his breakfast.

"Maybe he'll prefer the dining room this morning. Fanny can serve him as usual."

Abigail lowered her voice. "I heard everything yesterday morning."

Naomi's cheeks grew warm. "I'm sure everyone did—the study door was wide open."

"I think he would prefer having you serve him again," Abigail persisted.

"Has he asked for me?" she inquired.

Moving even closer, Abigail whispered, "He's still in his bedchamber."

Naomi felt like she was being led into a trap. She would not be manipulated by this woman, despite the fact that she was the head of the Hawkins household.

"I have far too much to do than take over someone else's job," Naomi said curtly. "I'm going to get something to eat, then start to work." Quickly grabbing a bowl of mush and a corn muffin, she exited the room without another word.

All day, Naomi made a conscious effort to stay in her room except for necessary reasons. Every time she heard footsteps in the hallway, she feared the master was sending for her. She felt certain he would reprimand her for being in the garden. But thankfully, she was left undisturbed all day.

Eating a light supper, Naomi slipped out of the house and headed to slave town. She vowed never to enter the family gardens again. While her heart ached at the thought of losing her place of prayer, the brief encounter with her master had left her greatly troubled.

Naomi knew everyone would be talking after a visit with Isaiah, but she longed to find out how his search had gone this morning. Besides, she was desperately lonely—she needed company.

Before even making it to Isaiah's cabin, Naomi was called over by a group of women on a nearby porch. They were working on a quilt and had been singing soulfully.

Approaching the cabin, Naomi noticed the beautiful wagon wheel pattern they were sewing. "We want ya to sees our work," one of them told her.

"It's lovely," she said, running her fingers along the edge. "You've done fine work."

All four women beamed. "Course we ain't got them fancy materials you got," one of them murmured.

"Oh, but you've found some bright pieces, and you're using them perfectly." Naomi's proclamation brought a smile to their faces. While the material was worn and thin, they were still doing a masterful job with what they had.

"How's things at the big house?" the oldest of the four probed. "We hears the massa be doin' poorly."

Letting out a deep breath, Naomi simply said, "It's true, he's struggled mightily. It's going to take some time." Then, quickly changing the subject, she said, "Why don't I bring you some of the scraps I've been collecting? I have several pieces I think you could use."

Nodding enthusiastically, the women told her that would be appreciated. "I'll come by again tomorrow evening," she said, then left the women to their work.

Isaiah saw her coming from where he sat on his porch. Quickly, he ran inside and brought out another chair. "So glad to see ya, Naomi," he said as she approached. "Come and sits with me for a while."

"First, I need to get a little loving from this fella." She reached down where Franklin was sitting on the porch step and swept him into her arms. "Oh, my, you're getting heavy. You must be ten years old."

Franklin grinned, shaking his head. "I's four," he said in a cute little voice.

"Four? I thought sure you were older than that." She kissed him on the cheek then on the forehead and squeezed him to her chest before setting him back down.

Isaiah stood until Naomi climbed the porch steps and sat down. She looked around at the other cabins. Not one of her kinfolk was indoors. It seemed they'd all come out to see if they could catch a bit of their conversation on the breeze. Naomi had been cooped up in her room so long, she didn't even care.

"How was your search, Isaiah?"

He gave her a forlorn look that made her heart ache. Dropping his eyes, he said, "I's goin' out again in the mornin'."

She felt like taking him into her arms. He reminded her of a lost little boy. Not daring to reach out, she quietly said, "I'm so sorry. I prayed earnestly for you to find her."

Isaiah's eyes were moist when he looked up. "I found one of the massa's horses. He be dead, o' course. But I's thinkin' Sarah's still out there somewhere."

Naomi felt a tug deep within her soul. What if he never found her? Would he ever be able to find closure?

Suddenly, an alternate thought came to mind. "Are you thinking Sarah might still be alive?"

"Anything's possible," he said with a more hopeful tone.

Naomi didn't know which was worse, searching for a body, or going on blind faith that the girl was still alive. She pulled in a deep breath. "Isaiah, I don't. . . ."

He held up his hand. "I knows what yer thinkin'. The chance o' my Sarah gal still bein' alive is . . . well. . . ."

His voice trailed off.

For a long time, the two sat in silence, watching the evening activity of their kinfolk. Songs and chatter filled the air. Franklin eventually joined in with the little ones playing in the yard.

Finally, Isaiah asked, "You wanna go talk to her?"

Naomi rested her eyes on his for a long moment, then simply breathed, "Yes."

Trying not to worry about the tales that would be told, Naomi followed Isaiah down the path to Ruth's grave.

❦

Returning to the big house at dusk, Naomi stopped at the pump outside of the kitchen for a drink. Even with the sun setting, the July evening was still overly warm and humid. She filled her hand with water, taking a long sip, then filled it again to splash the cool liquid on her face and neck. But her hand lingered on her neck as she straightened. She was suddenly reminded of the cruel hands that had encircled her neck and the bruises they had left behind.

Naomi's eyes instantly focused on the storehouse where Terrance had engaged her in polite conversation. If she had only foreseen his hostile intent. But he had lulled her into a sense of security until it was too late. A sudden shiver ran all the way up her spine.

Glancing back at the house, Naomi felt an oppressive spirit. Where normally lights brightly shone in the windows, the structure was wearing a shroud of darkness. She decided to walk around the yard a bit before going inside. This would need to serve as her place of prayer instead of the garden.

When the evening shadows faded into murky black, Naomi made her way into the front kitchen. She realized how late it must be—the house slaves had already gone to their quarters for the night. One light in the lower house still burned, aiding her as she left the kitchen. When she made it to the hallway, she realized where the light was coming from—the door to the master's study stood open.

Naomi froze. While she didn't have to pass directly by the door, she knew the creaking of the floorboards would give away her presence. It would be best to hurry to her room as fast as possible.

But before she could take a step, the master's shadow filled the doorway.

Chapter 21

N aomi fought to draw a breath. What if the master caught her standing here? It
seemed she was becoming entangled in one awkward situation after another.
The shadow remained motionless.

The longer the pause, the more uncomfortable the situation would become if he
were to step through that doorway. Should she move or should she wait?

After a few tense moments, the decision was no longer hers to make. Master
Hawkins stepped out into the hall.

"Naomi?" he inquired in a low voice.

Naomi released the breath she'd been holding. "Yes, sir, it's Naomi."

He stepped further into the darkened hallway. She could smell his scent—he had
recently bathed.

"Where have you been?"

"I was visiting with Isaiah this evening to see how he and Franklin are getting
along." She swallowed to calm her nerves. "I'm so sorry I disturbed you."

Master Hawkins didn't readily speak again. He seemed to be contemplating a
decision. Finally, he asked, "Would you come in and sit down?"

"If that is your wish," she answered meekly.

He stepped aside and allowed her to pass. Unsure of where to sit, Naomi waited
for him to instruct her. When he pointed toward the sofa, she sat as close to one end as
possible. To her great relief, he sat down in a nearby chair. She had to admit, the master
was looking better than she had seen him in weeks.

"Do you know what tonight is?"

His question caught Naomi completely off guard. She had no idea what the
master was talking about.

"Tonight would've been Isabella's coming out ball," he said solemnly.

The very thought of it slammed hard against Naomi's chest. Isabella's gown still
hung in her sewing room. She would've dearly loved to help her put on that gown
tonight. Tears immediately flooded her eyes. All she wanted to do was weep.

Master Hawkins reached into his back pocket and pulled out a handkerchief.
Leaning forward in his chair, he handed it to her.

While she felt like refusing, she knew if she didn't take it, she would certainly
humiliate herself. "Thank you," she said in a hushed tone.

He leaned back in his chair, a desolate look capturing his features.

After a long moment, Naomi was able to speak. "I'm so sorry," she managed to say.

Another extended silence played out between them. For some strange reason, it
was not disquieting to Naomi.

"I just wanted to thank you," he finally started again. "Last night, after visiting
with my sons . . . upon your urging, I realized how much I've been neglecting them and
little Catherine. I want to be a better father to my children."

She uncovered a slight smile but said nothing.

"I also wanted to talk to you about the garden."

Naomi dropped her gaze to her lap. She could feel the heat rising to her face.

"Please feel free to go there any time you like. You have my permission, Naomi."

She looked up. There was something in the way he spoke her name. His eyes were dark and searching. "Thank you, sir, but I know I overstepped my bounds. I should've never been there without your permission."

"But that's what I'm doing now," he declared. "I'm giving you permission to be there. I'm assuming that wasn't your first time."

Once again, warmth touched her cheeks. "No, sir, and I beg your forgiveness."

His brow wrinkled as he considered her words. Then, in a gentle voice, he said, "I forgive you."

Had she not heard those precise words, she would've never gone to the garden again. But the fact that she was invited and forgiven made her heart soar. After praying tonight in the yard where she had been attacked, she knew the garden was her sole refuge. She uttered a heartfelt *thank you.*

"You're welcome," the master said, coming to his feet.

Naomi immediately rose from the sofa to take her leave. Respectfully bowing her head, she walked to the door.

"Good night, Naomi," he called softly.

She turned to meet his gaze. "Good night, sir," then quickened her pace down the hall.

⁊⋙⋘⊱

The following evening Naomi made another visit to slave town. She had found some colorful swatches of material for the little quilting party. Not wishing to disturb their singing, she stood at a distance, taking in their haunting words.

Oh, my Lawd!
Oh, my good Lawd!
Keep me from sinkin' down;
Keep me from sinkin' down.
I see the angels beckonin' me,
Keep me from sinkin' down.

One of the women looked up from her work and noticed Naomi nearby. She waved her over. "We wasn't sure you was comin'," she said without compunction.

"I didn't forget about you," Naomi replied, realizing they may not have believed she would keep her word. In some ways, she was hurt by that, but in other ways, she didn't blame them a bit. Slaves in the big house were so much better off than the field slaves. If she knew how to rectify that situation, Naomi would do it in a heartbeat.

Carefully unfolding the batch of materials, Naomi displayed the pieces she had chosen for the quilters. Their eyes grew wide—it seemed they were almost fearful of touching the material. She held them out, "I chose these pieces especially for you."

The women speared their needles into the quilt, and each one reverently took a few pieces to examine. One of them smelled each swatch and brushed it against her cheeks. "Merciful Jesus," she whispered. "These is glorious."

Naomi's lips turned upward into a gentle smile. "I'm glad you like them. I'll let you get back to your work."

The women thanked her profusely before she left them. When arriving at Isaiah's cabin, he asked her to sit with him again, but she thanked him and told him she needed to get back to the house. Her soul was tugging her toward the garden in the worst way. She just wanted to know how his search had gone this morning.

Isaiah's failure to find Sarah was unsettling. This evening, Naomi didn't care what the others would think; she hugged him tightly as she would a brother and encouraged him to hold onto faith. She also promised that her upcoming prayer time would be centered on his quest.

Not long afterwards, the back gate to the garden creaked on its hinges. Naomi drew in a deep, cleansing breath. She closed her eyes and immediately thanked the Lord for his presence here. For the next several minutes, she allowed her feet to wander where they may as her prayers meandered to the ear of God. At times, her hands splayed open toward the heavens, and at others, she knelt upon the soft grass in humble reverence.

Rounding a corner to the very center of the garden, Naomi was drawn to the picturesque reflection pool. For a while, she sat on one of the smooth stones, trailing her hand through the water. Frogs hopped about on the stones, diving headlong into the pool, and occasionally a turtle popped its head to the surface.

Staring at her reflection in the calm waters, Naomi thought how tired she looked. Though she was finding it difficult to sleep, she hadn't realized the weariness in her expression. She hoped it was merely the water's distortion.

While she was lost in contemplation, another reflection unexpectedly appeared upon the surface. Naomi instantly jumped to her feet, taking a step backward and losing her balance. Immediately, the master's strong hands reached out to grip her arms, keeping her from falling into the pool.

"I'm sorry to startle you," he said. His face was flushed, and he quickly let go of her. "I should've said something before walking up on you like that."

Naomi pressed a hand to her chest. "No, it's all right. I was so lost in thought. . . ." She didn't know what else to say.

"Please, accept my apology." He stepped back to put more space between them. For a brief moment, his gaze explored her eyes, causing Naomi to feel vulnerable. But when he blinked, the expression was gone. "Would you walk with me?"

"If you like," she answered, dipping her chin in submission.

"Please," he said courteously, pointing toward the path.

At first, Naomi walked a half-step behind, knowing her place with the master was nothing like her relationship had been with the mistress. With Elizabeth, they had talked and loved one another as closely as dear friends. While she had had very little interaction with Master Hawkins, she had always admired him from afar—mainly because of Elizabeth's deep love and esteem for him.

From her position, Naomi no longer gazed at the beauty of the garden but was able to study her master's strong profile. It was obvious by the dark circles beneath his eyes that he was still not sleeping well. He had also lost weight in the last few weeks— his tailored shirt fitting a bit loosely. Still, his features were handsome, his shoulders square, his arms muscular. She had been quite aware of that fact when he reached out to keep her from falling into the water.

When he slowed his pace to match hers, Naomi quickly looked away.

"How is Isaiah getting along?" he asked.

"He's extremely disappointed that Sarah has not been found. He's been searching for her before sunup the last two mornings."

Samuel let out a long breath. "I wish we had been able to recover her body that day. I fear she was swept into the Kentucky river."

Naomi took in a shuddering breath, and the master suddenly stopped to face her. "I've ruined your peaceful walk in the garden. I'm sorry," he declared in a wretched tone. "I can't seem to free myself from this awful reality. Forgive me. I'll leave you now."

Her reaction came instantaneously and without regard to her position. Clutching his arm, Naomi told him, "Stay."

He didn't move, and immediately she dropped her hand, stepping away from him. She could feel the flames licking at her face. What had she done? Clasping her hands tightly together, she stared at the ground, waiting for a reprimand or at the very least a word of caution for her inappropriate gesture. But it never came.

"Naomi," he said gently.

Her head lifted slowly.

"We are both grieving for Elizabeth and Isabella." She noticed his hands clinching and releasing, over and over. "I'm afraid I haven't been handling it very well. I think it best for me to leave you now."

Naomi didn't speak. What could she possibly say? Truth be told, she was mortified by what she'd done and where her thoughts had led her.

"Oh, Lord," she prayed as he walked out of sight. "Help *me*."

Chapter 22

The next morning, Naomi didn't even bother to get out of bed. She felt guilty for the luxury of that one decision, knowing hundreds of her fellow slaves had already started their back-breaking toil in the fields. She was floundering in sorrow with nowhere to turn.

A few hours later, she startled awake, surprised by the fact that she had even fallen asleep in the first place. The room was now fully engulfed in sunshine, and someone was knocking on her door.

"Yes?" she called in alarm.

"It's Abigail," the voice behind the door called back. "You're wanted in the master's study."

"I'll be right there," Naomi said, ripping the bed covers away and throwing off her gown.

With no time to wash, she dressed hurriedly and began working on her hair. It was no use. She grabbed a head wrap and fit it in place. Checking her reflection in the tall mirror, she looked more like a field slave than a house slave. Maybe that's what she deserved for her thoughtless behavior last night. Taking in a deep breath, Naomi left her room, resolving to accept whatever the master decided.

The Hawkins' housekeeper stood near the master's study, pretending to dust the hall table. No doubt, Abigail would be listening intently at the door. Naomi ignored her and knocked.

Instead of calling for her to come in, Master Hawkins opened the door and ushered Naomi inside. "Have a seat," he said and promptly closed the door. "I have something important to discuss with you." His tone was matter of fact—his demeanor business like.

This time he pointed to one of the chairs at his desk. When she was seated, he went back around his desk to sit down. She felt her heart quicken as they faced one another.

"I've made a decision," he stated, "and I wanted you to be made aware. I'll be traveling to Nashville to visit my older sister. She's been writing me to come and bring the children so they can spend time with their cousins."

Naomi's inner reaction was a strong one. She did *not* want the master to leave. She was shocked by the realization of how much he meant to her. Finding it hard to focus, she sat up a little straighter.

"I have a job for you to do while I'm gone. I need you to go through Elizabeth's things and store them away. I plan to save some things for Catherine, but the rest can be given away later. I'll leave a wooden chest on her vanity table for you to store her jewelry and smaller items. Do you have any questions?"

His eyes were so benign, it almost hurt. She hoped her voice would sound normal. "Do you want *all* of her belongings gone from the bed chamber?"

"Yes," he said emphatically. "I've put some things away in my chest of drawers. The rest, I trust you to take care of."

"Yes, sir," she said quietly.

"I'll also need you to do the same with Isabella's things. I trust you to know what Catherine would want someday. The rest will be stored with Elizabeth's things in the attic. I don't want to make a decision about any of it right now."

Naomi dared to ask, "How long will you be staying in Nashville?"

Samuel let out a weary breath. "Don't expect us home until the first of the year."

Over five months? Immediately Naomi felt the warmth behind her eyes. Tears were forming—she had to willfully hold them back. Was she emotional because of Elizabeth or the fact that she would not see the master for such a long time? When he suddenly came to his feet, she was thankful for the brevity of their discussion.

"Micah will send help when you're ready for things to be taken to the attic. I don't want you to have to carry it up the back stairs alone," he said in a gravelly voice. Suddenly his eyes softened, and Naomi found herself utterly lost in them.

He cleared his throat. "I'm sorry you're the one to take care of this. I know it will be hard on you. But when I thought of anyone else touching Elizabeth's belongings, I knew it had to be you alone."

Coming around the desk, he stood close enough for her to touch him. Had she not been his slave, she would've taken hold of his arm again and asked him to stay. But the color of her skin made that impossible.

The master's next query caught her completely off guard. "Will you be walking in the garden this evening?"

Naomi's breath quickened. "Yes, if that's all right," she answered meekly.

For a moment the master looked as if he would say more, but instead, he opened the study door and quietly replied, "Always." Then, he stepped aside and allowed her to pass.

❧❧❧

Isaiah pressed the mule to a fast gallop along the low country terrain. In his left hand, he held the reigns, giving the mule his head. But in his right hand, he held Sarah's carpet bag. While it had been ripped open by the raging waters, a skirt remained caught within its folds. He had also found a comb and a shoe along this route before the trail eventually led to her bag.

All along the way, Isaiah chastised himself. He could tell by the pitch of the sun that it was far past midmorning. *Oh, Lawd, protect me*, he breathed with every stride of his mule.

This morning, he had almost made it to the Kentucky River, riding along low fertile farm land that usually flooded in heavy rains. He felt certain the water would've risen onto this land the day of the squall—and he was right. It had led him directly to Sarah's belongings.

Isaiah had yet to make it to the main road. Knowing he would need to cover the last two miles with all haste on the open road, he decided to give his mule a quick rest. The beast had taken him far this morning, and Isaiah was pushing him hard on the way back. The animal required water, and Isaiah would need a place to hide.

With the main road now in sight, Isaiah spotted a small pond not far away. He would have to ride in the opposite direction of the Hawkins Plantation, but there was no choice. The mule was tiring quickly.

A small copse of cottonwood trees provided cover for Isaiah, and he dismounted, leading the mule to drink. Isaiah quenched his thirst as well while the mule insatiably sucked up the water. Noticing the foamy, white lather on the mule's neck, he quickly removed the saddle and began splashing water on him. The last thing he wanted to do was run the animal into the ground.

"There now, fella. Let's get you cooled down a bit." Isaiah squatted on the shore, throwing handfuls of water on the mule's legs. The mule stomped his hooves in irritation but kept his mouth resolutely pressed into the pond while blowing air loudly from his nostrils.

After a few minutes, the animal raised its head. Isaiah was upset by how hard he was still breathing. He would have to lead him all the way into the pond. Taking the reins, Isaiah clicked his tongue. "Come on, les cool you off right quick."

The mule obediently followed him into the waist-deep pond. Isaiah continued to throw water onto his neck and back until his breathing finally slowed. Bringing him back out of the water, Isaiah knew the mule would need to dry before putting the saddle back on. They would have to ride once again at breakneck speed—the saddle could rub the mule's skin raw by the time they made it home if he was wet.

Taking a chance out in the open, Isaiah led the mule into the sunshine. Grabbing leaves and brush from around the pond, he rapidly rubbed him down in the warm rays of light. Isaiah shook his head in frustration. This was taking far more time than he could afford.

He heard the sound before he saw it—there was a wagon on the road. Isaiah grabbed up the reins again and trotted the mule back into the cover of trees. This was a busy road. How could he possibly know when the time was right to leave?

Leaning against a cottonwood, Isaiah began to pray. "Lawd, I knows you hear my heart cryin' out to ya. I needs ya right now. I's beggin' for ya to lead me safely back home to my little one. Thank ya, kindly, for hearin' my plea. I's puttin' all this in yer mighty hands. Through the name o' my Massa Jesus." Then, pushing away from the tree, he breathed, "Amen and amen."

"Alrighty, boy," he said. "Les get you saddled up."

Within ten minutes, Isaiah found himself on the open road. He pushed the mule hard, feeling like there was a big target painted on his back. The closer he got to the Hawkins Plantation, the more at ease he began to feel. Rounding a curve, he suddenly pulled the mule to a skidding halt. The road was completely blocked by a buckboard wagon.

Isaiah quickly analyzed the situation. The only way around the wagon would be to head down into the ditch. But at the moment, a well-dressed man, squatting down beside the back wheel of his wagon, was staring right at him.

Slowly, the man rose to his full height and trained his eyes directly on Isaiah. Not a word was spoken while he reached into the floorboard of the wagon, pulling out a shotgun. For the moment, the gun was pointed toward the ground.

"You just stay right there," he said in a rough voice, easing his way closer to Isaiah. He waved the end of his shotgun. "Now get down off that mule nice and slow."

Isaiah's nerves were on end, but there was nothing he could do but obey. When his feet were planted firmly on the ground, the man waved the barrel again. "What's that in your hand?"

For the first time, Isaiah felt panic rising up from his very core. He was holding a bag that contained a woman's clothing. How would he be able to explain himself? Swallowing back the bile in his throat, Isaiah humbly said, "This here belongs to my daughter, Sarah. I's just takin' it back to the Hawkins Plantation. Massa Hawkins be my owner, and he give me this paper that says. . . ."

The barrel of the gun instantly pointed to Isaiah's chest. "Put that hand down right now . . . and drop the bag."

Isaiah immediately did as he was told.

"Now back up and sit down."

Again, Isaiah complied.

The man picked up the carpet bag and rested the gun beneath his arm. Opening the clasp, he dumped the contents onto the ground, then threw the bag into the ditch. For a long moment, the man didn't move. He seemed to be mulling the situation over in his mind.

"How far is the Hawkins Plantation from here?" he asked.

"Not far, sir. Less than a mile."

The man glanced at the wheel of his buckboard, then back at Isaiah. For a while he rubbed the back of his neck. Then, through narrowed eyes, he said, "Don't you move." Backing away slowly, the man pulled a lead rope for his horse from the buckboard.

"Put your hands behind your back."

Isaiah submitted, and the man tied both wrists firmly together. "Get up," he barked, pulling up on the rope so Isaiah could come to his feet. The man then tied the other end of the rope to the wagon wheel.

Watching the stranger unhitch his horse from the buckboard, Isaiah tried once again to speak. "Sir, I's got permission from my massa to be out here. Please, just look in my front pocket here."

The man completely ignored him as he freed his horse and walked him over to Isaiah's mule, tying him to the saddle horn with one of the harness reins. After that was done, he untied Isaiah from the wagon and wound that rope around the saddle horn too. Mounting up with shotgun in hand, the man simply said, "Walk."

Within the half hour, Isaiah felt the humiliation of walking onto the Hawkins Plantation with hands bound behind his back. At least he could be thankful that the man hadn't taken him to the sheriff, or worse, shot him in cold blood. But he ached for Sarah's belongings. It bothered him to have them scattered about on the road.

The man rode all the way up to the front entrance of the house, dismounted, and looped the mule's reins through the hitching post ring. He left Isaiah standing in the drive as if he were one of the animals.

After knocking on the door, the man laid his shotgun on the porch at his feet. Abigail opened the door with a courteous smile. "May I help you, sir?" Then her eyes flew open wide, seeing Isaiah tied up with the mule.

"Get me your master right now," the man demanded.

"Yes, sir. Right away, sir," she muttered. "Would you like to come in?"

Looking back over his shoulder, the man said, "No. Just get your master."

Abigail disappeared, and the man picked up his shotgun again, descending the porch steps. Then, jamming the barrel beneath Isaiah's chin, he said menacingly, "If you've lied to me, the wild animals will be eating your carcass before sundown. You hear me?"

Isaiah couldn't have spoken if he wanted to. The shotgun was nearly cutting off his oxygen.

"What's going on here?" Samuel Hawkins yelled, storming down the front steps with a pistol in his hand.

The man with the shotgun backed away, raising the barrel to the sky along with his other hand. "I mean you no harm, kind sir. Is this your negro?"

"This is Isaiah, and he works for me. Untie him immediately."

The man didn't hesitate to do as he was told. When Isaiah was free, he rubbed his wrists and flexed his numb fingers.

"What is this?" Master Hawkins asked again.

The man cleared his throat. "I caught your slave out there on the road. I think he robbed a woman."

Samuel's brow wrinkled. "Isaiah? Why were you out this late in the day?"

Shaking his head apologetically, he said, "Massa, I found some o' my gal's clothes and her bag, but I's almost to the river by then. I's awful sorry to be so late gettin' back."

Master Hawkins turned to the stranger. "Did he show you my pass?"

"No, sir," the man said.

The master turned his gaze back on Isaiah. "I told you to have that pass with you at all times out there, Isaiah."

"I's got it right here, massa," he said, patting his pocket. "The man wouldn't let me show it to 'im."

Samuel Hawkins unleashed his indignation upon the stranger. Raising the pistol, he bellowed, "Get off my property right now, Mister! Take your horse and go."

The stranger put his palm out and nodded, backing away slowly. "I'm going. I'm going—just don't shoot." He immediately untied his horse from the mule and started down the drive without a backward glance.

Isaiah looked over at Master Hawkins. "Massa, that man be needin' some help with his wagon 'bout a mile back. He gots a broken wheel."

Samuel snorted out a laugh. "You mean after he tied you up and refused to look at your pass, you want me to help him out?"

Grinning slightly, Isaiah said, "Yessir, I specs so."

❧⬥☙

All throughout the day, the big house swarmed with activity. Everyone was pulling together to help Master Hawkins and his family pack for their trip to Nashville. Naomi made herself scarce, mainly because of the heaviness of the task before her. Elizabeth had always treated her with such respect and kindness. They had shared so much over the years. It had been pure joy to dream of new creations together and then collaborate closely on each project. Her mistress had been a beautiful woman outwardly but even more so inwardly. Naomi's heart continually struggled with such a profound loss.

As the day drew to a close, Naomi slipped into the garden to pray. She begged the Lord to give her strength for the coming days. A dread was sitting heavily upon her chest as she considered where to even start with her mistress' possessions. The gray clouds above left the garden in an uncharacteristic gloominess somehow befitting of her mood.

Rounding a corner near the back of the garden, Naomi stilled. There was the master, sitting on a garden bench, leaning forward, head bowed. She couldn't stop herself from studying him—taking in his strong hands, his dark hair that occasionally strayed onto his forehead, his handsome facial features, his. . . .

"Naomi," he said, coming to his feet.

"I . . . I'm terribly sorry. I didn't know you were here." She started to turn away.

"No, don't leave. I've been waiting for you."

Heat filled every part of her. She didn't know how to respond.

"Please, have a seat," he said, pointing to the wrought iron bench. He smiled sparingly. "I'm afraid it's not very comfortable."

For a moment all Naomi could do was stare at the bench. It was small. There was no way they could both sit there without touching one another.

"Please," he said again, taking hold of the back of the bench.

She moved forward, feeling her pulse thrum in her temples. Sitting down, she squeezed into the tiniest space possible. When he sat down beside her, their thighs met, and he kept his arm on the back of the bench to leave a bit of space between them.

Naomi could feel his eyes on her, but she didn't dare meet his gaze. She decided to look out into the garden instead. By doing so, some of her anxiety began to slip away. But not so for her companion. Naomi could literally feel an uneasiness radiating from him.

Without a word, he abruptly stood and backed away from the bench. His breathing was unsteady. "Maybe we should walk instead," he told her.

Naomi agreed and came to her feet.

Just like the evening before, Samuel determined the path they would follow. After a few moments, he spoke sincerely. "I hope I haven't given you too hard of a task while I'm away, Naomi."

Oh, but you have, she thought. The very idea of it overwhelmed her. But she bravely replied that she would manage.

"I also want to thank you for all that you did for Elizabeth. You made her so happy." His voice suddenly broke, and Naomi finally dared to look at him as they walked. It was obvious he was struggling with his emotions.

Tears sprang to her eyes, and this time Naomi didn't fight against them—she began to openly cry. In the past, when they'd been together, one of them had been able to withstand the other's emotions. But in this moment, the master too surrendered and started to weep.

Naomi's heart was pierced all the way through as Samuel turned away from her. He groaned through one sob after another. The sound of it was devastating. She could only take so much.

Barely able to see where she was going, Naomi made her way to the center of the garden. There, she stood beside the reflection pool, continuing to release the anxiety and grief she was struggling to come to grips with. The hurt wound its way throughout her entire being, threatening to drown her along with all of her dear ones.

Big drops of water started splashing into the pool, distorting her reflection. She felt them hitting her neck and back. The clouds were about to release their stores of rain. Just as she turned toward the path that led to the back gate, Samuel strode purposefully toward her. Though his eyes were still red-rimmed, he seemed to have found a semblance of composure.

"Come with me," he insisted. "It's quicker to go to the house."

Naomi didn't argue as the sprinkles suddenly turned into a downpour.

Chapter 23

Naomi found it difficult to run; her waterlogged skirt kept tangling around her legs. At one point, she stepped on the front of her hem, falling headlong onto the path.

Amidst the deluge, Samuel knelt beside her, apologizing profusely for not being more attentive to her situation. "Are you hurt?"

She took a quick inventory, then shook her head. "I don't think so."

His hands were gentle as he clasped her elbows, practically lifting her off the ground. She was taken aback by his grin. "No need to rush now—look at us."

He was right. They were both soaked to the skin.

Naomi turned her face upward, allowing the rain to rinse away her tears and momentarily wash away her sorrows. It felt gloriously cleansing.

When she lowered her face and opened her eyes, Samuel was watching her. His eyes were no longer sad—his despondency had momentarily dissolved in the rain. Coming along beside her, he stuck out his elbow. "We might as well enjoy it," he said with a hint of amusement.

A slow smile played on Naomi's lips. They weren't in any danger. There had been no thunder or flashes of lightning in the sky. It was truly the perfect rain.

Without a second thought, Naomi slipped her hand into the crook of his arm. But as they started to walk, she stumbled again. Laughing softly, she let go of him and gathered the front of her skirt in one hand so she could keep it off the ground. When she looked up, his elbow was still proffered in her direction. She thanked him and took it once again.

Instead of leading her toward the house, they walked a path that led into the stand of chestnut trees. The pitter-patter of raindrops on the jagged leaves played a hymn of welcome peace. They stood still beneath the canopy, listening to nature's song, moisture dripping onto them from the branches above.

Naomi released her hand from his arm, suddenly feeling self-conscious. Samuel didn't seem to notice as he reached out and ran his hand along the thick, deeply furrowed bark. "Do you know what a chestnut tree symbolizes?" he asked. His hand continued to follow the long curving swirl of the bark. When Naomi said she didn't, he turned to look at her. "It represents chastity and honesty and justice." He released a long breath and gave her an unsettling gaze. "I'm afraid you haven't been the recipient of justice during your lifetime."

Not knowing what to say, Naomi held her silence. This was her master, after all. Surely he wasn't trying to start a conversation about the injustice of owning another human being with his very own slave.

Thankfully he went on, obviously not expecting a response. But his next words overpowered her soul with an unexpected gift. "I'm truly sorry, Naomi, and I would like to give you your freedom."

His revelation threw her equilibrium completely off balance. Naomi's whole body quaked, and she went to her knees. She was having trouble just trying to capture her next breath.

Samuel knelt down in front of her, tenderly lifting her chin. "Elizabeth would've wanted it."

Naomi searched his eyes, scarcely believing what she'd heard. "How?" she breathed. Then a sudden fear gripped her mind. "Where would I go?"

Taking her by the shoulders, Samuel drew Naomi back to her feet. "You don't have to go anywhere . . . unless that is your wish."

"It is not my wish," she said emphatically.

He nodded and dropped his hands.

Still feeling weak in the knees, Naomi reached out to steady herself on the nearby chestnut tree. Her fingers moved into the deep grooves of the bark, tracing a path. An unexpected path to freedom!

⊰⚬⊱

That evening Naomi joined Samuel in his study. He had told her to meet him there when the household was quiet. This time he joined her on the sofa.

"I've been rethinking my request for you to clean out Elizabeth's—"

Naomi raised her hand to stop him. "No, I've been thinking about it too. I want to do this now more than ever."

He gave her a curious gaze, and she smiled warmly. "Now I will be taking care of my dear friends, Elizabeth and Isabella. It will be my pleasure."

"I understand," Samuel said. His eyes crinkled at the corners. His grin was heart-stopping. "This is for you," he said, holding out a folded sheet of paper. "This is your deed of manumission. It declares that you are a free woman."

Naomi pressed her hand to her chest and reached out to clasp her freedom with the other. She never dreamed this day would come. Her appreciation was heartfelt and earnest. "Thank you," she said softly.

Raising his brow, he replied, "It's *my* pleasure."

Naomi unfolded the paper and looked at it for a long time. After a moment, Samuel asked in an astonished voice, "Can you read?"

Naomi looked up, feeling her cheeks grow warm. "Yes. My mother could read. She taught me before she passed away when I was twelve." She now felt free to tell him one of her longtime secrets. "I've been hiding her Bible in my room since coming into the house. I read it every morning."

Samuel sat back on the sofa, letting out a low chuckle. "I guess we're both full of surprises today."

She nodded in agreement while reverently folding the paper. When she looked up, his smile had already faded.

"Is it too much for me to ask you not to tell anyone right now?" he asked solemnly. "I won't have time to explain everything to Micah before we leave in the morning for Nashville."

Naomi had already given that a lot of thought this evening too. "I don't want anyone to know either. I can't imagine how that would make the others feel. It's enough for *me* to know right now."

They talked comfortably for a long time until the clock in the hallway struck midnight. Naomi instantly came to her feet. "I'm so sorry, I've kept you up. I know you're leaving early in the morning and need your rest."

When Samuel rose from the sofa, he held her eyes with a probing gaze. "I have one more question before you go." Taking a long breath, he asked, "Will you be here when I return?"

A beautiful smile turned her lips. "I'll be here," she answered quietly, then slipped from the room.

&~&~&

While all of the house slaves had gone out to the front walk to say good-bye to Master Hawkins and his children, Naomi forced herself to stay inside. She headed upstairs to Isabella's room where she could watch the family without being noticed. She simply couldn't trust her emotions. Too much had transpired in the last few days for her to be a dispassionate bystander.

Naomi watched the master standing beside the carriage while Violet and Catherine entered, then young William. Master Joseph had already mounted his horse, awaiting to ride in front of the carriage with his father. Another wagon had been loaded with several trunks that would follow in the rear of the traveling party.

Before mounting up, Samuel Hawkins turned to speak to his overseer. It appeared he was giving Micah last-minute instructions about the plantation. When the conversation ended, Samuel didn't readily get on his horse. Instead, he turned and scanned the gathering. His eyes roamed back and forth before he dipped his chin to everyone and put his left foot into the stirrup. Just as he swung his right leg over the saddle, he looked up toward the house. That's when Naomi knew he saw her standing in the window.

While his horse pranced in the drive, Samuel held the reins tight. He didn't take his gaze away from the window where Naomi stood. She felt her pulse quicken and knew immediately that he had been looking for her all along. He took off his hat, holding it to his chest, then dipped his head in her direction.

Naomi immediately stepped away from the window for fear someone in the gathering would look up and see her. She worried that Abigail had already started looking for new fodder for gossip. In some ways, it was good that the family would be gone for several months. Maybe Abigail would turn her sights in another direction for a while. Not that Naomi approved of talking about others behind their backs, but for now, she didn't relish being the target.

Standing in Isabella's room, Naomi made the decision to start packing her missy's things first. She would definitely need to ease into the task of going through Elizabeth's belongings. It struck her for the first time why it was going to be harder than she originally thought. She was carrying a burden of guilt where her mistress was concerned. Letting out a long sigh, Naomi had to face the fact that she had fallen in love with Elizabeth's husband. Her chest squeezed uncomfortably just admitting it to herself.

"Oh, Lord," she whispered aloud, "help me get past this."

Dropping to her knees in front of Isabella's cedar chest, she rested her hands on the top. In some ways, five months seemed like an eternity, but in other ways, it seemed so brief. She would have to use the brevity of time to force her heart back into submission. She would never be free enough to love Samuel Hawkins the way Elizabeth had. Even with the manumission paper hidden away in her Bible, her station in life had been decidedly stamped on her skin from the moment of birth.

Loving the master was not the only alteration she would need to come to terms with. She began to think of herself as a stranger in this household. In one sense, she was extremely proud of her freedom, but in another, she was afraid to own it outright. She felt like the little frogs in the reflection pool—free to hop about as they wished, but stuck in the shell of the turtles, cautiously poking their heads out of the water.

From the time she could form a conscious thought, Naomi had known nothing but servitude and subjection. She had been forced to accept her lot as a slave—there had never been a choice in the matter. It was her only reality. Just the word *choice* made her head spin. She actually had the ability to decide whether to stay or go. The thought of it was irresistible and overwhelming all at once.

A convincing voice abruptly seized Naomi's attention, tossing her into utter confusion. *You should go before it's too late.*

She sat down hard on the floor, a rush of air escaping her lungs. Where did that come from? Was that the voice of the Holy Spirit warning her of trouble on the horizon, or was it the anxiety she felt of suddenly finding herself belonging to no man on earth?

For several minutes, Naomi sat on the floor, envisioning the possibilities that lay before her. Maybe she could go to a city up north and start a new life of her own. Surely as a qualified seamstress, she would be able to find a job. Or perhaps another family would want to take her in and pay for her services. It would be like a new birth. But just the thought of leaving made her nauseous. This was her home—her life was here . . . Samuel Hawkins was here.

Remembering her conversation with Samuel last night, Naomi once again sensed her heart longing for him. He had asked her if she would be here upon his return. Nothing had felt truer in that moment than promising that she would be.

"Precious, Lord, lead me. What would you have me do?"

For the moment, there didn't seem to be an answer to her dilemma. And why should she rush to a decision? Samuel had been gone for mere minutes. There would be plenty of time to seek the Lord's will before the family returned.

With another deep sigh, Naomi pushed herself off the floor and knelt again before the wooden chest. Lifting the lid, an aroma of cedar wafted into the air, filling her nostrils with a pleasant fragrance. But with one look at the contents within, a stabbing pain spread its wings and took flight, dragging her soul back into the dense blackness of sorrow.

Chapter 24

Isaiah needed advice in the worst way. Not about the thoroughbred he was training to take the racing saddle, but about his gal, Sarah. Today, he had not even bothered to go out searching for her. Part of him made the excuse that he wanted to be here to see the master off on his trip. He even used yesterday's incident on the road as justification for not going out today.

Mercifully, Micah had brought Sarah's property back after helping the man with his buckboard yesterday afternoon. Isaiah was thankful that her things were no longer scattered about on the road. It had felt like a violation of her privacy. His heart wrenched again just thinking of her body out there somewhere. The thought of it almost drove him mad. Other than begging for Massa Jesus to bring him peace, he knew no one else to turn to except Naomi.

After leading the thoroughbred back to its stall, he saddled two of the Hawkins' stable horses, one with a side-saddle. Maybe he could convince Naomi to take a ride with him on the plantation trails. He longed for a pleasure ride, as opposed to the macabre quest that he had been on for the last few days. And if he was being honest, he was in desperate need of companionship.

❦❧

Naomi stood in the middle of Isabella's room, tears trailing down her cheeks. The cedar chest lay barren, its contents strewn across the missy's bed. This had been her trousseau—all of the things Isabella had been collecting since childhood for her marriage. She had called it her *glory box*. In her mind's eye, Naomi could still see the missy pulling out her beautiful collection, telling Sarah make-believe stories about the man she would marry someday.

Steven Hardy and his family had come to pay their respects almost immediately after hearing of Elizabeth and Isabella's passing. Naomi had found it odd that the young man had asked if Isabella was wearing a diamond ring. He had wanted it back. It had made Naomi wonder if young Master Hardy had been a good match for Isabella after all. That was a question that would forever go unanswered.

A knock at the door startled Naomi back to the present. "Yes?" she called, not wishing to be seen in her state of grief.

"It's Tabitha. Can I come in?"

Taking in a deep breath, Naomi wiped her tears with a handkerchief she pulled from the pocket of her skirt. She let it linger on her face for a moment, relishing the fact that it was the one Samuel had given her.

Instead of giving Tabitha an answer, Naomi walked to the door to let the girl in. Tabitha froze, a worried look straining her features.

"I'm all right," Naomi told her. "I'm just emotional going through the missy's trousseau."

Tabitha's eyes grew moist. "I'll be ever so glad to help ya."

"Thank you, but I just started. Surely it will get easier," she lamented.

With a nod, Tabitha looked back into the hallway before closing the door. "There be someone outside for ya."

Naomi's brow wrinkled. "What do you mean?"

"I seen Isaiah ridin' to the back porch, pullin' another horse fer a female rider. Ya know, with one of them saddles where you sits sideways. He says he's wantin' to talk to ya."

Naomi glanced back at the bed—she had barely gotten started with her task. She exhaled a long breath. "Thank you, Tabitha. Tell him I'll be right out."

"Alrighty," the girl said before heading back downstairs.

Folding the handkerchief back into her pocket, Naomi left the room and headed down the back staircase. Thankfully, the inner kitchen was deserted, and she was able to get out of the house without anyone else taking notice.

Isaiah stood at the end of the gravel path, holding the reins of a horse in each hand. He smiled affectionately as she drew nearer. "I's hopin' you'd join me on a ride this mornin', Naomi. I's got somethin' I needs to discuss with ya."

When she came up beside him, he quickly added, "Course, if'n you wanna walk, I understands."

"No," she answered softly, rubbing her hand along the horse's muzzle. "I could use a good ride today. But I haven't ridden since I was a girl—and even then, I was riding bareback on a mule."

Isaiah chuckled. "Well, I specs it's time to get you into a saddle."

He threw the reins over the horse's head, then followed Naomi around to the left side. She gave him a nervous grin while patting the horse's neck. "What's his name?"

"It be a her, and we calls her Pleasant."

Naomi laughed out loud. "I hope her name suits her."

"Oh, it do," Isaiah said, clasping both hands and squatting down. "Just step in my hands and I'll give you a lift."

Naomi grasped a firm hold on the saddle with her right hand, then planted her left hand on top of Isaiah's shoulder. She hoped he didn't notice how much she was trembling.

In a matter of seconds, Naomi found herself sitting atop Pleasant. The horse didn't seem to mind one bit, putting Naomi's mind at ease.

"Here now," Isaiah said. "Puts your right leg up over that there part o' the saddle."

Naomi gathered her skirt while lifting her leg over the side pommel. She looked down when Isaiah took hold of her left ankle, guiding her foot into the stirrup.

"Do that feel like the right length for ya?" he asked.

Situating herself firmly into the seat, Naomi told him it was fine.

As soon as Isaiah mounted his horse, he turned toward the road to the stream at the back of the plantation property. "There be a nice trail we can take the horses down."

For a while, Naomi rode behind him, allowing Pleasant to have her head, but when they came to the trail in the woods, Isaiah pulled up for her to come alongside him.

"You feelin' comfortable now?" he asked.

"As a matter of fact, I am," she said, almost bragging.

He gave her a satisfied grin. "Ain't it perty through here?"

"It's beautiful, Isaiah. Thank you for bringing me here."

He nodded, then fell silent.

Naomi could tell there was more on his mind than just taking her on a ride. "Isaiah, did you want to talk to me about something?"

"Yes'm, I did. But now that I's ridin' out here with ya, I don't wanna spoil nothin'."

"Oh," she said softly, feeling his angst. "If you'd rather wait, that's fine," she added.

"I think so—least for a bit anyways."

They rode together in silence for a while, until coming to the stream that ambled closely beside the trail. That's when Isaiah's breathing changed. Naomi glanced over at him—he was noticeably struggling.

"What's wrong? You can tell me anything."

His voice was tight with emotion. "Maybe I shouldn't o' come to the stream. You mind if we goes back?"

"Oh, no, not at all."

They turned their horses around and headed back down the trail. "Do you mind if I take *you* somewhere, Isaiah?"

"That's fine," he breathed.

After a few minutes, Naomi turned Pleasant down a short path that led to the clearing where Ruth's prayer log had lain idle for many weeks. "Did you know this is where Ruth prayed?" she asked.

Isaiah dismounted and looped his reins across a low branch. "She never did tell me 'bout it, but I followed her here once or twice to see what she be up to. I couldn't help but watch her pray sometimes."

He came around to Naomi and lifted her to the ground, then made sure Pleasant was secured to the tree. Naomi immediately sat down on the log and asked Isaiah to join her. When he was sitting, she entwined her arm with his. "Tell me what's on your mind."

Isaiah dropped his gaze. "I think my gal be too far away for me to go lookin' for her. I don't know whether to keeps tryin' or. . . ." His voice trailed away.

"Or let her go?" Naomi offered.

He looked at her through anguished eyes. "How can I ever let her go? She ain't never gonna find peace."

Naomi leaned her head on his shoulder, feeling a terrible ache inside. "Isaiah, God knows exactly where she is. Her soul has already found rest in His arms."

"How can you know that?" he moaned.

"Because the Good Book says these bodies we're living in are like tents. We try to hang onto these tents, but they're not our eternal bodies. Someday our Lord is coming back, and we'll have new bodies—bodies that will never die. Sarah's tent is gone, but she'll have a glorious body on that day."

"So should I stop lookin' for her?"

"What does your heart tell you?" she asked.

"I guess it be tellin' me not to give up."

Looking into his face, Naomi told him, "Then there's your answer. But Isaiah," she said, squeezing his arm, "keep listening to your heart. There will come a day when you know it's time to move on."

He sucked in a deep breath and let it out slowly. "You think maybe you'd like to pray a bit whilst we're here?"

"Yes," she breathed softly. "I'd like that very much."

Leaning her head back onto his shoulder, the two finished the morning in heartfelt supplication to their Lord and Master in heaven, begging for tender mercies and pleading for Sarah's soul to be at rest.

When they were done, they walked back to the house, leading their horses behind them. As they came to the gravel path, Naomi handed Isaiah the reins. She stroked Pleasant's neck and told her what a good girl she was. Then, turning toward Isaiah, she said, "I needed this. Thank you so much."

Isaiah gave her a nod. "It be my pleasure, Naomi. Thank ya for prayin' with me. Ya think we could do it again sometime?"

"Absolutely. I'd like that." Then, without conscious thought, Naomi kissed him affectionately on the cheek.

"Thank ya," he said with a grin and watched her walk all the way back to the house.

"Isaiah's smitten," a cold voice called from beside the larder on the back porch.

Naomi swiftly turned to see Abigail coming out into the open. Apparently, she'd been watching them, or more likely, spying on them.

Without giving Abigail the satisfaction of a reply, Naomi headed straight into the house and back to Isabella's room.

❧❀☙

The next couple of weeks seemed to grind by slowly. Naomi took her time with Isabella's things. While she would've welcomed Tabitha's help, she remembered Samuel saying that he didn't want anyone else touching his wife and daughter's belongings.

All of Isabella's personal effects were now stored in wooden crates and trunks. They covered the floor of her room. It was hard to enter that room again—it felt so empty and lifeless. Isabella had brought such joy and delight to everyone's life. Naomi couldn't remember a day that the girl hadn't made her smile.

Turning her sights on Elizabeth's room, Naomi pushed the curtains back and opened the windows wide. It was obvious Samuel had not slept here since the accident. She had heard that he was using the guest room at the very end of the hall near the back stairs to the kitchen. She doubted he would ever return to this room that he had shared with his dear wife.

Where to start? Noticing the wooden chest on Elizabeth's vanity table, she decided to begin with her jewelry and smaller items. Naomi put the chest on the floor and sat down at the mirror. Her soul felt utterly crushed as she remembered Ruth standing behind Elizabeth, brushing her mistress' gorgeous hair. She could literally hear their voices in quiet conversation. It hadn't taken long for the two women to care deeply for one another. Naomi had been so proud of Ruth's accomplishments with Elizabeth.

Staring at her reflection in the mirror, she wondered what it would be like to be the mistress of this house. What had it been like to share this bedroom with Samuel? Closing her eyes, she felt ashamed of the very thought. It was inappropriate, and she would not allow herself to follow such a perilous path. Instead, she lifted one of Elizabeth's exquisite necklaces and held it up in front of her. Then on a whim, she clasped it behind her neck.

An angry voice from the doorway screeched, "You vile woman! You be from the devil hisself. Get out of—"

Naomi spun around to see Berthy standing in the doorway. The woman's face was contorted; her next words were so slurred they were unrecognizable. Drool began slipping from her mouth. Something was terribly wrong.

"Berthy, are you all right?" Naomi cried as she quickly crossed the room toward her.

Berthy couldn't answer. She was trying, but only gibberish was coming from her mouth. All of a sudden, she swayed wildly, and Naomi reached out to grab her just before she collapsed. Taking on Berthy's full weight, Naomi lowered her to the floor, trying to keep her head from hitting the doorframe.

Gurgling sounds came from Berthy's throat. Naomi feared she was dying. "Help!" she yelled loudly. "Someone, help!"

In a matter of seconds, Abigail came up the front staircase and Tabitha up the back steps. When they caught sight of Berthy and Naomi, they ran swiftly to their side.

"What happened?" Abigail frantically asked.

"I don't know," Naomi answered.

Berthy immediately started thrashing about on the floor, trying to make herself understood. But it was impossible.

Abigail went to her knees and held Berthy tightly to keep her from hurting herself. "I think she's having a seizure," she cried. "Tabitha, go tell Micah to fetch the doctor, then bring some men to help us get Berthy in the bed."

It seemed like it was taking forever for help to arrive. Naomi's stomach wound tightly into knots.

Finally, Moses the gardener and two of his young workers came up the back stairs. Abigail proceeded ahead of them into Berthy's room to prepare the bed. All three men carried her into her small room, laying her gently on the bed.

"Thank you," Abigail told them.

Moses tipped his hat. "I's awful sorry 'bout this." Then all three men left the room.

When Naomi came to Berthy's bedside, Abigail turned on her. "Get out!"

"Abigail, I'm concerned—"

The housekeeper cut her off, pointing a stiff finger into Naomi's chest where Elizabeth's necklace hung. "Get out, I said. You have no right to . . . to *this*."

Naomi reached up and fingered the beautiful necklace at her throat. She had completely forgotten about it. Obviously, it had upset Berthy beyond reason . . . and now Abigail. She quickly left the room and took it off, praying that her thoughtless act had not been the cause of Berthy's dire condition.

Chapter 25

It took four long hours for a doctor to come to the plantation house. By the time he arrived, Berthy was already gone. Naomi realized that Berthy had passed to the next life an hour earlier when she heard Abigail mournfully crying. But she didn't dare check on her. Instead, she spent the entire time praying in Elizabeth's sitting room.

Naomi no longer had the heart for the work she'd been given to do, but she also had no one to turn to in the house. It was obvious Abigail would blame her for Berthy's death. *Oh, God in heaven, how could I have been so careless? Forgive me.*

Ironically, slave town was the only place she could turn. Naomi felt certain that Abigail would poison everyone in the house against her. That realization made her heart long for Ruth all the more. *Would there ever be relief from this pain?*

Mired in a bog of loneliness, she quietly slipped away from the house. Knowing everyone else would still be working, she decided to visit Eula.

When Naomi walked into the cluster of cabins belonging to her kinfolk, Eula was indeed sitting on her porch, rocking. She fanned herself with a tattered rag to keep the bugs away.

"Well, looky here. What brung ya to ole Eula's cabin?" she croaked, as Naomi approached.

"I came to let you know about Berthy. She passed on today around noon."

Eula's rocker came to a standstill, and the old woman leaned forward. Her eyes were darkened by sudden grief. Naomi immediately sat down on the top step of the porch and reached for Eula's hand.

"Berthy and me go way on back—back to her first days on this here plantation. I used to cook at the big house, and we gots real close when she and the missus come to live amongst us."

Naomi gave her hand an affectionate squeeze. "I know, Eula, and I'm so sorry."

Eula wiped the rag across her misty eyes. "How'd she go?" she asked in a broken voice.

"It was a seizure. She was gone before the doctor arrived."

"Oh, sweet Jesus, have mercy on her soul."

"Amen," Naomi whispered.

Eula directed a weary gaze toward her unexpected companion. "You's lonely, ain't ya?"

Naomi slipped her hand away from Eula's and looked toward Ruth's cabin. "Yes," she admitted. "I am."

"I thought that's why you come back to your ole Eula." The elderly woman reached out and brushed the back of her wrinkled hand on Naomi's cheek. "You need your kinfolk in times like these."

Naomi sighed deeply and laid her head on Eula's knee. "I'm sorry I've stayed away so long."

"Well, yer here now. We never stopped lovin' ya just 'cause yer at the big house," Eula said, stroking Naomi's hair. "I knows what it's like to come back to your kinfolk. Kinda humblin', ain't it?"

Naomi closed her eyes and let out a quiet laugh. "It is." Then she straightened so Eula could go back to rocking.

For a bit, the two women shared each other's company without words. Finally, Eula broke the silence. "Maybe I could get ya to help me with somethin'."

"Of course," Naomi quickly agreed.

"I's been helpin' Isaiah feed hisself and his young'un'. Would ya mind takin' it to him this evenin'? My ole bones has been hollerin' at me lately." She leaned forward again, pushing heavily on the arms of her rocker.

Naomi immediately came to Eula's side, lifting her gently beneath one arm. "I'll be glad to help you prepare a meal for Isaiah and Franklin. As a matter of fact, you just come inside and sit down and tell me what to do."

"Now ain't that kind of ya?" the old woman crooned. "But we's not cookin' in my cabin." She pointed a gnarled finger toward the small, three-sided brick structure out back.

Naomi helped Eula down the steps, and the two women walked arm-in-arm to the community cookhouse where the old woman and Solomon prepared the noon meal for their kinfolk. Once Eula was seated on a splintery bench, Naomi allowed herself to be bossed around. The irony of the situation wasn't lost on her. Here she was, an utterly free woman, taking orders from an old slave. Naomi smiled inwardly. Something about it felt invigorating.

A stew had already been simmering in an iron pot over a low fire. Naomi stirred it with a ladle, noticing peas and turnips and potatoes. She even turned up a large ham bone at the bottom of the pot.

After kneading and forming some biscuits, Naomi slid them into the oven over hot coals, then started to sit down.

"No girl, ain't no sittin' down. Go over and get the pot from Isaiah's place. Fill it up with stew and get his fire goin' to keep it warm."

Naomi got the distinct feeling that Eula would've been able to perform every one of these tasks without her, but it felt good to be useful for a change. By the time she got the fire going at Isaiah's and hung the small pot of stew over the grate, the biscuits were a nice golden brown.

"Put enough in the basket for the three of ya," Eula told her with a wink. "You ain't eatin' at the big house tonight."

The thought of sharing the evening meal with Isaiah and Franklin hadn't even crossed Naomi's mind. While she was sure to be welcome at Isaiah's table, she didn't know how she felt about that seemingly innocent act. It was obvious, Eula was trying to push them together. If Naomi actually stayed for the meal, everyone would be talking. Thinking about it a little longer, she came to the conclusion that it would be better for the kinfolk to be talking about her and Isaiah than knowing her heart had been smitten with their master.

⁓⋄⋓⋞⋗⁓

Isaiah and Franklin walked along the path from Mammy Lou's cabin to the pump. Untying the bandana around his neck, Isaiah soaked it in water and scrubbed his face before supper. Looking down at his son, he told him, "We's headin' to the creek this evenin', little man. You and me's gonna get a bath." He lifted Franklin's arm and pretended to smell him. "Ooh, wee, you stinks somethin' awful."

Franklin giggled and sniffed his pappy's leg. "You stinks too," he said with a wry grin.

Isaiah grabbed up his son and threw him over his shoulder like a sack of potatoes. "Don't you be talkin' 'bout your pappy like that," he snickered.

They were both chuckling when Isaiah pushed through the door of their cabin. At the sight of the woman squatting down in front of their fireplace, Isaiah fell silent. When she stood and turned to face him, his heart took off on a wild race.

"Naomi," he breathed. "I's surprised to see ya here."

She gave him an amused smile and walked right up to him. He didn't know what she was doing until she reached up and covered his son's little bottom. Franklin never wore anything but a long cotton shirt to Mammy's.

"You know," she said, "maybe it's time for Franklin to start wearing more clothes." She patted his bottom and turned back around to the fire.

"Yes'm," was all he could think to say while lowering his son to the floor.

Naomi turned again, still squatting on the floor. She opened her arms, and Franklin didn't hesitate to fill them. Isaiah watched her hold the boy with great affection and even noticed how Franklin kept his arms tight around her neck. He was missing his mammy in the worst way. Naomi was obviously the next best thing.

"I came to visit Eula today. She wanted me to bring your supper this evening." She stood and faced him again. "Do you mind if I eat with you?"

"We would love to have ya, wouldn't we, young'un?"

Franklin responded by throwing his arms back around her legs.

Naomi laughed softly, then went back down to the boy's level. She kissed him tenderly on the cheek. "Did you have a good day at Mammy's?"

"Uh, huh," he said. "And me and Pappy's gonna get a bath in the creek. Wanna come?"

"Hey, now, little man," Isaiah chastised. "That's just fer me and you." Giving Naomi an apologetic look, he said, "Sorry, we's not smellin' too good."

She winked and began ladling stew from the pot. "I hadn't noticed."

Isaiah kept the door to the cabin open as usual to let a good breeze blow through. But this evening, he particularly wanted it wide open so his kinfolk wouldn't think something was going on with Naomi staying for supper. Yet all throughout the meal he couldn't help but stare at her. A few times he knew she caught him, and he was embarrassed by it. Ruth hadn't been gone long enough for him to be feeling the way he did about another woman. He kept telling himself that Naomi was kinfolk—she was like his sister. But he was pretty sure he shouldn't have this kind of feeling about a sister.

When the meal was over, Naomi got up from the table to clean the dishes.

"Here, let me help ya," Isaiah offered.

Waving him off, she said, "Oh, no. I've got this. Why don't you take Franklin down to the creek to wash?"

"That bad?" Isaiah mused.

"That bad," she answered, smiling playfully.

Gathering up clean clothes for both of them and a sliver of lye soap, Isaiah watched Naomi work for a minute. "You gonna be here when we gets back?"

"Should I be?" she asked quietly.

Isaiah knew for sure in that moment he wanted her. The realization caused him a bit of angst. Keeping his eyes trained on hers, he safely said, "Only if'n you wants." Then he and Franklin left for the creek.

⊰⊱⊰⊱

When Naomi finished cleaning the supper dishes, she sat down at Isaiah's table. Part of her wanted to stay and put little Franklin to bed. She loved that boy beyond measure. He had stolen her heart as a baby in Ruth's arms, but now, he was totally wrapped inside her. He made her realize how much she longed for a child of her own.

Being here tonight had done her heart so much good. She felt comfortable with Isaiah—she'd known him and Ruth all her life. Yet that was the problem; Ruth would always be there between them. She could never see Isaiah as a lover—he would always be her brother.

With that thought, she rose from the table and immediately left for the big house. It wouldn't be right for her to wait for Isaiah to return. She had seen the way he looked at her tonight. He hadn't been able to hide his obvious feelings for her.

If she was truly being honest with herself, it felt good being wanted by a man, especially a man as worthy as Isaiah. A few weeks ago, Naomi had believed that Samuel Hawkins cared for her. But how could she have been so naïve? She had read much more into him giving her freedom than she ought. After all, he had used the very words that it was what Elizabeth would've wanted. The master had done it for his wife.

Naomi paused in the road. *Oh, Lord, what are you telling me?*

Looking up into the blushing sky, she took in a deep breath. Then, summoning her nerve, she turned around and headed back into slave town.

Chapter 26

September rolled in, carrying a much-needed relief from the August heat. It had been two weeks since Naomi had eaten supper with Isaiah and Franklin. When she'd gone back to his cabin that evening, Isaiah had seen her walking in from the road. His expression revealed curiosity, but he didn't ask where she'd gone. So many of their kinfolk had been outside by that time, Naomi didn't have the courage to do anything but ask him if he had any clothing that needed mending. He had given her a pair of trousers, two shirts, and a pair of socks, all badly in need of repair. She had been glad to do it for him and left them in his cabin two days later while he was at the stables.

Isaiah hadn't come calling in all that time, and for that, Naomi was grateful. She felt incapable of trusting her own heart. Grief could play such ugly tricks on a person. She didn't want to hurt Isaiah by giving in to his affections too soon. Maybe in time, they could find a way to be together, but their wounds were far too fresh. There had been no escape from the terrible loss they were both suffering. Naomi didn't want to build a relationship upon mutual heartache.

Returning to her task in Elizabeth's room, she did her best to be dispassionate about her former mistress' belongings. But at times, Naomi found herself quietly sobbing in the middle of the floor, cradling one of the fine gowns she had made for Elizabeth.

Between such a highly emotional task and Abigail's obvious hatred, Naomi found it harder and harder to stay in the big house. Instead of wallowing in self-pity, she decided to make herself more useful in slave town by taking on extra mending for her kinfolk and occasionally helping Eula and Solomon with the noon meal. What a bizarre situation she found herself in—a free woman, willfully spending time in slave town instead of the big house.

When September surrendered to October, Naomi had taken all the abuse she could handle from Abigail and some of the other house slaves. She began to devise a plan to leave for good. Starting a new life was sounding better by the day. Yet even though she had completed her difficult work, and all of the trunks and crates had been stored away in the attic, an unexplained apathy had taken Naomi into its clutches. She couldn't seem to make a definite decision. She had given her word that she would still be here when Samuel came home Surely, she owed him that much for what he'd done for her. But how was she going to make it for three more months?

Feeling desperately alone, Naomi turned to the peace of the garden night after night. Thus far she had been able to slip out of the house without anyone knowing. But this evening, she had the distinct feeling that someone else was there from the moment she entered the back gate.

The further she went into the garden, the more anxious she became. This was not turning out to be the peaceful time of prayer she'd grown accustomed to. A footfall on dried leaves. A crunch on the gravel path. A bird taking sudden flight. It was nerve-wracking.

Naomi swiftly turned to leave, but her pathway had been blocked. A rush of emotions assailed her at the sight of the man standing before her.

"Naomi."

He had spoken her name so tenderly, she nearly fell apart. Warm tears filled her eyes.

Samuel Hawkins consumed her vision and her heart. She couldn't help it—she went to him.

When his arms opened to her, she allowed herself to be drawn into an ardent embrace. Laying her head against his chest, she could hear the steady rhythm of his heart. After months of loneliness and maltreatment, his body felt like home.

For a prolonged moment, they held onto one another. Eventually Samuel released his embrace but not his hold. He gently cupped Naomi's face with both hands. "I'm so thankful you're still here. I didn't know what to expect."

Naomi reached up to cover both of his hands. More tears came to her eyes. "You have no idea how difficult it's been."

A concerned look held his features. "I'm sorry for the hardships you've endured, Naomi. Tell me about them." He took her hand and led her to a rustic bench beneath one of the chestnut trees.

Sitting with him this time, Naomi didn't want any distance between them. It was apparent Samuel felt the same way. He slid his arm around her shoulders, pulling her close to his side.

Being in such an intimate embrace, Naomi didn't want to spoil it by reliving her anguish of the last two months. "It can wait," she said. "Please tell me what brings you home."

Samuel smiled down at her. "I've neglected my work far too long. I need to get back in the saddle again, so to speak."

Feeling a bit wounded by his answer, Naomi remained silent. But his next words made her heart take wing. "Truthfully though, I came home because I realized how much you mean to me." He took her hand and kissed it. "I forced myself to stay in Nashville to make sure my heart wasn't playing tricks on me."

"And is it?" she asked coyly.

"It most certainly is not," he said definitively. "My heart knows exactly what it wants."

❧❧❧

For the next several evenings, Naomi met Samuel in the garden at a designated time. They always came together beneath the chestnut trees at the very place he had set her free. They withheld nothing from one another in conversation—sharing their deepest feelings and most intimate thoughts.

"Do you miss the children?" Naomi asked him one evening as they walked.

He nodded with a grin. "Very much. But the boys are extremely busy. I'm thankful they're in school instead of being tutored here at home. I think it will do them both a lot of good."

"What about little Catherine?"

"My sister Amelia is completely enthralled with her." He laughed heartily. "I may have to steal her back after Christmas."

Naomi thought how wonderful it was to hear Samuel laugh. It had been a long time since she'd seen him so relaxed . . . and happy.

As shadows began darkening the garden, Samuel turned their walk toward the back gate. Naomi was disappointed that the days were growing short. It wouldn't be long before their evening walks in the garden would no longer be possible. Tonight, the time had passed so quickly.

Fortunately, Samuel lingered with her at the gate. "I'm finding it hard to let you go every night, Naomi." He took her in his arms and held her tighter than usual. Then, before she knew what was happening, he bent his face to hers and kissed her tenderly.

When he stepped back, his breath was uneven, and Naomi felt the warmth of her cheeks.

"Good night, Naomi," he said quietly and left her at the gate.

For a moment, Naomi stood at the edge of the garden, wondering if Samuel's kiss had been real. It had been so brief. She touched her fingers to her lips—he had been so gentle. It seemed like a dream.

The following afternoon, Naomi headed into slave town to help with the noon meal. As all of the kinfolk came in from their various locations around the plantation, they sat down together to eat. Naomi sat on a bench near the side wall of Eula's cabin. After a few minutes, Isaiah lowered himself down beside her.

"How ya been, Naomi?" he asked quietly.

"I'm doing very well, Isaiah. Thank you." She looked over at him, realizing how much she had missed seeing him and Franklin in these last weeks. But he held no attraction for her, and she definitely didn't want to lead him into thinking there might be a chance with her. Still, he was like her brother, and she loved him as such.

"How are you and Franklin getting along?"

"We's all right. Things has picked up a bit since the massa come home."

"Yes, I expect so." Naomi felt a warmth in her face that she hoped would go unnoticed.

Isaiah thankfully kept on eating. "Massa seem to be doin' a whole lot better than before. He's takin' an interest in the place again."

Naomi simply nodded, not wishing to be drawn into a conversation about Samuel Hawkins. She decided to change the subject. "Are you still going out in the mornings to look for Sarah?"

He let out a loud breath that sounded more like a moan. Naomi wished she hadn't brought up the subject. "I'm sorry, Isaiah, I shouldn't have asked."

"Oh, no, that ain't it." He looked at her through anguished eyes. "I done decided not to look no more. I ain't found any more of her things and . . . well, Franklin been wakin' up wantin' his mama lately. I just can't go off leavin' him like that no more."

Naomi took hold of his arm. Her heart was crushed to think that Franklin was missing his mother so. "I'm awfully sorry. What can I do to help?"

Isaiah shook his head slowly. "Don't guess there be much you can do, unless'n you wants to come around more often. He sure do love havin' you here with us."

Guilt immediately plagued Naomi. By staying away from Isaiah, she had unintentionally kept her distance from Franklin. She would have to figure out a way to spend time with the boy without making Isaiah think she reciprocated his feelings.

It suddenly occurred to her that the two of them needed to stop tip-toeing around the obvious. "Isaiah, do you have time for us to talk alone after you're finished eating?"

"I reckon so," he said. "You wanna meet me at Ruth's prayer log after a bit?"

"That would be perfect. Just give me some time to help Eula and Solomon clean up."

Isaiah nodded and looked around at the kinfolk, who were mostly trying not to get caught watching the two of them. Grinning, he said, "I'll head out in a bit, so's no one will see us go there together."

Their eyes met. "Thank you," Naomi said with a wry smile.

❦❦❦

The day had grown chilly, and heavy clouds were rolling in as Naomi took the pathway to the clearing. Isaiah was standing near the log waiting for her. When she was seated, he joined her.

Naomi had thought all the way here about how she should tell Isaiah her true feelings. The last thing she wanted to do was hurt him. But it was time to clear the air.

"Isaiah, do you know how much I loved Ruth?" He gave her a questioning glance but nodded. "She was as close to me as a sister—I don't think I could ever love another friend so deeply. And because she was like a sister to me, *you* have always been my dear brother."

He drew a long breath and leaned forward, placing his elbows on his knees. Naomi feared she was hurting him, but their relationship needed to be defined beyond doubt.

She went on gently. "I just wanted you to know that I do love you, but only as a sister loves her brother—there could never be anything more."

When he sat up, his dark eyes met her gaze. "I already know'd what yer tellin' me, Naomi. I know'd it deep down. That's why I didn't come 'round no more. But. . . ." He fell silent and looked away.

"But what?" she inquired softly.

"But me an' Franklin miss ya somethin' awful. I understands how ya feel, and you won't have no problems bein' 'round me—I give ya my word." His eyes filled with concern. "But Franklin be needin' his auntie somethin' fierce." Then he winked and added, "And I needs my sister."

"Oh, Isaiah, thank you for understanding," Naomi said in relief. "You have no idea how I've longed to be with both of you."

"We've been pinin' for you too," he said. "But ya know what this mean, don't ya?"

Naomi's brow dipped. "What?"

"The kinfolk'll be waggin' their tongues 'bout us."

"Let them wag," Naomi gladly pronounced. "That will be our little secret."

"Yes'm, it will."

Naomi pulled her shawl a little tighter around her shoulders. It was getting downright cold. Isaiah put his arm around her, drawing her close. She knew in her heart that he was merely trying to provide her with some warmth.

"I gots to get back to the stables," he said. "Would ya like to pray afore I go?"

"Yes," she agreed wholeheartedly. "And Isaiah, I'm going to join you and Franklin for supper tonight."

A slow smile turned his lips. "Thank ya," he said, then started praying.

❦❦❦

Naomi practically ran back to the house after supper. The wind brought with it a biting chill. It almost seemed like winter had arrived without an invitation. There was no way she would be able to meet Samuel in the garden tonight. Besides, it was nearly dark when she finally made it back.

Tabitha was still working in the upper kitchen when Naomi arrived. She was one of the few house slaves who had remained loyal, despite the rumors that Naomi had caused Berthy's death.

"You best get yourself in here, Naomi. It's cold out there."

Feeling a shiver, Naomi agreed wholeheartedly. "I may have to get a fire going in my room tonight." Then, joining Tabitha at the washbasin, she asked, "Is there anything I can help you with?"

Tabitha smiled, while drying some of the supper dishes. "No, I gots all this. Why don't you go on and get that fire goin'? Seems you been workin' hard in slave town."

Naomi pulled off her outer wrap. "I've been trying to help my kinfolk as much as possible. Without the women of the house, I don't have as much sewing to keep me busy."

Lowering her voice, Tabitha speculated, "I'm thinkin' you and Isaiah be gettin' close. Am I right?"

It was unlike Tabitha to get caught up in gossip, but Naomi was sure she was curious just like everyone else. For a good reason, she didn't correct the young housemaid. Maybe it would be better for everyone to think that she and Isaiah actually were together. It would completely throw the scent off her trail from the constant hounds in pursuit.

Naomi simply replied, "I love him and Franklin deeply, but we are both still grieving terribly over Ruth."

"Oh, I knows," Tabitha sympathized. "I hope ya didn't think I's tryin' to start troubles for ya."

"Not at all," Naomi answered, then told the girl she was turning in for the night.

When Naomi stepped inside her room, a note was lying on the floor. Someone had pushed it beneath the door. Too dark to read, Naomi lit the lamp on her bedside table and sat down.

Dear Naomi,

I'm afraid the weather will not permit a garden walk this evening. I have enjoyed our conversations tremendously and wondered if you would join me in my sitting room tonight after the household is quiet? It's much warmer upstairs, and of course, I am the only one living there at the moment. I completely understand if you feel that this is an inappropriate invitation, and I will not be hurt in the least if you should decide not to accept—only disappointed in not being able to spend time with you.

Sincerely yours,
Samuel

Chapter 27

Naomi folded the note from Samuel, then unfolded it and read it for the second time . . . and a third. She, too, had felt the disappointment of not spending time with him in the garden. While her heart readily accepted his invitation, her mind was trying to plead a more prudent case. She refolded the note and held it to her breast. Responding to the heady rush of Samuel's invitation, Naomi's thoughts suddenly fell into perfect stride with her heart's wild contractions. Without any more deliberation, she kindled a flame in the fireplace to wait for the household to turn in for the night.

The door to Samuel's sitting room stood ajar. A soft glow of light illuminated the hallway. Naomi peered inside. He was sitting in a chair near the fireplace, facing the door. It was obvious he had been waiting for her. Immediately he came to his feet and opened the door wider for her to enter. Then he closed it silently.

"Please, sit down," he said softly, gesturing toward the small sofa facing the fire. When she was seated, he went back to his chair.

For a while they made small talk about the garden and the sudden appearance of cold weather. Then Samuel said, "Micah tells me you've been spending most of your days in slave town."

"Yes," she confirmed. "I know it must seem strange, considering you've granted my freedom. But I feel more useful there than I do in the house."

His dark brow furrowed. "Is there something I can do to help you, Naomi? I'm ready to tell Micah that you've been given a deed of manumission. I just want it to be your decision."

Naomi shook her head. "I truly don't want anyone else to know—at least, not right now. I feel freer than ever before because I'm making my own decisions about where to go and what to do." Then, leaning forward, she added, "I hope that's all right with you."

He smiled handsomely, then left his chair, sitting down beside her on the sofa. "I'm ready to do whatever makes you happy, Naomi." He opened his arm to her, and she slid up against his side.

"I miss having a purpose," she told him. "I was able to use my God-given talents for Elizabeth and Isabella, but I have to confess that I'm feeling a bit lost."

Samuel was silent for several heartbeats, then he said, "I don't have the right to ask you for anything. You're free to do as you wish. Normally, Elizabeth would be asking you to make clothing for the house slaves for Christmas at about this time of year. But. . . ."

Naomi rose up to face him. "Then that's what I need to be doing." She experienced a surge of creative energy that she hadn't felt since the loss of her dear ones. "I long to be useful again."

"Then I'll pay you for your work," he said directly. "I can't have you doing all of this for nothing."

For a moment, Naomi was shocked by his statement. Although she was a free woman, she realized her mindset was still mired in slavery. Her first instinct was to tell him no, and she told him as much. But he wouldn't hear of it.

"Naomi, I'll be hurt if you don't accept compensation for your hours of work. It will be between the two of us."

She leaned back into him, knowing that she needed to accept his offer. The last thing she wanted to do was hurt the man she loved. "All right," she said softly. "I accept."

For a long time, they sat watching the glowing fire, feeling its heat, as well as their own warmth, sitting so closely together. Samuel rubbed gentle circles around her shoulder and caressed her arm tenderly. Naomi felt completely at ease with him, and her eyelids slowly dropped.

When her eyes opened again, Naomi was unsure of her whereabouts. All she knew was that she was completely warm and comfortable. A clanking sound against the fire grate brought her fully awake, and she lifted her head from the soft pillow.

Samuel turned from the fire, dressed in a different outfit than she remembered.

"Good morning," he said quietly.

"Morning?" Naomi questioned. It was still dark.

He came to the sofa and knelt down beside her. His knuckles brushed the smooth skin of her cheek. "I didn't have the heart to wake you last night. I hope you don't mind."

Her head plopped back down on the pillow. The blanket she was wrapped in felt glorious. "I can't believe I slept all night. I haven't done that since. . . ." Her voice fell silent.

"Since what?" Samuel asked with genuine concern.

Her face suddenly felt as warm as the embers in the fireplace. "Since the attack," she whispered.

Samuel slowly reached beneath her and lifted her into his arms. He sat down on the sofa, cradling her gently to him. Naomi encircled his chest with one arm and cuddled her face into the crook of his neck.

"I know you and Elizabeth talked about what happened that night," he said. "I want you to know how sorry I am. I've always felt responsible for that somehow."

"That wasn't your fault," she breathed against his warm skin. "It was mine alone."

Samuel held her away from him so he could look into her face. "Naomi, that was *not* your fault. There are men in this world who have no honor, and that man was one of them. You did nothing to deserve such treatment."

She closed her eyes and let out a languished breath. "I was so tired that night, I let my guard down. I should've stopped his . . . provocative words from the very start."

Pulling her a little tighter, Samuel breathed heavily—his voice was angry. "He should've been punished severely."

"No," she said, putting her hand on his chest and sitting up in his arms. "The overseers made the right decision. I couldn't live with myself if they had killed him for my ignorance."

Noticing how emotional he had become, Naomi went on. "It's fine . . . *I'm* fine now. Thank you for caring about me—even then."

Samuel nodded, and his demeanor gradually calmed, but his voice was still impassioned. "Naomi, I don't ever want to hurt you. Please don't let me hurt you."

She frowned slightly. "You could never hurt me. You've given me more than I could ever hope for. You've made me a free woman. And for that, I will always be grateful."

Taking in a deep breath, he let it out slowly. "Will you choose to come back tonight?" he asked, giving her a captivating grin.

Leaning up to kiss him on the cheek, she breathed next to his lips, "I'll be here."

Naomi didn't go to slave town on such a cold and blustery day. She knew Isaiah would understand, but she would dearly miss her time with Franklin. If the weather cleared, she determined to have supper with them tomorrow.

As for today, Naomi felt revived and valued in the household once more. She quickly sat down to write out a new order for material to give to Micah. She particularly had a very special order for the women this year. If there was any way to make amends for Berthy's terrible demise, she was determined to try it. She was so tired of living as an outcast.

Already possessing the measurements of the house slaves, she decided to start in with the material at hand. With a fire roaring on the grate, and several lamps lit about the room, Naomi felt a weight lifted from her shoulders for the first time since that dreadful day in June that took away her loved ones. *Thank you, Lord*, she breathed as her hands got back to the work that made her feel whole.

❧❧❧

Isaiah pulled his jacket up around his neck, trying to ward off the chill. The wind was brutal this morning—his body wasn't acclimated to such a drastic change in weather. He couldn't wait to finish inspecting the mules outside in the paddock and get back inside the barn. He rubbed one of the mule's necks with a gloved hand and noticed a winter coat of hair had already started growing.

This morning, Isaiah had actually dressed Franklin in long pants, a flannel shirt, socks, and shoes for the day. The thought of it made him smile. Naomi would be proud.

As much as he tried, Isaiah couldn't seem to get the woman off his mind. Naomi was not only beautiful in appearance, but her inner nature was incredibly appealing. Her walk with the Lord was evident to all and one that he desired to emulate.

"Lawd," he spoke aloud. "Help me look on her as my sister. And if'n you sees fit to change her heart someday, I'd be much obliged."

Finally getting in out of the weather, Isaiah went to work with the mules inside the barn. Most of them were females that were being used for breeding. The side door to the barn blew open and slammed against the wall, causing the lanterns to sway on their hooks. Isaiah looked up and saw Micah and the master enter. Micah immediately shoved the door closed against the wind.

"Mornin', massa," Isaiah called.

"Good morning, Isaiah." Samuel rubbed his hands together. "Seems like winter is upon us."

"Aww, it'll pass," Isaiah told him. "Probly be warm again tomorrow."

For the next half hour, the three men walked through the barn, inspecting the brood mares. Isaiah was thankful to see the master taking such an interest again. When their discussion concluded, he walked with Micah and Master Hawkins to the door.

"Thank you, as always, for your good work, Isaiah."

"It be my pleasure to serve ya, massa."

Then turning to Micah, Master Hawkins said, "I almost forgot. I need you to get to the house and see Naomi this morning. She's going to have an order for material you need to get as soon as possible."

"Yes, sir," Micah replied. "I'll get right over there."

When Micah opened the door, he stepped outside. "You comin', sir?"

Master Hawkins took a step back. "Not yet. I'll join you in my study after you take care of Naomi's request."

Micah bowed slightly and lowered his head into the wind. Samuel immediately closed the door and turned back to his trainer.

"I'm curious about something, Isaiah."

"Yessir?"

"Micah tells me that Naomi has been spending a lot of time with you lately."

Isaiah's heart turned over in his chest, and he worried why the master would be probing into his relationship with Naomi. He simply nodded as an answer.

"Do you think . . . well, I guess I was just curious if the two of you might be getting together? After all, it seems like the natural thing for both of you."

"Oh, no, sir. Whilst I enjoy her company an' all, she be comin' round to spend time with Franklin. He be missin' his mammy somethin' fierce."

Master Hawkins' shoulders dropped down. He seemed to relax. "I'm sorry to ask about your business like that. I just thought I might congratulate you if you all were making plans."

"That ain't the case at all, sir. Naomi done sees me as her brother, that's all."

The master buttoned up his coat, then put on his gloves. "All right, I'll leave you to your work."

"Thank ya, massa," Isaiah said while opening the barn door for him. Instead of going back inside, Isaiah stepped out under the eaves of the barn. His face had grown overly warm at the mention of Naomi, and he turned it into the wind.

"Lawd?" he petitioned again. "I's got it bad. If'n it's yer will, please take Naomi from my heart."

⊱⋅⊰

Naomi had waited anxiously all evening for the household to settle. Fortunately, everyone went to their quarters earlier than usual, hoping to find relief from the chilly downstairs rooms with their high vaulted ceilings. Without the family, there had been no need to keep a fire burning in the various rooms. Naomi smiled inwardly, thinking of the warmth of Samuel's sitting room upstairs.

The door to his room was in the exact position as the night before. Naomi didn't delay to walk inside and close it behind her. Samuel came to her immediately, taking her into his arms. The feel of his body against hers made her head swirl. If she weren't careful, she would lose all control with him.

Thankfully, he stepped back and brought her to the sofa. Tonight, he sat down with her from the beginning. She noticed his breathing was ragged. He didn't readily open a conversation.

Taking the lead, Naomi expressed her gratitude to him. "Thank you so much for sending Micah to get my order." Her look grew sheepish. "He was surprised when I gave it to him."

Samuel's head tilted. "Why would he be surprised?"

"The order normally came from Elizabeth. He obviously knows now that I can read and write."

A slow grin played on Samuel's lips. "I didn't think about that. Did he say anything to you about it?"

"He looked a little shocked but said nothing." Naomi smiled, recalling Micah's expression.

"I assure you, he'll be discreet," Samuel told her.

Naomi reached over and took his hand into her lap. "I'm not worried about Micah."

"Nor am I," Samuel said, scooting closer. "He's the furthest thing from my mind right now."

For a moment their gaze held steady. His eyes were ablaze with passion. Before another thought came into Naomi's head, Samuel's mouth covered hers, not nearly as gently as before. One hand kept steady pressure on the small of her back, while the other clasped behind her neck. His thumb caressed her jaw. She was completely swept away.

After a long moment, Samuel withdrew. Every part of her begged him not to stop—except her words. She knew with just one word from her, they would find themselves in the other room.

He stood and walked over to the fireplace. Naomi was quite aware that they had crossed a line from which there might be no retreat. His breath hitched. "Forgive me, Naomi. I will not be like the man who took you against your will. I respect you beyond words."

She sat motionless on the sofa, save for her quickness of breath. This was the most honorable man she had ever known. He was giving her a way out. If she didn't take it now, she never would.

Coming to her feet, she walked to the door. *Open it*, the voice in her head told her. But her hand remained on the knob. Instead, she spoke to him, keeping her gaze on her hand. "I love you with all my heart, Samuel." At his silence, she looked back into his eyes. "I want to belong to you."

His chest rose and fell, drawing one long breath after another. "Naomi," he said softly. "You have already belonged to *me*. My greatest desire is to belong to *you*."

With those words, Naomi's head began to spin, and her hand slipped away from the knob.

Chapter 28

Naomi made her way back to her room in the dark, long before any of the household slaves had awakened. If she'd had her way, she would still be in Samuel's arms. He had made it clear that it would've been his choice as well.

As she washed and dressed for the day, Naomi found it difficult to concentrate. She had used her freedom to make a choice she could've never fathomed. Her thoughts were drawn to the long conversation which had ensued after she'd made the decision to stay with Samuel.

Sitting on the rug in front of the fire, they had pledged their lives to one another. Samuel had slipped the ruby ring from his finger and put it on a long gold chain. Placing it around her neck, he held it to her chest. "Here and now, I give you my heart. Always and forever." Naomi had held her hand to his and pledged her undying love and devotion to him.

A soft smile turned her lips as she pressed a kiss to the ruby. While it would be safely hidden beneath her bodice, the feel of it against her skin would remind her of Samuel throughout the day. But a sudden weight fell upon her chest where the ring lay. How could their actions have been honoring to God?

Naomi sat down on the edge of her bed, rubbing her temples. She needed to pray, but no words would come. Her spirit felt shame for what she'd done. Normally, she would be lighting a lamp and reading her mother's Bible. But today, she pushed herself off the bed and headed to the lower kitchen. She would make herself breakfast, then get to work on her new project. Staying busy would be her solace for now.

By midafternoon, Naomi was ready to get out of the house. The weather had cleared, and she would enjoy a walk in the sunshine to slave town. As she strolled along the road, she caught sight of Samuel in the distance on horseback. She stopped to watch him, and her heart fluttered wildly when he glanced her way. For a long time, they observed one another from afar. She struggled with her desire to go to him.

Finally, Samuel removed his hat and pressed it to his chest the way he had on the day he left for Nashville. Naomi's hand automatically reached to the ring which lay hidden beneath her blouse. She could see his broad smile, even from where she stood. Dipping her head to him, she turned and continued on into slave town.

Eula sat on her porch, resting up from the noon meal. "So's you've come to be with Isaiah again?" she crooned.

Naomi laughed. "I've come to be with Franklin for supper."

"Tell yerself what you like," Eula said with a smirk. "I suppose Isaiah will be there too."

Naomi's smile was striking. "I suppose."

Eula stopped her rocker and stared intently into Naomi's eyes. The old woman's mouth dropped open. "Yer in love, ain't ya, girl?"

Feeling the heat from her body rise all the way up to her face, Naomi's smile disappeared. Eula could see right through her.

Noticing her reaction, Eula went on. "Sit yerself down, girl. I ain't gonna blab yer business everywhere."

Naomi sat down on the step but kept her racing thoughts to herself.

"I seen the way Isaiah looks toward ya. I reckon everyone else seen that by now." She smiled wryly. "I just didn't know'd how ya felt about Isaiah till I seen yer face today."

Relief swept over Naomi like a rushing tide. She would do her best not to lie to her kinfolk, but they could certainly surmise what they will. Relaxing her posture, Naomi settled in for a bit of feisty conversation.

When Isaiah and Franklin came into the cabin for supper, Franklin ran to her. Naomi barely had time to brace herself. She squatted down to his level as usual and held him tight against her. Then kissing him, she asked, "What was the best thing about your day?"

He gave her a smile that turned her heart to liquid. "Seein' you."

Naomi glanced up at Isaiah with tears in her eyes and pulled the boy back to her. Then standing up, she wiped her face, trying to rein in her sudden emotion.

"I's glad yer here," Isaiah said softly. "He sure is needin' ya right now."

"May I stay and put him to bed?"

Isaiah nodded. "He'd be mighty happy 'bout that."

When supper was over, Naomi washed the dishes while Franklin dried and Isaiah put them away. Then she pulled a chair over to the fireplace and took the boy into her lap. He laid his head against her chest, and she wrapped her arms around him. Isaiah set his chair up to the fireplace facing them.

A tinge of guilt passed through Naomi's mind. She was using Isaiah as a cover for her love affair with his master. Her eyelids closed for a brief moment as she let out sigh.

When her eyes opened, Isaiah was staring at her. "What's wrong?" he asked.

She shook her head. "It's nothing. I just have a lot on my mind right now."

"You still bein' hounded in the big house?"

"Not as much as before," she said.

"You think it be 'cause the massa come home?"

Naomi took a cautious breath. "Well, that could certainly be it. He does have a way of keeping order."

"Ya know, he asked me 'bout you yesterday."

Every muscle in Naomi's body tensed. She turned her gaze toward the fire. "Whatever for?"

"He be thinkin' we might have feelin's for one another. Ya know, with ya comin' here so much an' all."

Naomi glanced back at his face. "What did you tell him?"

"I done told 'im the truth o' the matter—that we's like brother an' sister. I let 'im know that you comes here to be with Franklin."

She nodded, then looked down at the boy in her lap. "You know it's not just Franklin I come to see. I care about you, Isaiah."

"I know'd that," he said. "I just wants ya to keep comin'. He needs ya somethin' awful."

When it was time for Franklin to go to bed, Naomi helped him into his nightshirt. She held the covers back as he climbed in. Isaiah had gone out onto the porch, so Naomi laid down beside the boy. Immediately he turned into her arms.

For a long time, she held him, singing softly while rubbing his back. When his breathing changed, she gently laid him on the bed and kissed his forehead before getting up.

Isaiah had been watching her from the door. "I'll walk ya back to the big house," he said quietly.

It was already dark, and Naomi appreciated the fact that Isaiah would be with her. "Thank you," she said. "But what about Franklin?"

"Ceceilia's comin' to watch over 'im till I gets back."

"Oh," Naomi said. Obviously, after tonight, there would be no doubt as to what the kinfolk would be thinking.

Ceceilia didn't wait to be invited in. She walked through the door, keeping her eyes fixed on Naomi.

Naomi offered a quiet hello. Ceceilia merely dipped her head, giving Naomi a knowing expression. But when she looked over at Franklin sleeping peacefully, she turned back with a kindlier gaze. "Thank ya, fer this," she said quietly. "I think Ruth would be glad."

Without pause, Naomi told her, "Franklin means the world to me."

Ceceilia picked up a chair and quietly set it beside the bed. Only the crackling fire in the hearth lit the cabin.

"Thank ya, Ceceilia. I be right back," Isaiah whispered.

She nodded. "Take yer time, Isaiah."

As the pair walked onto the road, Isaiah offered Naomi his arm. "I shoulda brung a lantern," he remarked.

She immediately slipped her arm through his. "I didn't realize it had gotten so late."

"Not really late. Just gettin' dark a lot earlier, that's all."

"Isaiah, I won't always be able to come to supper. But I want you to know that you can send someone for me if Franklin is ever having a hard time. I'll be here in a heartbeat."

He gave her arm a gentle squeeze. "Thank ya fer that. Franklin loves ya like his own mammy."

Naomi's heart swelled at the very thought of it. "I love him as my own," she replied softly.

The pair walked the rest of the way in silence. At the back door, Isaiah released her arm. "G'night, Naomi," he said softly.

"Good night, Isaiah." Naomi watched him turn and disappear into the inky night.

The house seemed quiet as she entered the darkened kitchen. Naomi decided not to go to her room but headed toward the back stairs to be with Samuel. Just before she got there, a voice called out from the shadows. "You been out with Isaiah?"

Naomi's heart about jumped out of her chest. She turned sharply. "Abigail? You scared me to death. Why are you sitting in here without a light?"

Instead of answering her question, Abigail spewed, "Does the massa know you been sneakin' around like this?"

"I'm not sneaking around. Everyone knows I spend time with little Franklin *and* Isaiah."

Naomi went straight to the table and found a candle with a match in its holder. She quickly lit the wick. "I've had enough of your games, Abigail. Let's take care of this once and for all."

Immediately, Abigail rose from the table and started for the door that led to the slave quarters. But Naomi would not have it. "No," she said forcefully. "You will not leave. If you have something against me, say it now to my face. This ends tonight."

Abigail's mouth pursed tightly—her eyes held undeniable malice, but she remained where she was.

"Is this about Berthy's death?"

Abigail's mouth curved downward, and she shook her head. "Started long before that."

"Why?" Naomi pleaded. But Abigail remained silent.

"If I've done something to hurt you, I deserve to know what it is. How can I make things right with you if I don't have a clue what I've done?"

Abigail folded her arms against her body. Her shoulders hunched, and she suddenly looked older than her years.

Praying for the Spirit to lead her, Naomi motioned toward the table. "Why don't we sit down. I'm ready to hear what you have to say."

A look of surrender crossed Abigail's face. Naomi was fairly surprised that she accepted the invitation.

The two sat across from one another at the table. When Abigail didn't readily speak, Naomi simply asked, "How can I help you, Abigail?"

For a long time, Abigail appeared to be wrestling with herself. Naomi was determined to wait patiently. She would take whatever the Hawkins' housekeeper had to dish out. In the flickering light of the candle, it appeared that Abigail's chin had begun to quiver. When she finally spoke, it was in a broken voice. "It's not you," she admitted, looking down at her hands. "It's not you."

Naomi felt pity for the woman. She seemed so shattered and forlorn.

"I've been strugglin' for a long time with the way you were always so close to the missus and missy. Seems like you were always so important to 'em."

Naomi began to breathe in relief. She'd been so tense, waiting for Abigail to deliver a hard punch. Instead, she received a heartfelt admission. "But they're gone now, Abigail. Why have you turned this household against me?" she pleaded.

Abigail's face crumpled. "The night of the gala . . . I watched how everyone looked at you to lead 'em, when it should've been me. Then hearin' all those compliments about the dress the missus was wearin', well. . . ."

Exhaling a deep breath, Naomi finally understood Abigail's insecurities. But how could Abigail still be so hostile toward her? "I'm sorry you felt that way," she offered. "You've always been very important to this household."

Abigail rubbed her face wearily. "Not anymore," she bemoaned.

"What are you talking about?" Naomi pressed.

"We're all afraid," she declared. "The master's probably decidin' who he wants to sell. He don't rightly need all of us anymore. But *you* . . . you seem to get whatever you want. You're in there sewin' again, and you got Isaiah. And of course, Isaiah is important to the master, so—"

"So that makes it all right to turn everyone against me?"

Abigail shook her head dolefully. "I know it's not right—I know it in my heart."

Naomi's eyes fixed on the woman across from her. "Thank you for admitting that," she told her. "We're all still grieving our terrible loss, Abigail. Maybe you and I should be working together to encourage this household, not *discourage* them."

The housekeeper didn't immediately speak again. It was obvious she was deeply worried about her position and status in the Hawkins' household. Finally, Naomi said, "Could you and I at least agree to a truce, after all that we've been through?"

Without warning, Abigail came to her feet, staring at the doorway behind Naomi. "Master Hawkins," she spoke humbly.

Naomi felt a charge run through her body. She stood and turned. Samuel had entered the kitchen, carrying a sconce with a single candle. "Have I interrupted something?" he asked.

Abigail nearly stuttered. "Uh, no, sir. We were just talkin' a bit."

He looked over at Naomi. She instantly dropped her gaze as if she were still his slave.

"May I help you with somethin', sir?" Abigail asked.

"Yes, I hope so," he told her. "I came in search of a snack. Seems I'm still a bit hungry from dinner."

"Did you get some of Mamie's blackberry cobbler, sir?"

"Actually, I did. But I'd sure love to have a little more."

Abigail picked up the candle from the table. "I'll go get you some, Master. Would you like me to bring it to your room?" she asked.

"No, I'll wait right here," he told her.

When Abigail headed down to the lower kitchen, Naomi raised her gaze toward his. "I think I should go to my room before she returns."

His smile nearly drove her over the edge. "Will you share the cobbler with me in a little while?"

"Don't eat it all," she whispered before departing the kitchen.

B y mid-December, Naomi's work was nearly complete. She had made every member of the household a brand-new outfit for Christmas, plus a uniquely special creation for each of them. At Naomi's urging, Samuel had purchased new shoes for every single one of his slaves this year.

By late afternoon on a snowy day, a knock sounded on Naomi's door. Quickly, she put her unfinished needlework out of view. "Yes?" she called.

"It's Abigail. The master wants to see you in his study."

Naomi quickly went to the door and opened it. "Thank you. Please tell him I'll be right there."

Abigail nodded and left her.

It was rare for Samuel and Naomi to interact together during the day but not altogether unheard of. She checked her appearance in the mirror, then headed down the hall to his study. The door was open, and thankfully, Abigail was nowhere in sight. While she and Abigail had found a way to peacefully coexist, Naomi still held onto the hope of achieving a better relationship with her.

"Good afternoon," she said benignly, just in case prying ears were nearby.

"Good afternoon, Naomi," Samuel responded with a gleam in his eye. He left his desk and closed the door.

A fire was roaring in the fireplace, making his study a comfortable refuge from the rest of the house. He reached for her hand and led her to the sofa.

"I have something to give you," he said, holding out an envelope. "It's payment for all of your hard work these past weeks."

While Naomi was gratified to be paid for the first time in her life, she also felt compelled to refuse. She didn't readily take the envelope.

A half-smile crossed Samuel's lips. "I hope you're not planning on hurting my feelings."

"I was thinking about it," she said with a quiet laugh.

He reached over and turned her hand upward, pressing the envelope into her palm. Closing her hand and covering it with both of his, he said, "You've earned every bit of this and more. Someday, when you're ready, you can use it as you wish."

Naomi looked down at his hands covering hers and felt an overwhelming gratitude. "Thank you," she said, before raising up to kiss him softly on the lips. He deepened the kiss, then cuddled her close to his side.

"There's something I need to tell you," he said. "I'll be heading to Nashville next week to spend Christmas with the children."

She sat up out of his arms. "For how long?"

"At least three weeks." He pulled her back possessively. "I wish you could go with me."

Naomi squeezed her eyes shut, thinking how lonely she would be without him. "The children will be coming back with you, I suppose."

"That was the plan. But if the boys are still thriving, I may allow them to finish out this school year in Nashville. It may actually be better for Catherine to remain as well."

"I know you miss them," she sympathized.

"I do. But I'll go back again in the spring for a visit. My sister Amelia is having the time of her life. She always wanted more than two children, and now she has five."

Naomi allowed herself to be held for as long as possible but knew she should probably leave Samuel's study soon. With a deep breath, she reluctantly sat forward. "I think I should go."

He nodded, but when they both stood up, he cupped her face tenderly in his hands. "I love you so much," he said in a husky voice. Before she could reply, he kissed her passionately.

Naomi could barely speak when he pulled away. She found just enough breath to profess her love to him. Then, gathering her wits, she pressed her hand to his chest. "Tonight," she whispered and left his study.

❧❧❧

On Christmas Eve, Abigail assembled the entire household staff for dinner. Another table had been brought up from the lower kitchen to extend the one in the upper kitchen. Tablecloths covered both tables along with fresh holly and bows of evergreen. The roast beef and potatoes smelled wonderful. Since Naomi had earlier shared the worries of Samuel's house slaves with him, he had made it clear that they would have no cause for concern. He told Micah to make sure they had everything needed for a Christmas feast.

Naomi was grateful for her newfound peace with the household slaves. Had it not been for Samuel these past months, she would've found it difficult to survive the malevolence that had been pressed upon her. During the gala, every one of them had looked to her with such respect, but people could be so fickle. All it had taken was Abigail's dissenting voice to turn the lot against her.

Tabitha sat down beside Naomi at the table, giving her a bright smile. Unexpectedly, the girl leaned over and kissed her cheek. "Happy Christmas."

This dear girl had never followed along with the rest of the household. She had faithfully and quietly remained loyal. "Happy Christmas," Naomi beamed.

Soon, the bounty of food was being passed among them. Lively chatter filled the air, giving Naomi great hope. While Micah had presented the household slaves with their new clothing and shoes this morning, Naomi was eagerly anticipating the time when she could give out her special gifts.

As soon as Mamie brought out her famous custard pies, Naomi stood. "I have a small gift for each of you," she told them. "I hope that it will be a comfort to all of us as we continue to remember our great loss this year."

A reverent silence permeated the kitchen while Naomi retrieved a box that she had slid beneath her chair. Placing it on the table, she opened the lid. Those who could see inside let out a soft gasp. "Abigail," she said, "this one is for you."

Naomi pulled out a beautiful, white lace handkerchief, much like the ones Elizabeth had possessed. Abigail stood up, a look of astonishment capturing her features. Naomi walked around the table to the housekeeper's position at the head, laying it gently in her hand.

Abigail accepted it, lightly rubbing the lace between her fingers. Naomi cradled one hand beneath Abigail's, then pointed to something she had embroidered on the handkerchief. "This is an A, which is the first letter of your name."

For a moment, Abigail simply stared at the letter, as if she could hardly comprehend what Naomi had told her. Then, with a sharp intake of breath, she looked up with emotion in her eyes. "This is the letter at the beginning of my name?"

Naomi gave her a soft smile. "Yes."

Abigail now traced the letter with her finger. Then, looking into Naomi's eyes, she said, "Thank you."

The gathering around the table erupted in applause, causing tears to flow freely from Abigail's eyes. She used the handkerchief to dab her eyes, then enveloped Naomi in a hug.

Feeling a tremendous relief, Naomi held her tightly, then proceeded to give out the rest of her gifts, taking the time to show each slave their first initial.

As they were all eating pie, a knock sounded on the back door. Abigail immediately rose to answer it. "Isaiah!" she said in a surprised voice. "Would you like to come in for pie?"

"Oh, no, but thank ya. I's sure sorry to interrupt you'ins, but I's wonderin' if I could speak with Naomi?"

"Well of course. She's right here."

Naomi immediately joined him at the door, and Abigail went back to the table. "Come in out of the cold," she told him.

But Isaiah was shaking his head. "We needs to talk, just. . . ." He glanced around her at all the people in the kitchen. "Not here."

"At least come in while I get my coat." Naomi took hold of his arm, urging him out of the cold. Reluctantly, he stepped inside and took off his hat.

"I won't be a minute," she said, disappearing down the hall.

When Naomi hurried back to the kitchen, she went straight to Mamie, who was still sitting at the table admiring her handkerchief. "Thank you for such a wonderful dinner."

Mamie reached out and grabbed her hand, nearly cutting off her circulation. "Oh, sugar, thank ya for this wonderful gift."

Naomi tried to squeeze the old cook's hand back, but it was no use. She kissed her cheek instead, then headed out into the dark night with Isaiah.

"I surely hates to take ya away like this, it bein' the eve o' Christmas an' all."

"Is it Franklin?" she asked immediately.

Isaiah's head bobbed. "He be needin' ya real bad. He's moanin' fer his mammy. Ain't none of the kinfolk able to help him."

Naomi didn't hesitate to hold onto Isaiah's arm. She was glad he'd remembered a lantern. He quickly snatched it off the porch steps and said, "It sure looked like a nice gatherin'."

"It was," she said. "I'll tell you all about it later." Naomi had no desire for small talk. Her steps quickened along with her anxious heart.

When they got to the cabin, Ceceilia and Phibe were doing their best to get Franklin to stop bawling, but it was obvious they were having no success. He was standing naked in the corner of the cabin, pressing his forehead against the rough wall.

"Oh, thank the Lord," Ceceilia cried as soon as Naomi came in. "We can't do nothin' with him tonight."

Naomi threw off her coat and went to the boy. Dropping down to her knees, she laid a gentle hand on his back. "Franklin," she said with such tenderness. "It's going to be all right. I'm here."

Instantly he turned to her, and Naomi wrapped him up tightly in her arms. She stood with him and held him against her, kissing his tear-streaked face. Taking him to the bed, she sat down, propping herself up against the head rail.

Isaiah brought a blanket, laying it over his son and Naomi's legs. The boy soon began to settle but continued to whimper against her chest. "It's all right, my little one. Hush, now. I love you, dear one."

Naomi kept her focus on the boy, not even aware when her kinfolk left the cabin. She rocked him gently back and forth, humming softly. Soon, he was fast asleep in her arms. He'd worn himself out crying.

Isaiah sat down on the other side of the bed. He laid his hand lightly on Franklin's back. "Ceceilia can come back and stay with 'im when yer ready to go," he said quietly.

The idea of leaving the boy tonight was unthinkable. "No," she told him firmly. "I'm staying."

Isaiah dropped his hand to the bed. "I got no right to ask ya to do that," he said.

"You have no choice, Isaiah. When Franklin wakes up, whether it's in the middle of the night or in the morning, I'm going to be here."

Swallowing hard, Isaiah seemed to be wrestling with how to respond to her. Finally, he nodded, then rose to his feet. "I'll get some blankets and head on over to the stables."

Naomi reached out and clasped his arm. "You'll do no such thing. It'll be freezing out there."

Isaiah's gaze held hers for long seconds. Tilting his head toward the door, he said, "Everybody be talkin' if'n I stay here with ya."

With a soft laugh she said, "Isaiah, they're already talking, remember?"

He gave her a humorless smile and sat down in the chair next to the bed. "Naomi," he said softly, "you don't deserve to have that kind o' talk goin' on. You's a godly woman, and I can't let people be thinkin' like that about ya."

Naomi felt her heart pinch. Her conscience was suddenly attacked by a barrage of fiery darts. *Godly* was the furthest thing from the truth—how far she'd fallen. If Isaiah were to know the truth about her, he would be devastated.

"You think too highly of me," she stated coolly.

Just then, Franklin began to rouse in her arms. Raising his head, he looked into her eyes. He was so innocent, so pure. He only made Naomi's heart ache more.

"I needs to take him out to do his business," Isaiah said.

"Where's his nightshirt?"

Isaiah picked it up off the floor. Holding it out to Naomi, he told her, "Ceceilia be tryin' to get him out from under the bed an' he come right outta his shirt. Couldn't none of us get it back on 'im."

Without much effort, Naomi put the nightshirt over Franklin's head. "You go out with your pappy, and I'll stay right here with you tonight," she said.

Before Isaiah took him, he went over to a wooden chest. "I still gots Ruth's night flannel. You be nice an' warm in it. If ya wants, you can put it on whilst we're at the privy." He reached over and took Franklin out of her arms.

"Let me go first," Naomi said, "then I'll change while you're out."

Isaiah nodded, and she quickly headed outside.

Late into the night, Naomi remained awake, holding Franklin, and staring up at the ceiling in the dim light of the fire. Isaiah softly snored on his pallet by the fireplace. She'd been cut to the core by his obvious high esteem of her virtue. He couldn't have been further from the truth. She closed her eyes and took in a long breath. *Oh, Jesus, please save me.*

Chapter 30

Naomi's resolve to be a better woman completely vanished the moment Samuel Hawkins came riding down the plantation drive in his carriage. By that evening, she was lying beside him on the rug in front of his fire, wearing one of his shirts. There was simply no way to resist the man she loved so deeply.

As May approached, Naomi had no idea how the household slaves had not the slightest inkling of what was going on upstairs. People's minds could be so easily fooled. After that one night in Isaiah's cabin on Christmas eve, no one had any reason to believe anything other than the fact that Naomi and Isaiah were in love. It troubled Isaiah to no end, but Naomi had asked him not to give any explanations to those who asked— simply ignore all the talk. Naomi constantly assured him that she was not hurt by it.

Spring cleaning had been going on for weeks. Abigail wanted the house to be in top shape for the arrival of the children and their aunt. Amelia Hawkins Bordeaux was coming for a visit. Her husband was Senator John Owen Bordeaux, who was currently living in the family's second residence in Washington, D.C.

The household staff lined the front walkway on their greatly anticipated day of arrival. Naomi tried desperately not to glance at Samuel, standing handsomely out front as the Bordeaux carriage made its way down the long drive. Master Joseph galloped ahead of the small caravan. Micah took control of Joseph's mount when he leapt to the ground and into his father's arms.

"Look at you," Samuel said, holding his son by the shoulders. "You've grown another foot since March."

Joseph laughed. "I wish."

Just then the carriage came to a halt beside the pair. William was the first to disembark, hugging Samuel with his naturally reserved demeanor. But Naomi was shocked to see little Catherine with her blonde curls bobbing, as she ran from Violet into her papa's waiting arms. She had changed the most, from just an infant to a walking, talking toddler.

Seeing little Catherine in Samuel's arms did something to Naomi. The child looked so much like Elizabeth. Naomi experienced utter shame for her behavior with this precious child's father. Feeling physically ill, she nearly turned to leave but feared the others would notice.

When Mistress Bordeaux appeared in the carriage doorway, Samuel held out his hand to assist her. He kissed both of her cheeks, and she smiled at him warmly. Naomi immediately noticed what she was wearing—how the cut of her dress accentuated her fine figure. Her face was handsome and her dark hair the same color as her brother's. She was a striking woman, who seemed to command the attention of everyone within her sphere.

"I'm so glad to have you here," Samuel told her. "I wish my niece and nephew had been able to accompany you."

Amelia took her younger brother's arm as they turned toward the steps of the house. Naomi could just make out her answer. "Well you know how persuasive John Owen can be. He insisted that Susan and Walker join him in D.C. for the month of

June. So it looks like I'll be living the country life with you for the next month. I'll be joining them in D.C. in July," she concluded.

Naomi had to admit it felt invigorating to have a full house once again. The place had seemed so forlorn at times without Isabella's exuberance and Elizabeth's genuine interest in the lives of those around her. It was hard to believe that, in a few days, it would be exactly one year since the dreadful accident that had taken them all away.

Walking around to the back of the house with the kitchen slaves, Naomi wondered what her dear ones would think of her now. She cringed at the very thought. She had worked so hard to keep those feelings buried deep inside.

Amelia Bordeaux had not been in the house long before Abigail came to Naomi's room. "Mistress Bordeaux would like to see you."

"Me?" Naomi asked in surprise.

"As soon as we got her settled in, she was askin' for you." Abigail eyed Naomi with curiosity. "You reckon she wants you to whip up a gown for her?"

Naomi merely shook her head. "Well, if that's the case, she certainly isn't wasting any time."

Abigail gave Naomi a cautious glance. "Just in case you didn't know, she's in Mistress Elizabeth's room."

Naomi greatly appreciated the forewarning. She hadn't even thought about where Samuel's sister would be staying. "Thank you for that," she told Abigail. "I assume she's in the sitting room."

"She is," Abigail said, before heading down the hall.

Taking in a guarded breath, Naomi headed up the back stairs. She glanced at the door to Samuel's room and suddenly realized the upstairs would be teeming with life. She would definitely stay in her own quarters tonight—and maybe longer.

When Naomi knocked on the sitting room door, she was instantly beckoned inside. Mistress Bordeaux was sitting on the sofa in the exact position where Elizabeth had always reclined. Naomi felt her heart squeeze with yet another reminder of her dear Elizabeth's death.

"You're Naomi?" Amelia inquired.

"Yes, ma'am."

Amelia's mouth dropped wide. "You're more beautiful than I was led to believe."

Naomi had no idea how to respond to such praise from a virtual stranger. "Thank you," she said softly.

When Amelia continued to look her over, Naomi asked, "Is there something I can help you with, Mistress Bordeaux?"

"You're very . . . articulate as well."

Naomi felt her cheeks grow warm. This woman had no qualms about speaking her mind. Once again, she responded with a quiet, "Thank you."

Amelia's eyes slowly narrowed. "Sit down," she ordered. "We need to get to know one another."

Immediately Naomi's heart took off at a gallop. Why would Samuel's sister be insistent upon meeting her so soon after arriving? Having no other choice, Naomi took a seat in the chair across from her.

"My brother told me about you," Amelia began. "But he certainly didn't do you justice."

Naomi could feel her cheeks reaching a new level of heat. Surely Samuel hadn't told his sister about their relationship. But at the moment, she feared that's what Amelia was intimating. That is, until the woman revealed her true purpose.

"I haven't talked to my brother about this yet, but my personal slave fell ill just before our trip from Nashville. I had to leave her at home. So, as you can see, I'm without a companion while I'm here. You will fit my needs perfectly."

Now it was Naomi's turn to drop her mouth open. She instantly closed it, realizing how that must look. Everything within Naomi screamed, *I am no one's slave!* She had the right to refuse this woman, but not without talking to Samuel first. He obviously hadn't shared her situation with his sister.

Humbling herself, Naomi simply said, "I will be glad to serve you, Mistress."

Amelia babbled on, mostly about the new gown that she wanted Naomi to make for her. Naomi, however, heard very little of her *new mistress'* chatter. She was feeling overwhelmed by the sudden demands being placed upon her.

"What do you think?" Amelia asked, drawing Naomi back from her despairing thoughts.

"I'm sorry, Mistress, I . . . I'm afraid I didn't hear what you said."

"Too busy dreaming of what you'll create for me, I see."

"Yes, ma'am. I'm sorry," Naomi quickly agreed.

"I was saying that I'll be attending the Independence Day Ball in Washington, D.C. I can't wait to see what you come up with. Samuel told me about your incredible gift. He said Elizabeth and Isabella were the envy of every party."

Naomi's head continued to spin out of control, but at least she was able to respond. "It will be my pleasure to create just the right gown for you, Mistress."

Amelia beamed in delight. "We'll get started first thing in the morning. But for now, help me get out of this travel outfit. I need a nap in the worst way. It's impossible to sleep in a carriage. You can come back to help me dress for dinner."

Swallowing back her pride, Naomi stood up. "Yes, ma'am. Right this way."

❧❦❧

That night, Naomi got into bed feeling a heavy burden of dread. Though she looked forward to creating a new ball gown after such a long hiatus, being Amelia's personal companion was going to be exhausting in multiple ways. She suddenly wished Amelia Bordeaux and Samuel's children had stayed in Nashville.

Naomi turned her head at a scratching sound on the floor, followed by a light knock. With a furrowed brow, she got out of bed. Just before opening the door, her foot stepped on something. A paper had been slipped beneath her door. Picking it up off the floor, she cautiously cracked the door open. No one was there.

Lighting a candle, Naomi set it on her sewing table and sat down. The note was from Samuel.

Meet me in the garden as soon as you can. I'll wait all night if I have to. S

Without a moment's hesitation, Naomi got dressed. Blowing out her candle, she silently left her room and tiptoed through the kitchen. Once outside, her feet instinctively led her to the back gate of the garden. He was there waiting for her.

"Samuel." Naomi said his name in relief. He was the only person in the world she wanted to be with right now, in spite of the fact that he was the source of her emotional turmoil.

He took her in his arms and held her close. "I'm so sorry for what my sister did to you. She completely overstepped her bounds."

Naomi looked up into his face. "I'm more than happy to make her a ball gown, Samuel. It's just—"

"I know," he interrupted. "The nerve of her taking you for her own without even talking to me. She got an earful from me at dinner tonight, believe me."

Naomi smiled just thinking about it. "Really?"

He slid his arm around her waist and led her deeper into the garden. "I told her she had no right coming into my house taking whomever she wanted for her own."

"What did she say about that?"

"She huffed a bit. Amelia always loved to boss me around when we were growing up. I told her she was welcome to choose another companion other than you."

Naomi immediately stopped and turned to him. "Will she be suspicious of your reasons?"

"Not at all," he said. "I told her you wouldn't have enough time to tend to all of her needs *and* create the gown of her dreams. But Naomi, if you don't want to make her a ball gown, you don't have to. Just say the word."

"Oh, no," Naomi responded emphatically. "I'm actually excited about this new project. It was . . . well, the rest of it was overwhelming, to say the least."

"I can only imagine how that made you feel," he said, as they continued to walk. "I'm sorry." When Naomi released a sigh, he turned to face her. "What is it?"

"I think we need to sit and talk about everything," she told him.

Immediately Samuel led her to the bench beneath the chestnut trees. A warm breeze rustled the leaves overhead. When he moved in close to her side, she inched away. Even in the dark, she could see the worry lines on his face. "Naomi, if I've done something to—"

"No," she declared, cutting him off. "You've done nothing to hurt me. It's just that all of these circumstances have caused me to think about everything that's going on in my life."

The bewilderment in his voice was obvious. "What do you mean?"

"Samuel, I don't think you'll ever begin to understand how I feel right now. I'm a free woman, but if I ever decided to leave here and start a new life somewhere else, it would be an almost impossible task. A woman of my heritage has no place in this white man's world—free or not." When he started to speak, she raised her hand and pressed it to his chest. "Please don't say anything. Just hear me out."

He solemnly nodded.

"Today, when Amelia treated me as a slave, giving me orders as if she owned me—I can't tell you what that did to me. It was like the person I am didn't even exist." She then gestured between the two of them. "And then, there's this."

Now Samuel looked panicked. He couldn't be silent any longer. "There's what? You and me? Naomi, please tell me you're not leaving me," he begged. "Please."

Naomi immediately reached for his hand. Turning it upward, she kissed his palm. "I'm not sure about anything, Samuel, but I think it's important for you to know how I feel right now."

When she released his hand, he quietly said, "I'm listening."

"I love you with all my heart—truly I do. The fact that you pledged your love to me and gave me this ring. . . ." She pulled the chain from beneath her bodice. "I can't tell you how that made me feel. But you will never be free to marry me. And Samuel, that is all I want right now. More than anything in the world, I want to be your wife. But that too is impossible."

Samuel leaned forward on the bench, placing his head in his hands. While they had been together for over eight months, they had never discussed what the future might look like for both of them.

"Am I destined to be your mistress for the rest of my life?" Naomi asked fervidly.

After taking in a ragged breath, Samuel sat up and looked her fully in the face. "Naomi, I can't live without you. It's you who brought me back to life when I thought everything inside of me was dead. You are the very breath in my lungs."

"And yet, here we are, sneaking around in the dark behind everyone's backs."

For a long time, the two sat silently, side-by-side, without touching one another. Finally, Samuel spoke. "I don't have an answer to this situation, but I want to do what's best for you. Just tell me what that is."

Naomi looked away from him, knowing her words were about to cut him to the core, but she couldn't help how she felt. Looking back, she told him, "As long as your children are here with you, I cannot be. It is nothing but a betrayal to the memory of their mother."

"Naomi . . . their mother is gone," he breathed.

"I know," she said softly. "I just didn't realize how it would make me feel to see them again."

Samuel stood up and paced a few steps in front of the bench. Turning back, he said, "You know we can't marry, but I gave you the ring as a symbol of my commitment to you. We are bound together in our own way."

"But not in the eyes of God or anyone else," she responded softly.

Samuel sat back down on the bench with a look of absolute misery. Naomi knew he was in pain—she was too. Here she was in the very garden where she used to pour out her heart to the Father above. She was sitting beneath the trees that symbolized chastity and honesty. This had been her sanctuary of prayer. And now, it had become a clandestine place to meet her lover. She was seared at the very center of her being with shame.

"Then what's the answer?" he asked.

"We need to separate," she simply told him.

"For how long?"

"I don't know." Naomi's voice was but a whisper. "I just can't do this while your children are here." She reached up and removed the chain from around her neck, holding it out to him.

Samuel looked at her in disbelief. "What are you doing?" He refused to take it from her.

She slipped it into the front pocket of his shirt before he could stop her. He pulled it out as if it were a burning coal. Both of her hands instantly covered his, not allowing him to give it back.

For a long time, they sat gazing into each other's troubled eyes. Naomi finally leaned down and kissed his hand then came to her feet.

Samuel immediately stood up. "Naomi, please stay with me. We can talk about this—"

"No," she interrupted, shaking her head. "This is the right thing to do. I have a lot to think about, and I can't do that when I'm with you." Softly brushing her knuckles on his cheek, she whispered, "I'm so sorry."

When she turned to leave, Samuel said her name with such deep emotion Naomi almost turned back. But her desire to make things right with her heavenly Father compelled her feet to move determinedly forward.

Chapter 31

O n her third day working with Amelia Bordeaux, Naomi was able to show her the beautiful royal blue taffeta material just in from Lexington. The two women had spent the previous two days sketching out the perfect gown for Amelia's figure. It would have a scoop back with a bateau neckline and a ruffled waistline across the back.

"I would like to add some embroidery work along the left shoulder and chest, then continue it from your right hip down the right thigh. It will be in a lighter shade of blue, but I want to throw in a hint of red and white at your shoulder and waist in honor of Independence Day."

Mistress Bordeaux's admiration for Naomi's creative talent was evident. "This is more than I could've imagined," she said breathlessly.

Just then, a knock sounded on the sitting-room door. "Come in," Amelia called.

Samuel opened the door and strode into the room. Naomi automatically rose to her feet.

"I'm sorry," Samuel stammered. "I didn't realize you were . . . in the middle of something."

Amelia's face beamed. "You're not interrupting. Come look at what Naomi is going to create for me."

Naomi felt like all the air had been sucked out of the room. Her face flushed intensely as he stepped closer. His eyes barely scanned Naomi's work of art. "That looks very nice, Amelia." Then, clearing his throat, he said, "I'm taking the boys into Lexington to a thoroughbred auction. We won't be back until tomorrow evening. I just wanted you to know why we won't be at dinner tonight."

Amelia shooed him with her hand toward the door. "Go see the horses with your boys. Naomi and I plan to relish having no men around for a while. Isn't that right, Naomi?"

Naomi realized all of her attention had been rapt on Samuel. She hadn't seen him since that night in the garden, and he didn't look well. His eyes seemed hollow—they were lined by dark circles.

"Uh, yes, ma'am," was all Naomi could seem to muster.

For a brief moment, Amelia looked between Naomi and Samuel. Naomi instantly dropped her gaze to the floor.

"Well," Samuel breathed, "I'll leave you to your work."

"Have a safe trip," Amelia called after him.

He merely dipped his chin and left the room.

Naomi quickly turned back to her sketch and the bolt of taffeta material, but Amelia Bordeaux's attention had been drawn elsewhere. Naomi's intuition began giving off sharp warning signals.

"You know, my brother doesn't seem to be doing well for some reason. He was so happy back in March when he visited Nashville. Come to think of it, he was in fine spirits when I arrived with the children just four days ago."

Naomi refused to be pulled into Amelia's speculation. She unraveled some of the material from the bolt and draped it across the woman's shoulder. "This is the perfect color for you," she said.

Amelia Bordeaux wasn't biting. She pierced Naomi with a shrewd gaze. "You're not his slave, are you?"

"Master Hawkins has owned me since the very day I was born on this plantation." Just saying it made Naomi wince inwardly. Now she could add liar to her list of sins.

Amelia let the material slide off of her shoulder. "Why do you think he's doing so poorly all of a sudden?"

"Mistress, it's none of my business—"

"No, I'm curious to hear what you think is going on right now."

Naomi released a deep breath, knowing that if she was going to play this woman's game, she would need to play it well. "I believe he's grieving terribly over the loss of his wife and daughter. We all feel terrible for him. Are you aware that tomorrow marks one year since the accident?"

Looking mortified, Amelia leaned back on the sofa. "Oh, dear. I mistook your look upon him as one of. . . ." Her sentence trailed away. Then, sitting forward, she said aloud, more to herself than to Naomi, "How could I have been so insensitive?"

Naomi busied herself with the taffeta, winding it neatly back onto the bolt. She needed to escape this room and Samuel's sister in the worst way. But she would have to wait to be dismissed.

Fortunately, Mistress Bordeaux waved her away. "You can go now, Naomi. I imagine you have a lot to do."

Naomi dipped her head. "Yes, ma'am," then left the room with all haste.

⟡⟡⟡

The next morning, Naomi was up long before the songbirds. Not even Mamie and the kitchen slaves had roused from their slumber. With Samuel away, Naomi had spent the past evening in the garden. She begged God to forgive her for being so weak and wanton. While she knew her heavenly Father was a God of forgiveness, she struggled with forgiving herself. She felt so unclean.

When Naomi had awoken so early this morning, she knew exactly what the Spirit was leading her to do. Taking a towel, she headed out the back door and down the road she and Isaiah had travelled on horseback. By the time she made it to the trail in the woods at the back of the plantation property, the pale light of dawn guided her through the thick trees.

Hearing the gurgling stream, Naomi's steps slowed. She left the wide trail and made her way to the edge of the water. Carefully stepping over a few small boulders and a fallen tree, she finally came to a deeper pool.

Naomi gazed at her reflection in the dark water before removing her shoes and all of her clothing. She walked into the stream, letting the cool water engulf her body.

Tears immediately filled her eyes, and she began to weep. She wept for the loss of her dear ones, Ruth and Elizabeth, Sarah and Isabella. She wept for the loss of her innocence and purity. She wept for the life of deception that she had been living.

"Oh, my Father," she cried out. "Cleanse me from my sins. Wash me, and I shall be whiter than snow."

Naomi took in a deep breath and bent her knees, plunging her entire body beneath the surface. When she arose from the depths, she turned her face toward heaven. "Thank you, Jesus," she whispered with tears continuing to pour from her eyes.

Naomi stood in the water until this new reality was planted firmly within her heart. She would never again give herself to Samuel. Her body would be a living sacrifice to God.

❧❦❧

With Amelia Bordeaux's departure for Washington quickly approaching, Naomi spent longer than normal hours working on the Independence Day gown. Considering all of the extra needlework, it had turned out to be her most challenging endeavor yet. In reality, Naomi was grateful for the commission and its short deadline. It had kept her hands and mind completely occupied and had delivered her from her weak-willed obsession with Samuel.

Hanging the dress on a rod near the window, Naomi inspected her needlework down the lower part of the gown. The midmorning sun provided optimal light as she trailed a slender finger along the intricate pattern. She smiled, realizing her creation was now complete. "Thank you, Lord," she said aloud, giving glory to the One who had gifted her so freely.

A knock sounded at her open door, and Naomi's attention immediately shifted from the finished gown. Surprised by her visitor, she lowered her eyes. "Mistress Bordeaux," she said. "I was just about to bring your gown upstairs."

Amelia Bordeaux's face held a look of awe, but strangely, her eyes were not on the gown. "The final fitting can wait," she said. "I have a carriage outside."

"The gown will be here when you return, Mistress."

"When *we* return," the mistress told her. "I would like for you to join me . . . please."

Naomi's heart quavered. There was something very odd about Amelia Bordeaux's demeanor. "Yes, ma'am," she said, then followed the woman through the house and out the front door.

A covered carriage was standing in the drive with an elderly slave named Ben standing at the door. He bowed to the mistress, then offered his weathered hand to help her inside. When Naomi sat down opposite of her, Ben folded the carriage step and closed the door.

As the two horses trotted down the plantation drive, Mistress Bordeaux kept her gaze outside the open window. Finally, she turned her attention fully upon her companion. Amelia's manner toward Naomi had completely shifted. Even her voice seemed gentler than in all of their previous encounters. "In case you're wondering, we're not headed anywhere in particular. I've instructed our driver to take us wherever he likes for the next hour."

Naomi sat back nervously against the carriage bench, waiting for Mistress Bordeaux to reveal her mysterious purpose.

"May I speak with absolute candor, Naomi?"

"Of course, mistress."

Amelia Bordeaux shook her head. "No more *mistress*. Please call me Amelia."

Naomi's pulse quickened—tiny dots of perspiration broke out on her brow. She held her tongue, fearing Samuel's sister was trying to lead her into a trap.

Leaning forward in her seat, Amelia said, "Samuel has told me about the two of you."

Amelia's startling revelation felt like a slap to the face. Naomi could've literally come up with a thousand different scenarios for this carriage ride and still not thought of this one. "Mistress—"

Amelia's hand flew up. "No, I'll not have a free woman, whom my brother adores, call me *mistress*." The corners of her mouth turned slightly downward. "I can see that I've caught you completely off guard. How can I put you at ease?"

Naomi's hand instinctively reached for the ring that had hung around her neck for eight months, but it was gone. She pressed her hand tightly to her chest instead. "When did he tell you?" she managed to ask.

"Last night after dinner. I couldn't stand to see him in such a sad state, so I compelled him to tell me the truth."

"Did he tell you it's over?" Naomi asked.

"That's where it gets a little sticky. He's not sure if you're coming back to him."

Naomi replied unwaveringly. "I'm not."

"Why ever not? He told me you love him."

"Oh, I do, with all my heart. But…."

"But what?" Amelia asked, her eyes showing deep concern.

Although she didn't owe Samuel's sister an explanation, something compelled Naomi to try. "I realized I could no longer live as his mistress. He will never be free to marry someone like me. So, I've made the decision to try to please the Lord and not myself."

Amelia's brow dipped and she sat back against the cushioned seat. Both women stared at one another for a suspended moment. Finally, Amelia said, "You know, we really are a God-fearing family. But I must confess, we don't live out our faith day-to-day as we probably should. I find your faith quite admirable, Naomi."

Naomi quietly thanked her.

"That still leaves the two of you in a quandary. I would like to help if I can."

Naomi let out a soft sigh. "We are at an impasse, miss…I mean…Amelia. If Samuel were to marry me, he would be ruined. Most people would stop doing business with him altogether. And then there's your family. I'm sure Senator Bordeaux could scarcely afford such a scandal."

Amelia's eyes glimmered with admiration. "You are a remarkable woman, Naomi. I can see why my brother is completely enamored with you."

"And I with him," Naomi responded softly.

"You are absolutely right on all accounts. This system in which we live is neither fair to women nor the negro race." Amelia surprisingly reached for Naomi's hand. "I am deeply sorry. While there's nothing I can do about our system of government at the present, I can certainly change my own heart. Would you please forgive me for the way I've treated you?"

A tear slid from Naomi's eye. Never had she dreamed that a white woman would ask her for forgiveness. Her throat tightened with emotion. "Yes," she said, squeezing Amelia's hand in hers. "I forgive you."

Chapter 32

On the day Amelia Bordeaux was to leave for Washington, D.C., the house slaves rose from bed before dawn. The mistress was not to be late—she had to catch a stagecoach in Lexington by noon. From there, she would travel to Cincinnati to board a train that would take her to the nation's capital. Isaiah had been chosen to drive the carriage that would convey both Amelia and Samuel. Master Hawkins wanted to make sure his sister was well taken care of on the first leg of her journey.

While Samuel and Amelia were eating an early breakfast in the dining room, Naomi went upstairs to check on the new ball gown. While she had given explicit instructions for how it was to be packed, she wanted to make sure her directions had been followed. Finding everything in perfect order, Naomi left Amelia's room intending to take the back stairs. Just as she headed down, she was caught completely off guard. Samuel was on his way up.

For a moment, both of them froze. Their paths rarely crossed in the house, especially on the back staircase.

Samuel took in a slow breath and advanced three more steps. "Naomi," he said. His eyes held hers with a depth of emotion that stirred Naomi's passion. Being in this confined space with him would most certainly cause her heart to stumble. She could not afford to walk this tightrope of temptation and turned to leave.

Samuel took the steps two at a time. "Stop, please."

Before she could even step into the hallway, he had caught up to her. "I just need a word with you."

Naomi looked into his face boldly. "No," she asserted. "I cannot be alone with you."

"I only have a favor to ask. Please."

Naomi took another step backwards into the hall. She needed to put more space between them. The desire she felt deep within her soul was akin to agony.

At that very moment, Amelia appeared at the top of the main staircase and headed their way. "Come into my sitting room," she said. "Both of you." Her manner was so authoritative, Samuel and Naomi complied without question.

Once inside the sitting room, Amelia closed the door. "You two can talk here undisturbed. I have last-minute packing to do."

Amelia disappeared into the bedroom, closing the other door.

"Samuel, I have nothing to say." When Naomi turned to leave, he reached out for her arm. A charge of energy swept through her, but she immediately pulled back.

Samuel withdrew his hand. "I'm sorry, but this is important."

"Then speak."

"Will you meet me in the garden tonight?"

Naomi was already shaking her head. "No. I can't do this again."

"I promise—Naomi, look at me. I promise to respect you in every way. I just need to talk to you about something important."

With great reluctance, Naomi conceded. "All right, I'll meet you, but I won't go any further than the gate."

"I'll take that," he said in relief.

Naomi turned and hurried from the room. Without a doubt, she would be spending this day in prayer. If she was going to be able to resist the man she had loved more than life itself, she would need God's Spirit to shore her up.

Back in her room, Naomi decided to busy herself by cleaning up her sewing area. It was in disarray after her latest project. Almost immediately, a quiet knock sounded on the door. Amelia entered quickly and closed it behind her.

"I wanted to see you before I left."

"I would've come to you, Amelia."

A soft smile turned her lips. "I wanted to come to you." Amelia instantly closed the distance between them and drew her into an unexpected embrace. She held Naomi for a long moment. When she stepped back, Amelia took both of her hands. "You have become dear to me, Naomi. Please know that I want the best for you."

There was a slight tremor in Naomi's voice. "Thank you."

"Thank *you* for the exceptional work you did on my gown." She pressed Naomi's hands, then reached into her handbag and pulled out an envelope. Setting it on the sewing table, her smile broadened. "This is for you. I'll see you in a month when I come to collect the children."

Naomi stared after Amelia, who left the room as briskly as she had entered. While she had found a certain level of comfort with Amelia ever since her startling apology, she still questioned the woman's motives. Would she have asked for forgiveness had Naomi not been a free woman? Would Amelia Bordeaux be willing to apologize to any of her own slaves at home? She suspected not. Asking forgiveness of an enslaved person would oblige her to grant that individual their freedom.

Sitting down at the sewing table, Naomi fingered the thick envelope. She wasn't ready to open it. Her thoughts were drawn to the conversation she had initiated with Samuel several months ago. She had asked him if he would be willing to free his other slaves. Why should she be the only one who had been manumitted?

Samuel had listened intently. Naomi knew he had given her question a great deal of thought. But he had come back to her a few days later with an answer. He didn't think he could survive the loss of so many plantation workers, and he wasn't sure he could afford to pay all of them if they decided to stay. It was a tricky proposition, but Samuel had promised that he would continue to consider it.

Still lost in contemplation, Naomi turned over the envelope to break its seal, but she was stopped short. Amelia had written a message along the top: *Naomi, do not open this until tomorrow morning. Yours truly, Amelia.*

⋘⋙

Franklin broke away from the little pod of slave children on Mammy Lou's front porch and leapt into Naomi's arms. For as long as she lived, this would be one of the sweetest feelings in the world. Not sure if she would ever have a child of her own, Naomi savored every moment with this boy and the feel of him in her arms. She couldn't think of a better companion for the afternoon.

"Oh, my goodness. I think you get heavier every time I pick you up."

Franklin giggled and kissed her right on the mouth.

"Mammy, do you mind if I take him now?"

The old nanny's eyes crinkled deeply at the corners. "He be all yours, Naomi. Ain't no one that boy'd rather be with than you."

Naomi offered her a grateful smile. Then giving Franklin a tight squeeze, she lowered him to the ground. "I can't think of anyone I'd rather be with than you, little man." Taking his hand, they headed toward Isaiah's cabin.

"Hold on, now. You two best be comin' over here to see ole Eula." The white-haired slave sat in the shade of her porch, rocking and smoking a corncob pipe.

Franklin gripped Naomi's hand a little tighter. He was a bit wary of Eula. Naomi knew it could be for any number of reasons—the old woman's raspy voice or piercing black eyes or loud guffaws. Whatever it was, when Naomi sat down on the porch steps, the boy immediately crawled into her lap.

Eula discharged a cloud of smoke from her throat. "Franklin, whatchu been doin' today?"

Franklin immediately turned his face into Naomi's neck. She gently lifted his chin with her thumb and forefinger. "Tell Eula what you did at Mammy's today." But the boy only stared into Naomi's eyes, remaining silent.

Eula slowly stood up. "I got just the thing."

When she disappeared inside her cabin, Naomi kissed the top of Franklin's head. "There's no need to be afraid of Eula. She loves you just like Mammy does." She felt him relax in her arms until Eula hobbled back onto the porch.

"Here now, young'un. Ole Eula knows what you want." She leaned down and handed him a clean wet cloth, twisted around a small amount of sugar. "I know you ain't a babe no more, but I specs you can suck on this fer a while."

Franklin shyly reached out to take the sugar-tit. He wasted no time slipping it between his lips.

Naomi supported her back on the porch post as Eula lowered herself down into her chair. Thankfully, she had left her pipe inside the cabin.

"I hear-ed the massa's sister left early this mornin'. She sure had you hoppin' whilst she was here."

A wry smile crossed Naomi's lips. "She commissioned me to make her a ball gown to take to Washington. I've never made a gown on such short notice."

"Well, I reckon you made her a perty one." Eula set her rocker in motion, leaning her head back against the smooth hickory wood. "What's she like?"

"Now, Eula, you know I won't gossip."

Eula coughed out a laugh. "Gossip be when ya tell somethin' awful 'bout a person who ain't here. I ain't askin' ya fer that kind o' stuff. She like the massa?"

"In a lot of ways, yes. They do look alike—you can certainly tell they're related."

"What else? I swears this'll be just for ole Eula's ears."

Uncertain about the truth of that statement, Naomi decided to impart a bit of information Eula had probably already heard. "She loves her brother dearly. No doubt, Amelia has helped him get through his great sadness by taking care of his three children so well."

"See now. That weren't so hard to tell, were it?"

Naomi laughed out loud. "That's all you'll get from me."

Eula's eyes narrowed. "Only one more thing. How's come it be so easy fer ya to call the mistress by her first name?"

Unnerved by Eula's astute inquiry, Naomi tried to shrug it off. "Did I say that? I meant to say Mistress Bordeaux, of course."

"Uh, huh," Eula murmured, rocking a little slower than normal. "Well, I reckon the massa'll be missin' her now that she's gone."

"I suppose so," Naomi offered.

Eula changed the subject altogether. "You waitin' to have supper with Isaiah?"

"Yes, I wanted to be here for Franklin in case his pappy's late getting back from Lexington."

"Well, come on then. Let's get on back to the kitchen."

Naomi looked down at Franklin. He had completely sucked all the sugar out of the cloth. Climbing out of her lap, he surprisingly handed it back to Eula.

"Well, looky here," she cackled. "I won ya over with a little sugar." Eula looked as proud as a peacock, especially when Franklin gave her an adorable grin.

As the women busied themselves in the communal kitchen, Franklin climbed around on the woodpile outside. Eula wasted no time prying further into Naomi's business. "I's a wonderin' if any o' the kinfolk be talkin' to ya 'bout nature's ways."

Naomi could practically feel the blood pulsing through her veins. "Eula, what on earth are you talking about?"

Eula rested a knobby hand on Naomi's arm. "I specs I'll just come right out and say it. You knows there's ways o' not getting' yerself in the motherly way, don't ya?"

Caught completely off guard, Naomi nearly choked on a response. "Eula, I have no need for such—"

"Hush now. We all knows what's goin' on 'tween you and Isaiah. Alls I'm sayin' is, if'n you don't want no baby, you better listen up."

Feeling like a trapped animal, Naomi had no choice but to go along with Eula's discourse, no matter how intimate the details. Now that she had chosen a chaste path, she felt keenly responsible for Isaiah's reputation. It hadn't really bothered her until now. But like spilt molasses, there was no way to stop the deception from spreading. The truth about their relationship, or lack of one, would never be able to be contained.

Later that evening, Naomi found it extremely difficult to be with Isaiah. Her sense of guilt was so intense she struggled just to make conversation with him. Thankfully, he didn't seem to notice. He was too busy telling Franklin all about the sights of Lexington.

Balancing his son atop his knees, Isaiah went on. "And did ya know, there be six horses harnessed to that stagecoach? They's needin' all six of 'em to pull such a heavy load." After giving Franklin a few more details about the stagecoach, he turned his attention back to Naomi. "You sure we can't help ya clean up the supper dishes?"

"No, it's fine. Really." Naomi desperately needed something to keep her busy. "Why don't you two head out onto the porch? I'll join you in a bit."

Isaiah thanked her and ushered Franklin through the door.

With the two outside, Naomi finally allowed her mind to wander to the meeting with Samuel later tonight. While she was nervous about being alone with him again, she had to also acknowledge the thrill that had risen up within her. *Lord,* she prayed silently, *your word says that I will never be tempted beyond what I can bear—you've promised to always provide a way out. Please, I beg you, provide that way out for me tonight.*

Chapter 33

C ome with me to the chestnut trees," Samuel pleaded.
Naomi drew a deep breath and folded her arms against her body. "Samuel, I told you I won't go any further than this gate. If you even knew how difficult it is for me to be here alone with you, you wouldn't ask this of me."

He let out an exacerbated sigh. "I give you my word, I won't touch you…unless that's your wish."

She laughed. "And there lies the problem. That's my base desire. But you need to know this, I've made a vow to God, which I will not break again. He has forgiven me. Samuel, you can have that same forgiveness if you'll only accept it."

Samuel wiped a hand across his face. His voice became less insistent. "I want that too, more than you know. I just need your help getting there."

"Well, we can't get there by venturing into this dark garden alone. As a matter of fact, I should probably leave."

"No."

The desperation in Samuel's tone compelled Naomi to freeze. She softened her expression. "Whatever it is you intend to say to me must be said right here. Please respect me on this."

Without warning, Samuel dropped down to one knee. Opening his right hand, Naomi could see the gold chain with his ruby ring glimmering in the moonlight. With great emotion he offered his appeal. "Naomi, will you marry me?"

For a moment, Naomi wasn't sure of her next breath. Was she dreaming? She fell to her knees in front of him. "I don't understand. How could you possibly take me as your wife?"

"Amelia helped me work through it—she showed me how it would be possible."

"Please tell me," Naomi urged.

"It's a bit complicated, but I promise it can be done. Do you trust me?" His eyes shone with irresistible sincerity, even in the scarce light.

Naomi suddenly felt a peace enter her soul that hadn't been there before. "I do," she said.

"Then will you be my wife?"

This time, there was no hesitation. "I will."

Relief seemed to wash over the pair as Samuel placed the chain about her neck. She took the ring in her hand and kissed it. Then, without thought, she leaned forward and pressed a tender kiss to Samuel's lips. True to his word, he kept his hands from touching her.

When Naomi withdrew, she softly laughed. "Let's stand up. I need to be in your arms."

Samuel immediately offered her his hand along with a generous smile, and they came to their feet. Naomi willingly stepped into his familiar embrace. She had missed his physical touch beyond words, but this time it was different. She would remain pure and holy until the day Samuel became her husband in the eyes of God.

❧❦❧

The next morning Naomi awoke to a note beneath her door.

Please join me on a ride today while everyone is at the noon meal and resting. I'll be waiting on the trail behind Micah's cabin. No one will see us leave from there. I love you deeply and forever. S

Naomi held the note to her breast. Nine months ago, she had shamelessly lost her way, but now her heart soared to heights unimaginable. Reading the note again, she was reminded of the envelope Amelia had left on her sewing table yesterday morning. With intense curiosity, Naomi broke the seal.

The envelope was filled with money, more than Naomi had anticipated. One thing could be said about Samuel's sister—she was indeed generous. A letter had also been enclosed.

Dearest Naomi,

By now, Samuel has hopefully offered you his proposal of marriage. I do pray that you have said yes to him for numerous reasons. First and foremost, I know how happy you will make my brother. His life seems utterly adrift without you. I fear that we might have lost him along with the others had it not been for you. Thank you, my dear, for bringing him back to us. And secondly, I want you to know that I will be most proud to become your sister. I'm counting on you to change our family in due course. Please be patient with us as we navigate these uncharted waters. But for now, it is my great honor to help you and Samuel start your new life together. I look forward to being with you at the end of this month.

With genuine affection for you,
Amelia

❧❦❧

When Naomi exited the upper kitchen before noon, she knew the house slaves would believe she was on her way to slave town. They had become accustomed to her dividing time between the big house and her kinfolk. Had anyone been slightly more observant, they would've noticed an extra spring in her step—a joy that she could scarcely contain.

Rounding a curve in the trail, Naomi's heart squeezed with emotion. The sight of Samuel overwhelmed her. He would soon be her husband.

Immediately, he came to her side, leaving the two horses tethered to a low-hanging branch. At first, he seemed hesitant to touch his intended. Naomi determinedly took the lead. Pulling his head down to hers, she kissed him boldly.

"Mm, that was nice," Samuel said, sliding his arms around her waist. "How about one more before we take a ride?"

Naomi's lips turned upward in a stunning smile. "Just one," she said, then drew him into an even longer kiss.

When it ended, Samuel was breathless. He simply took her hand and led her to their waiting mounts.

"What? No female saddle?" she exclaimed.

Samuel shook his head. "I didn't want anyone to be suspicious. I hope you don't mind riding astride."

"Actually, I prefer it," she told him. "But tell me about the horse you've chosen."

Putting his hand on the small of her back, Samuel led her to the bay mare. "Naomi, meet Amaryllis."

Naomi stroked her glistening neck. "Amaryllis, you're as beautiful as your name. Is she gentle?"

"Only the best for my future wife. Are you ready?"

Naomi nodded, then allowed him to help her mount up. Samuel held the reins taut while Naomi settled into the saddle and got her skirt situated. After setting the stirrups for her, he mounted his horse and patted his saddlebag. "I told Mamie to make me a big lunch. You don't mind splitting it with me, do you?"

"That sounds wonderful…Samuel, this is wonderful." She made a sweeping motion with her arm. Naomi hadn't felt this free since the day of her manumission. She actually allowed herself to start imagining what the future might hold for them.

At a leisurely pace, the horses meandered along the wooded trail while Samuel and Naomi conversed of nothing other than their mutual adoration for one another. They laughed and bantered back and forth, enjoying each other's company in a way they never had before.

Coming out of the woods, Samuel led them through a lush bluegrass pasture, then up a hill along a winding path. A small stand of trees crowned the hill, and he told her, "From up here, you can see nearly half of the plantation."

Inside the shade of the small grove of trees, Samuel dismounted and tethered his horse. Naomi was just about to swing her leg over the saddle when he came to her side. "Please, allow me." He took hold of her waist with two strong hands and lifted her to the ground. While Naomi wanted to linger there, she was well aware of her effect on him. She would need to be careful not to draw them back into a snare before they could properly wed.

Instead, she stepped away, slipping the reins over Amaryllis' head, and tying her next to Samuel's mount. He had already removed the saddlebag and started spreading a quilt near the edge of the shade. "This spot will give you the best view of our land." He captured Naomi's gaze with a sparkle in his eye. He had not called it his land, but theirs.

Sitting down, he reached into the other side of the bag, pulling out the food Mamie had prepared. "Ah, fried chicken with okra and biscuits. Do you think we'll survive on that?"

Naomi sat down beside him on the quilt. "We can try," she teased.

Before they started eating, Naomi reached for Samuel's hand. "Would you mind if we ask a blessing over the food?"

Samuel glanced down at his hand in hers and rubbed his thumb across her knuckles. "I'd like that." When he looked up, his eyes were moist. "Would you say it?"

She brought his hand to her lips, then down into her lap. Bowing their heads, she simply thanked their heavenly Father for all that he had provided and asked him to guide their way.

"Thank you, Naomi." Samuel cleared his throat, then told her if she wanted that chicken leg, she'd better get it fast.

"Is that your favorite piece?"

"Not if it's yours," he said with a sly grin.

Naomi laughed. "This is glorious. We have so much to learn about each other. Just think, this is our first meal together."

"And in the daylight, no less," he added, bouncing his eyebrows at her.

"Oh, Samuel. I never dreamed that we could be together like this."

His grin widened. "You have two seconds to get that chicken leg before it's gone."

She snatched it up and took one bite, then handed it to him. "We'll share it."

Naomi thought his laugh was the most wonderful sound she had ever heard.

When the lunch had been devoured, Samuel lounged beside Naomi, pointing out various landmarks on the plantation. "And see at the other end of that field of hay, that's where the corn starts. Of course, the hill next to us is where the family cemetery is."

For a while, the two somberly reflected on the memories of their loved ones. It had been a long and trying year, the likes of which neither wanted to experience again.

Naomi laid down on her back beside him. "How are we ever going to pull this off, Samuel?" She reached up and brushed back the stray hair on his forehead.

Resting on one elbow, he caressed her arm tenderly. "When Amelia comes back from Washington, she's going to commission you to make a new gown for her daughter Susan. You and I will accompany all of them back to Nashville. She's working on finding the perfect minister to marry us there. Of course, Amelia will be our only witness, as we can't even let the children know what's going on."

Naomi felt trepidation for the first time since being with Samuel today. "Are you sure about this, Samuel? I want you to be absolutely—"

He leaned down and kissed her, cutting off her next words. For a long moment only their mouths touched, as he made it very clear how certain he was about their future.

When he pulled away, she smiled. "Just checking."

He laid down on his back beside her. The warm afternoon shade lulled them into a comfortable state of relaxation. Naomi rolled onto her side, laying her head on his shoulder and draping her arm across his chest.

"What about children?" she asked.

Naomi's question was met with utter silence. If not for the change in his breathing, she would've thought Samuel had gone to sleep. But it was obvious that her words had stirred something within him.

Taking a cautious sip of air, Naomi rose up to look into his face. Samuel's eyes met hers with an expression akin to grief. Her brow immediately dipped. "What's wrong?"

"Naomi," he said hoarsely. "There must be no children."

Chapter 34

Naomi cherished every moment with Samuel leading up to their marriage. It was all so different than before. So pure. So right. She and Samuel purposely met one another during the day, slipping away to share a noon meal or going on rides to remote areas of the plantation. A few times, they even took walks in the garden before sunset. It all seemed perfect, save for one significant detail—Samuel's feelings about having a child.

There must be no children. Naomi couldn't seem to clear that one phrase from her thoughts. It was always lurking somewhere in the back of her mind. Her desire to be a mother was a strong one. Other than becoming his wife, there was nothing she wanted more than to bear Samuel's child. But perhaps she was incapable of having children. After all, she and Samuel had spent eight months together without precautions before Naomi had broken off their relationship.

If not for Eula's straightforward tutorial, Naomi wouldn't have had a clue how to prevent the conception of a child. However, on this particular morning, while Samuel was away for the day on business, Naomi nervously made her way to the healer's cabin.

Eliza the healer lived in the center of slave town where she was easily accessible to all of the women on the plantation, especially to those birthing babies. Eliza was not the same type of healer as Henry. She was strictly known for her female cures and remedies as well as midwifery.

Naomi stopped to ask directions from a small gathering of candlemakers. Their job was not an easy one on a hot June day such as this one. At least they had a lean-to roof over their heads to keep the direct sun off. Several children helped in the operation, collecting bayberries while the women dipped and molded the candles. Each of the women had hiked their skirts up and tucked them into their waistbands to keep them from catching fire over the flaming coals beneath the tub of wax.

"Where might I find Eliza?" Naomi called.

One of the slaves wiped her chin across the top of her shoulder as the sweat slid down her jaw. "That be her place over yonder." The woman merely tilted her head in the direction of Eliza's cabin.

After thanking her, Naomi made her way to the cabin door and knocked.

A voice called from within. "Hold on a minute, I got someone with me. Have a seat on the porch."

Naomi turned and looked back towards the group of women making candles. Every now and then, one of the slaves would look up with a curious glance. No doubt there would be gossip after she went in with the healer. It almost caused Naomi to lose her nerve and head back to the big house. But at that very moment, Eliza's door swung open. A very pregnant woman stepped out onto the porch, using one hand to support her back.

"I expect to be birthin' that young'un in three days' time. Just you wait and see," Eliza told her.

Naomi tried to give the expectant mother an encouraging smile, but it didn't seem to help the woman who was in obvious discomfort.

The healer turned inquisitive eyes on her new visitor. "What can I do for ya?"

Naomi stared at Eliza in shock, causing the healer to chortle. "You were expectin' someone a whole lot older than this, weren't you?"

"How old are you?" Naomi couldn't help but ask.

"Well, I'm none too certain. But if I was to guess, I'd say about your age, maybe younger." Eliza gave her a wide grin. "Do you happen to know how old you are?"

"Yes, I'm twenty-seven years," Naomi told her.

"Sounds about right. Let's go inside and you can tell me what you came for."

Swallowing back her anxiety, Naomi followed Eliza into the cabin. It was notably larger than the other cabins with an extra room on the back. Because of her great significance to the health of the female slaves, she had most likely been given a larger space to live in and work from.

Eliza pointed to a chair. "Have a sit-down and tell me what you need."

After Naomi was seated, Eliza pulled a chair right up in front of her so they were sitting practically knee to knee. For some reason, the young woman's close proximity gave Naomi a reassurance she hadn't felt earlier. "I'm in need of…well, I don't want…." Naomi's face felt flush, she didn't realize how difficult this would be.

Before she could try to convey her need, Eliza leaned forward and placed both hands on Naomi's thighs. "Are you wanting to keep a baby from comin' into this world?"

Naomi closed her eyes. That was just the opposite of her heart's true desire, yet it was entirely the reason for her visit. "Yes," she said quietly.

"You're Naomi, aren't you?"

Naomi's brow furrowed. "How did you know?"

Eliza's lips gave an upward tilt. "Everyone knows who you are. But I got somethin' to ask you before we get into this. Are you bein' used at the big house?"

A small gasp escaped Naomi's throat. "Oh, no, nothing like that. The master is a good man."

"I thought as much. We all fear the massa just like we fear the Lord. But…some are scared that somethin' might've changed him after the terrible loss."

This was getting a whole lot more personal than Naomi had anticipated. She didn't want to sit here and deceive Eliza, yet she had no choice but to rely on the healer's expertise.

"You need to speak the truth to me. Do you already have a baby inside you?"

Naomi slowly shook her head. "No…I just need to prevent that from happening."

Eliza patted Naomi's legs and sat back in her chair. "I got just what you need if you're not wantin' to produce offspring." Eliza rose from her chair and went to her row of shelves along the far wall. "Just so you know," she spoke over her shoulder, "you're not the only one. There's plenty who don't want to bring a babe into this world and make him a slave for the massa. Course, if you were needin' more help with your work and love your man, well, it makes sense to go on and add some extra hands to the family. But I expect that's not the case for you, is it?"

Naomi simply answered, "No."

After a long moment, Eliza returned to her chair in front of Naomi. She opened a small, round tin full of seeds. "These are the seeds of the wild carrot—the fancy name is Queen Anne's Lace." She put a few in Naomi's hand. "That's how many you need to chew. They'll do the trick."

Curious, Naomi asked, "When do I take them?"

For the next few minutes, Eliza explained how the seeds would work in her body and when to ingest them. "Now don't you go gatherin' these seeds by yourself. There's other plants out there that look just like the one these come from, but they're poisonous." She scooped the seeds from Naomi's palm and put them back inside the tin. "Come 'ere, I'll show you somethin'."

Naomi followed Eliza through the back door and into an extensive herbal garden. Some plants were growing in pots, while others were sprouting from the ground. Bamboo wind chimes heralded a soothing symphony, making it seem like a magical place.

"Looky here." Eliza squatted down in front of a patch of lacey white plants and Naomi joined her. "This is the real thing. See the fuzzy green stems? Smell 'em."

Bending close, Naomi caught the carroty scent.

Eliza spoke in a soft tone. "I'll take good care of you, Naomi. Come see me when you need more or if you're having trouble."

Both women stood. Naomi searched the healer's brown eyes reflecting the warmth of the sun. She knew unmistakably that this was a woman to be trusted.

"Thank you, I will."

Naomi followed Eliza around to the front of her cabin. Every candlemaker looked up from her work. As smoothly as possible, Naomi slipped the tin of seeds into her skirt pocket, then headed for the big house.

◈◈◈

The Bordeaux residence in Nashville was even larger than the Hawkins Plantation house in Kentucky. While it was not far from the center of town, there was enough land around it to support a sizeable stable of horses and several slave cottages.

Naomi followed Amelia up the massive spiraling staircase to a large suite of rooms on the third floor. "The nursery used to be up here," she told Naomi. "Of course, it hasn't been used in years. We're not even using it for little Catherine. No one lives or works on the third floor any longer."

Opening a door at the end of the wide hall, Amelia ushered Naomi into a spacious room containing a large four-poster mahogany bed. After closing the door, she lowered her voice. "This will be for you and Samuel after your wedding. There's even a hidden staircase beside the room he is supposed to be occupying that leads straight up to this floor. You two can spend as much time as you like up here with no one to disturb you night or day. Of course, Samuel will need to make his bed downstairs look like it's been slept in every night."

Naomi knew her cheeks were glowing. She hadn't anticipated such a blatantly personal conversation with Samuel's sister, but Amelia thankfully was already moving on. "Come with me. I have something else you're going to love."

Down the hall, Amelia led her into another room bursting with light from several windows. A magnificent sewing table stood in the sunlight, its glossy surface beckoning Naomi to glide her hand along the smooth top. "This is beautiful." Naomi had never seen anything like it.

"I had it brought in just for you. Maybe you will have the opportunity to create many gowns in this space in the years to come."

A content smile spread across Naomi's face. "I like the sound of that."

Amelia stepped closer to Naomi's side at the sewing table. "I've told my slaves that you are not to be disturbed unless you need their help. Someone will bring your meals upstairs and leave them on the table outside your door. It may be a little lonely over the next few days until you and Samuel are wed."

"I'll be fine as long as I'm working on a gown for Susan," Naomi conceded. "I'd like to get started tomorrow morning if possible."

Amelia nodded. "I've already told her to give you her full cooperation. Of course, I'll be with you as well."

"Of course." Naomi looked around and realized everything she would need was already available in this room. All Amelia Bordeaux had to do was speak, and her wishes were granted.

"Now," Amelia said, taking hold of Naomi's arm. "I'll allow you to get your bearings and have supper sent up to you in an hour. Later tonight, Samuel and I will join you in your sitting room to discuss plans for your wedding."

Naomi was suddenly overwhelmed with gratitude for this woman. It would've been so easy for her to deny this relationship between her brother and a former slave. And yet here she was, fully embracing it and working out all the intricate details. "Thank you for all of this, Amelia. Samuel and I owe you a great debt."

"Nonsense. It's the right thing to do. Besides, I am beyond thrilled for the two of you."

The two women shared a warm embrace, then Amelia left to let Naomi settle into her new surroundings.

That night in Naomi's sitting room, Samuel held her hand possessively as they sat on the sofa facing Amelia. "With a bit of discreet correspondence, while I was in D.C., I've found just the right man to perform the ceremony. Daniel Ward is an abolitionist minister out of Hendersonville. That's a good twenty miles from here, but he's willing to meet us halfway. I have directions to a small, country church near Dry Creek where he often preaches. His wife, Juliette, will be with him."

Naomi turned her face upward toward Samuel's. "Tell me this isn't a dream."

"It's not a dream, Naomi. We're about to become husband and wife." He leaned down and kissed her forehead, then turned his attention back to Amelia. "How are we going to pull this off? The three of us can't just head out together on Saturday morning for a carriage ride."

Amelia let out an amused laugh. "No, we can't. But you can leave on horseback whenever you like. You don't have to answer to anyone, not even your own sons. Naomi and I will leave shortly afterward in the buggy on a shopping trip. I hope you don't mind driving," she said, giving Naomi a sympathetic gaze.

"That won't bother me a bit. I'll do whatever needs to be done." She would swim all the way across the Cumberland River if that's what it took to finally marry Samuel.

"Then it's settled. I'll leave you two for now." Amelia came to her feet causing Samuel to do the same. After his sister said good-night and left the room, Samuel sat back down.

"I hope you don't mind if I stay longer," he said, giving her a sly grin.

Naomi looked into the depths of his eyes. There was nothing more she would rather do than spend the night in his arms, but just being alone with him in a secluded room was far too great a temptation. She inched away from him. "I'm not sure that's such a good idea right now."

He laughed and moved to the chair Amelia had vacated. "Maybe we could just talk for a while," he offered.

Naomi's smile was an eager one. "I'd like that."

Samuel, however, cast her a more serious gaze. "I haven't had a chance to ask you how things went with the healer. Will you be protected from childbearing?"

A sharp pain instantly stabbed Naomi's heart. Samuel simply had no idea the havoc he was inflicting upon her emotions. She felt the heat rise up behind her eyes and feared she would start crying.

When she didn't immediately respond, he said, "Naomi, if this is too personal, I understand. You don't have to tell me about it if you—"

"No, it's not that," she interrupted, wringing her hands in her lap. "I guess I need help understanding why you feel the way you do about children. I want nothing more than to bear your child."

Samuel's features melted into a look of concern. "Oh, Naomi, I've been so thoughtless. I should've talked to you about this a long time ago."

Tears suddenly spilled over her long lashes. There was no holding them back.

Samuel left his chair and sat down beside her again. He took her anxious hands into his. "Naomi, there are so many reasons why we shouldn't have a baby if we're going to keep this marriage a secret. If you suddenly became pregnant, it could be devastating for us. I hope you understand I'm trying desperately to protect us."

She let out a heavy sigh and accepted the handkerchief he pulled from his pocket. Of course, Samuel was right. How could she have gotten so carried away with thoughts of bearing a child? Her maternal instincts had completely overruled her practicality. "Samuel, I should be apologizing to you. I've allowed myself to wander down an unwise path. I'm truly sorry."

Giving her a compassionate smile, he drew her into his side and spoke tenderly into her ear. "Maybe someday it will be possible for us to bring a child into this world—I would love nothing more."

Naomi relaxed into his side, giving rise to hope once more. But his next words left her reeling.

"But, if we brought a child into this world now, he or she would have to be enslaved."

Chapter 35

J uliette Ward descended the two steps of the Dry Creek church building, waving to the buggy on the road.

"This is it," Amelia said, touching Naomi's elbow.

Naomi turned the horse onto a dirt trail leading up to the small, cabin-like building. She noticed Samuel's horse tethered near a water trough and couldn't hold back a wave of pure joy. In mere minutes, she would be married to her heart's one desire.

Naomi was instantly drawn to the middle-aged woman with the friendly smile. Instead of addressing Amelia first, she came to Naomi's side and offered her a hand down from the buggy. It must've been an afront to Amelia, but when Naomi glanced her way, Amelia seemed unfazed.

"I'm Juliette Ward, Daniel's wife, and you must be Naomi." The woman continued holding Naomi's hand in warm welcome.

"I am. And this is Mr. Hawkins' sister, Amelia Bordeaux." Naomi took a step back while the two women greeted one another.

When Amelia made a move toward the front door, Juliette raised a cautionary hand. "If you don't mind, Mrs. Bordeaux, we need to give the men a few more minutes. Daniel wanted to spend some time with Mr. Hawkins before the ceremony."

Amelia gave her a bemused look. "I assumed Samuel had already arrived long before we got here."

"Oh, he did," Juliette admitted. "They've been talking for nearly two hours."

"About what?"

Amelia's curiosity bordered on impertinence, which appeared to make Juliette uneasy. "Perhaps that's something for Mr. Hawkins to share with you at a later time."

Naomi laid a light hand on Amelia's arm while speaking to Juliette. "It's all right. We can wait as long as necessary." While she was every bit as curious about Samuel's visit with the minister, Naomi was willing to wait for him to reveal the purpose when he was ready.

Pointing to a bench on the porch, Juliette asked if they would like to have a seat until the men were done talking. "Maybe I can peek in and let them know you've arrived," she said.

That seemed to placate Amelia, but when Juliette opened the door, Amelia stepped inside right behind her. Naomi was quite aware that Amelia had not inherited the renowned Hawkins patience. It was obvious she was ready to take charge of the situation at hand.

Naomi sighed and took one step inside the door as well. Instantly, her heart fell. One look at Samuel's face bespoke of something dreadfully wrong. What if he had decided not to go through with the marriage after all? That had been a worrisome thought coursing through Naomi's mind ever since his proposal. She knew how difficult this marriage would be for him, despite his obvious love for her.

But there he was, her husband-to-be, sitting on the front pew with a downcast expression on his face. What had Mr. Ward said to cause such a discouraging countenance? She let out a tiny moan which drew Samuel's attention. When his troubled eyes met hers, Naomi thought she would weep. Immediately, she stepped back outside.

Rapid footsteps sounded on the wooden floor, and Naomi lowered herself onto the bench by the outer wall. Whatever Samuel had to say to her, she would need to be sitting down.

Striding onto the porch, Samuel quickly descended the two steps and searched the church yard with his gaze. Naomi knew she should let him know she was right behind him, but putting off the bad news seemed like a better option.

"Naomi," he called out frantically.

She sat completely still, remaining silent.

When he spun around, Samuel groaned in relief. "I thought you had changed your mind." He stepped up onto the porch and sat down beside her. "Are you all right?"

"Are you?" she asked. "What was going on in there?"

Samuel visibly relaxed. "It's a very long conversation that I plan to have with you tomorrow—or the next day. But for now, I plan to become your husband." The sparkle in his eye was irresistible.

Her gaze earnestly searched his. "You're absolutely sure about this? I don't want you to regret this marriage for the rest of your life."

A hearty laugh rumbled up from his chest. "Naomi, I plan to spend the rest of my life making you the happiest woman in the world. You are everything to me."

He abruptly dropped down to one knee and clasped her hand. "Will you please marry me now?"

Placing her free hand on the side of his face, Naomi thought her heart would burst with desire. "Yes," she said before passionately kissing his lips.

Daniel Ward tactfully cleared his throat. "Are you two about ready…or do you need a little more time?"

"We are," they both said eagerly.

The lanky preacher had a smile on his face and a glimmer in his eye. "Then follow me."

After the ceremony, the Wards joined Mr. and Mrs. Hawkins out on the porch. Amelia expressed her gratitude to the couple, then made her way to the buggy. Samuel offered his hand to Daniel. "I appreciate everything you've done for me today…and for us." He squeezed Naomi's hand in his.

Daniel Ward's face beamed. "I've never been more gratified to marry a couple than the two of you. Juliette and I will pray for you daily."

Naomi left her husband's side to hug the minister's wife. She found herself wrapped in a tight embrace. "If you are ever in need of a friend, Naomi, you know where to find me."

Juliette's sincerity warmed Naomi's heart thoroughly. It was nice to know there was someone to turn to if things should ever become difficult. Lord willing, she and Samuel would find a way to make this work. "Thank you," Naomi told the older woman, giving her a grateful smile.

Later that evening, Samuel and Naomi enjoyed a delicious dinner in Naomi's room on the third floor. Amelia had thought of every detail when it came to giving the newly married couple all that they would need. Privacy had been her top priority, but it was obvious that Amelia had also had a hand in the couple's first meal together.

Early the next morning, Naomi slipped out of bed, drawing back the heavy drapes on the nearest window. Faint light spilled into the room, giving her a clearer view of her husband soundly sleeping on his stomach. She smiled contentedly, taking his shirt from the back of a chair and putting it on. Overwhelmed with gratitude, she turned her gaze outside the window. *Oh Lord, you have given me far more than I deserve. Help me never take your blessings for granted.*

At that very moment, a pair of sturdy arms surrounded her body, and she leaned her head back into her husband's chest. "What are you thinking?" he asked in a husky voice.

"I was thinking how blessed I am." She started to turn in his arms, but he held her snugly up against him.

"Naomi, I'm the one who is blessed." He softly kissed the side of her neck. "You will be the one to save me."

She couldn't help but turn her face into his loving gaze. The earnestness in his voice had touched her very soul. "What do you mean?" she whispered.

But his answer came in the form of more tender kisses on her neck, causing her to completely forget that she'd even asked a question in the first place.

❧⁂❧

On their third day as husband and wife, Naomi knew she would have to kick this man out. He was thoroughly content to remain in her bedroom for the next week, but she had a gown to make, and this husband of hers was a major distraction.

"Samuel, if I don't start working on Susan's gown, we'll be here till Christmas."

His smile made him look like a scoundrel. "So."

Naomi rolled her eyes as she threw back the sheets. He reached for her wrist, but she deftly moved out of his grasp. "I mean it. After breakfast you need to find something to do. I'm sure your children have been wondering about you."

He turned over onto his back, clasping his hands behind his head. "You're forgetting my clever sister. I'm sure she's keeping the entire household occupied while we—"

"I mean it, Samuel. I have work to do."

He groaned good-naturedly and got out of bed. "All right, all right. I get the hint."

Naomi immediately pressed her forefinger to her lips. Both of them stood completely still until the breakfast tray was placed on the hall table and the sound of footsteps disappeared.

Samuel bounced his eyebrows. "That was a close one."

"Another reason why you need to make an appearance downstairs and I need to get into that sewing room."

After dressing, Samuel cracked the door open to check the hallway, then quietly went for the tray. Setting up breakfast on the small table in their room, he quipped, "They must think you eat like a horse."

She couldn't help but laugh. Nearly a double portion was being left in the hallway every day and not a bite left when the tray was returned to the table. Her reputation for eating would be hard to live down.

After Naomi asked the blessing, she sat back in her chair, watching Samuel divide up the food on their one plate.

"Would you like to use the fork or the spoon today, madam?"

When she didn't answer, he slowly placed the silverware beside the plate and leaned back. His voice took on a more serious tone. "It's time, isn't it?"

She nodded solemnly. "I need to know what you and Daniel Ward were discussing."

He hauled in a deep breath and rubbed his hand across his mouth. He seemed to be weighing his words carefully. "Our conversation was two-fold, really. He first wanted to know if I'd given my life to Christ."

Naomi immediately sat forward. Samuel had never been eager to discuss spiritual matters with her. But her strongest desire was to know the answer to that one question. Her voice was soft and imploring. "Have you?"

He didn't readily answer but looked down at his hands. When his eyes lifted, they held the appearance of bewilderment. "I don't know. I know that sounds strange, but maybe I did when I was a boy. I always believed in God, and I used to pray, but it's been so long ago. And then after the accident...I think I lost whatever faith I may have had."

Naomi's heart broke for him. His struggle was palpable. Her first impulse was to try to fix him somehow. She wanted to infuse him with words from the scriptures. But the Spirit compelled her to remain silent. She sensed that she would need to win him to the Lord over time. Today would be the beginning of a very long race—one that Naomi eagerly yearned to run with him.

"The other part of our discussion was much more complicated." He looked down again, his face turning a light shade of red.

After the space of several breaths, Naomi couldn't hold back. She went to him, kneeling beside his chair. Their hands found each other as did their eyes. "You can tell me anything, Samuel. We'll work through whatever this is together."

He leaned his forehead down onto hers, then reached beneath her arms and pulled her into his lap. Her arms encircled his neck, and she laid her head on his shoulder. "Tell me," she whispered.

When Samuel finally spoke, his voice was strained. "Daniel told me that surrendering my life to Christ would come at a cost." His hands drew Naomi a little tighter. "If I was truly going to follow Jesus, then how could I possibly own my fellow brothers and sisters?"

Oh, Lord, Naomi prayed within her soul, *don't let this be the stumbling block that keeps his heart from you.*

The two of them stayed in that same position until the breakfast had long grown cold. Naomi knew that this was a decision Samuel would have to come to on his own. They had discussed it once before, but that had been months ago. One thing was certain, Daniel Ward was right. How could anyone follow Jesus while cruelly enslaving another human being?

The longer Samuel held her the further Naomi carried her thoughts. Even though she had become his wife, she certainly hadn't become a slave owner.

Or had she?

Her chest constricted painfully, and that one ominous question suddenly terrified her beyond words.

Chapter 36

Coming home to the Hawkins Plantation was much harder than Naomi could've imagined. If she had been bewildered by her sudden gift of freedom a year ago, it had been nothing in comparison to her torment over owning slaves. How had this monumental issue never entered her mind? While she wasn't the mistress of the plantation in the way that Elizabeth had been, she was still Samuel's wife. She was one with him in every way. But not in this—she could not be complicit in this one thing.

Naomi knew that she would need to press Samuel persistently, but it would have to be done gracefully. A well-placed word. A thoughtful story. A scripture verse like the one in Galatians that said, *There is neither Jew nor Greek, there is neither slave nor free, there is neither male nor female; for you are all one in Christ Jesus.* Even her dreams were haunted. She could find no true peace until her husband laid down his life to Christ and freed his slaves.

Every morning, as she awoke in her husband's bed and slipped back down to her room, she whispered, *For such a time as this.* God had allowed her to enter in this covenant of marriage with an influential man for such a time as this. *Whatever it takes, Lord,* she prayed every morning. *Use me to turn Samuel's heart to you and free our sisters and brothers.*

❧ ❧ ❧

By December, Naomi began to detect a softening of her husband's heart. With colder weather upon them, he not only allowed her to talk more freely about spiritual matters, but Samuel also showed great delight while she read the scriptures by the fire on long winter evenings.

Naomi closed her mother's Bible and looked at the man she deeply loved. He was sitting beside her on the sofa and seemed lost in his own thoughts. "Do you want to talk about the passage?" she asked.

The corner of his mouth turned upward. "I think I was a little distracted tonight."

Putting her Bible on the end table, Naomi scooted up to Samuel's side. He wasted no time pulling the soft quilt over her and surrounding her with his arms. "What are you thinking about?" she asked.

He took in a deep breath and released it slowly. "I received a letter from Amelia today. They're in the midst of a hard winter. They've already had two severe ice storms that haven't even melted away yet." His voice took on a tone of disappointment. "She suggested we stay home this Christmas."

Naomi put her hand on his thigh and sat up. "And not be with the children for Christmas? How do you feel about that?"

"I'm not happy about it, but she suggested we come in the spring. Amelia said she'll need a new gown by then, and she won't worry so much about us being on the road as she would now."

Naomi's head dropped back down to his shoulder. "I'm so sorry. I know how much you were looking forward to your time with the children."

"Maybe it's not such a bad thing," he said. "Perhaps we could plan a big celebration here on the plantation."

His statement surprised her. "Are you ready to start entertaining again?"

"No, definitely not that kind of celebration. I'm talking about for our slaves."

While Naomi's heart leapt at the thought of a Christmas celebration with more than two hundred souls on the Hawkins Plantation, her heart was struck a hard blow when he referred to the slaves as *our* slaves. She couldn't let it pass. Raising up to look into his eyes, she said, "Samuel, they're your slaves, not mine."

He swallowed hard, then looked toward the fire. His breathing became shallow as he appeared to be grappling with his wife's words. Without moving his gaze back to hers, he said, "You're right. I don't know how I didn't realize that before now."

Naomi silently thanked the Lord for cracking open a closed door within his heart. God had blessed this moment with an eternal purpose. She prayed that Samuel would keep talking about it without her having to push him.

"You must think your husband is an insensitive man."

He sounded so dejected; Naomi moved out of his arms completely. "I think no such thing. It didn't even occur to me until after we were already married."

"You don't regret marrying me, do you?"

She laughed softly. "Not in the least. Please don't ever think that again." She leaned up and brushed a sweet kiss on his lips.

The slow smile he gave her was hard to resist, but she wanted to keep him talking. "I know that as your wife what belongs to you also belongs to me, but I refuse to take ownership of the human beings on our plantation."

"I understand," he said thoughtfully. "And I'm working on it. I'm working on a lot of things. It's just going to take some time." Now it was his turn to lower his mouth to hers. After a long moment, he pulled back slightly, his warm breath on her lips. "Keep being patient with me, my love."

"Always," she whispered, drawing his mouth back to hers.

᭪᭬᭪

Three giant bonfires blazed along the road from slave town to the plantation house at midday. Each one was in an area with no overhanging trees. A small band of fiddles and African drums played within a few yards of the middle blaze, and nearly every able-bodied person on the plantation was dancing. Some had a partner, while others frolicked in jubilant clusters. Children played and danced among the throng—the sound of boisterous merriment must have resounded for miles around.

Five long tables of food stood nearest the plantation house. Mamie and her kitchen staff had outdone themselves and so had Naomi. She worked from early morning Christmas Eve to Christmas Day without rest, determined that this would be a celebration like none that her people had ever experienced.

Lugging a huge platter of ham to one of the tables, Naomi wiped the perspiration from her brow. Christmas had turned out to be a mild, overcast day, perfect for an outdoor celebration. She searched the crowd for her husband, finally spotting him near the second bonfire. He was clapping his hands to the lively music. Occasionally, he patted someone on the shoulder or conversed with one of his slaves. Her heart nearly leapt from her chest with gratitude for the changes God was steadily making in his life.

Someone cleared their throat nearby, drawing Naomi's attention away from Samuel. Isaiah stepped into her view. He was wearing his nicest suit, the one she remembered seeing on the night of the gala, which now seemed ages ago.

"Naomi," he said earnestly. "You been workin' way too hard. I's thinkin' you need to enjoy some o' this merry-makin'." He held his hand out to her.

She was already shaking her head. "I couldn't possibly leave Mamie with all this work."

"Oh, sure ya can, child!" Mamie had come right up beside her, fists pressed hard to her hips. "Now go on. Shoo!"

When Naomi started to argue, Mamie grabbed her hand and forced it into Isaiah's. He immediately clamped his hand securely around hers. "You heard the woman. Les go 'fore we gets her upset."

"Uh, huh, that's right," Mamie crooned.

But Naomi had ideas of her own. "Then you're coming with us!" She grabbed Mamie's hand and pulled her along too.

Mamie let out a robust hoot and allowed herself to be dragged into the swarm.

Naomi was immediately caught up in the music and revelry. While she would much prefer to be dancing with her husband, Isaiah was the next best thing. She did worry what Samuel would think if he should see her, but she threw caution to the wind. She'd worked far too hard for the past two days, and this was a welcome distraction.

Isaiah's hand clasped hers while his other rested on her hip, and he twirled her about to the rhythm of the music. It must've been half an hour before the music stopped, and Isaiah led Naomi out of the crowd while keeping his hand on the small of her back. She noticed numerous heads turning their way, including that of Eliza, the young healer. She suddenly felt sorry for Isaiah. His reputation was being tainted by her, but he was as much aware of what they were saying as she was. Naomi felt guilty for the charade that she was forced to play and longed for the day when her relationship with Samuel could be made known. *Lord, haste that day.*

Isaiah led her to a large log that had been placed on the side of the road, and they sat down together. He moved closer to her side than usual, but Naomi's lack of sleep left her oblivious to that fact. The longer she sat there the sleepier she became. Her head listed toward Isaiah and landed against his strong shoulder.

᎒᎒᎒

Carefully looking down, Isaiah couldn't help but stare at her while she slept. He had never seen such a beautiful woman in all his days. Knowing how she felt about him hadn't deterred his desire for her in the least. He prayed constantly that her heart would soften and she would come to him. He inwardly vowed that if that day should arrive, he would treat her like a queen for the rest of her days.

After a while, Isaiah spotted Franklin coming their way. He held a finger to his lips, and the boy smiled sweetly. "She be sleepin', little man. Les try not to wake her."

Franklin stepped in between his pappy's legs and leaned against him, never taking his eyes off of Naomi. Isaiah half-smiled. His boy was as smitten with her as he was. She would make such a fine mother for him.

Looking out over the crowd, Isaiah noticed Massa Hawkins watching them. Something about the massa's eyes made him uneasy. But at that very moment, Franklin laid his head on Naomi's lap, causing her to rouse.

"Oh, there's my boy," she said sleepily. "Come 'ere and sit with me." Naomi sat upright and pulled Franklin onto her lap. She kissed his neck, causing him to giggle.

Naomi hugged Franklin snuggly to her breast, much the same way Ruth had when she was still alive. Isaiah hadn't moved from his position, but Naomi scooted over slightly. She must've realized how there had been no space between them.

After playing with Franklin for a while, she looked up at Isaiah. "Thank you so much for making me take a break. This was nice." She lowered Franklin to the ground and stood up. "I'll come by for supper sometime next week."

"You sure you won't stay a while longer? We's enjoyin' your company."

Naomi's eyes searched the crowd for a moment, then turned back to his. "I'm sorry, I really should get back to Mamie. I'll see you soon." She leaned down and kissed Franklin, then both Isaiah and his son watched her walk all the way back to the big house.

⋙⋘

Samuel had stayed at the celebration until well after dark. Micah finally told him to get inside; he would tend to the fires until they were burned out and all the slaves were back in their quarters.

Naomi had already washed in her room and headed straight up the back stairs into her husband's bed. She must've fallen asleep because the next thing she remembered was wakening to Samuel gently kissing her shoulder and neck.

"Oh, did I wake you?" he teased.

Her answer was a bit lethargic. "Yes, you did, mister. But I'm glad." She pulled him down to her.

Samuel raised his head and looked into her eyes. "Are you sure about this? You've been up for two straight days."

"I'm absolutely sure." She laughed softly in his ear. "Just try not to be upset if I don't remember this in the morning."

Chapter 37

Naomi had been sick for days. She'd done her best to hide that fact from Samuel, but she began to worry about passing the illness on to him. It was time for her to seek out Eliza.

Tugging her shawl close, Naomi now wished she'd worn something more substantial. The late January wind seemed to slice right through her. At least the chilly air held her nausea at bay. Hopefully, Eliza would have something she could take to settle her stomach.

The young healer opened her door before Naomi even had a chance to knock.

"Come sit by my fire and warm yourself, Naomi." She even brought a quilt over to cover her legs. As she'd done before, Eliza drew her chair right up to Naomi and laid her hands on the top of her thighs.

Naomi could feel the extraordinary spirit emanating from this woman. It brought a much-needed comfort.

"You're feeling sickly, aren't you?"

"How did you know?"

"Your colorin' doesn't seem right. Your face is pale. Tell me what you've been dealin' with."

Naomi's spine straightened. "I can't seem to keep anything down. I can hardly even bear to look at food right now, much less eat it."

Eliza's eyes narrowed. "How long has this been goin' on?"

"All this week. I think it started last Saturday."

"In the mornin'?" Eliza asked, leaning in a bit closer.

"Mostly, but sometimes in the afternoon too. Thankfully, I've been feeling better by evening."

Eliza's eyes took on a softness that brought out an unexpected emotion in Naomi. She could feel tears welling up for no apparent reason.

"Naomi, I need to ask if you've been chewin' the wild carrot seeds I gave you."

Without the slightest hesitation she answered, "Yes."

"Every time?"

"Yes…why?"

"Have you had your cycle this month?"

Naomi's mouth dropped open, and she pressed her back into the chair. Closing her eyes, she whispered, "No." Then, letting out a soft moan, she said, "Now that I think back, there is one night that I forgot to chew the seeds."

"I'm thinkin' Christmas."

Eliza's ability to see right into her was uncanny. The one night she had forgotten to take precaution was indeed when Samuel had awakened her on Christmas. A tear slid down her cheek. "Am I with child?"

"I'd say more than likely."

The emotions roiling through Naomi were almost more than she could handle. Part of her wanted to shout praises to God above, while the other part of her wanted to lay down and die.

"I could examine you, if you like, just to make sure."

All Naomi could do was nod her head, releasing more tears onto her cheeks.

Eliza brushed them away with the back of her hand, then stood up. "Bring the quilt. We'll go in the back room."

After the healer's examination, she helped Naomi sit up. "Let's go back to the fire and talk a while."

Feeling completely numb, Naomi followed her back to where their conversation had begun. With Eliza's hands atop her legs, Naomi asked her, "Am I?"

Eliza's expression was both comforting and distressing. "You are, but no more than four weeks at the most, plus a couple of days if we're countin' from Christmas. You have a choice, you know. If you don't want this baby, I have exactly what you need to take."

Just the thought of doing such a thing made Naomi's stomach churn. She lurched, and Eliza was quick to grab a bucket. Naomi emptied the meager contents of her stomach into the bucket and accepted a clean cloth to wipe her mouth.

For a long moment, Eliza observed her patient with great interest. "Course, you could marry him, you know. Most of the unattached women in slave town would give anything for Isaiah just to look their way."

The sound that came from Naomi's throat was part sob part mirth. If Eliza only knew. She wished she had the luxury of telling her everything. Naomi desperately needed someone to share this burden with. But for the time being, her only choice was to tell Samuel. The very thought of doing so made her nauseous all over again.

A knock sounded on the healer's door, and Eliza called out, "Are you dyin'?"

"No," the voice answered.

"Then give me a minute. I'll be right out."

The sound of footsteps shuffling across the porch and the creak of the bench was Naomi's cue to leave. She stood up, Eliza rising with her.

"Would you like me to give you something to take, Naomi?"

Naomi shook her head. "I can't make that decision right now." She expelled a deep breath. "I need to think and pray."

Eliza tenderly held her arm and walked her to the door. "Don't take too long. It gets lots harder as time goes by. Come back in the mornin' if you want to talk about it."

"I will," Naomi said before stepping out into the chilly afternoon.

༄·༇·༄

That night, Naomi sat in a daze on the end of the sofa. She couldn't even open the Bible in her lap. Samuel looked worried but didn't seem to know what to do. He had already asked if she wanted to read a passage but received no response. When he asked if she'd rather talk, her eyes stared at him blankly.

Finally, he reached for her hand. "Are you feeling sick?"

She gazed into his deep brown eyes, wondering how to give him the news. This would be devastating as far as he was concerned. Naomi struggled with whether to take the herbs Eliza had offered and keep Samuel from having to bear the burden of killing their child. But everything within her rebelled against it. Their child was growing inside of her. How could she possibly make a decision to end its life?

"I *am* feeling sick," she admitted. "But not in the way you think."

His brow pressed downward. "Has something happened, Naomi? Please tell me."

There was no way to soften the blow. Her voice held a tremor when she told him the startling news. "I'm with child."

Instantly, his hand withdrew from hers. If the look in his eyes was any indication of what was about to come out of his mouth, Naomi didn't want to hear it. She had to deliberately keep herself from fleeing the room.

"That can't be." He raked a hand through his hair. "I thought you were taking something for that."

"I was."

"Did you stop?" His voice bordered on accusation.

"No, Samuel, I didn't stop...on purpose."

He suddenly stood up. "What do you mean?"

"Please, sit back down," she begged. "We just need to talk through this."

A cynical laugh escaped his throat. "Did you expect me to be happy about this? I can't sit here and have a conversation about this knowing it will ruin us."

"Samuel, the Lord will give us strength to—"

"The Lord?" he mimicked. "Naomi, God has done nothing but make my life miserable. He's taken away everything I loved."

Samuel could have plunged a knife directly through the middle of her heart and not caused as much pain as that one statement. It was so hurtful she didn't even know how to respond. She sat without emotion—it's as though his very words had killed her.

He stepped across the sitting room with his hands on the top of his head. His back was to her as he stared into the fire. All Naomi could do was pray, *Lord, help us.*

Samuel stood there for so long Naomi was finally able to find her voice. Tears began to spill from her eyes. "Have I made your life that miserable?"

When he turned around, he too was crying. "Never," he said. "You are everything to me. You are my love." He went to her and dropped down to his knees. "I should never have said that. Can you forgive me?"

She cupped his face in her hands and leaned her forehead into his, but the damage had been done. Naomi gave no response.

"Please, I'm begging you to forgive me." He was now openly weeping and sat back on his heels. "I have this...this darkness still inside me. You're the only...light in my life."

"Samuel," she said softly, "the only thing that's good in me—the only light is from the Lord. Let him fill you."

He sent his hands back through his hair and let out a deep sigh. "I'm trying."

Samuel gave Naomi his handkerchief, then went into the bedroom and retrieved another for himself. When he came back into the sitting room, he took a seat in the chair across from her. Naomi could feel the chasm between them. She didn't know if it could be breached.

"Samuel, I have a child growing inside of me. Our child."

He closed his eyes, releasing more tears. "Go to the healer. She'll take care of the situation."

"There has to be a way...."

"Naomi, I told you from the beginning we couldn't bring a child into the world. Not now, and I'm sorry to say, maybe not ever. You have to take care of this before it's too late."

She sat in stunned silence. As far as she was concerned, it was already too late. But his mind was set, and he had made it obvious there was nothing she could say to change it. The shattering pain in her chest overwhelmed her.

When she stood up, Samuel came to his feet as well. But instead of going into the bedroom, she headed for the door. His voice sounded desperate. "Where are you going?"

Letting out a languid sigh, she said, "I'll sleep downstairs tonight."

Samuel was at her side before she could reach the door. "No, my love. Please stay with me. I'm sorry for what this is doing to you." He tenderly caressed her arm. "Stay. I just want to sleep beside you tonight."

Even though she needed desperately to pray, she didn't want to be alone either. Giving in to his plea, she turned to him, feeling a deep sadness. Their gazes held for the space of several breaths before Samuel lifted her gently into his arms and carried her into the other room.

∽♥∾

Eliza rose before dawn, knowing Naomi would be early today. She could feel it in her bones. After eating her usual gruel, she hung a pot of water over the fire and was adding her favorite herbal tea with leaves of mint when a light knock interrupted the silence. "Come in," she called from her place by the hearth.

This morning, Naomi had protected herself against the late winter chill. She was wearing a heavy wool coat and scarf that covered her hair and neck.

"Come warm yourself by the fire and we'll have some tea."

Taking off her outer wraps, Naomi quickly made her way to the source of the cabin's warmth.

Eliza pointed to the waiting chair. "Tea'll be ready in a bit."

Before the healer could even pull her chair into position, Naomi spilled the contents of her heart. "He wants me to get rid of the baby."

In all her years as a healer, Eliza had never seen such a look in another woman's eyes. She knew in that moment the baby didn't belong to Isaiah. It was another man's.

Eliza laid her hands on Naomi's thighs. "Before you do it, I think you need to unburden yourself of more than what's been conceived."

Naomi's chair scraped against the floor, and she stood up, backing away. "How do you know so much about me?"

"I don't mean to scare you. I'm sorry." Eliza patted the chair. "Sit back down, I won't push you. Only tell me what you can."

A relieved look washed over Naomi's face, and she slowly came back to the chair in front of the fire. "Could you please not touch me right now? It seems like you know what I'm going to say before I say it."

Eliza put both hands in the air. Her lips tipped into a smile. "I think what you need right now is a friend you can trust." Out of habit, she started to put her hands back onto Naomi's legs but caught herself and clasped them in her lap instead. "Whatever is said in this room is never spoken of again by me. If you want me to help you carry your heavy load, please let me do it. I care about you, Naomi, and I want you to make the decision that's best for you."

A tear escaped Naomi's eye. "There is no decision that will be best for me."

Something about Naomi's statement gave Eliza the clue she'd been searching for. She leaned forward in her chair but didn't touch her. "You don't belong, do you?"

Naomi's eyes grew wide. "What do you mean?"

"I'm thinkin' you don't belong in slave town nor the big house."

A crimson color worked its way up Naomi's neck and onto her cheeks. Eliza could literally feel the spirit of confusion battling inside of her. Forgetting restraint, she laid her hands back on top of Naomi's legs. Naomi instantly covered them with her own.

"I can't do this alone," she whispered.

Eliza slid in closer. "I would die first before telling anyone else your secret. Let me help you."

Naomi's beautiful eyes held hers for a long moment, then looked away toward the fire. For an instant, Eliza thought she would share whatever was on her heart. But when Naomi looked back, her chin tilted upward. "I can't."

A quiet sigh escaped from Eliza's throat. She patted Naomi's legs and sat back. "It's not my way to beg. But know this, I'll be here when you're ready."

⚜

Making her way through slave town, Naomi decided to stop by to see if Eula and Solomon needed help with the noon meal. Maybe she could share this meal with Franklin. She didn't know when she would feel like eating with him again, but for now, her stomach seemed to be settled. Perhaps it was the herbal tea Eliza had given her.

Sliding her hand into her coat pocket, Naomi felt the leather pouch that held the bark of the cotton root. While she could chew it as it was, Eliza had told her how to brew it into a tea and drink several cups in the course of the day. She quickly took her hand away—the feel of it made her heartsick. Eliza had told her it would produce the desired results within a day's time.

Eula kept a close eye on her companion but never asked about her despondent disposition. Naomi was grateful to work in silence, allowing her mind to think through the grim decision that had been forced upon her. A few times she had to dab away the warm tears that came without warning, but she was able to disguise her action as if she were wiping her brow.

When all preparations were done, Naomi knew she wouldn't be able to stay and eat with her kinfolk. She couldn't live with the acute anxiety any longer.

"Nay!"

The welcome sound of that little voice pulled her up short. Franklin was running toward her with open arms. She bent to his level and took the full impact of his body against her own. Today, she hugged him tighter. Held him dearer within her heart. Felt his arms bring healing and peace. He was a much-needed refuge for this moment, and she drank him in.

Thankfully, Isaiah hadn't come from the stables, so Naomi sat with Franklin while he ate. When he was done, she kissed him lovingly and headed for the big house, her hand nervously stroking the soft leather pouch in her pocket.

Chapter 38

S amuel didn't say anything when he slipped into her bed. Naomi scooted as close to the wall as she possibly could to give him room. Her husband took up most of the tiny space. His arms encircled her body with great tenderness, bringing a welcome warmth to a frigid day.

Neither one spoke as she lay in his arms. Naomi was grateful for his silence. Samuel's words would've heaped an extra weight upon her unscalable mountain of guilt.

Night after night, Samuel came to her. And in the day, while all of the slaves were resting and eating, the two found a way to be together for conversation. But in all the month of February, not a word was ever spoken about the child they had conceived. Only once did Naomi tell him, "I will come to you when its time." He had given her such a compassionate look. "Only come when you're ready." Naomi admired his patience and prayed with all her heart that it would continue.

As the days rolled on toward spring, Naomi constantly felt herself drifting between two worlds—the world of slavery and the world of freedom. Eliza had been astute in her observation. Truthfully, she didn't fully belong to either. But even more so, her life had taken on a surreal quality, hovering somewhere between the temporal and the ethereal. She couldn't seem to reconcile one with the other.

In the second week of March, Samuel opened the door to his bedroom. He had been unbuttoning his shirt, and his hands immediately froze. For a long moment, he remained still, until his eyes took on a sparkling glimmer. His voice was low and husky. "Are you sure about this?"

Naomi slipped out of bed and finished unbuttoning her husband's shirt, tugging it off of his shoulders and letting it drop to the floor. "I'm sure," she said, drawing his mouth down to hers.

Nearly two weeks later in the dead of night, Samuel sat straight up in bed. Naomi immediately awoke and turned over. He had been cuddling close behind her, his arm draped across her abdomen.

"What is it?" she asked drowsily. "Did you have a nightmare?"

He didn't answer. Naomi thought he must still be asleep. She gently laid her hand on his chest, urging him to lay back down. But he was taking shallow breaths, she could feel his heart racing wildly.

Scooting away from her, he dropped his feet to the floor on the other side of the bed and raised the wick on the oil lamp. When Naomi saw the expression on his face, it scared her. Something was horribly wrong.

"What have you done?" he whispered.

A shockwave of heat rose up through Naomi's core and flooded her face. Her chest rose and fell rapidly—every breath threatened to choke her. She knew the time had been quickly approaching, but not now, not like this. She had practiced her words a hundred times, waiting for just the right moment. And this most certainly was not it.

Naomi swallowed hard, knowing there was nothing she could say to ease the obvious tension. She had betrayed her husband with her silence. She didn't blame him if he never spoke to her again. Truthfully, she feared that he would divorce her and send her away. Maybe that's what she deserved.

"You're still carrying the child," he said, not hiding his incredulity. He wiped his hands across his face. "I felt it move."

Naomi briefly closed her eyes, drawing in a deep breath while searching for the words she had rehearsed. "Samuel, I prayed fervently for God to help me do the right thing. I came so close to taking the remedy." The memory of that fateful day came rushing back, threatening to demoralize her. Naomi had stopped by Ruth's prayer log and opened the leather pouch. She poured the cotton root bark into her hand, ready to ingest it until something bizarre happened. It had actually felt like the palm of her hand was on fire. There had been no time to put the bark back inside the pouch. Naomi threw it across the clearing before she could stop herself.

"Why didn't you take it?" His voice had acquired a more severe tone.

Reminded of her ardent prayer on that day, she boldly answered her husband. "Samuel, God gave me the peace and strength to do *his* will…and not yours."

He let out a low huff. "I trusted you to take care of the situation. How could you have done this to me…to *us*?"

Samuel's reaction was everything she had feared, and yet, deep down inside, Naomi knew she had made the right decision. If only he could understand how she felt about the life growing within her.

Samuel bent forward, placing his head in his hands. Warily, Naomi scooted across the bed and laid her hand on his back. "I'm truly sorry I kept this from you for so long." She pressed her body up against him, resting the side of her face on his shoulder. She had intentionally waited past the time that the remedy would've been safe to take. "Can you find it in your heart to forgive me?"

The ticking of the clock on the mantle was the only sound in the room. Without turning to look at her, he said, "What you've done could undo everything I've worked for. I will forgive you, but you need to go back to the healer. There are still ways to take care of this."

Surely she had misheard him. Was he so willing to rid himself of the child which only a few moments ago he had felt moving beneath his hand? And was he prepared to put *her* very life at risk? Wasn't it he who should be asking forgiveness for asking her to do such a thing?

Letting her hand drop from his back, Naomi slid over to her side of the bed. She thought she was going to be sick. Slowly pulling the sheet over her body, she laid down facing away from him. She would never be able to express how deeply he had injured her.

When the lamp light was lowered, Samuel moved up close behind her again, gathering her into his arms. His breath was warm on her neck. "I love you," he whispered.

Naomi closed her eyes tightly and tears of anguish fell onto her pillow. She loved him deeply and unconditionally, but she had no way of expressing those words to him—not in this moment of heartbreak. *Oh, God, help him see things differently in the light of morning.*

But when the sun came up, Naomi was left in bed alone.

At ten minutes past noon, she slipped into Samuel's study unnoticed by the household slaves. Lunch had already been delivered, and he stood from the sofa when she entered. His eyes instantly roamed to her belly, causing Naomi to feel a sharp cramp.

He pointed to the food. "Sit and eat with me."

"I'm not hungry," she said, shaking her head.

"Then, please sit."

Nodding, Naomi deliberately sat close to him on the sofa. In one swift motion, she reached for his hand and laid it on her abdomen before he could withdraw. "Samuel, this baby was conceived on Christmas. Does that not hold meaning for you?"

At that very moment the baby flopped inside of her, causing them both to marvel at the movement. His reaction brought a hopeful smile to Naomi's face.

"I've never felt anything like that. Does it hurt?" he asked.

She looked at him in surprise. "Sometimes. Samuel, didn't you sit like this with Elizabeth when she was with child?"

His expression turned sheepish. "Never."

Naomi's brow wrinkled. "Why not?"

He shrugged. "Elizabeth didn't think it was proper."

For a while, they sat in silence, contemplating the woman they had both loved. Then Samuel said, "I think I've come up with a solution."

Naomi immediately sat a little straighter, wondering what her husband might offer.

"At first I thought about Daniel and Juliette Ward. I know they would be so happy to take you in while you're with child. But…."

"But what? I would be willing to go to them," she said eagerly.

"And they would no doubt be glad to have you. But as their friends, we can't put them in jeopardy. We already did that when Daniel agreed to marry us. What he did was illegal."

Naomi sighed deeply, realizing how much they owed the Wards. She would never want to put them in any danger.

Samuel continued resting his hand on Naomi's midsection. "What if you go to Amelia until the baby is born? You would have all the privacy you need, plus access to the best doctors in Nashville. It might solve all of our problems."

While Naomi didn't relish the thought of being hidden away in seclusion, she quickly warmed to the idea. It could definitely be an answer for the short term.

But within two days' time, an unexpected letter arrived from Nashville. Senator Bordeaux had taken seriously ill, and while he was expected to recover, Amelia and the Bordeaux children were going to be with him in Washington. Apparently, the Senator's recuperation period was predicted to be a long one. In the meantime, all of the Hawkins children would be coming home.

That night, Samuel shared the news with Naomi as they talked in his sitting room. "I had hoped this would be the answer to our quandary, but since it's not, you'll need to go to the healer tomorrow."

In that very instant, Naomi knew that she would go to the healer, and when she did, she would not be coming back.

Chapter 39

With a sense of utter desolation, Naomi packed a carpet bag with her most needed belongings and left it in her sewing room at the big house. She had some ground to till with her kinfolk before moving into slave town. The conversation that was weighing most heavily on her mind was the one with Isaiah. He would be so disappointed in her. Oh, how she longed to tell him about her marriage to Samuel, but she couldn't risk it. No one must know.

While it wasn't yet obvious that she was carrying a child, it wouldn't be much longer. Before talking to any of her kinfolk, she first needed to have a visit with Eliza. Unless Eliza had already had one of her eerie premonitions, the healer had no idea that Naomi hadn't taken the cotton bark remedy two months prior.

When there was no answer to her knock, Naomi wandered around back to the herb garden. Eliza straightened at the sight of her.

"I wasn't expectin' to see you today." She immediately wiped her hands on the apron at her waist and came to Naomi's side. "Would you like to come in?"

Naomi glanced around to make sure they were alone. "If you need to keep working, we can talk out here."

Eliza intently studied Naomi's eyes, then she splayed her hand across Naomi's abdomen. "It didn't work, did it?"

Naomi didn't know why she even bothered to talk to the woman. Eliza practically knew everything before she could say it. With a sigh she told her, "I didn't take it."

Clasping her arm, Eliza led Naomi toward the back door. "I think we better get inside."

In the back room, Eliza handed her a quilt. "Get yourself undressed while I wash."

Taking a deep breath, Naomi did as she was told, all the while marveling at Eliza's gift as a seer and a healer. She wanted to know more about her and where the gifts had come from.

After the examination, Eliza told Naomi to get dressed and come to the front room.

"Is everything all right?" Naomi asked as they sat knee to knee.

"Well, I'm a little concerned about where the baby's sittin'. You're carryin' it a bit high for goin' on four months. Has it been hurtin' ya?"

Naomi had to admit there had been discomfort. Her brow furrowed deeply. "Is that a bad thing?"

"Not always. I'm sure it'll drop down soon. We'll have to keep an eye on things. You're gonna have to come see me a little more often."

"That's about to get easier," Naomi told her. "I'm moving into slave town."

At last, Naomi said something that surprised the healer! She couldn't help but smile.

"And you're fine with that?" Eliza asked.

"It's my choice."

Eliza tilted her head to the side and sat back in her chair. "Who's takin' you in?"

Naomi sighed. Truthfully, she was a little worried about that one. "I don't know yet."

Eliza stood up and shuffled about the cabin. She folded a blanket and laid it on the foot of her bed, then went to the shelves with her herbal remedies and began straightening them. Turning toward the table, she dipped a ladle in the water bucket and took a sip.

Naomi watched her closely, wondering if she should leave.

Eventually Eliza sat back down. "You can stay with me."

"Oh, no, I couldn't impose on you like that. Besides, women from all over the plantation come here to—"

Eliza raised a hand to stop her. "I don't ever let anyone stay here with me, not even a woman in labor. But somethin' is tellin' me this is where you need to be."

Naomi had to admit, Eliza's offer would solve a huge dilemma. But she adamantly shook her head. "Thank you, Eliza, truly. I just can't do that to you."

"Yes, you can, and you will. Course, I need to warn you, I get knocks on my door in the middle of the night sometimes. But we can put a bed for you in the back room, and you'll sleep right through it."

If it hadn't been for Eliza's strong insistence, Naomi would've held her ground. But something was telling her this was the perfect answer to her problem. "All right, but I don't want to be a burden, so I'll be glad to help you any way I can."

"Then it's settled. I'll tell Micah to bring me an extra bed and covers. Go do what you need to, and I'll see you back here this evenin'."

When the women stood, Eliza gathered Naomi in a warm embrace. "Truth be told," she said, "I could use a friend."

❦

Naomi's first of many difficult conversations started with Eula. The old slave was sitting on her porch as Naomi made her way from Eliza's cabin, which was some distance away. Without waiting for an invitation, she climbed the steps and sat down in her usual spot.

Eula's rocker creaked to a steady rhythm as she welcomed Naomi to her top step. "Where'd you come from, gal? You been visitin' somewheres?"

Having already made the decision not to mince her words, Naomi said, "I've been with Eliza. I have something to tell you."

The rocker came to an immediate halt and Eula leaned forward. There was nothing she liked better than gathering information no one else had heard. "I's listenin'."

It was hard for Naomi to look her in the eyes, but she forced herself to do it. "I'm with child."

Eula's eyes grew wider than Naomi thought was possible. "Ya don't say. Do Isaiah know it yet?"

Naomi felt the heat rush to her face. "No," she said quietly.

Eula's hand cupped Naomi's chin. "He's gonna be a mighty happy man."

Tears escaped Naomi's eyes before she could stop them. Misconstruing them for tears of joy, Eula's face brightened into a wrinkly smile. "I specs there'll be a weddin' soon."

It was all Naomi could do to sit there and listen to such talk. But she wasn't going to set Eula straight—not yet. Word would get out soon enough that the baby didn't belong to Isaiah. She supposed it was a good thing Eliza had offered her cabin. Naomi's kinfolk were going to be awfully upset with her.

Naomi came to her feet and squeezed Eula's hand. "I need to go."

Eula set her rocker back in motion. "Let me know how Isaiah takes to the news."

If the cramping in Naomi's stomach wasn't from the baby, it certainly was a symptom of her profound angst. Capturing a deep breath, she straightened her shoulders and headed for the stables. Naomi hated to take Isaiah away from his work, but this was a burden she didn't intend to carry any longer. *Lord, give me the words that will protect his heart.*

Naomi found him immediately upon entering the stables. He was talking with a young stable worker beside one of the stalls. When he caught sight of Naomi, he patted the boy's shoulder and strode toward her.

"Whatchu doin' here this mornin', Naomi? Is everythin' all right?"

That wasn't a question she was ready to answer. Instead she said, "Good morning, Isaiah. I was wondering if we could go somewhere to talk…that is, if you're able to get away."

Grinning widely, he said, "Sure, there's nothin' that can't wait. You wanna go outside?"

"Could we? We should talk in private."

When they came out into the sunshine, Isaiah led her to a bench at the far end of the stable wall. No one would disturb them there.

It felt a little awkward sitting here with him. She wished they could be in the privacy of his cabin, but that wouldn't be appropriate for such a conversation. Besides, she didn't want Franklin to be there.

Turning sideways on the bench to face him, Naomi decided not to be quite so blunt with Isaiah as she had been with Eula. "Isaiah, I have some difficult news to share with you."

Immediately his face took on a look of concern. "I's here for ya, Naomi, whatever it is." When he covered her hand, it made her want to weep.

She gently slid her hand from his and glanced away. "I wish Ruth were here."

The confusion in his voice was obvious. "Naomi, what this be all about?"

Looking back, she said, "I'm really sorry to have to tell you this. You know I'd do anything within my power not to hurt you."

His expression was so compassionate, Naomi cringed at the thought of the wound she was about to inflict. "There's no way to make this easy," she said. "I'm with child."

By the look on his face, if Naomi had told him she was dying, he might've been able to handle it better. Isaiah literally looked like he couldn't catch his breath. He suddenly stood up and turned, pressing both hands to the stable wall. Lowering his chin toward his chest, he let out an anguished moan.

Tears once again formed in Naomi's eyes. Isaiah's grief sliced through her very core.

Finally, he wiped a hand down his face and came back to the bench. "I's gonna stand by ya, Naomi, no matter what. If'n you'll let me, I'll take you as my wife. I promise to raise the child as my very own."

If there was a man on earth with greater kindness and humility, Naomi had yet to meet him. It caused the tears to stream down her cheeks. This time she reached out and took both of his hands in hers. "I can't marry you, Isaiah, but I thank you with all of my heart for your selfless offer."

"Then what'll you do?"

"I'm going to live with Eliza the healer for now. That's all I can tell you."

Isaiah was shaking his head. "If'n you been treated wrongly, that man's gonna have to answer to me."

"No, Isaiah. I want you to know that this was not forced upon me. I fully accept this child that I carry. Please don't worry about me in that regard."

They sat on the bench holding each other's hands for a few moments until Naomi withdrew. "You're one of the finest men I've ever known. Please don't worry about my situation. I'll make sure the kinfolk know that the baby isn't yours. There's no need for you to have to put up with all this gossip anymore."

Isaiah lowered his gaze and let out a deep sigh. She knew he would struggle with this news for a long time. With nothing more to say, she leaned over and affectionately kissed his cheek, then stood and walked away. To her dismay, the sound of Isaiah's sobs followed her.

࿐ ࿐ ࿐

That evening, Naomi moved into Eliza's cabin. After the gut-wrenching conversation with Isaiah that morning, she had decided to spend the remainder of the day at the big house. She spent most of the afternoon writing a letter to Samuel. In it, she expressed her deep and sincere love for him and prayed that he would not see her decision as a betrayal. Yet she wanted him to know that she was following her convictions and that betraying God was not a road she was willing to travel.

After supper in the kitchen with the house slaves, Naomi took her bag and left for slave town.

"I hope you don't mind," Eliza said. "I had Micah put your bed beside mine. I decided it was best to have you right here with me."

Something in Eliza's tone sent a fragment of worry through Naomi's mind, but a smile was already touching her lips. She needed the companionship more than she could say. "I don't mind a bit."

"There's the dresser Micah brung for all your belongings. And if you have some things to hang, there's plenty of space in the corner cabinet."

Eliza seemed most anxious to take care of her every need. "When you're settled, come sit with me on the porch. I've made us some lavender tea."

Naomi hadn't brought a lot from the house, so in a few minutes she was joining Eliza on the bench outside. She noticed the smoothness of the wood, probably from hundreds of visitors to the cabin over the years.

Eliza threw a light quilt over their legs to ward off the early April chill. Then, reaching down beside the bench, she picked up a steaming cup of tea for Naomi, watching until she took a sip.

"What do ya think of my lavender tea?"

"It's amazing," Naomi said. "And it smells as good as it tastes."

Eliza giggled. "Kind of like drinking the flower itself. It's good for calmin' your mind."

Naomi could already feel herself relaxing after a stressful day. She wasn't ready to talk about the difficult conversations she'd had this morning, but she hoped to find out more about her new companion. "Could I ask how you became the Hawkins' healer?"

Eliza wrapped her slender fingers around the teacup, leaning back into the cabin wall. "My grandmammy started as the Hawkins' healer for Master Joseph and his wife. I learnt all my healin' methods from her before she passed on some twelve winters ago."

Naomi was a bit taken back. "You mean you became the healer when you were fifteen years old?"

"Somewhere in there. I might've been fourteen. By then, I'd already birthed scores of babies on my own. But I didn't become the healer just 'cause my grandmammy passed on. Mistress Elizabeth chose me."

Just hearing Elizabeth's name evoked a deep emotional response in Naomi. "Did you know the mistress well?"

"Oh, yes. Mistress Elizabeth took great interest in the babies born to this plantation. She came and sat right there where you're sittin' now and held my hand after I lost my grandmammy. She comforted me all day long, then told me she wanted me to take over as the new healer."

Naomi shook her head. "How did I never know about this?"

"Well, if you had no need for a healer, you wouldn't know such things. Besides, the mistress always brought in the doctor from town for all you'ins at the big house."

"What about your mother? Was she a healer too?"

Eliza took a long swig from her teacup, then set it at her feet. "My mammy didn't make it out of childbirth. I never knew her. It was awful hard on my grandmammy that she couldn't save her own daughter."

"I'm so sorry," Naomi breathed compassionately.

Eliza nodded. "You know, my mammy was a seer. She had a gift straight from above, and the good Lord saw fit to pass it on to me—leastwise, that's what my grandmammy told me."

"So, you received the gift of healing from your grandmother and the gift of seeing from your mother. You're an amazing woman, Eliza."

Eliza looked down at her hands, a little shy after hearing such praise. "Thank you," she said softly.

That night in the darkness of the cabin, Naomi lay in her bed, thanking the Lord for the way he had provided for her. Eliza hadn't been the only one in need of a friend. Naomi had needed a confidante in the worst way, and God opened the door to what she hoped would be a lasting friendship.

Eliza's voice softly broke into her thoughts. "Naomi? You still awake?"

"Yes," she said.

"Can you tell me about that ring hangin' around your neck?"

Chapter 40

Naomi's hand instinctively covered Samuel's ruby ring resting beneath her nightgown. Eliza must've seen it when they were getting ready for bed. While Naomi had no intention of hiding the truth from her new friend, she had been caught completely off guard by her question.

Perhaps due to the ensuing silence, Eliza spoke up again. "Course, if you're not ready to tell me, I'll respect that. I suppose I'll need to win your trust first."

With Naomi's kinfolk, it had always been a foregone conclusion that anything you told one, you were telling all the others. Except for Ruth. She had been different. Which was probably why she and Naomi had built such a strong bond. Trust was one of the most important attributes in any relationship of substance as far as Naomi was concerned. The question that plagued her now was whether she would be breaking Samuel's trust by sharing their well-kept secrets?

Finally, she said, "Eliza, I'm aware that you can see things others can't. I could probably guess what you're thinking right now. But I'm just not ready. I'm sorry."

"No apologies needed," Eliza offered. "I fully expect when the time is right, we'll be able to bear our souls with one another."

Naomi liked the sound of that. She would dearly love to bear her soul to a woman she could trust beyond measure. She just had to hope that the Lord would let her know if and when the time was right.

The next morning, while the women were sharing breakfast, a hard knock sounded on the door. Eliza immediately went to open it. Micah was standing on the porch, a slight scowl on his face.

"The massa sent me to fetch Naomi."

Eliza's brow immediately pressed downward, and she looked over her shoulder. Naomi rose from the table, trying desperately to slow her breathing. Was this Samuel's way of getting her to move back to the big house, or did he just want to talk? Whatever the answer, it was not a question she had the luxury of asking. "Tell him I'll be there in an hour." She hoped her voice didn't sound as strained as her nerves.

"He told me to take ya back to his office. I got a buggy here." Micah ran his fingers along the brim of his hat. "I reckon I can wait till yer finished with breakfast."

There was no chance of doing that. Naomi's appetite had completely vanished. "Just give me a minute."

Micah dipped his chin, then turned to sit down on the bench.

Naomi went to the table between the beds and poured water from a pitcher into the basin. She splashed the cool water onto her face, then held her hands to her cheeks. She'd forgotten a towel, but Eliza was quick to bring her one.

"Thank you," she breathed.

"You gonna be all right?"

Drawing a deep breath, Naomi simply said, "Yes." Then noticing the worry in Eliza's gaze, she told her, "I'll be back. There's no need to be concerned."

Eliza nodded thoughtfully, then stepped aside to let her pass.

All the way to the big house, Naomi caught Micah's glances, but he never said a word, for which she was grateful. It was obvious he had no idea why she was living with the healer, but at least he had the decency not to ask. He helped her down from the buggy and led her to the side door. After removing his hat, he knocked twice.

Samuel immediately answered the door and acknowledged his overseer. "Thank you, Micah."

Micah nodded and turned away.

Stepping back, Samuel beckoned Naomi to come inside. She tried desperately to read his expression, but he was masking his emotions well. He waited until she sat down on the sofa before joining her. His silence was unnerving.

"Did the children arrive safely?"

He nodded. "Just before dark."

When he offered no other details, she asked, "How are they doing?"

"They're all still in bed. The trip wore them out, but they seemed fine last night."

"What about their tutor? Is he—"

"Naomi, I didn't ask you here to talk about the children."

"I know," she said quietly.

He reached over to the table and picked up the note she'd left for him. His voice was calm, at least for now. "I don't understand this. Are you deliberately going against my wishes?"

Her spine stiffened. "Of course not. This really has nothing to do with your wishes...and in some ways, not even mine."

When he started shaking his head, she quickly went on. "Samuel, the reason you don't understand this is because you're still caught up in a life without hope. We're living in two separate worlds." She placed her hands across the child in her womb, her words spilling out with great passion. "I am carrying a child of God, and there is nothing you can say to compel me to destroy it."

The look on his face was one of utter shock. Had she finally gotten through to him? It was obvious he was searching for a response. She could only pray that it would be a good one, but it wasn't quite what she was expecting.

"This plantation has been in my family for three generations. The very cabin that Micah lives in was the first house on this land. My grandfather built it with his own hands. Look at this place now." His arm swept across the room where they were sitting. "This is one of the largest, most thriving plantations in all of Kentucky. I've worked hard to continue what my grandfather and father have built—and someday, it will all belong to my son, Joseph."

He took his gaze from her and swallowed hard. "I can't allow you to compromise everything I've worked so hard for."

Naomi struggled to answer her husband—tears of anguish pooled in her eyes. When she finally spoke, her voice came out as a whisper. "Oh, ye of little faith."

After hearing her response, Samuel stood up and momentarily paced the room. When he sat back down, he had obviously decided on a different approach. Taking Naomi's hands in his, he said, "I love you beyond words, Naomi. Please...I'm begging you...."

Naomi pulled her hands away and placed them on his face. Raising up, she gently kissed his lips once and then again. "I will pray for you," she said, before coming to her feet.

Samuel stared after her in frozen silence as she quickly departed the house.

✦❧✦

Ten days later, in the middle of the night, Naomi was awakened by a shout. Coming out of a deep sleep, she realized a man was in their cabin, waving a lantern like he was trying to stop a train.

Eliza's voice broke through the haze. "Wake up, Naomi. Get dressed."

Naomi immediately put her feet to the floor. "What's happening?"

"A baby!" the man yelled.

"John, get yourself outta here so we can get dressed. We're comin'."

Flashing a pair of wild eyes at the two women, the man named John turned on his heels and fled the cabin. Eliza went to the door and kicked it shut while buttoning her blouse. Then, opening a cabinet, she pulled out a satchel. "Finish your dressin', then go get the birthin' stool in the back room. You need to witness this before it happens to you."

Naomi suppressed her apprehension while tying her boot laces. When she returned from the back room, Eliza had already descended the porch steps.

"Come on," Eliza called out just before breaking into a run.

Both women were breathless as they arrived at John's cabin. His wife, Jessie, was being comforted by three of their kinfolk.

"John," Eliza hollered. "You're takin' up too much space in here. Get outside right now!"

When the man didn't move, Naomi took it upon herself to lead him toward the door. "John, I'm Naomi. Come outside with me." She glanced over her shoulder, noticing Eliza's quick, efficient movements. "Your wife is in good hands."

As soon as she got him outside, Naomi asked, "Is this your first?"

He shook his head vigorously. "This be number six."

Naomi couldn't help but laugh. "Then you know all will be well. Stay out here and I'll let you know when the babe has arrived."

Heading back for the door, John followed her, but Naomi put her hand forcefully on his chest. "John, where are your other five children?"

His head jerked toward another cabin. "They're with my mammy."

"All right, then that's where you're going." She gave him a stern gaze and stood her ground. She could hear Eliza's confident instructions inside and didn't want her to have to worry with the baby's father. Naomi took hold of his shoulders and turned the big man completely around. "Go, now," she ordered. Thankfully, John didn't argue. He stepped off the porch and disappeared into the darkness.

"Oh, good, you're back," Eliza said when Naomi appeared. "Hold the light up for me."

Naomi took the lantern from the table and realized she was practically breathing as hard as Jessie, who was already on the birth stool. Each of the other three women were holding her steady—one supporting her back and the other two allowing her to grip their arms. One of the women looked almost identical to Jessie. It must've been her sister.

"Take a deep breath now and let it out nice and slow. That one's passed. Let's wait for another contraction 'fore we start pushin'."

Sweat poured down Jessie's forehead and into her eyes. Eliza took a clean cloth and wiped her face, giving her soothing words.

Jessie's eyes landed on Naomi's, then slid down to her belly. "You's expectin' too, ain't ya?"

"I am," Naomi admitted, placing her hand over her slightly protruding belly.

"When's it comin'?" Jessie asked.

But the woman never heard Naomi's response. She writhed in pain and let out a piercing cry.

Eliza moved in closer, taking hold of her thighs. "That's it, Jessie. This is the one." She dropped to her knees into position to catch the baby. "Let's push now," she said. "That's it. Keep pushin'."

A few minutes passed while Eliza safely delivered the child from its mother. Naomi marveled at the awe-inspiring miracle of birth. It overwhelmed her, and a sob worked its way up, escaping from her throat.

"I know how you're feelin'," Eliza said softly, not looking over her shoulder at Naomi. "It's all so beautiful and pure."

When the baby made its first cry, Eliza smiled broadly and laid it onto Jessie's chest. "Your angel is a boy." With great tenderness, Eliza's hand covered the child, and she quietly blessed him with words from the Good Book. "Before I formed you in the womb, I knew you. Before you were born, I set you apart."

Jessie kissed the crown of her tiny boy's head before the healer lifted him from her. While Eliza cleaned the baby, the other women ministered to Jessie, eventually getting her into the bed. Soon, the baby was cleaned and swaddled and laid in Naomi's arms.

"Here," Eliza told her. "Take him to his mother to nurse."

For an extended moment, Naomi held the baby close. Tears clouded her eyes as she imagined the day that she would hold her own child this way.

Walking across the room with the tiny bundle, she sat down on the edge of the bed. She gently laid the babe in his mother's open arms. As exhausted as Jessie had been moments earlier, she perked up at the feel of her newborn son. Naomi smiled as the babe found his mother's nourishment and began to suckle.

As Eliza continued to clean up after the birth, she told Naomi, "See if John's outside on the porch. Tell him he's got himself another son."

"He left to be with his mother and children."

"Well, go find him. No need lettin' him worry any longer."

Naomi wasn't sure which cabin he'd gone to, but apparently she needn't worry. As soon as she stepped out onto the porch, John came running.

"What's it be?" he asked breathlessly.

"You have a son."

John let out a whoop that startled nearly everyone inside the cabin, including his son, who began to cry.

"Hush yer mouth, John," Jessie called out. "You's keepin' our babe from eatin'!"

John slipped into the cabin with a shamefaced grin. "Sorry, gal. Didn't mean to disturb ya none." He went to one knee beside the bed, and before touching his son, he lovingly stroked Jessie's arm. "Is you all right?"

Jessie gave her husband a weary smile. "I's fine."

A sob rumbled up from the big man, and he leaned forward, pressing his lips for a long moment to his wife's forehead. "That's good, that's real good," he whispered.

The tender scene tugged at Naomi's heart, causing her to wipe fresh tears from her face. When she looked away, her gaze met Eliza's. The healer had obviously been staring at her.

She knows. Those two words echoed through Naomi's mind. It only confirmed that there would be no way to keep any secrets from her extraordinary companion. On one hand, that realization felt freeing, while on the other, it felt like she was being unfaithful to Samuel.

Naomi looked back at the couple and their son, praying that the Spirit would give her wisdom.

A couple of hours later, Eliza and Naomi walked slowly toward their cabin, basking in the warm morning sun. They were both exhausted, but in a satisfying way.

"Anything surprise ya?" Eliza asked, bumping Naomi's shoulder lightly with her own.

Naomi's brow rose. "Yes, I wasn't expecting so much blood."

Eliza laughed softly. "Did it bother ya?"

"Not really. I just never thought it would be like that."

"Uh, huh," Eliza muttered. "What else?"

Naomi glanced at her friend, who was staring at her again, eyes shining in the sunlight. "Well, I found myself hoping I would be able to handle the pain."

"When the time comes," Eliza said, "you'll be strong. After it's over, you'll forget all about the pain with that young'un in your arms."

The two women continued walking slowly in comfortable silence.

Finally, Naomi spoke up, turning the conversation in a new direction. "After we get back, I'm going to change clothes and go to the big house."

Eliza looked concerned. "For what purpose? You need to rest."

"I made a blanket not long ago that will be perfect for Jessie and the baby. Plus, I want to get some extra food from Mamie to give to the family."

Eliza laid a hand on Naomi's arm, pulling her to a halt in the road. Her head tilted slightly to one side as her eyes narrowed. "Takin' a blanket and food to the family of a newborn is a fine thing. You know, that's just what Mistress Elizabeth always did."

Naomi's pulse quickened as they started walking again. It dawned on her for the first time that she had truly taken Elizabeth's place on this plantation, save for one thing—owning these dear people.

Naomi could literally feel a supernatural energy emanating from Eliza, and the two words she had already heard today resounded even louder than before.

She knows.

Chapter 41

I'm goin' with ya to the big house," Eliza announced. She had already washed and changed and was now standing at the cabin door. It was clear, Naomi wouldn't have a choice even if she wanted one.

Truthfully, she preferred to have Eliza's company for more reasons than she could count. At the top of her list was the reaction she was expecting from the house slaves. Loose women on the plantation had always been spurned by the others. Why should she expect to be treated any differently?

All was quiet as the two women walked by the cabins of Naomi's kinfolk. She could see smoke rising from the common kitchen and knew Eula and Solomon would be working on the noon meal. Hopefully they could make it back through before everyone came in from the fields. If not, they would have to walk the long way around.

Entering the lower kitchen, Mamie was bent over the oven checking on her renowned biscuits. "Jed, is that you? I done told you to bring me some more—" Her words fell away as she turned around. Immediately her gaze traveled to Naomi's midsection.

"Hello, Mamie," Naomi said quietly.

When the old cook's eyes moved back to Naomi's, tears had already formed there. "Child, I been awful worried 'bout ya." She opened her arms wide. "Come let Mamie hold ya."

Naomi took in a shuddered breath, then collapsed into Mamie's ample arms. This was a gift she had not expected to receive.

For a long time, Mamie held her without any words being spoken. When she finally let go, the older woman stepped back and dabbed her eyes with the apron at her waist then glanced at Eliza for the first time. "What brung the two o' you here today?"

"A new birth on the plantation," Eliza proclaimed. "John and Jessie have another son."

"Well, that calls fer somethin' special. I already done made apple pies, and I'll send Jed back to the smoke house, if'n I can get his sorry carcass back in here." Mamie quickly pulled a chair away from the table. "Sit yerself down and take a load off, child."

Naomi was already shaking her head. "Thank you, but I need to get a blanket from the sewing room. I'll be right back."

Eliza instantly said she would stay and help Mamie gather up the food, and in a short time Naomi was back.

Mamie's brow dipped. "Did ya see Abigail?"

"No, she must be upstairs."

"That's good," Mamie responded, causing Naomi to wonder if the housekeeper had slipped back into her old ways.

It took several minutes for the food to be collected, and when it all sat on the big block table, Mamie looked at the two women with concern. "You got a wagon waitin' outside?"

"No," Naomi told her. "I wasn't expecting this much."

Mamie's voice took on a reverent tone. "Well, John and Jesse already has a passel o' mouths to feed. I specs the missus, Lawd rest her soul, would've wanted 'em to have plenty." She put her hands on her hips, searching for a solution.

"I tell ya what, Jed'll go fetch a cart and help ya get it there. How's that sound?" Before they could even answer, Mamie let out a holler. "Jed! Where you done gone?"

When the boy didn't appear, Eliza said, "I'll go find him."

"Check to the side o' the storehouse. He sets his lazy bones on a barrel in the shade out there."

When Eliza was gone, Mamie pulled her biscuits from the oven and set them on the table to cool. "Come 'ere and sits with me fer a minute. I gots somethin' to ask ya."

The two women sat down in the rickety kitchen chairs, facing one another. Mamie reached over and claimed one of Naomi's hands. "I's curious, child, if you can tell me why Isaiah done disrespected ya like this? We's all wonderin' what's wrong with the man."

A doleful sigh escaped Naomi's throat. "Mamie, there's something you need to know, and I suppose you should let everyone else in the house know it too. This baby doesn't belong to Isaiah."

Mamie sat back in her chair so hard it nearly toppled over. "You don't mean it?"

"It's true. Isaiah is a good and honorable man. He didn't know anything about… this." She spread her hand across her abdomen.

The look on Mamie's face was one of utter disbelief. Naomi was certain of the question she would ask next but wanted to cut her off at the pass. "I'm sorry to disappoint you like this, but I've made my peace with God. That's all I can tell you."

Mamie captured her lower lip in her teeth, obviously trying to decide whether to push Naomi further. But suddenly her eyes softened, and she brought Naomi's hand to her chest. "I'll stand by ya, child. If you wanna move back to the house, you can always come to Mamie. Ya hear me?"

Naomi's smile conveyed enormous relief, as Mamie leaned forward and drew her back into a smothering embrace.

The sun was directly overhead as Naomi and her two companions made their way past her kinfolk's cabins. Jed trailed behind the women, pulling a small cart. He had already quipped that he felt like a mule, for which Eliza told him he looked like one. That caused him to chuckle and pick up his pace a bit.

To Naomi's chagrin, all of the field slaves began making their way in for the noon meal. She had so hoped to be well out of the area and would've been if it hadn't been for Jed's indolence. Most of them cast her a wary glance, but when Phibe and Ceceilia caught sight of her, they made a wide birth, refusing to even look her way. Eliza caught her hand in a firm grip and walked beside her with an air of self-confidence that kept Naomi's feet moving boldly forward.

The farther they moved away from Naomi's kinfolk, the more often Eliza turned to look behind them. Finally, Naomi asked, "What are you looking at?"

"Not sure," she responded. "I'm thinkin' someone's followin' us."

Naomi immediately stopped to look back but only noticed slaves wandering in from their places of work around the plantation. Nothing seemed to be amiss. Still, Eliza continued her vigilance until they arrived at John and Jesse's cabin.

Once inside, Naomi couldn't help but smile. The place seemed to be in utter chaos as children of all ages ran amuck. But all Jessie had to say from her resting place in the bed was "chill-ins!" and every one of them settled down. Big John had just made his way in from the gristmill for the noon meal.

The couple looked exhausted but thanked the women profusely for such a bounty of food. Jessie particularly made over the beautiful blanket Naomi had given her. "It be the pertiest blanket I ever did see."

"I hope you'll enjoy using it for many years to come," Naomi told her.

Not wishing to remain long, Eliza examined Jessie quickly and told her all was well. "I'll come back to check on ya again tomorrow."

John followed the two women onto the porch. "I reckon ya know you gots a shadow."

Eliza nodded. "You've seen him?"

"He be squattin' behind that tree when I gots here, but he ain't there no more."

"Did you recognize him?" Eliza asked.

"Naw, I ain't never seen him a fore. I reckon he be hungry and follered yer cart. We'll share with him if he comes 'round."

Eliza nodded. "That would be kind of ya, John. Take care of Jessie and your little one."

A deep laugh rumbled out of John's chest. "Oh, I intends to."

The first thing Eliza did when they arrived at the cabin was stir the coals in the fireplace and hang a giant iron pot over the heat. Making one trip after another to the pump, she filled the pot with water, then added more logs to the fire. Naomi hadn't even bothered to notice Eliza's efforts. She barely made it to her bed before collapsing in exhaustion.

A few minutes later, Naomi felt embarrassed when Eliza unlaced her boots for her and removed them. She started to sit up, but the healer pressed her shoulders back down to the bed. "You lay there for a bit while the water heats up. You're gonna get a hot bath in the tub in the back room."

The very sound of it caused Naomi's muscles to finally relax. She hadn't realized how tense she had been, walking through slave town earlier.

After several trips to the back room, Eliza announced that the bath was ready. She gave Naomi a towel and closed the door so she could be alone, although Eliza peeked in several times to check on her. "I don't want ya fallin' asleep and slippin' under the water," she told her.

Nearly an hour later, Naomi came back to the front room, dressed in her nightgown. She had no plans but to sleep until the next morning. However, Eliza told her she couldn't sleep just yet. "Prop yourself up in bed. I'll bring ya some soup and bread. You need to take care of that little one inside ya."

Naomi didn't argue. She realized how famished she was after such a long night and day of work. While she and Eliza shared their meal together, both women were surprised when the door to the cabin slowly creaked open.

Eliza quietly put her bowl on the table between the beds and tiptoed to the door. No one seemed to be there, so she pulled it wider. That's when she saw a quick movement at the side of the porch.

"Who is it?" Naomi called out, but Eliza pressed a finger to her lips and disappeared out of sight.

Soon, the healer was back, but she wasn't alone.

"Nay!" the boy called, running toward Naomi's bed. She had just enough time to put her bowl on the bedside table before Franklin threw himself into her arms.

"Franklin, I'm so glad to see you!" She pulled him close to kiss his cheek.

Eliza brought a wet cloth and thoroughly cleaned his hands and feet. "Naomi's already had a bath. I should probably dunk you in that water too, young'un."

He giggled but didn't protest against Eliza's ministrations.

Naomi cupped his chin and turned his face upward. "Was that you following us?"

His eyes twinkled as his head bobbed. "Yes'm."

"What about your pappy and Mammy Lou? They'll be missing you."

His mouth scrunched to the side, and he squirmed in a little closer to Naomi. "I wanna stay with you," he said.

Naomi caught Eliza's gaze, and Eliza must've read her mind. "I'll go find his pappy."

"Thank you, dear one. I'm sorry you have to do that. I know you're exhausted."

"Nah, it's all right. I don't mind a bit. Besides, that'll give the two of you some time to catch up."

Before Eliza left, she brought Franklin something to eat and left the two in Naomi's bed.

∽∾∿∾∿

Isaiah's hand covered his brow to ward off the midafternoon sun. He could see Eliza walking swiftly toward the stables. Something about her manner made him think he should check on her. He took off at a jog and caught up to her just before she reached the door.

"Eliza?"

She turned and offered him a relieved expression. "Isaiah. I was just lookin' for you."

"What's a matter. Is it Naomi?"

"Well, it's Naomi *and* Franklin. He followed us to my cabin this afternoon. He's there with her right now."

Isaiah hauled in a deep breath. "I's so sorry. I'll go fetch 'im right away."

Eliza reached out and touched his arm. "No need. Naomi seems glad to have him there."

"My boy's been missin' his mammy somethin' fierce. But Naomi's filled her place." Isaiah chuckled. "I's thinkin' he'd rather be with her than me most days."

"Well, I just wanted you to know where he is. Don't stop your workin'—we'll take good care of him till you get there."

One thing Isaiah knew, Naomi would always care for his boy like her own. "Thank ya," he said in relief. "Could I ask ya somethin' 'fore you go?"

"Course ya can," Eliza said readily.

"I's wonderin' if I should make myself scarce-like when I comes to get 'im. I don't wanna upsets Naomi none."

Eliza's brow dipped. "Isaiah, I don't know what's gone on between the two of you, but she has nothin' but the highest regard for ya. You're more than welcome to come in when ya get there."

Isaiah nodded in relief. "Thank ya, Eliza. I be there later."

Smiling thoughtfully, the healer turned and headed back the way she'd come.

Several minutes later, Eliza dragged herself up the back steps to her cabin and quietly entered. She wanted to let Naomi and Franklin have all the time they needed alone. After dumping out the bath water, she realized there hadn't been a peep from the front room. Curious, she peered around the corner and instantly understood why. Naomi was sound asleep on her side, her arm draped over Franklin.

Moving closer, Eliza realized the boy wasn't asleep at all. He was facing Naomi, eyes wide open. His hand was resting on her abdomen, moving in slow, gentle circles.

Eliza experienced a sudden stirring in her soul. It started deep in her gut before washing through her heart and mind, leaving her breathless. And in that very moment, she knew beyond all doubt, that this boy and Naomi's baby were profoundly connected by fate.

October 1858

M *iserable* was the only word that came to Naomi's mind. The sweltering afternoon heat coupled with the fact that the child she carried had yet to drop, caused discomfort nearly every hour of the day and night.

"Come on, let's get ya cooled down," Eliza told her. "The tub's ready for ya."

Eliza helped her undress and get into the cool water. All Naomi could do was lean back and moan. Occasionally, she had trouble just catching her breath.

"Isn't there anything…you can do to get the…baby to drop?"

Shaking her head, Eliza knelt beside the tub and sponged the perspiration from Naomi's brow. "Your babe's got a will of its own. I promise, it'll drop when it's ready to come."

"But it's already…over a week…past," she groaned.

"I know, I know. We just gotta let the baby set its own birthdate. It won't be long now. Try to take deep breaths and relax."

Naomi closed her eyes and concentrated on her next breath. But the deeper she drew into her lungs, the more painful the outcome.

Eliza patted Naomi's shoulder. "I gotta go check on supper and make sure Franklin doesn't come burstin' in." The boy had been coming for supper every night for the last four months. "You gonna be all right till I get back?"

Forcing out a slow breath, Naomi nodded. "I'll be fine."

While Eliza was gone, Naomi tried to occupy her mind with something other than her discomfort. She was so grateful for Eliza's constant attention but feared the woman was working herself to death. She not only had Naomi to care for but countless other women on the plantation. Naomi didn't know how she managed it all with such grace.

Turning slightly onto her hip to relieve an ache in her spine, Naomi thought back to the night in May when the Spirit led her to bear her soul with Eliza. While her dear friend had already surmised that the baby was Samuel's, and even the fact that they were married didn't completely surprise her, Eliza had been thoroughly stunned by the fact that Naomi was a free woman. The reverential treatment Naomi began to receive after that almost made her feel unworthy.

Several minutes later, Eliza sailed back into the room, a towel over her arm. "I'm sorry to tell ya this, but your little man is already out on the front porch." She set the towel on a chair and stepped behind the tub, slipping her arms beneath Naomi's. "Ready?"

Naomi nodded and clenched her teeth. When she was out of the tub, Eliza wrapped the towel around her and told her to holler if she needed more help. "I don't trust that boy to stay put."

For the first time today, Naomi actually laughed. She could just picture Franklin nudging his way through the door uninvited. For some reason, which Naomi had yet to figure out, he was more consumed with her now that she was carrying a child. Eliza had noticed it too and seemed to know more than she was willing to share.

When Naomi was dressed in a loose cotton shift, she made her way to the front room. "He's waitin' for ya," Eliza said, tilting her head toward the porch. "I told him to be careful with ya."

Naomi greatly appreciated the reminder and stepped outside.

"Hello, little man," she said fondly.

Franklin hopped off the bench and came to her slowly, arms open wide. But they were not open to her. He surrounded her belly gently, then kissed where the baby lay. The child in her womb instantly responded, and Naomi had to suppress a cry from the resulting sharp pain. Franklin had never done that before. It caused an overwhelming emotional response within Naomi, and she started to weep.

Stepping back, Franklin gave her a wide-eyed stare. Naomi carefully lowered herself onto the bench, wiping the tears away with her hands.

"Did I hurt ya?" he asked sheepishly.

"Oh, no, sweet boy…you didn't hurt me. Here…come sit down." She reached over and tapped the bench.

For a while, she kept him occupied, talking about the horses, but then, his hand slid over onto her abdomen. It was almost as if he couldn't help it. He smiled when the baby reacted again.

"She's happy," he said.

Naomi regarded Franklin's innocent brown eyes staring up at her. "She?"

The boy's head nodded and a chill crept all the way up her spine. Between Franklin and Eliza, Naomi felt like her life was completely laid bare. She leaned her head back against the wall.

"Franklin," she said. "How do you know?"

But he was silent, staring off somewhere in the distance.

❦❧

Another week passed before Eliza started worrying. She'd seen a few women carry their baby a week or so past its due date. But in most of those cases, the woman had miscalculated the last day of her cycle. That certainly wasn't true with Naomi. There was no arguing the exact date that this baby had been conceived.

What bothered Eliza the most was the size of the baby. She feared that it might've grown too big for Naomi to deliver safely. It was time to prompt the labor process along.

Naomi had been awake most of the night sitting, standing, walking—trying anything to find a comfortable position. It seemed like every half hour, she headed to the chamber pot in the back room.

Just before dawn, Eliza got up and dressed, then started a fire. It was time to try red raspberry leaf tea. The raspberry leaf was known to soften the birth canal and hopefully cause Naomi to go into labor.

When it was ready, Eliza poured a cup for Naomi and took it to her. She was sitting on the edge of her bed, rocking herself. "Thank you," she said in a shaky voice.

Eliza sat down on the bed beside her. "Before the sun gets over the trees, we'll go for a long walk. If that doesn't do the trick, I have something else I can try."

Naomi took a long sip, then turned an exhausted gaze upon her. "What is it?"

"It's a bit hard to explain. There's a sac surroundin' the baby, and I can gently separate it from your womb. That usually helps things along. But…."

"But what?" Naomi moaned.

"Well, I've only done it once before…mind you, it worked, but let's just hope this tea does the trick."

After two more trips to the back room, Naomi said she was ready for a walk. Eliza linked arms with her, and they took a road that led toward the cotton fields.

Slaves dotted the landscape, as it was near the end of the cotton-picking season. Noticing a few women with their nursing infants tied to their backs or chests, Eliza felt a pang in her heart. She had delivered those babes into this wretched life. Every now and then one of the slaves would straighten and massage their lower back. Curious laborers watched Eliza and Naomi walk by but scarcely had time nor energy to even nod their way. It made Eliza want to bawl.

When she glanced at Naomi, her face was pale. She shouldn't have walked her this way. She knew how Naomi felt about freeing all of the master's slaves. The woman was on a quest. Naomi had made it clear that after the delivery of this baby, she would pick up the gauntlet again with her husband. But for now, this scene was causing her dear friend a great deal of anxiety.

"Come on, I think we've gone far enough. Let's head back home."

Naomi didn't argue but leaned a little more heavily on Eliza's arm.

Four more cups of tea and two more short walks still had not caused the baby to drop or contractions to begin. That evening, after Isaiah came by to take Franklin home, Naomi had had all she could take. "I want you…to do…the…whatever it is…."

"You mean separate the baby's sac from your womb?"

Naomi nodded vigorously. "That."

Eliza felt her heart pounding in her ears. She didn't want to do it. "There is one more trick," she said awkwardly.

Naomi sat down on the edge of her bed, rubbing her temples. "I'll do anything."

Clearing her throat, Eliza said, "You could get intimate-like with your husband."

"What?" Naomi practically yelled, causing Eliza to laugh.

"Some say it gets everything primed and ready to go."

Naomi heaved in a short breath. "Not…happening."

"I didn't think so. Then why don't we wait till mornin' and see if something starts on its own."

Shaking her head, Naomi would have none of it. A stream of tears slid down her cheeks and she turned a pleading gaze toward the healer. "Now…I'm begging you."

Hauling in a deep breath, Eliza nodded. "Let's get you to the back room."

⋰⋱

It only took an hour for Naomi to feel her first contraction. Eliza had put a pillow on the bench out front for her to sit on while they talked. It felt like someone had fastened a belt around her midsection and cinched it tight. She leaned forward, letting out a moan.

Eliza held her hand tenderly until it passed. "That's a good sign. Somethin's happenin'."

As the evening turned into night, the baby still hadn't dropped, but the contractions gradually got more severe and closer together. Naomi was trying hard to bear up under the pain, but it felt like the baby was sitting on her lungs—she could hardly breathe at times.

Once, in the middle of the night, she turned to Eliza in panic—it felt like she was drowning. Eliza stood her up and wrapped her arms around from behind, trying to push the baby downward so Naomi could breathe.

Lanterns burned all night inside the cabin. Both women knew in their heart this was going to be a long, slow process. By morning, Naomi started vomiting until nothing remained in her stomach. Her lips were pale.

"Here, drink this," Eliza told her. "You gotta sip as much water as you can all day."

At midmorning, there was a knock on the healer's door. It was Jessie with four-month-old Jackson on her hip. "I's wonderin' if you can take a look at his rash?" she said. But one mournful cry from Naomi inside brought a sympathetic look from Jessie. "Naomi finally be in labor? What can I do to help?"

Eliza invited her in. "The baby still hasn't dropped. She's strugglin' to breathe."

Jessie handed her infant over to the healer and immediately went to Naomi's bed. "That happened to me once. Here, sit yerself forward a bit." Jessie climbed in the bed right behind her and leaned Naomi back against her. She started gently massaging down from the top and helped press the baby downward. Naomi instantly felt the relief. It was good to finally take in a normal breath.

The healer took little Jackson into the back room to examine him and moments later came back with a salve for Jessie to use. "I put some on him. He should be good as new in a couple of days."

Jessie nodded and continued her massage until Jackson started squalling. "I's so sorry, Naomi. That boy's gotta eat."

"That's…all right. Thank you…for helping me…breathe."

"I tell ya what," Jessie said. "I's gonna feed 'im and leave 'im at the nursery, then I be right back to help." She patted Naomi's leg and quickly took Jackson from Eliza.

True to her word, Jessie came back within the hour. The first thing she did was go right to the healer. "Gal, you need to lay down and rest. Ain't seen you lookin' like this in a long time."

Eliza was already shaking her head, but Jessie took her by the shoulders and marched her straight over to the bed. "What good you gonna be if'n you's too tired to help get this baby out?"

For the first time, Naomi realized how exhausted her dear friend must be. All she'd been able to think about was her pain and her next breath. "Dear one…I insist that… you rest. Jessie's here…now."

When they finally talked her into lying down, Naomi told Jessie, "Let's go…for a walk." She wanted to give Eliza as much sleep as she possibly could.

When Jessie got Naomi down the porch steps, she asked, "Ain't yer kinfolk comin' to help ya deliver?"

Naomi took several small sips of air before answering. "I don't…think so."

Jessie shook her head vigorously. "They ought ta be ashamed o' theirselfs leavin' you all alone like this."

"It's all right," Naomi told her before a hard contraction doubled her over. The two women stood still in the road while Naomi moaned and Jessie held her.

"Ya wanna go back?"

For a long time, Naomi couldn't speak. It was all she could do not to collapse in the dirt. But when the spasm passed, she shook her head. "Keep…going."

Eventually Jessie led her to the nursery where all the weaned babies in the area were taken care of. Much like Mammy Lou's, these were the children too young to work on the plantation but too old to be in the fields with their mammies. Jessie pointed out her twin sister holding baby Jackson on the front porch. Naomi recognized her from the night Jessie had given birth.

"Come on, you need to sits and rest fer a minute." Jessie led Naomi over to the porch, and they both sat down on the edge. "This here's my sister, Jane."

All Naomi could do was wave a weary hand to her. After sitting through two more contractions, Naomi knew she needed to get back to her bed. If she didn't go now, she might not make it.

By then, the slaves were coming in for the noon meal. Big John called out as he came down the road, but when he saw Jessie struggling to get Naomi to her feet, he ran to them.

"Hang on, gal, I gots her." John picked Naomi right up off the porch like she was a young child. "Put yer arms 'round my neck, Naomi. I's got ya."

When John got Naomi back to her bed, Eliza rolled over. She'd obviously been able to sleep, which turned out to be a blessing, since Naomi began to scream in agony.

Chapter 43

"Get back to your pappy right now, Franklin! This is no time for you to be here." Eliza had stepped out on the porch, closing the door behind her.

"What 'bout supper?" he asked.

"You're gonna have to eat with your pappy tonight. Go on."

When Naomi let out an ear-piercing cry, Franklin darted around Eliza for the door. But she was quick to grab his arm and turn him around. Swatting his backside, she said, "I mean it. This is no place for a boy."

The rascal still held his ground. Eliza finally squatted down and took hold of his shoulders. "Franklin, Naomi's gonna have her baby today. Why don't you go on home and let your pappy know?"

That did the trick. He gave her a nod, then turned and ran his bare feet as fast as they could go toward home.

Within minutes another knock sounded on the door. Since Jessie was still straddling behind Naomi, Eliza answered it. This time it was Isaiah, breathing hard. "Naomi gonna be all right?"

"NO!" Naomi yelled through one of her debilitating contractions.

Isaiah's eyes grew wide. "Hows can I help?"

"Pray," was all Eliza could think to say. But just before closing the door, she had another thought. If Naomi's water were to break, they were going to need more help.

"Stay right there," Eliza told him and closed the door in his face.

Eliza knelt by the bed and covered Naomi's hand. "Isaiah's outside. I need to send him for two more women. Do you want him to ask your kinfolk?"

Naomi's head wagged back and forth. "Big house…Tabitha…and Mamie."

Eliza went back outside to tell Isaiah, and he instantly shot off the porch in the same manner as Franklin had. She watched him sprint out of sight, then scanned the trees around the cabin. There was no doubt the boy was standing behind one of them, but she couldn't worry about that now.

When Eliza re-entered the cabin, she found Naomi weeping while Jessie continued to hold her. Kneeling down, Eliza laid her hands on the top of her thighs. "Shh, now. It's gonna be all right."

"I can't…do this," Naomi sobbed.

"Oh, yes you can. You're not giving up on me now…you hear me? You're strong, Naomi. It'll be over soon, and you'll forget all about it."

All Naomi could do was groan and writhe in abject misery.

Mamie and Tabitha arrived at the exact moment that Jane came bringing little Jackson. "Good timing," Eliza told them. "Jessie's gotta nurse her young'un."

"What can we do?" Tabitha asked, casting an anxious glance toward Naomi.

"As soon as Jessie gets her through this contraction, I need you two to get her up and walk her 'round the room."

Mamie had already lowered herself onto the bed, patting Naomi's hand. "I's here for ya, child. You just lean on yer ole Mamie."

Naomi choked on a sob and lowered her head onto Mamie's shoulder.

Hours later, sometime after midnight, the baby dropped down and Naomi's water broke. She'd been walking with her arms around Tabitha and Jessie when she felt it happen. Naomi looked down at the floor and started crying. "I'm sorry, Eliza."

Emotional tears flooded Eliza's eyes. "Oh, thank you, Lord," she breathed. "Don't you worry about a thing, Naomi. This is what we've been waitin' for." She beckoned the women into the back room and helped Naomi onto the examining bed. But all Eliza could do was shake her head. "Not yet."

For several more hours, one contraction after another ravaged Naomi's body. Eliza soon began to worry in earnest. She had seen many difficult labors in her time, but none so long as this. If the baby didn't come soon, Naomi wouldn't have enough strength left to help with the delivery.

At dawn, after her third examination, Eliza told the women to put Naomi on the birth stool. It took all of them to get her there. Mamie immediately braced herself behind Naomi, supporting her back and spouting words of love and encouragement. Jessie and Tabitha held her arms tightly to keep her in place. Naomi could hardly sit up.

Eliza moved in between her thighs and raised Naomi's listless chin. "Look at me, sister, this is it. You give me all you've got."

Naomi's eyes were clouded by days' worth of pain. She was barely conscious. Eliza's heart started racing—she feared they would lose her.

"Push, hard!"

All the women joined in the chorus with Eliza, urging Naomi to give what she had left.

It worked.

The baby girl came sliding into Eliza's hands, wrinkled and bloody. The healer went right to work on her, clearing her mouth and nostrils. A tiny cry sounding like the bleat of a lamb, brought a welcome relief to all of the women, save for one—Naomi. She had already slipped into unconsciousness.

Eliza was torn between the newborn child and Naomi. The women continued to hold her on the birth stool while she delivered the afterbirth—all three were crying. When the time was right, Eliza quickly tied off the umbilical cord and cut it. She'd done it so many times, she didn't even have to think about it. Her mind was overrun with saving Naomi.

"Can you get her on the bed?"

They all nodded. Jessie directed them to work together. Eliza was thankful Jessie had been through so many births—she knew exactly how to care for Naomi after the delivery.

Watching the women work on her dear friend, Eliza dared to ask, "Is she breathin'?"

Tabitha dropped her head onto Naomi's chest. "She is. I feel her heart beatin'."

"Jessie, come swaddle the babe for me." As soon as Jessie took over, Eliza helped the other two get Naomi into her bed in the other room. She still hadn't come around.

Pouring water into the basin, Eliza dipped a cloth in it and bathed Naomi's face. With great relief, that action seemed to bring her back. When her eyes fluttered open, the women let out a collective sigh of relief.

"Welcome back, sister," Eliza said, kissing her forehead tenderly.

It was obvious Naomi was still in a haze, but she had the wherewithal to ask about the baby. "Is she all right?"

At that moment Jessie brought her into the front room. "She be perfect, Naomi. And she be wantin' her mama in the worst way."

A feeble smile touched Naomi's parched lips. She raised her hand toward the baby. "Oh, my precious girl."

Mamie moved to the other side of the bed. "Here, child, let us help ya sit up."

After arranging pillows behind her back, Mamie stepped away so Naomi could receive her babe from Jessie. "Thank you, Father," Naomi breathed, looking at her precious daughter. Tears of joy and gratitude spilled from her eyes.

Jessie sat down beside her and opened Naomi's gown. "See if she can suckle."

But after several attempts, the babe was frustrated and began to cry loudly. Naomi's body had nothing to offer. Through tears of anguish, she pleaded, "What can we do?"

Jessie looked down at herself and softly laughed. She worked her way into the bed next to Naomi. "You hold her whilst I feed her."

Naomi looked stunned. "Are you sure? Will you have enough for Jackson?"

This time Jessie laughed a little louder. "Trust me, gal, there be plenty to go 'round."

That evening, Isaiah walked Mamie and Tabitha back to the big house. He had stayed outside Eliza's cabin all night and all day. Franklin had been there too. The only time they left was to pick up some food at the noon meal and bring it back to Eliza's porch.

Earlier that afternoon, Phibe and Ceceilia had come calling, but Isaiah turned them away. "She be in good hands," he told them. When they argued, he didn't hesitate to give his kinfolk a piece of his mind. "You'ins ain't got no right comin' to Naomi after the way you's treated her. Go on home." Completely flabbergasted, they did as they were told.

Big John brought his youngest to the cabin at feeding time. Jessie told him she was spending the night and would keep Jackson with her. He offered Naomi a thoughtful gaze when his wife told him she would need to feed two babes for a while. As soon as husband and wife went out on the porch to talk, Eliza sat down on Naomi's bed. She was deeply worried about her friend. Naomi's face remained pale, and her heart rate was weak.

She laid the back of her hand on Naomi's forehead, then her cheek. A thankful smile turned her lips as she looked at the sleeping child in her arms. Placing her hand lightly on the baby's back, she uttered the profound words of the Almighty. "Before I formed you in the womb, I knew you. Before you were born, I set you apart."

"Rachel," Naomi breathed quietly. "Her name is Rachel."

"Beautiful name for a beautiful child," Eliza said. "Just like her mama."

For a long moment, both women admired the little miracle in Naomi's arms. Then, glancing over her shoulder, Eliza made sure they were still alone. "I have a question for ya before it gets too late."

"What is it?" Naomi asked.

"Should I go to the big house and let the master know he has a daughter?"

Naomi's eyes moistened. "He needs to know. But the way news travels in the house, I'm sure he's already heard." She looked down at her daughter. "It's late, you should go in the morning."

Eliza nodded. "I'll give Jessie my bed tonight and make a pallet right here on the floor by you."

"There's room for the three of us," Naomi said quietly.

"Oh, no. You and Rachel need to rest. I'll be just fine."

During the night, when the baby girl began to fuss, Eliza got up and changed her linens, then swaddled her for feeding. Jesse slipped into bed with Naomi, and Eliza laid down with Jackson until the baby girl was satisfied.

It was on the second feeding of the night, near dawn, that Jessie discovered something dreadfully wrong. "Eliza," she called out in panic, "light a lantern. Naomi's strugglin'."

Eliza was up before Jessie could finish her sentence. In the light of the lantern, Eliza could see that the bedsheets were completely soaked. Naomi moaned softly when the healer laid a hand on her forehead—she was burning up with fever.

The little newborn was still bawling, begging for comfort and sustenance. "I gotta feed her," Jessie said over the noise of her pitiful cries.

"Go on, then. I'll tend to Naomi, but as soon as you're done, I need ya."

Jessie took care of little Rachel, then crawled back into bed beside Jackson to feed her. "What do ya think's wrong?"

Eliza knew exactly what it was. She could smell the infection before even checking. "It's her womb—she's infected."

Jessie's brow creased. "Can ya do somethin' for her?"

Yanking the sheets back, Eliza began applying cool, wet cloths to Naomi's face and chest. She bathed her arms and legs to bring the fever down, all the while whispering, "You stay with me, Naomi. You hear me? Your fight's not over yet. Keep fightin'."

Naomi moaned but didn't open her eyes.

"We're gonna need more help. I can't get her in the tub alone," Eliza said.

"You go," Jessie told her while still nursing. "Get John."

Eliza nodded and bolted onto the front porch, running smack into little Franklin, knocking him off his feet. "Franklin, what are you doin' out here this early?" she bellowed.

Franklin couldn't answer. She'd knocked the air right out of him. Squatting down to him, she pulled his arms above his head. "There now, catch your breath, young'un."

It only took a few seconds before Franklin was inhaling again. He stood up, but Eliza stayed down on his level, grabbing his shoulders in a vice. "I need ya to do somethin' awful important, Franklin. All right?"

He looked her intently in the eyes and nodded unwaveringly. "Yes'm."

The words that came out next surprised Eliza herself. "Go find your pappy and tell him to get the master right now." She shook the boy hard. "You hear me?"

He nodded again, then shot out like an arrow from a bow when she released his shoulders.

Back inside the cabin, Eliza went to work on a poultice that she hoped would draw out the infection in Naomi's womb. Jessie had just finished nursing Rachel and laid her in the bed with Jackson, surrounding them both with blankets and pillows.

"Is John comin'?" she asked.

Eliza shook her head. "It's someone else." Then, without elaborating further, she told Jessie to start filling the tub with cold water.

After several trips to the well, the tub was finally ready. Eliza stepped out on the front porch in time to see a horse galloping down the road, the master pushing his animal at top speed.

Samuel didn't bother to tether his horse when he jerked it to a halt. He jumped down and leapt onto the porch. "What's happened?" he asked the healer.

"Before you go in, Master, you need to know somethin'."

Panic dominated Samuel's eyes. "Is she all right? Please tell me she's all right."

"She had a terrible labor, Master. It took over two days to deliver your daughter, but she's got an infection inside her that we gotta stop from spreadin'." She grabbed his sleeve and tugged him toward the door. "I need ya to help me get her in the bathwater. Her fever's too high."

Samuel strode inside the cabin scarcely glancing at the babies in the other bed. His eyes were only for Naomi. Kneeling by the bed, he stroked her face. "Naomi," he said in a broken voice. "I'm here, my love."

She let out a soft moan, and her hand searched the bed for his. He immediately held it and brought it to his lips. Then in one swift and gentle motion, he lifted her to his chest, following the two women into the back room. Bending down, he laid her in the tub, gown and all.

The shock of the cold water on her body brought a gasp from Naomi, and her eyes opened for the first time. They were murky with fever, but she recognized Samuel immediately and started crying.

He cupped her face in his hands and leaned forward, kissing her tenderly on the lips. With enormous effort, Naomi professed her love for him.

Jessie's eyes were the size of half-dollars. She pierced Eliza from across the tub with an astonished gaze. Eliza merely nodded her head, and Jessie's attention was immediately drawn back to the unexpected scene before her.

"You're John's wife, aren't you?"

Startled by her master's inquiry, Jessie quietly answered, "Yessir."

"I need you to go find Micah. Tell him he needs to bring Doc Burgess right away."

When Jessie jumped to her feet, he urged her to hurry.

Eliza took no offense that Master Hawkins wanted the doctor from town. She would take all the help she could get to save Naomi's life.

Naomi soon began to shiver uncontrollably, so Eliza ran into the front room, hastily returning with a chair and several towels. Samuel removed Naomi's gown while she was in the tub, then lifted her onto the towels covering the chair. He held her steady while Eliza dried her and got her into a new gown.

"Put her on my exam bed. I've gotta work on stopping the infection." She looked at her master with a sympathetic gaze. "You may wanna go outside for this."

He was already shaking his head. "I'm not leaving her." He knelt beside her and took her hand, drawing it to his mouth. "I'm not leaving you."

Naomi gave him a faint smile, then mashed her eyes shut, a guttural cry escaping her throat.

"I'm so sorry," Eliza told her. "I know this is painful."

The piercing cries continued, causing Eliza's vision to blur. She knew there would be no relief for Naomi from the agonizing pain. Blinking back tears, she told her master, "Stay with her while I change the linens on the bed."

He nodded, and she noticed the tears glistening on his dark beard.

"Oh, thank the Lord," Eliza called out as she entered the front room. Tabitha and Jessie were already there, taking care of the two babies. Mamie came inside utterly winded from such a hard walk but immediately started helping Eliza with the linens. "Master," Eliza said, lightly touching his shoulder. "You can bring her to the bed now."

Just lifting Naomi into his arms brought another scream of pain that cut through every heart inside the cabin. When he laid her in the bed, Naomi grasped his arm and held on tight. "Stay with me," she begged Samuel.

He gazed about the room into the faces of the four women whom he owned. Every one of them urged him with a nod to do whatever Naomi wished of him. He immediately removed his boots and sat down on the bed, drawing Naomi into his arms.

Eliza cleared her throat, hinting to the others that it was time to go outside. Even though she knew the couple needed privacy, she didn't want to leave Naomi's side. "I'll just be over here if you need me." She moved to a chair near the fireplace.

Samuel dipped his chin to the healer, then turned his full attention back to Naomi. Eliza observed the two, all the while praying that the infection would leave Naomi's body.

"Have you...seen our daughter, Samuel?" Naomi could scarcely project her voice above a whisper. "She's so...beautiful."

Samuel stroked her arm and kissed her hair. "So is her mother." He drew her a little closer to his chest, continually expressing his love for her.

"Her name...is Rachel."

He nodded thoughtfully.

She turned slightly in his arms to see his face. "Samuel?"

"Yes, love, I'm right here." He bent his ear low toward her mouth.

With great effort, she told him, "I want you...to know Christ. You will...never be free until...you give your life to him."

"I will," he said without hesitation. "Just stay with me and help me. Please stay with me...I need you." His plea was intensely emotional.

Naomi's eyelids closed tightly while the crease in her brow deepened. Eliza sat forward in her chair, certain that her pain was excruciating. Naomi groaned as she massaged her temples with shaking hands. "My head."

Samuel immediately glanced at Eliza, a look of fear overshadowing his features.

The healer moved quickly to their bedside. She laid her hand on Naomi's throat, feeling the rapid heartbeat. Eliza reached for a cup of water and lifted Naomi's head, pressing it to her lips. "Naomi, take a sip for me."

Surprisingly, she took more than one sip, then collapsed back onto her husband. After a suspended moment, her eyelids flickered open. "Help me...sit up."

Samuel eased out of bed and worked in tandem with Eliza to get her into a sitting position with pillows behind her. She moaned through the whole process.

"What can I do for you, my love?" Samuel asked.

Naomi didn't hesitate. "Hold...our daughter."

Eliza nodded to her master. "I'll bring her to you."

Chapter 44

Eliza was shocked by the sheer number of people standing outside her cabin, but her eyes only searched for one. Jessie was sitting on the bench, cradling the baby girl, Franklin mashed up against her side. His hand rested on the top of Rachel's head. Isaiah sat on the other side of his son, elbows pressed upon the top of his thighs, obviously praying.

"Jessie, come with me." Eliza scanned the solemn gathering once more, hoping to see Micah and Doc Burgess, but they were nowhere in sight. She put her hand on Jessie's back, ushering her inside the cabin.

Master Hawkins had already gotten back in the bed with Naomi, holding her with great love and tenderness.

"Naomi?" Jessie said softly. "I gots yer baby child for ya."

Naomi's eyes opened and a brief smile illuminated her face. Her eyes were shining as she accepted Rachel into her arms.

For a long moment, the couple sat in silence, eyes riveted on the sleeping baby. Samuel's arm finally enclosed the child within his embrace.

When Naomi spoke, her voice rasped from her throat. "Samuel…Rachel is free. Promise me…she will be educated…in the house."

Samuel sat unmoving. Naomi gripped his shirtsleeve with surprising strength, her voice louder than before. "Promise me!"

Lowering his lips to Naomi's shoulder, then close to her ear, he said, "I promise."

Naomi immediately relaxed, then her eyes encompassed Eliza still standing nearby. "Dear one," she breathed, beckoning her to come close. Eliza's face bent to hers, but Naomi was incapable of even kissing her dear friend. Eliza turned and tenderly pressed her lips to Naomi's cheek instead. Tears tumbled from her eyes as she withdrew, still holding Naomi's gaze with deep affection. She loved her so.

When Eliza stepped away from the bed, a look of peace bathed Naomi's features, delivering her from the last few days of relentless pain. Her eyelids slowly and gently closed. "Free…" she whispered, as one final breath was expelled from her body.

The silence inside the cabin was unbearable. No one moved—not Samuel nor Jessie nor Eliza—not even the tiny babe whose eyes had opened. It seemed as if a bright light had been eclipsed by the horrendous power of death.

Samuel's face suddenly crumpled in anguish, and he bent his head low, kissing Naomi's face. Silent sobs began to well up, and he dropped his face to the top of her head. His body convulsed over and over again with one soundless sob after another.

Eliza couldn't bear to watch. She turned an agonizing gaze toward Jessie, then fled to the back room and out the door. As soon as she entered the herb garden she fell to her knees, grabbing handfuls of dirt and slamming her fists to the ground. Her sobs turned into wailing, as she bent her forehead to the earth.

Someone dropped down beside her and surrounded her with strong arms. His chest pressed into her back as he tightened his grip. Not until he spoke did she know it was Isaiah. She rose up and leaned into him, expending her grief unashamedly.

It was a long time before Eliza was able to capture a normal breath. When she finally did, Isaiah loosened his hold, and they both sat down in the dirt side by side. Another wave of grief came bounding back, and she bowed her head, covering it with both hands. "I couldn't save her," she mourned. A violent shudder ran through her as tears poured down her cheeks. "Why couldn't I save her?"

At that moment, a thought so dreadful entered her mind it made her want to follow Naomi into the grave. What if the procedure she had used to prompt Naomi's labor had caused the infection? "Oh, Lord, no," she sobbed, as the darkness threatened to destroy her.

Isaiah embraced her again until she was able to bring her wild thoughts and emotions under control. He'd only spoken once since being with her, and he made no attempt to speak now. She was so grateful for his presence. He had kept her from going through these heart-wrenching moments by herself.

"Thank you," she said softly, turning her eyes to his.

Isaiah met her gaze with grief stamped all over his face. She knew his heart was painfully shattered. All he did was stand up and offer his hand to her. When she came to her feet, he let go, then turned away, leaving her all alone.

Eliza slowly walked back inside her cabin, but it was disturbingly empty. The oppressiveness of it caused her to quickly step outside again onto the front porch. Jessie was waiting for her, holding the newborn in her arms.

"The massa had Naomi took to the big house. Mamie and Tabitha's takin' care of her."

Eliza's heart throbbed with a terrible ache at the very thought. "What about Rachel?"

Jessie looked down at the baby girl, then back at Eliza. "I's to keep her."

Eliza's mouth dropped open. "But...."

"I knows," Jessie said. "But he's the massa. Sides, I's the only one that's feedin' her."

Turning her gaze down the road toward the big house, Eliza noticed Franklin for the first time sitting on the edge of the porch, staring at them. Poor fella. He'd already lost the two most important women in his life by the age of six.

"What will ya do?" Jessie asked her, clearly not wanting to leave the young healer alone.

Eliza had no clue. She knew she couldn't stay in her cabin tonight. She shook her head, feeling utterly lost.

Just then, Franklin stood up and pointed down the road. A horse and buggy were coming—it was Micah. He drew the horse to a stop in front of her cabin and addressed Eliza directly.

"Massa wants me to bring ya to the house. He says Doc Burgess needs to talk to ya."

Guilt and remorse instantly came rushing back. But as insidious as those two emotions were, another one rose up to take their place.

Panic.

What if the master blamed her for Naomi's death?

❧❧❧

Eliza was led into the side door of Master Hawkins' study, but the master was nowhere in sight. Instead, Doc Burgess rose from his chair as she entered. The two had never had occasion to meet, but Eliza would've given anything if he had made it to the plantation a few hours earlier.

"This is our healer, Eliza," Micah told the doctor. The overseer made no move to leave the room. It was obvious he was to be the eyes and ears of Master Hawkins.

Doc Burgess was not a young man, probably in his late fifties if Eliza were to guess. His salt and pepper hair, along with a matching beard, made him look grandfatherly and wise.

"Pleased to meet you, sir," Eliza said quietly.

The doctor nodded in response then took a seat. He didn't invite her to do the same, so she nervously stood before him.

"Tell me about the deceased woman's labor. Was it long?"

Clearing her throat, Eliza said, "Yes, sir. It was the longest I've ever seen. She struggled for a full night, all the next day, and then another full night before the babe was delivered."

Doc Burgess sat forward in his chair. "Having contractions of labor the entire time?"

"Yes, sir."

Taking out a small notebook and pencil, the doctor continued. "Do you know the woman's due date?"

"It was to be the 25th day of September, but she was two weeks past."

"And did you induce?" he asked.

"Induce?" Eliza had never heard that term before.

A half-smile turned the doctor's mouth. "That means to help get the labor process started."

Distressed over what she had done to Naomi, Eliza suddenly felt light-headed. She had had so little food and even less sleep over the last three days. That, coupled with the profound grief she was dealing with, made her feel like she was about to faint. When she started to sway, Micah instantly threw his hat on the desk and grabbed both of her shoulders. He led her to the chair facing Doc Burgess.

"Young woman, what's wrong?" the doctor asked.

"I'm sorry," she said, lowering her head between her knees. Immediately, she could feel the blood rushing back to her face.

Micah knelt beside her chair. "What do you need?"

Raising up slightly, she looked into his eyes, mentally noting his concern. "A glass of water will be fine," she said, slowly leaning back in the chair.

Micah quickly stood up and left the room.

Doc Burgess stroked his beard while piercing her with a curious gaze. After giving her a short time to recover, he finally asked, "Are you prepared now to answer my question?"

Eliza closed her eyes and took in a deep breath. When she opened them again, she tried to muster as much confidence as possible to tell him what she had done. But at that very moment, Micah returned, handing her a glass of water. She accepted it with thanks and took a long swig. There was something about Micah's presence that gave her the courage she needed to tell what she'd done.

The doctor listened intently, jotting down notes as she spoke. She told him about the red raspberry leaf tea and the long walks and how neither had been effective. When she was ready to speak about the procedure she had performed, Eliza was fully aware of Micah's rapt attention. While she had no qualms about sharing such things with a medical doctor, she had never talked of such an intimate subject in the presence of another man. She could feel the heat rising from her neck into her face, and she quickly glanced in Micah's direction. His demeanor told her that if she could handle it, he could too.

Expelling a deep breath, Eliza explained the method she had used to prompt Naomi's labor. As the doctor pressed for more and more details about what had happened, Eliza could feel that she was once again close to tears. *Don't fall apart,* she told herself. *Hold it together a little longer.*

Eventually, Doc Burgess closed his notebook, tapping his pencil on the cover. He sat forward with a satisfied gaze. Eliza waited nervously for his opinion.

Looking down, the doctor dropped his notebook into the black leather satchel at his feet. "There are two things I think you should know as a healer," he began. "Number one, inducing labor was the correct decision to make. It was obvious the baby's size was going to be a problem—you couldn't have waited any longer."

Eliza felt a small portion of her heavy burden of guilt slip away. But there was still so much more she was dealing with.

The doctor suddenly came to his feet and said, "Come with me."

Micah quickly went to the inner door to the house and opened it, allowing Eliza and the doctor to pass. "I hope you don't mind," the doctor said, leading her into the quarters of the household slaves. "But there's something I want to show you on the deceased woman."

Eliza's feet came to an abrupt halt. Micah nearly ran into her. "I can't," she said emphatically.

The doctor turned to look at her through narrowed eyes. "Young lady, I am trying to help you learn something today. I've spent thirty-six years in the medical profession, and I have seen this condition more times than I care to count. If this is your first time to encounter it, then you need to let me help you learn from it." He promptly turned and opened the door to Naomi's sewing room.

Still, Eliza's feet remained stationary. She was terrified of breaking down at the sight of her dear friend.

A gentle hand pressed the small of her back, and she turned to see Micah's sympathetic gaze. "Go on, now. You can do it," he encouraged. "I'll be right here if you need me."

A warmth filled Eliza that seemed to give her the strength to do what she knew she should. Turning back toward the door, she slowly stepped inside the room.

Naomi was lying on her sewing table. Eliza silently thanked the Lord that someone had covered her body with a sheet. She couldn't have handled looking upon the beautiful face of the one she loved as deeply as a sister.

It felt like a violation to examine Naomi after her death, but the doctor had been correct in doing so. He was able to enumerate the signs she should be watchful for in the future. Perhaps it could save another's life.

"Let's step outside in the hall," he said. "I have something to tell you before speaking with your master."

True to his word, Micah was still standing there, hat in hand. He took a step toward the healer when she left the room.

"The second thing you should know is this," the doctor pronounced as he pulled the door closed to Naomi's room. "For reasons which are currently unknown, when a woman suffers through an exceptionally long labor, she is highly prone to an infection of the womb. The longer the labor, the higher the risk." Doc Burgess' expression turned empathetic for the first time since they'd met. "I have never known a single woman to survive."

A rush of air escaped Eliza's lungs. It was as if her soul had run away from a life condemned to prison. She leaned back hard against the wall as the doctor passed by, heading toward the main hallway. As soon as he was gone, she bent at the waist, placing her hands on her knees. Without warning, the relief she had just felt twisted back into unimaginable grief, and this time, she spent it all in the arms of Micah.

Chapter 45

If Isaiah had thought about Naomi once, he'd thought about her a thousand times since she'd gone to be with Jesus over two weeks ago. There was an ache in his heart that he thought might never go away. He had felt the same way about his Ruthie, believing he would never be able to move on in life without a cloud of grief hanging over him. But it had been Naomi who had lifted that dark cloud. She had awakened his heart in a way he hadn't even thought possible, and now she too was gone. Where would he ever find comfort?

Oh, Lawd, forgive me, he silently prayed. *I knows you be the onliest one that can bring me peace.*

A large hand clamped down on Isaiah's shoulder, tugging him out of his painful reverie. "Try it now." Amos' deep voice matched the mountain of a man that he was. No one could rival the size nor strength of the Hawkins Plantation blacksmith.

Isaiah accepted the horseshoe and stood up from a low wooden stool. He roughly ran his hand down the rump and back leg of his master's horse. The animal lifted his hoof obediently while Isaiah sized it up. Nodding curtly, he said, "That be it, Amos."

Grasping the nails from his pocket, Isaiah clenched all but one between his teeth and lips. He straddled the rear leg and picked up the hammer off the ground. In a matter of seconds, he had finished nailing the last shoe to the animal. Then, pulling an iron file from his back pocket, he started shaving the hoof around the shoe when Amos fastened a tight hold on his wrist.

"You gonna shave that hoof plum off the massa's horse?"

Isaiah straightened, dropping the horse's hind leg to the ground. He hadn't realized how he was taking out his anger against the massa on his innocent animal.

"Somethin' eatin' at ya today?" Amos asked, releasing his grip.

Exhaling a long breath of frustration, Isaiah simply said, "I's all right. Just got things on my mind, that's all."

"Well, whatever it be, you best let it go." He nodded his head toward the road. "Massa done comin' fer his horse."

Isaiah turned around to see Master Hawkins striding toward the blacksmith's shop. A great sadness lingered in his massa's eyes, which only served to fuel Isaiah's resentment. He would've done anything to protect Naomi, even if it meant defending her from the man who owned him. He had always held Master Hawkins in high regard, but not now, not after the way he'd defiled Naomi and spoiled her reputation. He couldn't help but blame the man for her death.

Master Hawkins slapped his hand down on top of his horse, causing the animal to pull against the two ropes tethering his halter. "All done?" he asked Isaiah.

"Yessir, he be shod and ready to ride."

The master nodded his head, then disconnected both ropes. Instead of using a lead rope, he took hold of the halter and began guiding his sorrel gelding toward the stables. "Walk with me," he told Isaiah.

Isaiah immediately laid the tools on the blacksmith's bench and bobbed his head. "Thank ya, Amos."

The big man nodded, sweat glistening on his face and neck. "You's welcome."

The sound of iron clanking on iron faded into the background as Isaiah quickly fell in step with his master. "Can I takes him from ya, sir?"

Samuel merely shook his head. "I just wanted you to know that Micah and I have been talking about Franklin. We want him to start working in the stables full time. I know he's been with you for a long time anyway, but that boy's too valuable to be going to the mammy."

"Yessir," he said, keeping his eyes trained on the ground.

"There's something else I want you and Franklin to do. I need you both to go with me to Winchester next week. I'm taking Prince to a breeder there who will keep him for the next year. He's paying a hefty price for Prince's services."

Isaiah didn't respond. All he could think about was how his master was caught up in making money for himself while Naomi was lying somewhere in the cold ground. He didn't even know where she'd been laid to rest. And then there was the baby girl—the master's very own daughter living in slave town instead of the big house.

Master Hawkins yanked on the halter and pulled his horse to a standstill. "I asked you a question."

Looking up, Isaiah was caught completely off guard. He'd been so deep in thought he hadn't even heard what his master was saying. "I's sorry, massa."

Something flickered in Samuel's gaze that set Isaiah's nerves on end. Surely the man couldn't read his thoughts. "I asked if it would be all right for Franklin to ride atop Prince on the trip?"

"Massa, that's fer you to decide," he said flatly.

Now the master's eyes narrowed. "Why don't you just come out and say what's on your mind, Isaiah."

Isaiah's jaw clenched. He should've known better than to act like this around his master. But at the moment, he could barely stand to be near the man, much less give him respect that he didn't deserve.

The two men stood staring at one another for the space of several heartbeats. Isaiah noticed the rims of his massa's eyes growing red. When Samuel spoke, his voice held a raspy quality. "Here. Take my horse back to the stables." He handed him off to Isaiah, then lowered his head and walked briskly away without another word.

Isaiah watched the man until he was out of sight, a shade of guilt penetrating his heart. Who was he to judge the man? He'd done things in his own life that he wasn't proud of, but Isaiah knew for sure he would never treat a woman so disrespectfully. He would've given anything if Naomi had agreed to become his wife.

Kicking at a dirt clod, Isaiah released a deep sigh. If he couldn't figure out a way to get his emotions under control, it was going to be a hard trip to Winchester next week with Master Hawkins. The one saving grace would be having Franklin along.

With that thought, Isaiah's mood perked up a bit. He quickly took the master's horse to the stables, then headed to Mammy Lou's to pick up his son for the last time. But when he got to Mammy's, Franklin was nowhere to be found.

❧⸱❧⸱❧

It was rare for Jessie to ever raise her voice, but John should know better than to come between her and one of her children. "For the third time, I ain't lettin' you take her to the big house. That ain't our choice no how."

"But we's already got more chillins than we can feed and—"

"Get outta here right now, mister! I don't wanna hear no more o' yer whinin'."

Big John's eyes grew wide at his wife's sudden demand. Jessie could tell she'd finally gotten through to him. She lowered her voice, hoping not to wake up the two sleeping babies. "Listen up, mister, you ain't havin' to feed no extra chillins. I am! I's the one feedin' these two precious young'uns. Whatchu all afeared for anyway?"

John lowered his big frame onto a stool by the fireplace where Jessie had a meager soup simmering for the evening meal. He pulled the ladle up from the liquid and examined it. "This ain't hardly enough to go 'round," he murmured.

"Well, maybe you oughta thought about that 'fore you plowed this field again." She patted her midsection and raised her brow.

John dropped the ladle back down in the pot and gazed toward the cradle. "Look at her," John said. "Not a patch o' brown skin on her. You's actin' like that white baby belong to us."

Jessie's man was sliding out on mighty thin ice. He had never once cradled that baby girl in his arms or used his very own body to give her nourishment. But she had. And knowing that sweet baby's mama was gone just made Jessie want to protect her all the more. "As far as I's concerned, she *do* belong to us."

Turning an imploring gaze on his wife, John said, "Jessie, she be the babe of a loose woman and—"

"Well ain't that just like a man to be sayin' such! Naomi be no different than you or me. If the massa done took her fer his own, what choice do she got?"

"Somes at the mill say they seen her with the man all eager like."

Jessie shook her head adamantly. "Ain't none o' our business what went on tween the massa and Naomi. None a t'all. But it be our business to take care o' this baby child. She be all innocent-like. She gots no control over what brung her here, so I don't wanna hear another word about it."

John's mouth opened to speak, but Jessie wouldn't allow it. "You hear me?" she said emphatically. "No more!" Then, pointing toward the door, she told him, "Now, go tell our young'uns to get in here fer supper."

All John could do was shake his head, letting out a groan of defeat. He stood up and reluctantly headed outside. In her heart, Jessie knew her husband was right about one thing—they barely had enough food to keep their family nourished. John set traps in the woods near the stream, but an occasional rabbit or squirrel didn't do a lot to fill her supper pot. At least the noon meal with their kinfolk provided most of their daily sustenance. However, Jessie knew it was about to get harder in a few months when

Jackson was weaned. That would put one more hungry mouth at their table—a mouth they would barely be able to feed.

∽৵৵৽

Isaiah had spent the better part of the afternoon looking for Franklin while still trying to get his work done. Maybe the boy had gone to Eliza's for supper out of habit. But when Eliza opened her door, she shook her head. "He's not been back here to eat since Naomi passed on," she told him in a somber voice.

Taking a step back, Isaiah stared out across slave town, rubbing his neck in frustration. "Massa wants 'im to work in the stables with me, but how's he gonna do that if'n I can't find him?"

Eliza stepped out on the porch and closed her door. "Come on. I think I know where you can find him."

A few minutes later, Eliza was knocking on John and Jessie's door. John answered, giving Eliza a welcome nod, then turned his gaze on Isaiah. "You lookin' fer the boy?"

"I is."

John jutted his chin toward the inside of his cabin. "He be with us. You can come get 'im."

When Isaiah stepped inside, he noticed John's family all around the supper table, save for the two babies in the cradle. But Franklin was leaning over the cradle, playing with the little ones. He appeared to be keeping them well entertained while everyone finished their meal.

Isaiah immediately turned his gaze toward Jessie. "I's so sorry. He be disturbin' you'ins?"

"Oh, no," Jessie said, rising to her feet. "He gots a way with babes."

"Well, he ain't gonna disturb ya no more. Massa done wants 'im workin' with me in the stables." Franklin didn't look up when he heard his pappy's proclamation, but a slow smile tipped his mouth.

"Come on, little man. Les get home and has some supper of our own."

Franklin trailed a gentle hand down Rachel's arm, then headed toward the door with his pappy. Jessie followed the threesome onto the porch as her husband sat back down at the table with all their young'uns.

Lowering her voice, Jessie turned to Eliza. "You reckon you could do somethin' fer us?"

"Anything, Jessie. What do you need?"

"John's got a burr under his saddle 'bout not havin' enough to feed our little uns. Truth of it be, I's worried 'bout feedin' the big man hisself. And then when Jackson gets weaned, well...."

"Say no more," Eliza told her, laying a gentle hand on her arm. "I'll go to Micah first thing in the mornin' and see what can be done. After all, you're takin' care of the master's baby. I'm sure he'd be more than happy to supply your family with some extra food."

Isaiah crammed his hat down on his head and stormed off the porch. He hated the way he felt about his master, but it seemed the man's true character was coming to light. He paced back and forth in the dirt, kicking up a cloud of dust.

At the sudden silence, Isaiah glanced toward the porch. Jessie had already gone back inside, but Eliza and Franklin stood staring at him. Removing his hat, he scratched the top of his head, feeling a bit silly. "You'ins ready to go?" he asked.

Eliza's eyes narrowed as she stepped down off the porch. Isaiah turned, and both of them started walking slowly toward her cabin while Franklin ran on ahead. For a long time, they walked in silence until Eliza plunged right to the point. "You need to give the man a chance."

Isaiah wasn't sure he'd heard her right. "Who you talkin' 'bout?"

"The master," she said.

All Isaiah could do was shake his head. He would never speak the unkind things he was thinking out loud. It wouldn't be right. Yet he knew the Lord could see clear down into his heart. Just thinking such ill thoughts toward another was practically the same as saying them. But he could at least control what came out of his mouth.

"Aww, Eliza, I's all right. T'ain't nothin' fer ya to worry 'bout."

He could tell by the look on her face that Eliza thought otherwise. "Well, I won't poke into your business, but I do want to tell you one thing that might help. Naomi had the chance to rid herself of the baby, but she wouldn't do it. That baby back there meant everything to her."

When Isaiah looked over at the healer, her eyes held his intently. "Do you understand what I'm sayin' to you? She wanted the child she carried, and she wasn't ashamed of where it came from."

The hurtful conversation he'd had with Naomi outside the stables suddenly penetrated the depths of his soul. Isaiah had offered to marry her and take the baby as his own, but she had refused. If he remembered correctly, she had told him that she fully accepted the baby she carried.

Isaiah mulled that thought over in his mind until they were all the way back to Eliza's cabin. While he wasn't quite sure what to make of it, he started feeling some of the tension about his master loosen its grip. There was no doubt that Naomi had shared her private thoughts with the healer, but he had no right to ask about any of it.

"You and Franklin want to come in for supper?" Eliza asked.

"Thank ya, but Eula done already gots supper waitin'. You's welcome to come with us."

Eliza's mood seemed sad, despite the fact that her lips turned upward. Maybe it was the despondent look in her eyes that tugged at his insides. He knew a lonely heart when he saw one—after all, he'd spent the better part of the last two years in its clutches.

"Are ya sure?" he asked again, hoping for her sake that she'd change her mind. But suddenly, her eyes brightened.

"I'm sure," she said. "I just remembered there's somewhere else I need to be." And without so much as a word of good-bye, Isaiah watched her take off down the road toward the big house.

Chapter 46

Approaching Micah's house, Eliza's pace slowed to a crawl. She chided herself for walking all this way when the likelihood of actually knocking on the overseer's door was slim at best. She came to a halt beside a sizeable woodpile several yards away from his porch. Resting her hand on the axe handle embedded in a weathered stump, Eliza stared at the log house. There was a light burning in the window—obviously the man was inside.

Why hadn't she waited till morning? Dusk was already settling in. With that thought, she turned on her heels and started for home.

"Eliza? That you?"

Eliza could feel the heat creeping up her neck as she turned back around. All she could think to do was wave.

Micah was off the porch in no time, his sturdy legs striding toward her. "What brings ya to the big house?" he asked.

It wouldn't do at all to tell him the truth behind her coming—that she was lonely and preferred his company over anyone else's on the plantation. Maybe the feelings stirring in her heart over the past two weeks had been hers alone. What if she'd misread Micah's tenderness toward her on the day of Naomi's death? She had been so distraught, maybe he was just being kind.

Reining in her rampant thoughts, she apologized for coming so late. "I meant to wait till mornin'." She started to back away. "I'll come again tomorrow."

A look in Micah's eyes arrested her attention. It was the same look she'd seen there two weeks ago. "No," he said, pointing toward the house. "Please stay."

"Are ya sure?"

"Come on in, it's gettin' chilly out here." He stepped closer, urging her to join him.

Once inside, Eliza was struck by the overseer's living space. It was not only neat and tidy, but one wall was half-covered by a shelf full of books. The light she'd seen in the window illuminated a comfortable chair with an open book turned upside down in the seat. Micah had been reading. Eliza looked from the book to the man.

A slow grin spread across his clean-shaven face, making her heart race. "Do you read?" he asked quietly.

She shook her head. "It's my dream. I still have Naomi's Bible at my place. I sure do love the feel of it in my hands."

Micah quickly reached for his half-eaten supper on the table by the lamp and started to dump it into his scrap bucket when Eliza stopped him. "Oh, no, don't do that. Please finish your supper."

He stood still for a moment, looking down at her. "Have you already eaten?"

Her hand went to her empty belly. "Well, to be honest, I haven't eaten since breakfast. It was a busy day."

Immediately Micah pulled a chair away from his table and waited for her to sit down. Then he went to the fire and put a helping of Mamie's meatloaf and sweet potatoes and peas on a plate. When he set it in front of Eliza, he told her, "Mamie loads me up every night for supper. She thinks I need more meat on my bones." He sat down across the table, nodding for her to eat. "I'm glad to have someone to share it with," he said.

Forgetting all about the reason for her visit, Eliza found herself enjoying Micah's company immensely. They easily traded stories about their lives, even sharing their hopes for the future. She admired his ease with conversation and his quick wit that caused her to laugh out loud more than once. That seemed to bring the man a great deal of satisfaction.

Supper had long been over, but the two were still sitting at the table when a knock sounded on his door. Before Micah could even get to it, the master stuck his head inside. "Micah, can I talk to you for a—" His words abruptly ended as he noticed Eliza. "I'm so sorry." The master laid his hat against his chest. "I didn't know you had company."

Micah went to him. "Sir, it's fine. What can I do for ya?"

"It's nothing that can't wait till morning. You know how I get when something's running through my mind."

Eliza came to her feet. "Master, it's getting late, and I need to be on my way. Please stay."

Micah looked distressed. She was certain he had planned to get her home safely in the dark. But she didn't fear the night. Eliza was used to traipsing all over slave town in the dark to deliver a baby or take care of a woman in need.

Suddenly remembering her original purpose for coming and feeling empowered by all that she had witnessed between Naomi and the master, she decided to address the man directly. "Master, the reason I came here tonight was to ask a favor for John and Jessie."

Samuel stepped fully inside the door and closed it behind him. "Is it about the baby?"

"Part ways, sir. They're strugglin' to feed such a big family, and now with Jessie takin' care of Rachel, well…."

Without hesitation, Samuel turned to his overseer. "Whatever they need, Micah, you see to it." He momentarily stroked his beard, contemplating the situation at hand. "I know John works at the gristmill, what about Jessie?"

"She's a dairymaid over in the cow barn."

"No more," the master said, shaking his head. "From now on she stays home to take care of all the children in their household."

Eliza couldn't believe her ears. Such a heavy burden was being lifted from John and Jessie's dear family. "Thank you, sir," she said. "You have no idea how much that will mean to them."

Micah chimed in. "I'll see to it first thing in the mornin', sir. Is there somethin' else I can help you with before then?"

Master Hawkins didn't answer his overseer. He stood for a long moment, staring at Eliza. She instantly read his thoughts as though they were her own. A great wretchedness dwelt within the man—she was certain he was blaming himself for Naomi's death.

The poignant words left her mouth before she could stop them. "She loved you without measure."

Samuel took in a shuddered breath while slowly nodding. Then he opened the door and quietly said, "Good night."

Micah held Eliza's hand all the way back to her cabin. It didn't seem uncomfortable in the least. As a matter of fact, all she could think about was how natural it felt. How had she known this man for so long but never once looked at him in this way until two weeks ago? It was obvious now that his feelings equaled her own.

When they arrived at her cabin, he walked right in without so much as an invitation. Immediately he went to her fireplace and worked until she had a roaring blaze. Then, before she knew what was happening, he bent his face to hers and kissed her sweetly.

"G'night, Eliza," he said in a low voice.

"Good night, Micah," she replied, before touching her fingers to lips that no man had ever kissed...until tonight.

෴

A small crowd had gathered at Chester Brant's stables in Winchester to get a good look at the champion racehorse. The Prince of Madagascar was putting on quite a show, particularly since a six-year-old boy was riding him around the large indoor paddock. Isaiah felt a sense of pride as he listened to the words of praise for Prince and Franklin alike.

Brant's negro trainer stood next to Isaiah, shaking his head in disbelief. "I hear-ed that boy be atop the Prince when he won the race in '55. That be true?"

A half-smile turned Isaiah's lips. "It weren't supposed to be that way, but that's exactly what happened. The boy only be four at the time."

"Ooh, wee. Sure woulda liked to seen that," the trainer said.

"I's wishin' I hadn't," Isaiah quipped. "Liked ta scared me ta death."

The two men watched as Master Hawkins entered the paddock, both hands in the air, indicating for Franklin to bring Prince to a halt. The stallion obediently submitted to Franklin's will, drawing a sedate round of applause from the onlookers.

When Franklin slid to the ground, his master kept him close by the horse as he led him out of the arena and into a nearby stall. Isaiah couldn't see his boy with so many men gathering around. Mr. Brant's trainer worked his way through the onlookers and into the stall, taking Franklin with him. Like everyone else, Isaiah figured he'd heard the stories about Prince's antics at the race three years ago. Just thinking about that day put Isaiah's nerves on end and opened an old wound of sorrow over his Ruthie. He missed her something awful.

It was a good hour before Master Hawkins was satisfied with Prince's care. He had been paid half of the stud fee now and would collect the rest upon his return the following year. Isaiah didn't know how much it was, but it was enough that the master had a pistol strapped to his hip and a shotgun in the wagon for protection.

"Come on," Master Hawkins said to Isaiah. "It's getting late, and I want to show you some property before dark."

Isaiah dipped his chin while he and Franklin headed to the mule wagon out front. It was only about a fifteen-minute ride outside of Winchester before the master nodded toward a steep, narrow road through the trees. "Head the mules up that way," he told Isaiah.

"Yessir," Isaiah said, turning the mules off the main road. He guessed this would be the place where they would spend the night.

Coming out of the woods, Isaiah instantly admired the beautiful bluegrass pasture that seemed to go on and on. A line of trees rimmed the pasture in the distance, but a magnificent oak tree stood in a nearby corner all alone. The autumn leaves had already turned orange and yellow, and they shimmered in the waning light.

"This land belonged to my grandfather, Joshua Hawkins," the master said. "It was compensation for his outstanding service in the Continental Army. He never built on the property, but it has an unusual feature." He pointed across the pasture. "Take the wagon that way."

Isaiah did as he was told, driving the mules through the grass. When they made it to the line of trees, Isaiah realized they wouldn't be able to go much further. A giant rock formation was just beyond. He pulled the mules to a halt, and they strained at the harness, anxious to get a mouthful of bluegrass.

Master Hawkins jumped from the wagon and turned to the boy. "Come on, Franklin. I've got something to show you." He reached into the back of the wagon and pulled out a lantern. Isaiah quickly tethered the mules to a tree and followed behind the pair. As they rounded the outcropping of rocks, a gaping hole stood before them.

"My grandfather actually lived inside this cave for a while after the war for independence," the master said. He reached into his pocket and took out a tin of matches, then quickly lit the lantern. As they moved deeper into the cavern, Franklin trailed his hand along the limestone wall while Isaiah walked behind the two.

"Grandpa Hawkins lived in here, along with his horse and a few chickens and cows, after the war with the British ended."

It wasn't long before the cavern they traversed turned into a winding passageway. The ceiling got to be so low near the end, both of the men had to duck down a bit. When they exited the narrow passage, all three came into another sizeable cavern where the dim evening light drifted in from a spherical opening above. An old rickety ladder stretched from the floor of the cave to the opening up top.

Master Hawkins grasped one of the rungs and shook the ladder. Little clods of dirt fell from above, causing him to take a step back. "It's pretty old. I doubt it would hold any of us now."

Isaiah was thoroughly intrigued by the cave hidden beneath the bluegrass pasture overhead. Franklin, on the other hand, seemed fascinated by the ladder and looked as if he was ready to make good use of it. Isaiah positioned himself between the boy and the ladder, just in case he decided to give it a go.

"Well," the master said, "we best get back to the entrance and set up camp before it gets too dark." He moved toward the opening of the passageway. "What do you think about this, Franklin?" he asked.

Franklin gave his master a broad smile. "Can I live here?" he asked.

A loud guffaw echoed through the cave, as Master Hawkins put his hand on the boy's shoulder and led him into the narrow opening. "Then who would train my horses?" he asked, still chuckling as they made their way back to the other end.

By the time the trio had a good blaze going just inside the entrance of the cave, the sun finished its journey below the horizon. Mamie had sent a box loaded with cornbread, brown beans, and a slab of ham, which they all eagerly devoured.

Isaiah laid out his and Franklin's bedrolls a short distance from the fire. After taking the boy outside to do his business, he got him settled under his blanket for the night and sat down beside him.

"Pappy?"

"Uh, huh?"

"I likes it here."

Isaiah laid a gentle hand on his son's chest and smiled. "I's likin' it here too. That be a fine bluegrass pasture up top."

"Is we gonna get to come back?" Franklin asked, his eyelids starting to droop.

"I specs we's gonna be back this time next year when we come fer Prince." Isaiah leaned down and lovingly kissed Franklin's brow. "You get some sleep now. I loves ya, little man."

After a big yawn, Franklin said, "I loves you too, Pappy."

Isaiah continued to sit beside his son, praying and watching over him until he fell asleep. When he looked up, the master's eyes caught his. Samuel had leaned back against the wall and taken off his boots. His legs stretched out toward the fire. "Come warm your feet, Isaiah."

While that sounded awfully good at the moment, Isaiah still struggled with his feelings toward Master Hawkins. In all the long hours on the road today, they'd barely exchanged a handful of sentences between them. But he obviously couldn't refuse the man's request.

Isaiah moved around the fire and sat down near Samuel, pulling off his boots. He pressed his back to the wall beside his master and had to admit, it felt nice.

For a long time, neither man spoke. Isaiah stole a quick glance at his master—the man seemed to be struggling with something. He'd already let out several deep breaths and cleared his throat a couple of times. Whatever it was, Isaiah wasn't going to ask him about it. Better to just sit here in silence than dredge up memories too painful to even speak of.

Finally, Isaiah yawned and reached for his boots. "Well, massa, I best be turnin' in with my boy."

But Master Hawkins had other plans. "Not yet, Isaiah," he said quietly. "There's something I think we need to talk about." He turned his gaze fully upon Isaiah, emotion flickering in his dark eyes. "I saw you with Naomi last year on Christmas day." While his voice was quiet, it had an edge to it that made Isaiah more than a little uncomfortable. "Did you have feelings for her?"

Everything within Isaiah rebelled against answering his master's pointed question. If only he had the right to refuse—but he didn't. Yet if he admitted that he'd loved her, what would the man do to him? The master had completely demolished the bond of trust that had once existed between them. Feeling trapped, yet unwilling to lie, Isaiah begrudgingly nodded his head. "Yessir," he breathed.

Samuel leaned his head onto the limestone wall, turning his attention toward the fire. After a couple of beats, he looked back at his trainer. "I owe you an apology, Isaiah."

Isaiah's brow dipped. That wasn't at all what he'd been expecting to hear.

Without a pause, the master said, "I'm going to tell you something that no one else can know. Maybe it will bring you some peace." Hauling in a deep breath, he quietly said, "Naomi was my wife. We got married last year in August."

Isaiah's mouth gaped open not unlike the entrance to the cave where they sat. He was having a hard time trying to comprehend his master's words. Had he heard him right?

Master Hawkins' mouth twitched, but his eyes remained doleful. "I can only assume that you thought I…mistreated Naomi, but that's not the case at all. I loved her like I've never loved another." Looking away again, he said, "There's something else I think you should know."

Isaiah pulled his mouth closed—emotions roiling like waves on the ocean.

"Naomi was a free woman," Samuel told him. "I manumitted her just a few weeks after the accident. I wanted her to have the freedom to reject me if she chose to do so."

Isaiah's eyes now brimmed with tears of shame. He felt an overwhelming sense of guilt for carrying such a strong desire for Naomi while all along she'd been another man's wife. His master's wife, no less. Isaiah's chin dropped toward his chest. "I's so sorry, massa. I woulda never looked at her if I know'd she be yers." His voice broke with regret. "I's so sorry."

After an extended silence, Isaiah raised his head, noticing the streak of tears on his master's face. Both men had been severely wounded by unimaginable sorrow. Each one had lost a wife and daughter on the same day, and now Naomi too was gone—a woman they had both loved. But Isaiah's disgraceful behavior coiled a hurtful pathway through his conscience. No wonder Naomi had turned down his offer of marriage. He now felt foolish for thinking he could've ever made her happy.

Rubbing both hands across his face, Isaiah turned to his master. "You's not the one needin' to make an apology, massa, I is. Can ya forgive me?" he begged.

Samuel shook his head emphatically. "It wasn't your fault, Isaiah. You had no way of knowing Naomi was a married woman. I'm just sorry we couldn't tell you."

With that, Master Hawkins reached for his boots and pulled them on. When he stood up, Isaiah quickly did the same. The two men stood facing one another, Isaiah feeling his trust in the man slowly returning. The massa hadn't disgraced Naomi after all.

Master Hawkins locked his eyes on Isaiah with an earnest gaze, then held out his hand. "Can I count on you to keep this information just between you and me?"

Isaiah gripped his master's hand firmly and nodded. "I swears never ta tell another living soul."

"Thank you," Samuel said, squeezing his hand before letting go. Then, picking up his hat, he told him, "Get some sleep, Isaiah. I need to go out for some fresh air."

"Yessir," Isaiah said, watching him disappear into the darkness.

Walking over to his bedroll, Isaiah removed his boots again and laid down, pulling the blanket up to his chest. For a long time, he watched the flickering patterns of firelight dance against the wall and ceiling until his mind began to ponder events of the past two years. The massa's confession certainly brought everything into clearer focus, but still, there was something bothering him. Something keeping his thoughts stalled in confusion. And then it hit him—why had Naomi moved into slave town to have the baby? Had it been purely to be near the healer, or had something happened to make her leave the big house?

Rolling over, Isaiah checked on his son, who continued to sleep peacefully by his side. Isaiah's thoughts, however, were anything but peaceful. Whatever had happened all centered around the fact that Naomi had gotten pregnant. Isaiah's eyes narrowed as he remembered the healer's recent words. Naomi had been given the chance to rid herself of that baby, but she refused. Had his massa been the one who wanted to do away with the child? Maybe that explained why he had left his own baby child in slave town.

Isaiah turned back over, staring at the ceiling of the cave. It would be hard to find sleep with so many questions running through his head—even if those questions were none of his business. While only a few minutes ago he had felt the old, familiar respect return for his massa, Isaiah wasn't quite sure what to do with the man if he was truly willing to leave his own daughter in the hands of his slaves.

One thing was certain, discovering that Naomi had been married did very little to take away the agony of her loss. Isaiah had loved her.

He would always love her.

October 1859

At his master's request, Isaiah pulled the wagon over to the side of the road. They had gotten an early start this morning and were over halfway to Winchester to pick up Prince. Master Hawkins planned to make the trip there and back all in one day, which shouldn't be a problem.

Franklin stood up in the back of the mule wagon, using his right hand to shade against the midmorning sun. A sea of people stood nearly, shoulder to shoulder in an open pasture—all of their attention rapt on one man perched atop a large stump right in the middle. His voice boomed out into the wide expanse, yet he turned an almost tender gaze upon the audience that hemmed him in on all sides. The man's sleeves were rolled up, and perspiration dotted his brow despite the cool breeze.

Samuel Hawkins stepped down from the wagon and walked to the edge of the crowd. Tapping a man on the shoulder, Isaiah could hear his master ask, "What's going on here?"

"'Tis a stump meetin', sir."

Samuel's brow wrinkled. "A stump meeting? What is that?"

The farmer now turned his full attention on Samuel, but when he noticed Isaiah and Franklin in the wagon just off to the side, he seemed to weigh his words carefully. "Ever heard of John G. Fee?"

Shaking his head, Master Hawkins told him no.

The man slanted his eyes toward the wagon again, then back at Samuel. "Maybe you should give 'im a listen."

It was obvious that Master Hawkins' curiosity had been roused. He slid into the crowd, moving closer to the man on the stump.

When Franklin hopped to the ground, Isaiah quickly did the same, grabbing his son's jacket. "Nuh, uh, little man. You stays right here."

Even though the crowd had a fair amount of negroes, Isaiah's main concern was keeping Franklin from getting lost. Furthermore, should Master Hawkins return, they would be expected to still be with the wagon.

"Come on, Son, you needs to get back in. Sides, you can see better up there."

The boy immediately did as he was told, causing Isaiah to relax his guard. He stepped back up in the front of the wagon, trying to concentrate on the man's message, even though he could only grab snatches when the preacher turned their way.

"'Tis my constant plea—love thy neighbor as thyself," Isaiah heard him say.

"I, like the Apostle Paul, have been beaten, whipped, nearly hanged to death, cursed, clubbed, held at gunpoint, burned out of my own home, disinherited by my slave-owning father...."

The rest of the man's words drifted in another direction. Both Isaiah and his son leaned forward to pick up what they could. "But I will not retaliate," they heard him proclaim. "Nay, I willingly accept such hardships for the cause of Christ, and for the love of all of God's children." And though he faced away, the preacher's next words bellowed loudly into the crowd. "God's love is impartial—and so should our love be! For how can we call ourselves followers of the Almighty, while we cruelly enslave our own brethren? We must obtain true equality in this country for ALL or there is NONE for any."

As the preacher made another quarter turn on the stump, Isaiah found himself watching the crowd. Some of the men raised their hats in the air in agreement while others seemed edgy, even bordering on angry.

"My brothers, I implore you with love to free your slaves! Let no man or woman be enslaved to another…save to our Lord and Savior Jesus Christ and him alone."

Isaiah reasoned they must've gotten in on the tail end of the man's sermon. He watched him wipe his brow with a kerchief, then proffered one more earnest plea to the crowd. "I beg you to join this movement of love. It is our Christian duty to cooperate with one another. May God's will be done here on earth as it is in heaven."

A smattering of *amens* resounded throughout the audience as the preacher stepped down from his stump. Several people crowded around him, but when the man began coughing, a woman, presumably his wife, stepped forward and took his arm. The two walked through the pressing throng toward a long line of wagons and buggies parked along the road.

Assuming the crowd would disperse, Isaiah sat down on his side of the wagon bench, waiting for the return of his master. But almost immediately, another preacher stepped up onto the stump. He was an older man by the look of him, strands of gray streaking through his dark hair. He was much taller than the other fellow and lankier in build. Unfortunately for Isaiah, his voice didn't carry as far as the one before him, and he found himself wishing he too could move closer.

Since several people left once the man named Fee finished his message, that gave others the opportunity to step in closer. To Isaiah's surprise, he saw Master Hawkins work his way up to the very front. And if he wasn't mistaken, the two men actually acknowledged one another. It was obvious, even from Isaiah's distance, that the massa and this preacher had met before.

"Pappy, I can't hear 'im."

"Me neither," Isaiah agreed. "I's thinkin' maybe we could move up a bit, since Massa be all the way in the front."

Franklin's face beamed at the prospect.

Isaiah stepped down from the wagon and stood in front of his son. "Come on, fella, let me give ya a ride."

Even though the boy had grown quite a bit from his sixth to seventh year, he still wasn't as heavy as a feed sack. Isaiah easily carried the boy astride his shoulders.

Not wanting the massa to be out of his view, Isaiah only moved partially into the crowd, careful not to get in the way of someone else's view.

While this preacher's message was along the same lines as the other, his words were less fiery and more sympathetic toward his listeners. "Folks, this is a heart issue," he told them. "Unfortunately, many among us are sick with a disease, not with physical infirmities but with the infirmity of sin. Our hearts are full of greed, hatred, slander, and envy. As the Apostle Paul says in his letter to the Galatians, 'Brethren, ye have been called unto liberty; only use not liberty for an occasion to the flesh, but by love serve one another. For all the law is fulfilled in one word, even in this; Thou shalt love thy neighbor as thyself.'"

The man went on for several long minutes. His words and manner were so compelling, many in the crowd began to weep. Isaiah reached up to wipe away the moisture from his own eyes, wishing to renew his commitment to Christ. He longed to be the kind of man this preacher described. He knew in his heart that he had fallen far short of the mark.

"But God, in his tender mercy, has brought us to the foot of his beloved Son's cross." The man's kindly eyes searched the crowd with heartfelt emotion. "Who among us is carrying a heavy weight of sin and guilt? Those who carry such are the true slaves among us. But Galatians chapter five and verse one tells us that it is for liberty that Christ has set us free. Stand fast, then, 'and do not be burdened again by the yoke of slavery'—that is, slavery to sin."

Finishing with an emotional plea, he begged the slave owners to set their brothers and sisters free from bondage. Then he concluded with a scripture from the book of John, chapter eight. "'If the Son, therefore, shall make you free, ye shall be free indeed!'"

As soon as the preacher finished his last phrase, he stepped from the stump right into the embrace of Samuel Hawkins.

∽∾∾∽

"Follow that buggy," Master Hawkins pointed out. "We're going to their house for the noon meal."

"Yessir," Isaiah said, pulling the wagon back onto the main road. Though he was mighty curious as to how Massa Hawkins knew the preacher, he could only hope that his massa would enlighten him before arriving at their destination.

It was slow going as the crowd scattered in different directions, but Isaiah was able to get close behind the buggy carrying the preacher, his wife, and another couple. After only a mile or so, the buggy turned off the main road to a white, two-story farmhouse. The barn out back was nearly triple the size of the house with pasture land surrounding both structures.

Isaiah followed the buggy around the back of the house and noticed a stable on the other side of the barn previously hidden from view. As soon as he pulled the mules to a halt, both couples in the buggy disembarked and came toward the wagon. Master Hawkins stepped down, but Isaiah and Franklin held their positions, awaiting instructions. He assumed that they would spend their time at the stables until the massa was ready to leave. But surprisingly, the preacher came to Isaiah's side of the wagon. Stretching out his hand, he said, "I'm Daniel Ward."

Isaiah tentatively gave the preacher his grip. "Isaiah, sir."

"Pleased to meet you, Isaiah. And who is this strapping young fella back here?"

"Oh, that be my boy, Franklin, sir."

The preacher moved to the back of the wagon and offered his hand to Franklin. "Nice to meet you, young fella." Then, turning back toward Isaiah, he said, "Come on in, you two. Lunch will be served soon."

Isaiah instantly moved his gaze toward the massa. Maybe the preacher man had misspoke. But Samuel Hawkins had signaled for Franklin to follow, and the boy didn't hesitate one bit.

Daniel moved aside for Isaiah to step down from the wagon. "I'd like you to meet my wife, Juliette. Juliette, this is Isaiah."

Isaiah removed his hat and held it to his chest. Bowing slightly, he said, "Pleased ta meet ya, ma'am."

Juliette offered a kindly greeting, then lightly took Isaiah's elbow, leading him toward the back porch. "Uh, ma'am," he said. "I needs to take care o' the mules."

"Done," the driver of the buggy said. "My sons will take care of it for you."

Isaiah looked over his shoulder and sure enough, two boys, a few years older than Franklin, were already leading the mules toward the stables. The man extended his hand. "The name's Marvin…Marvin Bennett."

"Isaiah, sir."

"Welcome to our sorghum farm, Isaiah. Come on in and we'll all get acquainted."

Feeling his mouth go dry, Isaiah reckoned he'd entered into some kind of mixed-up world. While he'd heard the preacher's sermon, his mind had yet to wrap itself around this kind of interaction with white folks. He wanted to stop and say, 'Is you sure?', but Juliette Ward still held his left elbow and Franklin had plum already disappeared inside the house. All Isaiah could do was go along with the rest of these folks. Maybe it would all come to rights when they got inside the house.

But it didn't.

"Rose," Marvin called out, "come meet Isaiah. Isaiah, this is my wife, Rose."

The woman had already donned an apron and was busy in the large kitchen into which they had entered. Wiping her hands down a white apron, she offered Isaiah her right hand and a welcoming smile. "Ever so pleased to meet you," she said.

"I's happy ta meet you too, ma'am."

Rose gave him a friendly pat on the arm. "Now go on with the men in the other room. Us girls will have lunch done in no time. I'll introduce you to my daughters when it's time to eat."

At that moment, one of the Bennett's young sons burst through the kitchen door. "There you are, Taylor," Rose said. "Go get the boy in the other room. His name's Franklin, and this is his daddy."

Just like the others, Taylor extended his hand toward Isaiah. "Is it all right for Franklin to come outside with me?" he asked eagerly.

Putting Isaiah's mind at ease, Rose told him, "The boys can play outside for a while till the meal is ready…if you're fine with that."

"Yes'm. He be likin' that, I's sure."

Taylor disappeared into the other room, then seconds later scampered through the kitchen with Franklin in tow.

"Don't be late when the bell rings," Rose called as the boys headed outside.

"Yes, ma'am," Taylor shouted, letting the door slam behind him.

Mr. Bennett was still standing in the doorway to the other room and motioned for Isaiah to join the men. "Come on in and have a seat," he said, pointing to a chair beside the preacher.

Daniel Ward was leaning forward, intently talking to Samuel, who sat in the chair across from him. They seemed to be in a spiritual conversation of sorts as the preacher had an open Bible in his hands. After a fairly lengthy discussion about God's forgiveness, Mr. Ward sat back in his chair, turning his attention to Isaiah. "Are you a believer?"

"Oh, yessir," Isaiah told him. "I's belonged ta Jesus since I's a boy."

Isaiah moved his gaze to the massa and noticed the wrinkle lines across his forehead. It was obvious he was contemplating the things he'd just heard. Isaiah wondered if Massa Hawkins had ever given his life to the Lord. While the man had treated his slaves with dignity, he now wondered whether it was because of a faith in the Almighty or just out of the natural kindness of his heart.

After several more minutes of scripture talk, a bell clanged from somewhere outside. Mr. Bennett immediately stood. "That's the dinner bell. Let's not keep the women waiting."

In another room just off the kitchen, one of the longest tables Isaiah had ever seen stretched nearly from one wall to the other. Children of all ages and sizes came from every opening in the house, jostling one another until they made it to their places behind their chairs. Franklin was led by Taylor to a chair next to his, and Rose pointed out the seats for their other guests near the head of the table. No one sat down until Mr. Bennett pulled out his own chair and nodded. Then, the sound of chairs scraping the wooden floor filled the room until all occupants were settled.

Marvin Bennett offered a hand to his wife on one side and to Daniel Ward on the other. Everyone else around the table did likewise as the family chain was connected. Marvin addressed the preacher. "Brother Ward, would you be so kind as to bless our table?"

Daniel nodded while looking around the table. "Let's pray," he said, and everyone bowed their heads.

By the time the bounty of food had been consumed, Isaiah felt like he and Franklin had been adopted into the Bennett family. He had been introduced to their three daughters and six sons, all ranging in age from four to nineteen. Every one of them had a specific job on the farm and was prompted to tell their lunch guests all about it.

Mr. Bennett told Isaiah, "I'll give you a tour of the sorghum operation in our barn after we eat dessert. Rose makes the best apple sorghum pie this side of the Mississippi," he boasted, causing Rose to blush with satisfaction.

As the afternoon wore on, Isaiah began to wonder if they were going to even make it to Winchester before dark. They were due to pick up the Prince today after his yearlong service with Chester Brant, but the massa and Daniel Ward had been sitting out on the front porch for hours.

Isaiah had to admit, he was enjoying the company of Mr. Bennett and his sons. He was told that the sorghum harvest had just come to an end, and Isaiah was fascinated by the milling operation inside the barn. Marvin had even given him a jar of sorghum and told him it was Kentucky's syrup. "Put it on your breakfast biscuits and you'll never want jam again."

While the sun slowly traveled its downward path through the autumn sky, Samuel Hawkins and the Wards made their way out to the barn. When Isaiah saw his massa, he knew something was different. He couldn't quite put a finger on it, not until the preacher told them, "Samuel has made a decision to follow Christ. We'd like for everyone to join us at the pond to witness him putting on his Savior in baptism."

Isaiah's chest tightened as his gaze met Samuel's. The humility he saw in his massa's eyes filled him with unexpected emotion. Isaiah dipped his chin in respect to the man who had owned him all his life, and in return, he received a tenderhearted smile.

Later that night, while Marvin and Rose were seeing to it that all of the children got into bed, Isaiah sat by the fire in the front room with his massa and the Wards. Isaiah was told that Mr. Ward had been the one to perform Samuel and Naomi's wedding ceremony. As the discussion now centered on Naomi, Juliette had waited all day to find out what had happened to her. Hearing that Naomi had been lost in childbirth caused the dear woman to break down and cry. "Naomi was…such a precious soul," she said through her tears. "I'm deeply sorry for your terrible loss."

Samuel leaned forward, resting his forearms on his knees. His voice was low and full of emotion as he stared into the fire. "I've struggled mightily this year without her."

Isaiah, too, hung his head. He had witnessed his master's dreadful battle with grief all these months, even carrying that same heartache within himself. He had tried so hard to rid himself of it, knowing he had no right to feel the way he did, especially since Naomi had chosen to be with his massa. But for some reason, Isaiah's heart was taking its sweet time in moving on. It made him empathize with Massa Hawkins all the more.

Just then, Marvin and Rose entered the room, looking exhausted in a satisfied way. "We've doubled and tripled up some of the children in the beds so each of you will have a bed to sleep in," Rose announced. "And just so you know," she said, pinning her gaze on Isaiah, "Taylor is as happy as a lark in the meadow to have Franklin sleeping next to him tonight."

Isaiah sat back in his chair giving her a grateful smile. "Thank ya kindly, ma'am."

She patted Isaiah's shoulder on her way to the sofa. "You're not to be calling me *ma'am*. Please call me Rose."

Swallowing hard, Isaiah didn't know if he could actually do that. There had never been a time in his life that he hadn't addressed white folks as *sir* and *ma'am*. He kept wondering how this family could feel the way they did about a man like him. Honestly, he thought that at any moment they would realize the error of their ways—but they didn't. For the next hour, they pulled Isaiah into every conversation as if his opinion actually mattered.

Early the next morning, after a fine breakfast, two of Marvin's sons brought the mule wagon around to the back porch. If this family's welcome had been earnest the day before, it was nothing compared to their loving farewell. Handshakes were no longer in order. Isaiah and Franklin both found themselves being hugged by all—same as Samuel Hawkins.

Isaiah climbed up onto the wagon bench, taking the reins in his hands. He noticed his massa still on the back porch in deep conversation with Daniel Ward. After a while, the two men embraced tightly, and the preacher continued to keep his hand on Samuel's shoulder with a few more parting words—serious words, if Isaiah was reading it right.

Young Taylor ran alongside the wagon, shouting goodbye to Franklin until his papa called loudly for him to come back. Although the boy stopped running, he stood still and waved until the wagon turned onto the main road.

Isaiah glanced over his shoulder at Franklin and was contented by the look of joy on his face. He was so grateful that his son had been treated as thoughtfully and kindly as he had been. But one look at the massa told Isaiah a different story. While Isaiah was thankful that now he sat beside his brother in Christ, there was obviously something troublesome eating away at the man.

Chapter 48

After collecting Prince from Chester Brant, along with a hefty payoff, Master Hawkins instructed Isaiah to go by the property outside of Winchester. "Even though it's out of our way, we should have plenty of time to make it home before dark."

Isaiah didn't mind at all seeing that property again. It was the most beautiful piece of land he'd ever laid eyes on. He snuck a peek around his massa to get a better view of Prince and Franklin. His son looked right at home on top of the powerful stallion. Every time the boy pulled ahead of the mules, Isaiah cleared his throat, and Franklin backed him down. He could tell the beast was ready to run—muscles rippling in the late morning sun. It was almost mind-boggling the way he obeyed the tiniest pressure from the bit in his mouth. Yet if Franklin were to give him his head, Prince might not stop running for miles.

"We won't go back to the cave," the master told him when they came out of the woods onto the bluegrass pasture. "Let's head over to the oak."

Nodding, Isaiah led the mules to the massive tree near one corner of the property. He set the brake on the wagon just outside the shade of its sprawling branches so the mules would have access to the sweet bluegrass. Their response to the gift was immediate as they commenced to chomping loudly.

Master Hawkins took Prince's reins from Franklin before the boy slipped to the ground. "We'll tether Prince to the back of the wagon and give him some oats. I don't want him grazing with the mules and getting a grass belly." He winked at Franklin while removing Prince's bridle, then attached a lead rope to the stallion's halter to secure him to one of the back wheels.

Isaiah stepped out into the pasture, tugging a couple of blades of grass to chew on. A low chuckle rumbled up from his chest when Franklin did the same. Soon, the master joined them, and all three stood with their back to the tree, admiring the land that God had made.

"I've decided what I want to do with this property," Samuel said in a quiet voice.

"What's that, massa?"

Laying a hand on top of Isaiah's shoulder, he said, "I want you to have it. I can't think of anyone who deserves this piece of land more than you, Isaiah."

Thinking he heard wrong, Isaiah's gaze instantly slid to the man who owned him. "Massa, I's not understandin' yer meanin'."

One corner of Samuel's mouth turned upward. "You heard it right. I'm going to give this land to you as a gift for all that you've done for me."

"But Massa, I's a slave. How's I gonna own property—'specially property so fine as this?"

"Well, that's because this property isn't the only gift that I want to give you. I'm also giving you and Franklin your freedom. As soon as we get home, I'll draw up the manumission papers."

The news hit Isaiah's chest so hard he thought he'd been sucker punched. He hauled in a deep breath through his nose and let it out through his mouth. "Massa—"

he said in a trembling voice, but no more words would come. Tears blurred his vision and he was overcome with emotion.

Samuel's laughter bordered on a sob. He grabbed Isaiah's shoulders and hauled him to his chest. Then, patting his back hard, he let go. "I knew the moment I came up out of that water yesterday, that it was a sin for me to own you, Isaiah." His breath caught, and he briefly looked away while wiping tears from his face. "You're my brother…my equal."

While this was the moment Isaiah had dreamed of all his life, it suddenly didn't feel right. He slowly shook his head. "Sir, I's thinkin' I can't accept this."

"What? The land?"

"No, sir…my freedom."

Now it was Samuel's turn to look shocked. "I don't understand."

"Massa, I know'd you freed Naomi, and I understands why you done that. But I's thinkin' I can't be set free no matter how bad I want it if'n everyone else ain't set free too."

Samuel rubbed the back of his neck and let out a soft sigh. "I'm not stopping with you and Franklin. Naomi…." He'd choked on her name and looked away. After taking in a couple of deep breaths, he said, "Naomi pushed and prodded me every way she knew how to get me to this point. I only wish she—" This time he couldn't continue. He was completely overwhelmed by emotion. Turning away, he walked to the wagon and sat down on the back, bowing his head.

Sensing the man still needed to talk, Isaiah followed him, taking a seat beside him on the wagon bed. "Massa, I's here for ya."

Slowly raising his head, Samuel nodded, then his tear-filled eyes narrowed a bit. "You know, I've watched the way you handled all the tragedy we've been through, and I want you to know how much I admire you. I'm thoroughly convinced it's because of your faith. Naomi tried so hard to bring me to the truth." He looked away and let out a guttural sound from deep in his throat. "I was so…stubborn!"

"She'd be mighty proud o' you now, sir. I's thinkin' the Lawd done gave her a glimpse o' what you done yesterday."

A sad smile came to Samuel's lips. "I can only hope."

For a while, the two men sat in silence. Isaiah was fine to sit with the man in his pain if that was all he was wanting. But there was more that Samuel needed to get off his chest. "I know my sins were washed away yesterday, and believe me, I feel a heavy load of guilt lifted off of my shoulders, but I don't think I'll ever stop blaming myself for Naomi's death. That will go with me to my grave," he said in an anguished tone.

"Sir, if'n you'll let me, I wanna help ya with that."

When Samuel turned his eyes on Isaiah's again, they were full of years worth of pain and grief. Such aching only the Lord should bear, but it was obvious the man intended to carry it himself.

Isaiah went on. "This I recalls to mind, *therefore I has hope.* Through the Lawd's mercies we be not consumed, 'cause his compassions never fails. They be new *every* mornin'; great is yer faithfulness. The Lawd be my portion, says my soul, therefore, I's got hope in him!"

Raising his chin higher, Samuel searched Isaiah's gaze. "Is that in the scriptures?"

"Yessir, it be in the Good Book. I's not knowin' where, but my mammy used to say that very thing every single mornin'. No matter what the day before be like—good or bad, she be teachin' me to trust the Lawd again and again, even if I don't rightly understands it."

Isaiah let that sink in with his master for a bit. "Massa, the good Lawd above done cares for ya. He be ready to carry yer burdens if'n you'll let him. T'ain't no need to hold on ta regrets."

The master sat in contemplation, nodding his head. "If I had only…." He allowed the rest of his words to go unspoken.

Isaiah assumed his massa's regrets all hinged upon Naomi and the child. He longed to ask him about his baby girl in slave town. Did he plan to be her pappy, or was he planning to leave her there like he had for the past year? And Isaiah wasn't the only one troubled by that. Every time he saw Eliza, she asked if the massa had mentioned little Rachel. Maybe now that the man had given his life to Christ, that would change. There would be no way of knowing presently because that was a question he could only ask as a freedman. And he had no intention of accepting his freedom today if by refusing, it would hasten the day for the rest of his people on the Hawkins Plantation.

Somewhere on the breeze, a high-pitched cry rose up. It seemed far away, but both Isaiah and his master turned their heads toward the direction it had come from.

"What was that?" Samuel asked.

Isaiah was on his feet in an instant, anxiously scouring the landscape. "Where's my boy?" But he already knew the answer to that question. "The ladder!" he shouted and took off at a sprint across the pasture.

Samuel's voice held alarm as he ran behind Isaiah. "Be careful of the opening. You're headed right for it."

Slowing his pace, Isaiah jogged the rest of the way to the gaping hole in the ground and dropped to his knees. "Franklin," he heaved. "Is you down there?"

"Pappy!" The boy's voice was panicked. "Pappy, I's down here!"

"Is you hurt?"

"No, sir, but I needs ya to come get me."

The two men frantically searched around the opening in the ground. "I don't see the end of the ladder," Samuel said.

"Son? Where's the ladder?"

There was a long pause. "Pappy?"

"Young'in—where's the ladder?" he questioned fervidly.

"It be down here. I's a climbin' up when it fell."

Master Hawkins looked over at Isaiah. "Do we have the lantern and matches in the wagon?"

Isaiah's head dropped. "No, sir. I shoulda know'd better."

"That's not your fault. We didn't plan to camp this time."

Both men remained on their knees, searching their brains for a solution. Finally, Samuel asked, "What about a rope? Do we have something to lower down to him?"

"I gots a coil o' rope in the wagon! I always has it there just in case. Only now, I's gonna keep matches in there too."

"I'll get it," Samuel said. "You stay here and keep your boy calm."

Isaiah nodded and watched his massa run back across the pasture.

"Little man, how's ya doin' down there?"

Franklin's voice was jittery, despite his brave words. "I's fine, Pappy. I ain't scared no more."

"Alrighty, young'in. We's gonna get you outta there in no time."

After a few short minutes, Samuel returned with the rope. "Should we tie a loop in it and pull him up?"

Isaiah gave a slow shake of his head. "I's thinkin' that might be awful scary to 'im. What if we has him tie it on the end of the ladder and we pulls the ladder back in place?"

"Then we could have him loop the rope on before he climbs up," Samuel added. "Just to be safe."

"That be a fine idea," Isaiah agreed. "Son?" he called. "We's lettin' a rope down to ya. Can ya tie it onto the last rung o' the ladder? We's gonna put it back in place for ya."

"Yessir, Pappy."

Both men could see the boy standing in the ring of sunlight that shined down through the hole. Isaiah thought he detected moisture glistening on his son's cheeks.

"Are all the rungs still on the ladder?" the master asked.

"Yessir," the young voice called while grabbing the end of the extended rope.

After a minute or so, Franklin called up. "Pappy, I gots the rope tied."

"All right, Son. Step away from the ladder. I don't want ya to get hurt."

Franklin disappeared into the darkness of the cavern while both men worked to pull the ladder off the ground. When Isaiah was able, he grasped the end of the ladder and set it back in place. "That's a mighty long ladder, ain't it?" he quipped.

"Would have to be to get down in that hole." Samuel untied the knot Franklin had made, then secured a loop on the end of it. Lowering it back down, he called out to the boy. "Before you start climbing, put the loop over your head and under your arms. Your papa's going to hold that ladder and I'm going to hold the rope."

"Yessir," Franklin said, grabbing the loop that his master had lowered.

Franklin took the rungs at a snail's pace, but when he got to the last two, he practically leapt out of the ground. Shrugging out of the rope, he bounded into his pappy's arms. Isaiah scooted away from the hole while still on his knees, hugging the boy snug to his chest.

It took a while for Isaiah's heart to stop racing, but when it did, he kissed his son on the head and loosened his hold. To his surprise, Franklin turned and went right into the arms of Massa Hawkins. The massa stood all the way up with him, holding him tight. Franklin's arms remained around his neck for a long moment before Samuel lowered him to the ground.

Then, to their amazement, Samuel bent to his knees and shoved the ladder back down into the cavern below. "Maybe next time we come out here we'll cover this hole with wooden planks."

"Sounds like a fine idea," Isaiah said. He'd already coiled up the rope and flung it onto his shoulder. Then, taking his son's hand, they turned from the cavern and started back across the pasture. But before they'd even gone two steps, Franklin and the massa joined hands too, all three breathing a sigh of relief.

&⳥⳥&

It was after dark when Micah leapt from his porch and ran to the road beside the big house. Isaiah pulled the mule wagon to a halt near the side door to Master Hawkins' study, and Samuel stepped down.

Micah was breathless. "Sir, we've all been worried sick about you. We were expectin' you yesterday."

Samuel removed his hat, sliding a hand through his hair. "It's a long story," he said.

A woman's voice came from the shadows, and Eliza ran into view. "Is everyone all right?" she asked in a concerned voice.

"We're all fine," Master Hawkins said wearily. "Just tired and hungry."

Micah pointed back to his house. "We have plenty of food, or I can get Mamie out of bed and—"

"No, no, don't do that," Samuel interrupted. "We'll be glad to eat whatever you have to offer."

"Truth of it is," Eliza said, "Mamie made a big meal last night and tonight, expecting you to be home. She brought all the leftovers to Micah. I'll go in and get it heated up for you."

Micah took hold of the mule's harness. "All of you go in and make yourself comfortable. Isaiah, let me take the wagon for ya."

"The wagon can wait," Samuel said. "Let's just take care of Prince before supper."

Isaiah liked the sound of that. "I gots 'im, sir," he said. Reaching up to Franklin, he lowered the boy to the ground. "Go on in with the massa and Micah, little man. I's gonna be right there."

For a moment Isaiah stood smiling, watching his massa reach for the boy's hand. When he got to the stables, he was thankful that one of his most trusted stable hands was still up. Isaiah immediately handed Prince off to him. "Brush 'im down good and feeds 'im. I reckon he's happy to be home."

Rushing back to Micah's cabin, Isaiah found his son and the massa sitting at the table with Micah, while Eliza had already set out three plates. She was just putting the food on the table and offered him a warm smile. "I'm thankful you all are back safely. We were so worried."

Obviously, Master Hawkins hadn't shared the reason for their long delay, but it would be a welcome story if he should choose to tell it. Samuel instantly started filling his plate with food, but Isaiah and Franklin remained with their hands in their laps.

"Go on," Samuel said. "You don't have to wait for me."

But Franklin said, "Pappy, ain't we gonna say a blessin'?"

Everyone turned their gaze onto Master Hawkins. His hands froze, one holding a corn muffin to his mouth, the other reaching for the spoon to the potatoes. Color ran to his face as he put the muffin on his plate and swallowed the bite he'd taken. The boy now lifted both of his hands, palms up, toward the massa and his pappy.

Without hesitation, Samuel reached for the boy's hand, then accepted Isaiah's as well.

Franklin trained his gaze right on Master Hawkins. "Massa," he said. "My mammy done told us if'n we eats before the blessin', we's the one that has ta say it."

"Well, now—" Isaiah started, but the master cleared his throat.

"I reckon that's a pretty good rule, Franklin," the master said. "I guess that means I need to say the blessing then."

Franklin merely nodded, causing Samuel to chuckle. Then, bowing his head, the master led a prayer for probably the first time since his youth.

When the three started eating, Eliza joined them at the table. It was obvious she was curious as to what had delayed them so long and more than curious about the master's demeanor. But so far, the conversation was centering around Prince and Chester Brant.

Finally, as their appetites began to be satisfied, Master Hawkins looked between Micah and Eliza. "When are you two going to decide to get married?"

Eliza let out a soft laugh and turned a loving gaze toward Micah. "Are you gonna tell him, or should I?"

Micah's smile lit his face. He reached for Eliza's hand. "Sir, I asked her to marry me yesterday, but I'm sorry I didn't run it by you first. If you like, we can talk about it tomorrow and—"

Holding up a hand, Samuel silenced his overseer. Then, turning his gaze to Eliza, he asked, "What was your answer?"

Her smile broadened. "Sir, I told him yes!"

Slapping his hand lightly on the table, Samuel gave them both a hardy congratulations. "When can we expect a wedding?"

"That's what I need to talk to you about, sir," Micah answered. "We don't want to wait too long. We're ready." He smiled down at Eliza and squeezed her hand.

Master Hawkins slid his chair back from the table but only enough to stretch out his legs. He leaned an elbow on the tabletop, giving his overseer an earnest gaze. "I want you to come to my study first thing in the morning. I have a lot more to discuss with you than your wedding plans."

Micah leaned forward. "Anything you want to talk about tonight, sir?"

Samuel looked around the table and blew out a long breath. "I think we'll leave it till the morrow. But I do want to say one thing to all of you before I leave."

The room took on a quiet hush as the master seemed to be wrestling with how to express his feelings. He pulled his legs in and sat a little straighter. "All of you are important to me, not for what you can do for this plantation, although what each one of you does is significant, but for *who* you are." He swallowed hard. "I just want you to know that I see you as…well, as the children of God that you are."

For a long moment, no one spoke. Emotion tinted everyone's features. When Eliza blinked, tears spilled down her cheeks.

Master Hawkins continued. "I think it's fitting that I start with the four of you around this table and ask for each of you to forgive me. Daniel Ward has helped me understand that my highest calling as a Christian is to love others…*all* others without self-interest. For what I have done to you—and Micah to you as well, by forcing you to do my bidding—has been all for my own interests."

Eliza was now openly crying, and when the master turned his gaze on her, he too allowed his unshed tears to fall. "Will you forgive me?" he asked.

Immediately, Eliza said, "I will."

"I forgive ya," Isaiah said, his heart brimming with emotion.

"Sir," Micah said in a strong voice. "I forgive you and seek forgiveness for myself."

Turning into his arms, Eliza buried her face in Micah's chest.

That left one soul at the table who had yet to speak. Franklin's eyes were so pure, drinking in the scene before him. The boy slipped out of his chair and went straight to the master, easing into his lap. For the second time today, he wrapped his arms tightly around Samuel's neck. His master responded by pulling the boy close to his chest.

"You's forgiven," Franklin said with sweet innocence.

Samuel briefly closed his eyes, then turned them toward the other three at the table. Still holding the boy in his arms, he quietly said, "Thank you."

Then, lowering Franklin to the ground, the master came to his feet and dipped his head in respect. Without another word, he picked up his hat and left Micah's cabin.

New Year's Day 1860
Hawkins Plantation

Though the sun shone brightly overhead, the chill in the air kept most folks huddled near one of the three bonfires. A New Year's Day celebration had commenced in place of the one at Christmas since Master Hawkins and his children had been away in Nashville over the holidays. What's more, all of the slaves had come to witness the wedding of the plantation overseer to their beloved healer. Not a soul had been left in slave town on this bright afternoon.

Already a bountiful feast had been consumed—music and dancing would soon follow the greatly anticipated wedding ceremony. The crowd now moved in unison to the front of the big house. Micah and Eliza would be getting married on the front porch.

When Master Hawkins opened the door of the house, a hush came over the expectant onlookers. He stepped outside followed by his two sons, then by Floyd Johnson, the slave's well-loved preacher. Floyd was known for his high-spirited sermons in the middle of slave town every Sunday evening. Grinning widely, Floyd nodded to the assembly gathered out front.

Next, Micah stepped onto the porch wearing a fine-looking suit. "Mm, mm," some in the crowd murmured. He humbly dipped his chin, awaiting the appearance of his bride-to-be.

In the parlor, Eliza stood nervously wringing her hands. Jessie and Tabitha smoothed out her beautiful gown, which Master Hawkins had given her the privilege of choosing from the trunks in the attic. For days, she and Tabitha had wrestled with the decision—there had been so many to choose from. But in the end, she had selected a simple, cream-colored gown belonging to Isabella. The missy had been more to her size, the gown requiring no alterations.

"Oh, my," Jessie crooned. "Micah gonna sweep you off that porch 'fore you can even say, 'I will.'"

Eliza let out an anxious breath. "I may faint before I get out there."

Tabitha clucked her tongue. "You deliver babies and take care o' sick people like it ain't nothin'—now you's about to pass out?"

Fanning her hand wildly in front of her face, Eliza took several shallow breaths. "In case you hadn't noticed, gettin' married isn't somethin' you do every day."

"You'ins comin'?" Preacher Floyd had stepped back in the house, wondering if the bride had changed her mind.

Jessie reached up to adjust the lavender wreath in Eliza's hair. "We's comin'," she barked. "She gots to be married to the man the rest o' her life. What's the hurry?"

That caused Eliza to laugh, subsequently settling her nerves. Taking in a deep breath, she headed for the front porch. When she stepped outside, her attention was instantly drawn to Micah. Just glimpsing her fine-looking man made her go weak in the knees. She wasn't sure if she was supposed to do it, but she reached for his arm if for no other reason than to steady herself.

Micah had told Floyd to keep his remarks short and sweet. And while they were indeed animated, he didn't take long to get right to the point. "Micah Simmons, will you take Eliza to be yer wife fer the rest o' yer days?"

Eliza knew in that moment, she would never forget the smile on Micah's face, nor would she ever want to.

"I will," he said in a husky voice.

The crowd of slaves began clapping. *Amens* filled the crisp afternoon air.

"And what about you, Miss Eliza? Will you take Micah to be yer husband fer the rest o' yer days?"

"Oh, I certainly will!" she said.

Hearing her enthusiastic response, the gathering cheered even louder with *hallelujahs* and *amens.*

Floyd raised his hand to quiet down their exuberance. "And Massa Hawkins, do this be in accordance with your will fer these two to belong one to another?"

"It is," he said with a wink to the couple.

"Then Micah, you's welcome to kiss yer wife."

Eliza pressed her lavender wreath down with one hand and cupped the side of Micah's face with the other. Lowering his lips down to hers, Micah kissed her thoroughly, leaving no doubt how much he desired his wife. When he was done, Eliza fanned her face again, causing some in the crowd to clap and whistle.

With joyous smiles, Micah and Eliza stepped down from the porch, leading a procession back to the bonfires. As soon as the fiddlers were in place, dancing and merrymaking began, lasting late into the afternoon.

Just before sunset, two large wooden boxes were placed near the band of fiddlers. Master Hawkins stepped up on one box and Micah on the other. The master's sons, Joseph and William, stood on the ground beside their father, as did young Catherine, holding tightly to her brother William.

When Master Hawkins raised both hands in the air, the crowd slowly quieted down. Micah also raised a hand, beckoning the slaves to move in closer. "Master Hawkins has an important announcement to make," he shouted. "Gather 'round so you'ins can hear it."

Mamie moved right next to Micah and tapped him on the arm. He leaned down so she could speak into his ear, then he straightened, smiling at Samuel. "She wants me to tell 'em about the food."

Samuel chuckled and nodded for him to go ahead. "Folks, Mamie here says she made some extra food for all of you to take home tonight. So don't be forgettin' it."

"Cause I's not deliverin' it to ya!" Mamie shouted.

Laughter rippled through the crowd, and Mamie leveled a stern gaze at them to reiterate her point.

Samuel's eyes were full of mirth. "Can I speak now, Mamie?"

She nodded authoritatively. "Be my guest, massa."

Clearing his throat, Master Hawkins addressed his slaves. "This has been a long time coming, and honestly, it should've been done much sooner. But I want you all to know how thankful I am for each of you and the hard work you've done to make this such a prosperous plantation." He let his gaze wander over the people, many nodding their heads with gratitude for his words.

"Only a few of you know that I recently became a Christian—a true Christian. I've always been a believer in God—but not the way I should. And that's changed." Raising his brow, he declared, "*I've* changed."

Glancing at his overseer, Micah nodded reassuringly, hoping to infuse the man with extra courage.

"There was a belief passed down to me by my father from his father. It was the belief that the only way this plantation could thrive would be on the backs of its slaves. But my father was wrong! And so was his father! There is no way to justify owning another human being—a human being made in the image of God."

Mouths gaped open in the crowd. Restless movement swelled among the slaves as they packed in closer to hear what their master would say next. A sense of anticipation thickened the air.

"And for that reason, I declare on this first day of January, in the year of our Lord, eighteen hundred and sixty, that I am emancipating all of my slaves. Each and every one of you are free and—"

"We's FREE!" someone yelled loudly, and the rest of Samuel's words were completely cut off by the jubilation that broke out among the people. Many began leaping and dancing. Some shouted, "Praise the Lawd!" Others hugged their family members. Even small children were thrown into the air and caught. A refrain of "hallelujahs" floated toward the sky. Voices were singing jubilant praise. Surely only heaven itself would be able to rival such euphoria, Micah thought.

Samuel Hawkins allowed the rapture to continue for as long as the people wanted. When Micah reached over and clapped him on the shoulder, the man pulled him into a strong embrace.

"I couldn't have done this without your help," he told Micah.

Micah laughed heartily. "No, sir, this was all your doing."

Samuel was already shaking his head and pointing upward. "No…it was all his!"

When Micah perceived the time was right, he raised his hands again to quiet the crowd. "Mr. Hawkins and I will be meeting with each family at the big house to finalize your manumission. For the last few weeks, we've talked about how the plantation will continue to thrive with freed men and women working here, if that should be your choice. It will all be explained in your meeting over the next several days."

Samuel broke in. "Some of you already have a family name, but for those of you who don't, you are welcome to the Hawkins name. Be thinking about that before your meeting time comes." He reached over and clasped the back of Micah's neck, giving him a good-humored shake. "All of the meetings tomorrow will be with myself and my son, Joseph. This man right here has other things to tend to for the next couple of days."

A slow smile worked its way across Micah's face, and he searched the crowd for his wife. Spotting her near the road, he jumped down from the box and pushed his way through the gathering. With one swift motion, he swooped Eliza off her feet and kissed her. As he carried her toward his house, the crowd whooped and hollered for all they were worth. The fiddlers broke their silence, playing a lively jig, and Micah took the two stairs of his porch with one giant step.

Eliza grasped Micah's neck tighter as he turned back toward the people and bowed, drawing loud applause and laughter. She reached to open the door, and the couple disappeared inside, Micah slamming the door with his foot.

All night long, Samuel Hawkins' former slaves celebrated their freedom. When the fiddlers needed a rest, lively singing broke out. There would be no peace and quiet for the newlyweds. But that was all right. They weren't sleeping anyway.

❧❧❧

On January 3, John and Jessie Tillis were summoned to the big house. All six of their blood children, along with little Rachel, now fifteen months old, joined them. Micah ushered the large family into Samuel Hawkins' study. Abigail, now a free woman, brought sweet treats for the children and warm drinks for all. Samuel stood behind his desk until all were seated. Micah stoked the fire, bringing extra warmth to the room, then took a chair on the other side of the desk next to John and Jessie.

Samuel started the meeting by thanking them for the work they had performed on his plantation since the day of their births. "First, and most importantly, we want to give you your manumission papers. John, your paper is just for you, while Jessie, yours also provides the names of your children."

Micah handed the papers to John and Jessie, shaking both of their hands in congratulations.

Looking up from the open ledger on his desk, Samuel continued. "The gristmill has served as great importance, not only to this community of people but for our neighbors as well. John, you have been one of the primary reasons for its success. I would like to offer you the same job that you perform now, with the addition of a salary to be paid on a monthly basis." He nodded toward his overseer. "Micah will explain the wages you are being offered and the banking system we're setting up on these premises."

For the next several minutes, Micah read John's contract out loud, describing his current job, the pay he would receive, and how he could invest his pay to provide for his family. "Mr. Hawkins will not require rent at this time, but food and clothing can be bought here on the plantation at a low cost to you. You'll be expected to maintain your living quarters and are welcome to add on, if you so choose. We're also offering children aged fifteen and older a paid job. Are we correct that your oldest is fourteen?"

John nodded. "Yessir, my son Job."

Samuel leaned forward, placing his elbows on the desk. "Does this sound fair to you, John?"

At the moment, John looked a bit overwhelmed. Jessie laid a gentle hand on his arm. It was a lot to take in. John's eyes slid to his wife's—he needed reassurance. She swallowed back her own nervousness and nodded to her husband.

"Of course," Mr. Hawkins added, "if you choose to leave the plantation, you are free to do so. We'll help you all we can, but I would require a two-week notice before your departure."

Finally, John found his voice. "Sir, I's mighty grateful to has my freedom…and even more grateful for our chillins growin' up free." He gave his former master a grateful nod. "I's acceptin' yer offer for the job, and I plans to keep workin' for ya. But…."

Big John's voice trailed off, and he glanced behind him at all his children lined up on the sofa in their clean clothes and spit-shined shoes, the older ones holding the younger ones in their lap.

Micah broke in. "Is there something troublin' you, John?"

John fingered the slouch hat in his lap, beads of sweat breaking out on his upper lip. "I's wonderin'." He swallowed hard and started again. "Sir, I's wonderin' if Rachel's name be on Jessie's paper there."

Samuel drew in a deep breath. "That was something I wanted to discuss with you both today. I'm sorry I didn't lead with it first." He glanced around Big John at all the children, Rachel being held by the Tillis' oldest daughter. "I want to thank you for taking care of the child so well over the past year. Jessie, she wouldn't have survived a day without you, and I will compensate you for the care that you've given her. But now that she is fully weaned, I will take her in where she belongs, and—"

A high-pitched wail left Jessie's throat before she could hold it back. "Please, sir. No!" Her eyes were full of passion, and her words even more so. "From the very moment the babe went to my breast, she be like my own. I's felt as if she come from my own body, just like the rest of my chillins." She swept her arm broadly toward the passel of children behind her.

"I know she be yours, massa...." Jessie's mouth gaped open, eyes wide with shock. "Beggin' yer pardon, sir, I mean, *Mr.* Hawkins. But she be mine too." Her voice trembled and quaked with emotion. She couldn't bear to lose her baby child. "Please, sir, has mercy." Tears of grief flooded her cheeks—she slid to her knees on the floor in front of his desk. "Please, sir. I'm beggin'."

The look on Samuel's face was one of utter dismay. He cleared his throat, obviously struggling with the situation at hand. His words came slowly and quietly. "I had thought that you would welcome this news. I assumed she was a burden to your family." He now turned his eyes on Jessie's husband. "John, how do you feel about this?"

John's brow furrowed deeply. He was distressed over his wife's reaction—even more so when he looked back at his crying children. Wiping a hand across his mouth, he shook his head, a deep moan rising up from his chest.

"Sir, she be yer blood child, I knows that in my mind." He paused, briefly glancing at his wife, then back to Samuel. He lifted a fist to his chest. "But she be Jessie's child in her heart, and a baby sister in the hearts of our chillins." He paused again and dropped his eyes to his hands. "I's not knowin' what to tell ya 'cept it be yer decision, sir."

For a full minute nothing else was said as the clock on the mantle ticked away the seconds. Finally, Samuel Hawkins stood up, John and Micah rising with him. Samuel went to the door that led into the house and opened it. "I'll give you some time with Rachel—as much time as you need. Violet will be just outside the door to take her when you're ready." He dipped his head, offering a quiet apology, and left the room.

Chapter 50

The following week, Micah drove a buggy over to John and Jessie's. He knew the big man would already be at the gristmill, but that was of no consequence, it was Jessie he was aiming to see. Knocking on their cabin door, he was greeted by the Tillis's eldest daughter, Julia.

Micah removed his hat. "Could I talk to your mammy?"

"She's washin' 'round back. You wanna come through?"

Hearing the commotion from the children inside, Micah decided to walk around. "That's all right. Thank ya, anyway."

When he got to the back of the cabin, Micah found Jessie hanging wet clothes on a rope stretched between two fence posts. He cleared his throat, not wanting to startle her. Instantly Jessie turned to meet his gaze, causing his chest to tighten. Her eyes held obvious signs of grief.

"What brung ya here, Micah?"

"I've been asked to take you to the big house."

She was already shaking her head obstinately. "Not comin'."

"Mr. Hawkins asked for you to come."

Jessie threw a wet pair of trousers over the line and slammed her fists to her hips. "Well, he ain't my massa no more, so's I expect I can be sayin' no." She turned back to the basket of wet clothes without waiting for a response.

Micah sighed and stepped closer. "Jessie, I expect you're gonna want to come."

Her voice broke with emotion. "What fer?"

"I'm not certain, but I think it has somethin' to do with little Rachel."

Jessie roughly wiped her hands over her eyes and spun back around. "What about her?"

He shook his head. "All I know is Eliza's been called to the big house more than once in the past few days to check on her."

Worry plastered Jessie's features. "She bein' treated poorly?"

"Oh, no, I wouldn't expect that to be happenin' at all. Mr. Hawkins wants to take good care of his child. But it seems like somethin' must be wrong if he sent me for ya."

"Well, why didn't ya say so in the first place? Just give me a minute to change. I's all wet from washin'."

Micah watched her run through the back door of the cabin. He pressed his hat on, then headed out front to wait with the horse and buggy.

When they got to the big house, Eliza ran out from the kitchen to meet them. Micah stopped the buggy right beside his wife, and she reached for Jessie's hand. "You need to come in right away. It's little Rachel."

Jessie gave Eliza a pained look, then jumped to the ground and took off running for the kitchen door. Eliza caught up with her and took hold of her hand again before she could go inside. "No matter what you see in there, Rachel is all right. I promise."

The look in Jessie's eyes turned from pain to distress. "Take me to her!"

Eliza led Jessie through the kitchen and up the back stairs. The fit of crying could be heard before the two women even entered the long upstairs hallway. "Oh, Lawd. Tell me that ain't my Rachel?"

Confirming that it was, Eliza quickly led her to where the pitiful cries were coming from. When Eliza opened the door to the nursery, Jessie froze. Samuel Hawkins was holding the child in his arms, pacing the floor. The poor baby's face was red and distorted in anguish. Violet stood nearby, wringing her hands.

Samuel instantly turned so Rachel could get a glimpse of Jessie. The girl kicked and fought with all her might to get out of her father's arms. He bent and released her on the floor, and the child wasted not a second running to Jessie. "Mam," she sobbed, hurdling herself into Jessie's outstretched arms.

Jessie stood with the child, showering her with kisses, then hugged her close to her breast. "Shh, now baby child. You's all right. Shh, baby."

With little gasps and hiccups, Rachel slowly began to calm. She nestled her warm face into her mammy's neck. Jessie responded protectively, wrapping her into a tighter bundle. "She's lost weight. I's feelin' it."

Eliza stepped forward, laying her hand on Rachel's back. "I've kept a close eye on her every day, making sure she's taken care of."

Jessie now pierced the nursery maid with a hard gaze. "Whatchu been feedin' her?"

Violet's eyes darted from Jessie to Mr. Hawkins. She seemed reticent to answer until he gave her a solemn nod. "Truth of it is, we can't get her to eat nothin'."

"Oh, my Lawd!" Jessie cried out. "How's she been survivin'?"

Stroking Jessie's arm, Eliza told her, "I made sure she got her nourishment in the milk. At least we could get her to drink."

Closing her eyes in anguish, Jessie shook her head. "You'ins shoulda got me long before now."

Samuel stepped forward and the baby clung even tighter to her mammy. "I want to apologize to you for that, Jessie. I thought by being here with me and our family, she would be fine. I kept thinking, *just one more day*. But it's obvious that Rachel thinks of you as her mother. I just didn't realize the bond was so strong."

"What are we ta do?" Jessie asked. "I can't be livin' at the big house."

Samuel gave her a somber smile. "I know. That's why, as hard as this is for me to say, I think she needs to live with you. You and John have already done a fine job raising her, I trust that she will continue to be nurtured with great care."

"Oh, yessir," she whispered passionately.

"What about John?" he asked. "Will he be all right with this?"

Jessie laughed despite the tears on her cheeks. "John ain't got no choice in this matter," she declared. "He knows what's good for 'im."

Samuel moved closer and touched his child's soft, dark hair. She worked her way tighter to Jessie's chest, causing his smile to fade. Clearing his throat, he said, "Let me know if there's anything your family needs. When she's old enough, she'll come to the house for lessons. She and Catherine will share a tutor."

"Yessir," Jessie replied.

"I'll also compensate you each month for taking care of her." Then, taking one more prolonged look at Rachel, Samuel thanked her and left the room.

Eliza pressed her hand to Jessie's back, leading her out of the nursery toward the back staircase, but they were not alone in the hallway. Samuel's eldest son, Joseph, was standing on the upstairs landing. Joseph, at age sixteen, had already outgrown his father in stature. His dark looks were similar to Samuel's, but his blue eyes were unmistakably his mother's.

Looking into those eyes, Eliza's spine tingled. Though the young man regaled the women with a smile, it was not one of kindliness. It was the look of someone who had devised a scheme and saw it unfold in the exact way he had planned. Eliza stored the troubling observation in the back of her mind and hurried Jessie down the stairs.

As the women made their way outside with Rachel still clinging snugly to her mammy, they noticed Micah leaning against the buggy. Immediately he came to Eliza's side. "Mr. Hawkins and I have another meeting. Do you mind taking Jessie back home?" He gave Jessie a benevolent grin. "And Rachel too, by the looks of it."

Eliza smiled at her husband, loving this man more and more by the day. "Not a problem."

He bent and kissed her sweetly. "I'll see you at supper."

"All right," she called, watching him stride quickly toward Mr. Hawkins' study.

Eliza helped get Jessie and Rachel settled in the buggy before she went around and stepped up beside her. "Oh, Jessie, I couldn't be happier for you. It was all I could do not to sneak you into the big house days ago."

Wagging her head, Jessie replied, "That explains why I couldn't find no peace at all. I just knew somethin' was wrong."

"That was your motherly instincts tellin' you that."

Jessie poked Eliza with her elbow. "You'll be seein' what it's like one o' these days. If you think lovin' yer man is somethin' glorious, you just wait till you has a young'un of yer own. T'ain't nothin' in the whole world like a mammy's love fer her child."

Eliza clicked her tongue and slapped the reins, turning the buggy back onto the road. "Well, I'll have to trust you on that one. But when, and if, the time comes for me to give birth, I'll want you by my side, Jessie."

Jessie nodded enthusiastically. "I'll be there, sister, fer as many times as you been there fer me, and more."

Laughing loudly, Eliza gave no other response.

That evening, when Big John came home from the gristmill, he was met outside by three of his six children. The way they playfully danced around him, he thought maybe their mammy had finally come out of her doldrums. He rubbed the tops of their heads hoping for the best.

The moment he walked inside the cabin, John spotted the little white girl toddling around on the floor. A shockwave worked its way through his entire body. "Jessie, whatchu done, gal? You done stole the man's child?"

Jessie turned from her cooking pot with a smile, the likes of which he hadn't seen since their first kiss. "I ain't stole her, mister. She been given back to us."

"Whatever for?"

"On account o' the fact that she wouldn't eat nothin' at the big house. All she done was cry and cry and cry. They finally wised up and figured that she be needin' her mammy."

John's face scrunched in confusion. "So's they just give her back? Just like that?"

"Just like that. She be ours to raise now, John, so's you best be wrappin' yer chowderhead 'round that."

John watched the little girl totter about, chewing on one of Jessie's wooden spoons. He had to admit she was a beautiful child—the spittin' image of Naomi. But she wasn't his. She was the offspring of a loose woman and his former master. Chowderhead or not, he couldn't seem to accept that fact.

❧

Isaiah and Franklin cleaned up after their simple supper of beans and rice, then sat down together in front of the fire to stay warm. A blistering cold wind had blown all day, leaving both of them chilled to the bone.

"Pappy, when's we goin' back to the cave?"

Isaiah chuckled, wondering where that boy's mind was wandering tonight. "Ain't ya scared o' that cave after what happened to ya?"

Franklin's head vigorously shook. "Nuh, uh. I likes it there."

"That so? What else do ya likes about it?"

The boy scrunched his mouth to one side. "Well, I sure do likes the big tree, and I likes all the grass." He shrugged his shoulders. "I just likes all of it."

"Me too, little man. Me too."

"Is it really ours?"

"That be a fact. I's got a paper right over yonder that says me and you owns it."

"What if someone else goes ta livin' on it, Pappy?"

Isaiah's brow dipped. "I reckon that ain't gonna happen. T'ain't no one gone and lived on it before now. I specs it'll be fine." Stretching his legs out toward the fireplace, Isaiah actually contemplated that question for the first time. What if someone did try to squat on that piece of land? It was mighty fine property.

Franklin continued with his fanciful musings. "You reckon Mr. Samuel would wanna come live with us if'n we build a house there?"

This time Isaiah laughed. "Son, Mr. Samuel done already gots a big house ta live in with all his young'uns. T'ain't got no need fer another house." However, that got Isaiah to thinking. "But maybe you an' me'll build us a house there fer the two of us. We could raise some mighty strong mules on that sweet bluegrass. Yessir, we could."

Franklin laid down on his stomach on the rug by the hearth. Propping himself up on his elbows, he stared into the fire. "I's thinkin' we could build a house right on top o' that hole in the ground. Then I could go up an' down the ladder alls I want."

An amused chuckle left Isaiah's throat. "If'n we built us a house atop that hole, I's thinkin' we'd make us a staircase goin' right down in there."

For a long time, the two sat quietly, thinking about the remarkable property they'd been given. Finally, Franklin turned over on his back. "Ya know what else? We wouldn't need ta build no barn."

"How's come?"

"Cause, Pappy, the Lawd done already built us one right under the pasture."

Isaiah sat forward in his chair, curiosity sparking his imagination. The boy was right. The entrance to the cave would make a perfect barn. All he would need to do is build a gate to pull across the opening. He needed to mull that over in his mind a bit, but Franklin was already moving on.

"Is we kin to Mr. Samuel?"

"Whatchu talkin' about?"

"Ain't we got his last name now?"

A slow grin spread across Isaiah's face. "Yessir, we gots the man's name now. But so do lot's o' other folks on the plantation. We's not the onliest ones."

"Is we gonna get all mixed up?"

"Son, we ain't gonna get mixed up. We know who we's belongin' to. It just be me and you."

That seemed to satisfy him for a while, and soon Franklin's eyelids grew heavy. Isaiah reached down and shook the boy's shoulder. "Come on, les get out back and do our business right quick. You's tired."

There was no arguing that fact. Franklin rolled over and pushed himself off the floor. But he had one more question left in him. "Pappy, is Mr. Samuel gonna let us leave here so's we can live on our land?"

Isaiah swallowed loudly. "Son, we ain't ready fer that yet. But I reckon now that we's freedmen, we can do whatever we likes."

Putting on their coats to ward off the frigid night air, Isaiah opened the door and steered his son ahead of him. But it was a long time before the man was able to sleep. All he could think about was whether Samuel Hawkins would ever let him go.

Chapter 51

October 1861

Micah lingered in bed, knowing he should've gotten up before now. He trailed a hand down his wife's arm and along her abdomen, then let his hand gently rest there.

Eliza grinned. "Did ya feel that one?"

"I did. He's got a strong kick, that son of ours."

"Don't be so sure it's a boy," she countered. "I have a feelin' otherwise."

He leaned over and kissed her belly, then rolled out of bed. "We'll see."

Eliza threw back the covers to get up. "I'll make you some—"

"No, ma'am! Stay right where you are." Micah went around the bed and gently pushed her shoulders back to the mattress. Covering her up again, he sat down on the blanket to trap her. "Stay in bed. You got in late last night. I'll make sure you're not disturbed this mornin'."

"What if someone needs me?" She started to make an escape on the other side of the bed, but Micah reached across and pinned her completely in.

"Anyone else havin' a baby soon?" he asked.

"Well, no. Not after last night."

"Good. That means you're the only one, so you can sleep all mornin'." He gave her a winsome smile, confident he'd won the battle.

"But what about breakfast? Don't you want me to make you somethin'?"

Micah's gaze narrowed. "Let's see. How many years did I live in this house without you? Oh, yeah, seven. I think I know a thing or two about cookin' breakfast."

"It was nine," Eliza smirked.

"Well, see, I guess I know more than I thought."

She laughed, and Micah loosened his grip on the covers. For a moment, Eliza held his gaze with such tender eyes it made him want to get right back in bed with her. He caressed her cheek with the back of his hand. "Promise me you'll rest this mornin'."

Yawning, she said, "I promise."

Satisfied that she would stay put, Micah got dressed and headed into the front room. Even though the room lay in shadows, he immediately noticed the note partially under the front door. Picking it up, he stepped onto the front porch, peering out into the half-darkness. All was quiet, causing him to wonder when it had been delivered. He moved to the edge of the porch for better light.

The first thing he did after opening the paper was glance at the signature. It belonged to Samuel Hawkins.

Come to the house as soon as you get this. It's urgent.

With all haste, Micah went back inside to let Eliza know why he wouldn't be making breakfast, but she was already asleep. Inwardly satisfied, he grabbed his hat and quietly left the house.

Sprinting all the way to Samuel's study, Micah arrived, breathing hard. With two firm knocks, he entered without waiting to be summoned. Samuel was bent over in a chair, head in his hands.

Micah sat down in the chair across from him. "What's happened, sir?"

When Samuel looked up, it was with grief-stricken eyes. Micah's first instinct told him someone had died. He wondered how this man would be able to handle yet another death in the family. Instead of answering Micah's question, Samuel pushed a note across the table.

Seizing it, Micah read quickly, his mouth dropping open as he went. When he was done, he slowly folded the note and slid it back across the table. He didn't know what to say.

After a long minute, Samuel leaned back in his chair, letting out an anguished moan. "He's gone."

"Had he been talking about this at all, sir?"

Samuel's voice was thick with emotion. "Not a word. Not one."

Being a man of action, Micah's muscles tensed. "Do you want me to go after him?"

"It's too late," Samuel said, letting out a long breath. "Joseph left early yesterday morning, saying he was visiting a friend in Richmond. When he didn't come home last night, I found that note on his bed. He's already joined up with the Federals by now."

Micah nodded solemnly. "And to bring him home now would make him a deserter."

Just then the door to Samuel's study opened, and fourteen-year-old William walked in, still wearing his nightclothes. When he glanced at Micah, he hesitated near the desk. "Papa, I don't think Joe came home last night."

"Come sit down," Samuel said in a quiet voice, pointing to the sofa.

Micah grabbed his hat from the table. "Should I leave, sir?"

Samuel shook his head. "Stay."

As soon as William sat down, Samuel handed him the note Joseph had left, giving him a moment to read it. When William looked up, his eyes held emotion but not surprise.

Samuel's brow wrinkled. "What do you know about this?"

"I didn't know he was going to do it this way," William said in a confused voice. "He's been talking about it since his birthday in May."

That instantly raised Samuel's ire. "And you didn't tell me about it?"

William's chin trembled. "I-I thought he'd been talking to you too."

For a long time, the two sat staring at one another until William broke his gaze, looking down at his hands. After a while, he raised his head. "I'm sorry, Papa."

Running his hands roughly through his hair, Samuel sighed. "It's not your fault, Son. Just tell me what you two talked about."

"Well, he mostly got serious about it when Polk's army invaded Columbus last month. Joe said Polk had no right trying to force Kentucky into the Confederacy. When he read that our legislature asked the Federals to help us resist Polk's advance, Joe said he was gonna enlist." William shook his head vigorously. "He made me think that you approved."

"Why would I want one of my sons fighting in a war? Especially when we live in a neutral state! We don't have to get involved in this conflict," he practically shouted.

Micah could literally feel the man's stinging disappointment. He couldn't imagine having a son make the willful decision to take up arms, especially when he didn't need to. Even more so, Micah understood Samuel's incredible frustration, since he had just turned the entire mule business over to Joseph upon his 18th birthday in May. The young man had let his father down in a monumental way. Micah found himself hoping now that Eliza was carrying a girl after all.

Samuel perused the note Joseph had written one more time, then crumpled it up, throwing it toward the fireplace. It missed the mark, but he didn't bother to get up. Straightening in his chair, he addressed Micah. "There's nothing we can do about any of this now. We'll just have to go about our business as usual. I'm afraid you'll have to take over the mule operation again."

Immediately William sat forward. His features took on an expression of determination. "Papa, I can do it."

"Maybe in a couple of years, William. You're too—"

"I'm not too young, if that's what you're about to say. I've been watching and learning for a long time."

Micah's head bobbed. "Sir, he's right. William's been asking lots of questions. He's picked up the new way of things around here mighty quick."

Samuel's eyes narrowed as he observed his youngest son. "Is that right?"

"Yes, sir," William said confidently.

For a long moment, Samuel looked at his son as if he were seeing him through fresh eyes. "I tell you what, let me and Micah talk it over first. I'll let you know what we decide."

That seemed to satisfy the boy. William quickly stood to leave his father's study, but Micah noticed him retrieve Joseph's note off the floor, straightening it as he left.

After the door closed, Samuel turned a strained gaze toward his overseer. "Shoot straight with me, Micah. Is the boy capable?"

Leaning forward in his chair, Micah gave him his honest opinion. "Sir, that young man is more than capable, especially with a little help from Isaiah. William's a quiet one, but he's got your mind for business. And not to be disrespectful to your eldest son, but William's got your heart too."

Samuel Hawkins visibly relaxed. "Thank you for that, Micah."

But Micah could still see the lingering anxiety in the man's eyes. "Sir, if you don't mind me sayin', you'll just need to trust the Lord above to take care of Mr. Joseph. He's in God's mighty grip now."

Samuel nodded. "I know he is. It's just hard not to worry," he said, rising to his feet.

Micah stood as well. "Will there be anything else, sir?"

Shaking his head, Samuel quietly said, "That'll be all for now. I think I should go give William the news. Do you mind if he joins you in a little while at the mule barn?"

"Not at all, sir. Tell him I look forward to it. And sir," he said before opening the door, "Eliza and I will be prayin' earnestly for Mr. Joseph every day."

❧❧❧

While the weeks passed by slowly for Samuel Hawkins as he waited for word from his eldest son, the new year came with great anticipation for Micah and Eliza. Soon they would be welcoming a new child into the world. Eliza's greatest joy was that this new little soul would be born into a life of freedom.

When the time finally arrived, all Micah could do was pace across his front porch and pray. He heard Eliza's agonizing cries from inside the house, and it took every ounce of restraint not to go to her. But Jessie had given him a stern warning. "This ain't the place for no man," she'd told him, nearly shoving him out the door.

Tabitha and Mamie had come over from the big house as soon as they were summoned. Mamie had nearly hugged the life out of Micah before she went in. Now he wished he'd remembered to put on his heavy wool coat. As soon as the late January sun disappeared over the horizon, it grew painfully cold outside. He'd chopped wood before dark, just to keep warm, but now he couldn't even feel his hands or feet.

"Micah," a voice called out of the darkness. "I heard Eliza's in labor."

Just as Mr. Samuel stepped up on the porch, Eliza let out a primal groan. The man turned a sympathetic gaze on his overseer. "I know how hard this is. Just hearing Elizabeth in labor…well, it made me feel so helpless."

"That's it, sir. That's exactly it! I just wanna help her somehow."

Samuel clapped him on the back. "Well, there's nothing you can do, unfortunately. Come on, let's go to the house and get warm."

Micah's head was already shaking. "Can't do it, sir. I can't leave her like this."

A slow smile played on Samuel's lips. "How do you think Eliza is going to feel when she finds out her husband froze to death while she was giving birth? Come on," he urged. "This could take a while."

It was a mighty tempting offer to warm up by the fire in Samuel Hawkins' study. But everything within him kept his feet grounded to that porch. "No sir, I can't do it."

With a long sigh, Samuel unbuttoned his coat and held it out. "Then the least you can do is put on a warm coat. Just send Tabitha over to let me know when the baby is here."

"Could be late, sir."

"No matter. I'll wait up in my study."

Micah was already slipping into the coat. "Thank ya kindly for this."

Samuel gave Micah a thoughtful grin, then quickly headed back to the warmth of his own house.

With excruciatingly numb fingers, Micah was finally able to button the coat. He now felt certain he could make it through the night if need be. He reckoned if Eliza had to go through such pain to bring a child into this world, why shouldn't he.

By the grace of God, Micah only had to wait another hour. Tabitha stepped out onto the porch. "Micah, yer babe's here."

Micah hadn't heard a cry or any noise to indicate the baby had been born. "Is it all right?"

"Perfect," she answered.

He briefly closed his eyes and breathed, "Thank you, Lord."

When he got inside, Tabitha motioned him toward the back room, but Micah shook his head. "I can't be goin' in there till I get my hands warm. They're blocks of ice."

He quickly shed Mr. Samuel's coat, then stuck his hands close to the fire. Tabitha grabbed a rag and took a kettle of hot water off the grate, pouring some into a basin. She added a ladle full of cool drinking water from the bucket so it wouldn't be too hot. "Here, set yer hands in this for a bit."

While he couldn't wait to get into the back room, Micah quickly pressed his hands into the basin, ignoring the jabbing needles of discomfort as they began to thaw.

"Can you do somethin' for me right quick?" he asked Tabitha. "Mr. Hawkins is waitin' in his study for news of the baby."

She instantly nodded, grabbing her coat. "I's glad to do it."

When she disappeared out the door, Micah took a towel and dried his hands. Hopefully, they would be warm enough to hold his woman and child. Stepping into the back room, he noticed Eliza on the bed. She was lying on her side, propped up with pillows, tenderly caressing their baby child.

Hearing him enter, she turned her eyes upward. Tears immediately spilled over her lashes. "It's a girl," she whispered.

Micah felt his knees start to buckle. Thankfully he made it to the side of the bed before kneeling beside his two loves. "A girl," he repeated emotionally. He wanted to touch her but feared his hands were still too cold. He didn't want to wake her. Instead, he cupped his wife's face and kissed her tenderly. "Are you all right?"

Eliza nodded. "Mostly tired."

"What can I do for ya?" he asked.

"Do you want to hold her?"

His eyes shone with wonder. "Can I?"

Letting out a soft laugh, Eliza said, "She's yours, you know."

Micah gently slid his hands beneath the sleeping baby and picked her up, cuddling her tenderly to his chest. He kissed her little forehead, amazed by her tiny features.

Mamie helped Eliza sit up in the bed, arranging feather pillows behind her back. She and Jessie had finished with all of the cleaning and were getting ready to go home. "Thank you for everything, Mamie. I wouldn't have been able to make it without you."

The old cook bent down, pulling Eliza's head into her bosom. "I's honored to help bring this baby child into the world." Then she straightened and briefly grasped Micah's arm. "I'll be bringin' y'all some food come mornin'."

"No hurry," Micah laughed. "You go home and sleep. I expect we can take care of ourselves in the mornin'."

When Mamie departed, Jessie sat down on the side of the bed. "Well, sister, I's thinkin' you knows what ta do from here." She leaned in and kissed Eliza's cheek. "I be back ta check on ya tomorrow."

Tears once again coursed Eliza's face. She laid her hands on the top of Jessie's thighs. "Thank you, sweet sister, for everything."

Jessie covered Eliza's hands with her own. "Small payment for alls you done fer me an' mine."

The baby began to stir and fuss in Micah's arms. He looked at Eliza with a hint of fear. She held out her arms to him. "Here, let me have her. You can take Jessie home whilst I feed her."

Micah was relieved to hand the baby girl to his wife. He didn't want to be the cause of her crying. Then he turned to Jessie. "Do you mind walking with me to the stables, and I'll ride you back to your place? It'll be faster, and we'll be warmer ridin' double."

Jessie laughed. "Long as Big John don't see us." She headed into the front room to put on her coat.

Before leaving, Micah took one long gaze at his wife and baby child at her breast. His heart was so full of love for them both. "I've been thinkin' about a name for our girl," he said.

"What is it?"

"When I get back, I'll tell ya." He turned and quickly headed out with Jessie.

After nearly an hour, Micah returned to a sleeping mother and child. He banked the fire in their room and added enough logs to get them through the night. After undressing, he slipped into bed up close behind Eliza.

"Mister, you're a chunk of ice."

"Sorry 'bout that," he whispered close to her ear. "I'll get warmed up here in a minute."

"You better."

Micah could hear the teasing in her tone.

For a while, neither one spoke. Micah was basking in the warmth of the bed and feeling awfully grateful for the healthy baby girl on the other side of his wife. Finally, Eliza turned her head slightly. "Are you gonna tell me what name you're thinkin' of?"

Just the thought of it made him giddy. "It's really two names. I thought we should name her after your grandmammy Ann. But I also thought we'd put a name before it."

"What?" Eliza asked softly.

"How do you like the sound of Liberty Ann? Do you think your grandmammy would've ever dreamed that you and your daughter would be free?"

"Oh, Micah," she said with a depth of emotion that caused his throat to constrict. "It's so...." Her voice broke and she began to cry.

Micah's arm came around her, and he rested his hand lightly on their daughter. "Perfect?" he asked, hoping that was the word she'd been searching for.

All she could do was nod her head at the moment. Finally, gaining her composure, she said, "Yes...it's perfect."

"Just like our daughter and her mother," he added, causing Eliza to start crying all over again.

August 29, 1862

The ground quavered and shook with every thundering boom. Jessie prayed hard while trying to keep her young'uns calm, despite the fact that her own nerves were tattered beyond mending. John came home to be with his family midmorning, telling her that the gristmill had shut down for the day, as did the sawmill and all other operations on the plantation. All of the workers headed in from the fields, and many were standing in small clusters, speculating as to what they should do.

At the sound of a wagon on the road, John and their eldest son, Job, stepped onto the porch. Jessie peered through the open door but remained inside to bar her other children from heading out with them. To her surprise, it was more than one wagon, and both had come to a halt directly in front of their porch. Even more startling was the fact that Samuel Hawkins was driving the lead wagon, and his son William was driving the other.

John quickly descended the porch steps. "Mr. Hawkins, sir, does ya know what's goin' on?"

Samuel hopped down from the wagon, giving John an apprehensive gaze. "We've come to take your family to the house with us. We want all of you to be safe."

John's head tilted to one side. "This be the war comin' our way?"

"Yes," Mr. Hawkins said hastily. "What we're hearing now is artillery in Richmond less than seven miles from here. If the Federals get the upper hand, the battle will head this direction. If the Confederates win, they'll be going north. We just need to be prepared either way."

John's brow dipped low, and his head angled even further. "Wus gonna happen ta all these other folks? Is ya just comin' fer us, sir?

"Well…yes," Samuel said quietly.

"On account o' Rachel?"

Mr. Hawkins nodded.

Jessie could read her husband's mind as sure as she was looking at him. He was thinking about refusing the man's offer—she knew it. She cleared her throat. "Uh, John, can ya come 'ere fer a minute?"

John rubbed the back of his neck for a couple of beats, then turned to meet his wife's gaze. He was angry. She could see it in his eyes. But his feet remained planted firmly in place. Another loud blast broke the silence, sending thousands of dust particles from their roof into the air and onto their porch.

He turned his gaze back to Mr. Hawkins. "We be stayin' right here with our kinfolk. But thank ya kindly."

Samuel Hawkins' lips pressed tightly together, and he didn't respond for a long moment. After letting out a deep breath, he said, "I didn't want to do it this way…I'd prefer that all of you come…but I'll need to take Rachel back to the house."

To Jessie's chagrin, John stepped to the side, sweeping his big arm toward the open door. "Be my guest."

"John!" Jessie cried out. "What are ya doin'?"

"If Mr. Hawkins be wantin' to protect his girl, he gots a right ta do that. Give 'er to 'im."

Staying where he was, Samuel said, "Jessie, do you mind sending her out?"

Though Rachel was soon to turn four, she still had a mighty strong attachment to her mammy. Jessie wasn't sure if the girl would go with him. Knowing it would just be for a day or two did nothing to calm her anxious nerves over the situation. "Sir," Jessie said, "do ya reckon we be in too much danger if we all stays here?"

Samuel stepped closer, his eyes taking on a more empathetic gaze. "I have no way of knowing the answer to that. I just want to make sure she's safe." He glanced toward John, then back at Jessie. "I want *all* of you to be safe…if you'll just come."

"John?" Jessie asked imploringly.

But the big man was shaking his head.

Jessie hauled in an anxious breath, now seeking a compromise. She stepped out onto the porch, and in doing so, Rachel appeared in the doorway. "What if all us females were ta go to the big house? Would ya be fine with that, John? Surely it ain't gonna be fer long."

"Maybe just for the day," Samuel interjected.

John lowered his head, stroking his chin. Then, looking up, he nodded. "I specs that'll work."

Mr. Hawkins visibly relaxed and reached out to shake his hand. "Thank you for allowing them to come."

John slowly gripped the outstretched hand with only a nod.

When Jessie and the three girls came out of the cabin, it was obvious where Samuel's gaze was fixed. He couldn't take his eyes off of Rachel. Jessie knew why. The child looked exactly like Naomi, save for her creamy skin.

Coming around to the other side of the wagon, Mr. Hawkins offered his hand to help Jessie up to the bench, then picked up his daughter and set her on the seat so she would ride between them. Twelve-year-old Julia and eight-year-old Jenny climbed into the back. William had already turned his empty wagon around and headed back toward the livery.

"I see ya soon," Jessie called to her sons and husband. "You'ins stay safe."

"You too," John said, nodding somberly to his wife.

She turned on the bench, watching her husband and four sons till the wagon took the bend in the road. Turning back around, she began to notice the interaction between Mr. Samuel and his daughter. Every time he looked down at her beside him, Rachel looked up at him. It wasn't hard to notice the emotion in his eyes. But by the crease in his brow, the man obviously seemed conflicted. Not for the first time, Jessie wondered if he might be feeling guilty over Naomi. While she hadn't been privy to Naomi's situation, it seemed that Mr. Hawkins had abandoned her in slave town to carry and deliver his child. Maybe if he'd been concerned enough to have her cared for in the big house, she might still be alive today. Either way, she had personally witnessed the obvious love they held for one another when he came to be with Naomi in the end. It was an act of devotion that she would certainly not forget.

At the sudden *boom, boom, boom,* Samuel's arm protectively took in the child, and, to Jessie's amazement, Rachel didn't shy away. In fact, she leaned into him for security.

Samuel snapped the reins on the two mules, causing them to quicken their pace. Jessie could tell the man was worried…she was too. *Oh, Lawd, place yer mighty hand o' protection on us*, she prayed fervently within her soul.

Mr. Hawkins brought the wagon right up to the front porch of the big house and leapt to the gravel drive. He reached up for Rachel, and, surprisingly, she allowed him to take her into his arms. He held the girl close to his chest as he came around to offer Jessie his hand. But as soon as Jessie was on the ground, Rachel leaned out to her mammy. Mr. Hawkins gently placed the girl in her arms.

Jessie had only been inside the front of the big house once, and that was on the day of Eliza's wedding. Still, she tried not to let her mouth flap open at such beautiful surroundings.

"Come this way," Mr. Hawkins said. "You can stay in the parlor. You'll be safe there. Micah's already sent a few men to surround the house on all sides, and some will patrol through the woods in case soldiers start coming this way." He swung open the double doors. "But try not to worry. I'm sure all will be well."

As soon as they walked into the parlor, Jessie's heart instantly found a scrap of relief. Eliza turned from her pacing and came straight to her, pulling her into a tight hug. "Where's the rest of your family?" she asked.

Jessie shook her head. "John said he ain't comin'. He an' the boys is stayin' put."

Samuel Hawkins cleared his throat. "Well, Abigail will see to your needs." His dark gaze fixed upon Rachel for a prolonged moment, then he turned back to the women. "If the battle continues into the night, we've prepared rooms for you to stay." He bowed slightly. "I'll take my leave."

Jessie turned toward her former master. "Thank ya, sir."

Nodding, he quickly strode back across the hall. Jessie watched him open a drawer in the large mahogany table near the entryway and pull out a holstered pistol. Strapping it to his hip, he removed the gun and inspected the chamber. Apparently satisfied that it was loaded, he crammed it down into the holster and grabbed a box of ammunition before quickly heading out the door.

Worry once again consumed Jessie's thoughts. She needed a distraction. Glancing around the room, she asked, "Whatchu done with Liberty Ann?"

Eliza pointed to a cradle in the corner. "I've never in all my days seen a baby sleep so good."

Just then, a succession of mortar shells reverberated loudly from a few miles away, but the little one didn't even flinch. "What did I tell ya? When the girl wants to sleep, nothin' can stop her."

"Not even a war," Jessie said soberly.

The women occupied the girls as best they could and were able to spend time in prayer despite the alarming disturbance of artillery shells. At noon, they all joined the house workers in the kitchen for lunch and remained there for the better part of the afternoon. All of the women in the house felt more comfortable huddling together. Thankfully by evening, the artillery shells fell silent. But they had merely been replaced by a constant *pop, pop, pop* of rifle fire.

❧❧❧

After a sparse supper, the women cleaned the kitchen and remained around the table. Mr. Samuel and William entered the kitchen just before dusk. Eliza quickly came to her feet, still holding seven-month-old Liberty Ann in her arms. "Where's Micah, sir?"

Samuel's face gave her no reassurance. "I'm not sure. He and Isaiah were heading into the hills at the back of the property earlier this afternoon, but I haven't seen them since." He must've noticed Eliza's angst and softened his voice. "But I'm sure they'll be here by dark. We weren't supposed to meet back at the house until then."

Trying to relax her nerves for the sake of her child, Eliza sat back down at the table. It was all she could do not to head out to the back of the property to search for her man. But for the babe in her lap, she would've already been gone.

Regrettably, when darkness overtook the landscape, there was no sign of Micah and Isaiah. When Mr. Hawkins came back into the kitchen, he calmly addressed the women, although the anxiety on his features was unmistakable. "Why don't all of you go to bed and get some rest. William and I will stay awake in the house. I'm confident all of our men are safe and well. Please try not to worry."

Eliza knew that would be an impossible task but could see the wisdom in getting rest while they could. Abigail led Eliza and Jessie with their children upstairs to show them to separate rooms, but they didn't want to be separated. "Do you mind if we all go to the nursery instead?" Eliza asked.

"Are you sure? These rooms'll be a lot more comfortable for ya."

"We know, but there's plenty of space for all of us in the nursery. We'll feel a lot better being together."

Abigail nodded. "It's clean and tidy, so you're welcome to it." She nodded toward a room across the hall. "Violet's stayin' with Catherine in her room." Then, handing Eliza an oil lamp, she quickly retrieved another lamp from one of the prepared rooms. After leading the women and children to the nursery, she gave them a weary gaze. "You know where I am if you need anything. I'm thinkin' no one'll be findin' sleep tonight except the children."

The women nodded, thanking the housekeeper and telling her good-night.

It had to be well past midnight when Eliza startled awake to someone calling her name. She instantly rose up from her pallet on the floor beside Liberty Ann's cradle. William was standing in the doorway with a low-burning oil lamp. "You're needed in the lower kitchen right away."

Noticing Jessie sit up in the bed she was sharing with Rachel, Eliza hastily told her to stay with the children. "I'll be back as soon as I can. Try not to worry."

William stepped into the hall and ushered her toward the back staircase. "There are wounded men in the kitchen. One of them is a general," he said. "Papa and Mamie are with them right now."

When they reached the landing to the upper kitchen, Eliza grasped William's arm. "I need you to do somethin' for me. There's a satchel inside the cabinet to the left of the door in our house. You need to bring it to me right away."

William nodded, not hesitating to do her bidding. He ran across the kitchen and headed out the back door. Eliza quickly took the stairs into Mamie's domain. She counted four soldiers, all in Union blues—one lying unconscious on the large block table in the middle of the room. A steady stream of blood dripped to the floor.

Mr. Hawkins stepped away from the table when Eliza entered. "It's their general," he told her.

Eliza didn't bother to look at the other three men. She was already assessing the general's wounds. "Are the rest of you hurt?"

"Not like our general," one of the men replied from his chair in the corner. "We can wait."

Quickly glancing at Mr. Samuel, she asked, "Have you sent for Henry? I'm gonna need some help."

"Yes, Isaiah just left to get him."

Eliza's blood pulsed through her temples. "What about Micah?"

"He helped Isaiah lead the soldiers here. He's all right. But he's gone back to his post."

That information brought an ounce of relief to Eliza. At least she knew he was safe. She quickly prayed for the Lord to keep him that way.

With a head and chest wound, Eliza used Samuel and Mamie to help cut off the general's jacket and shirt while she tended to the deep gash on his forehead. She assumed the head wound had come from a fall after being hit in the chest by a bullet.

"Mamie, I need you to press a towel onto the chest wound. Hold it tight to stem the bleeding. And Mr. Samuel, I'm gonna need a lot more light than this. Bring a couple o' more lamps."

No sooner had Samuel left on his mission than his son came charging through the kitchen door with Eliza's satchel. He brought it right to her. "What do you need me to do?" William asked, breathing heavily.

"Look in my bag and get a bandage roll. You need to wrap it around the general's head nice and tight. I'll stitch the wound later. This chest wound needs tending." She briefly lifted the blood-soaked towel beneath Mamie's hands, and blood gurgled up. "Oh, Lord, not an artery," she pleaded.

Samuel hurried in with a lantern and an oil lamp. "Oh, good, hold it up high. Are any of you able to stand and hold a lamp?" she asked the other soldiers in the room.

"I can," a voice called out from a dark corner of the kitchen. When he came into the light, Eliza thought he looked more like a boy than a man. Shaking her head, she told Mamie, "Keep pressing down hard. I need to get somethin' from my bag." Wiping her hands on her skirt, she opened the satchel, grabbing her smallest forceps and a razor. Then, looking at the stove, she asked, "Is there water in the kettle?"

Mamie nodded. "But it ain't hot. I's got it there ready to warm up in the mornin'."

"Good." Eliza grabbed it and gave Mamie an unyielding stare. "When we take the towel away, I want you to start slowly pouring water over the wound while I work. Not too fast, just keep a steady stream goin'."

Mamie nodded confidently. "I's got it."

Before removing the towel beneath Mamie's hands, Eliza took hold of Samuel's wrist and pulled his lantern into a better position. "Hold it right there." Then, turning to Mamie, she said, "Grab the kettle."

When Mamie let go of the sopping towel, Eliza tugged it to the floor where it made a sickening splat. While the water poured over the wound, she quickly stuck her finger into the hole and felt instant relief. The musket ball hadn't lodged too deeply—it sat just below the clavicle. That was good news. It hadn't punctured his lungs and was nowhere near the general's heart. She now suspected that it hadn't even nicked an artery. Perhaps it was because the general was so heavy-chested. Leaving her finger in the wound to staunch the blood flow, Eliza said, "I'm gonna need more clean towels."

William had just finished tying off the bandage on the general's head. "I'll go get some." He quickly turned and headed for the stairs.

"No, no, Mr. William. I's got plenty right over yonder," Mamie cried out. "Looky there in that cabinet." William instantly moved in the direction she had jerked her head, then came back to the table with a stack of kitchen towels.

Eliza wasted no time giving the young man another order. "When I pull my finger out, Mamie's gonna stop pouring water, and William, be ready to wipe the blood away and hand me my forceps when I tell ya."

"All right," he said, taking a position on the other side of the table.

Eliza clasped the straight razor, then removed her finger from the wound. While she made an incision that would accommodate her forceps, William did everything he was told. "More light!" Eliza practically shouted when she could barely see what she was doing. Both Samuel and the young soldier moved into a better position, Samuel changing the lantern to his other hand. "That's it," she said in a softer tone.

When the incision was long enough, Eliza plied her fingers to stretch the opening but was unable to use the forceps at the same time. Her hands were too slick with blood. Mamie tried to help her, but the cook's fingers were too plump, and Eliza didn't want to extend the incision. Glancing across the table, she said, "William, I'm going to hold the wound open. Can you get the ball out?"

He didn't hesitate. Wiping his hands on his shirt, he took the forceps and quickly went to work. In seconds, he said, "Got it!" then pulled it free from the general's body.

A collective sigh of relief filtered through the stagnant August air in the kitchen. Eliza pressed a fresh towel over the wound, then instructed Mamie to hold it there while she retrieved a sewing kit from her satchel. When she finally started making her first stitch, Henry and Isaiah entered the kitchen.

Eliza shook her head. It would've been nice to have Henry by her side earlier, but she briefly glanced at the other faces around the table. None had flinched from their gruesome duty. And if the general lived, it would be because of their absolute fearlessness.

Chapter 53

While Isaiah helped Samuel and William carry the general to the bed in Naomi's old room, Eliza continued to help Henry patch up the other three soldiers in the kitchen. Their wounds were minor compared to the general's but could prove fatal if infection were to set in. The men were so filthy, it was hard to get them clean enough for the task at hand.

Abigail had agreed to sit with the general and monitor his breathing and heart rate. Eliza didn't want him left alone until she knew he was stable. It had been a blessing that he'd remained unconscious during her operation. Henry had also done a masterful job stitching the general's head wound.

Just after three o'clock in the morning, Isaiah came back to the kitchen. He looked so worn out, Eliza wanted to tell him to go home and rest. But she was fairly certain of the response he would give her. And the truth of it was, she preferred it if Isaiah would go back out to be with Micah. Now that the worst of the crisis was over with the general, her mind went back to worrying about her husband's welfare.

Putting the final touches on a homemade sling, Eliza told the young soldier who'd called himself Garrett that if he wanted his shoulder to properly mend, he would have to keep it in that position for at least a week. It had been wrenched out of socket so badly she didn't know how the man had made it here without passing out. "If you go back to usin' that arm too soon, it may never be right again. You gotta keep it in this position."

His bloodshot gaze met hers, and he slowly nodded. "Thank you, ma'am. I will."

Mamie danced around everyone in the kitchen as if no one was in her way at all. Tabitha had joined her in cleaning up from Eliza's surgery, and Mamie now started cooking breakfast for the men. When Isaiah headed for the door, Mamie chastised him. "Mm, mm, mister. You stay put till you get some o' Mamie's bacon an' eggs."

Isaiah rubbed the top of his head and let out a weary breath. "I's thinkin' I best get back to Micah...but thank ya."

Eliza joined forces with Mamie and took Isaiah by the arm. "Sit down for a little bit and tell me what's happenin' out there. After you eat you can take some food to Micah." Seeing his hesitation, she softly added, "Please."

Giving in, he took a seat at the small table by the wall where Mamie usually rolled out her dough. Eliza carried a stool over to sit beside him. "How did you find these men?"

"They found us," he said. "They's been in a terrible battle all day and some o' the night."

Eliza kept her voice low. "Did they say who's winnin'?"

"They ain't said nothin' to me or Micah. I think they's waitin' to talk to Mr. Samuel. You reckon he's comin' back down here?"

"Most likely. I'm sure he's gettin' cleaned up after...." Eliza's voice trailed away. She didn't even want to think about the ordeal they'd just been through.

Soon, Mamie brought Isaiah a plate full of eggs and bacon with two biscuits straight from the oven. The other men in the kitchen also accepted a hearty breakfast with thanks. All conversation ceased while the men devoured the food as if they hadn't eaten since the war began. While Isaiah was still eating, Mamie prepared a bag of food for Micah. Eliza knew how hungry he would be after missing supper last night.

"Don't you go eatin' Micah's food 'fore you get it to 'im," Mamie scolded.

Isaiah took a swig of coffee and grinned. He picked up the bag she'd set beside him on the table and stood. "I reckon some of it'll get to 'im." Then, wiping his mouth with the back of his hand, he said, "Thank ya, for the food and coffee, Mamie. It was just what I's needin'."

Eliza patted his arm. "I told you so." Then, with a more serious tone, she said, "Please tell Micah I'm prayin' for him…and for you too."

"Thank ya," Isaiah said, then headed back out into the blackened night.

Eliza quickly went upstairs to check on Jessie. Finding the children asleep, she quietly told her friend all that had happened, then suggested she continue to sleep while she could. Thankfully Eliza had brought some clean clothes with her, so she went down the hall to one of the rooms Abigail had prepared. It felt good to wash up and put on the fresh set of clothes. She wasn't sure she'd ever be able to get the bloodstains out of the blouse and skirt she'd worn while working on the general.

By the time Eliza got back to the kitchen, Mr. Samuel was already there and so was William. They too had changed clothes, and Mamie had made them sit down to eat. "You gots to keep up yer strength like the rest of 'em."

Instead of sitting at the table, Samuel took the stool and sat down near the most veteran officer of the group while he ate. "What's your name, soldier?"

"Sergeant David Rice, sir. I'm aid to Major General Bull Nelson."

Samuel looked shocked and hooked his thumb over the top of his shoulder. "That's Bull Nelson we were working on?"

"Yes, sir."

Samuel set his plate aside. "Sergeant Rice, I'm Samuel Hawkins. My son Joseph is under General Nelson's command. Do you know him?

"I do, sir. It's because of your son we came here. He gave us directions, but we thought we'd lost our way. If it hadn't been for your slaves out there, we wouldn't have made it."

Eliza and William moved closer to hear the conversation. Samuel didn't bother to correct the sergeant's assumption that his men were slaves. "So my son is all right?"

Sergeant Rice gave him a wary gaze. "He was when we left with the general."

"What about the battle in Richmond? Is your army winning?" Samuel's query was laced with fret.

The sergeant bowed his head, breaking eye contact with Mr. Hawkins. "Sir," he said quietly, "we were losing miserably."

Samuel abruptly stood up. "Oh, God, help them," he moaned, raking his hands through his hair.

⊰⊱

As soon as the shadowy light of dawn appeared across the fields, gunfire rang out from only a few miles away. Isaiah exchanged glances with Micah from their posts at the top of the hill—both men shook their heads. Apparently the battle would be raging for yet another day. The fact that it wasn't moving south in their direction didn't bode well for the Union troops. While it was of some comfort to know that the Hawkins Plantation was being spared from the violence, it was troubling to think that the Confederates might be winning.

Isaiah headed into the trees on the downside of the hill to take care of his business. On the way back to his lookout post, he stopped by the Hawkins family cemetery. Yesterday, quite by chance, he discovered where Naomi had been buried. It was hard to describe how it had made him feel. If it hadn't been for Micah, he would've never recognized it, not being able to read the marker.

Isaiah had been most grateful that the overseer pointed out Naomi's resting place as they came up the hill. Had Micah remained silent, he would still be wondering about Naomi's fate. While she wasn't buried near the family, she and Berthy, along with a handful of other slaves from old Master Joseph's time, had their own section outside of the fenced property containing the family plots.

Laying his hat over his chest, Isaiah breathed, "Be at peace, Naomi, till I see ya again," then he made his way over to where Micah sat with his back against the smooth bark of a sycamore tree.

"Why don't you go check on Franklin? I bet he's wonderin' about you," Micah told him.

"I's thinkin' 'bout that. But you's the one that needs to go by the big house and see yer family. Eliza be worried about ya."

"She told you that?"

"Not with words. I seen it in her eyes."

For a while the two men sat in silence, keeping a keen eye on the landscape. They would have the best vantage point to be able to warn the rest of the folks on the plantation should the battle move in their direction. Both were hesitant to abandon their post, even if for a short time.

Isaiah leaned back into the oak tree only a few yards from Micah. His mind drifted across a sea of thoughts, settling upon his son. Franklin was probably already in the stables with the thoroughbreds. The boy was beginning to grow in strength and stature. If Isaiah was correct, ten years had passed since his birth. Ruthie would've been proud of the kind of young man he was becoming. Always grateful; never unkind; honest and humble. Isaiah was aware that his son's ability with the horses had far surpassed his own. The Lord had blessed Franklin with a rare gift indeed.

The morning sun slipped across the sky and started its steady descent into midafternoon. The two men had become familiar with the pop and whiz of gunfire. Even though the air was thick and warm, the repulsive sound travelled unhindered through the summer heat. Isaiah found himself lulled into a state of lethargy. His eyelids grew heavy with fatigue. Soon, he was fast asleep in the shade of the oak.

Micah suddenly leapt to his feet, yanking Isaiah back to reality. "They're comin' out of the woods. You see 'em?"

Isaiah quickly stood, his gaze following the direction Micah was pointing. It wasn't hard to spot them. A band of men in blue uniforms were making their way across the hay field. This was no slow march—they were running for their lives.

"Go warn the house!"

Isaiah didn't have to be told twice. He took off at a sprint down the hill, wishing he'd thought to bring a horse or a mule. It would've gotten him to the big house twice as fast. Although with adrenaline pumping through his veins, he'd be giving a mule a run for its money.

Charging through the wide-open kitchen door, Isaiah found no one inside. He took the stairs two at a time to the upper kitchen and found Abigail with the women of the house around the table. Startled by his hasty entry, Abigail stood up, clasping her hand to her chest.

"What's happened?"

Isaiah's feet continued on toward the hall. "We's got more men comin'. Best be prepared."

"Blue or gray?" Abigail called out.

"Blue!"

Hearing voices in Mr. Hawkins' study, Isaiah entered without knocking. To his surprise, the general was leaning back in one of the room's easy chairs, his long legs stretched out on a footstool. Mr. Hawkins immediately stood from his chair. "What is it, Isaiah?"

"We's got more Yankee men a comin'. Looks like they's on the run, sir."

"How many?" the general bellowed.

Isaiah turned his gaze on the barrel-chested man. "Can't say fer sure. I seen a dozen or so runnin' through the hayfield, sir."

When the general put his feet to the floor, he groaned. "Did you see any Rebs?" The general added a string of curse words to express his disdain for the Confederate soldiers.

"No, sir, but Micah's on the hill, waitin' ta bring 'em here."

The other soldiers came across the hall from the parlor. "Sir, it's time to get you to the attic till we know it's safe."

General Nelson nodded, then winced when his men helped him up. It took a long quarter-hour to get the six-foot-four-inch general into the attic and well hidden behind the boxes and trunks. All of the men had their weapons at the ready. They couldn't allow their general to be taken prisoner.

❧❦❧

Eliza had heard the men's voices below but was powerless to do anything at the moment. She looked down at Liberty Ann taking her sweet time nursing. Knowing the babe would sleep for a few hours after eating, she didn't want to cut her off too soon.

Jessie must've read her mind. "I'll find out what's goin' on." Then, turning to her oldest daughter, she said, "Keep an eye on Rachel and Jenny. I be right back."

When Liberty Ann's eyelids slowly closed, Eliza whispered, "Finally." Placing the child on her legs, she covered herself, then lifted her onto her shoulder, patting the girl's back.

Jessie raced back into the nursery. "Give 'er to me," she said softly. "More Yanks comin'. They may need ya."

Eliza didn't hesitate to transfer her daughter into Jessie's arms. Leaning in, she kissed the baby, then held Jessie's arm with purpose. "Don't forget what to do if Rebels come through the house." Mr. Hawkins had told the women that they would be hiding the Union soldiers in the attic. At no time were they to even look in that direction should they be questioned. He wanted to avoid a gun battle at all costs.

Jessie nodded, eyes ablaze. "I 'member."

By the time Eliza made it down the back stairs, Union soldiers were pouring into the lower kitchen. It felt like they were sucking the air right out of the house. Mr.

Samuel and William were already there to meet them, watching the soldiers enter one by one. Isaiah had gone back outside to help Micah get them all in.

Eliza pushed her way past the men to see how many were yet to come. A premonition abruptly settled in her gut like a heavy sack of flour. She was certain it had something to do with one of the last soldiers. After stepping through the door, she instantly whirled back around. "Mr. Samuel, you need to get out here!"

Samuel slid past the men by the kitchen door and made it out back just as Micah was bringing the last man across the yard. The soldier's head was hanging down, his arm draped around Micah's shoulder. He looked as if he might collapse at any moment.

Running to help, Samuel took the soldier's other arm, then came to an abrupt halt. "Joseph?"

The soldier's head slowly came up, his face so grimy it was nearly unrecognizable. But the eyes were unmistakable—they belonged to Joseph Hawkins.

Joseph had enough strength to let go of Micah and fall into his father's arms. Samuel held him up, wrapping him securely to his chest while sobs shook his body. He kissed his son over and over again until his face was nearly as bloodied as Joseph's.

Eliza went to her husband and kissed him on the mouth. "Can you stay?" she asked.

Micah ran an affectionate hand down her arm. "No, I gotta make sure the Rebs didn't follow 'em here."

She let out a weary breath before kissing him again. "Be careful, Micah. I need you somethin' fierce."

Giving her a tight smile, he pulled his wife into a strong embrace. "I'll see you soon. Try not to worry," he said before heading back across the yard.

Eliza watched him walk away, then turned to help the men get Joseph into the house. Once inside the kitchen, Isaiah stepped forward and picked Joseph up, carrying him all the way to his room on the second floor. Eliza spread a blanket across his bed to lay him on. Then swiftly she helped get him undressed to see where he'd been wounded. But to her astonishment, she could find nothing more than cuts and bruises.

Without warning, Joseph's lips turned pale, and he moaned miserably. Then, turning on his side, he convulsed, vomiting on the floor. There was nothing they could do but let it happen. When he was done, he rolled back over on his bed, and Eliza cleaned his face with a wet cloth.

"Get as much water in him as you can," she told Samuel and William. "He's completely dehydrated."

While Eliza cleaned his wounds and his body, the men held his head up and forced Joseph to drink. Every minute she would tell them, "Again."

Tabitha soundlessly entered the room, cleaning the floor, then taking Joseph's filthy clothes away.

As soon as Eliza finished her ministrations, Samuel lifted his son while she yanked the sullied blanket onto the floor and turned down the bedsheet. Gently laying Joseph back on the bed, they pulled a nightshirt over his head, then covered him with the sheet.

Samuel turned a pleading gaze upon Eliza. "What do you think?"

Laying her hand on Joseph's forehead, she softly said, "He'll recover. He's completely exhausted and dehydrated. Do you want me to stay with him?"

Already shaking his head, Samuel pulled a chair next to Joseph's bed. "I'm not leaving his side."

"That's good, sir. Just make sure he keeps drinking water. I'll have Mamie send up a broth to get some strength back in him."

By nightfall, none of the Confederate army had materialized on Hawkins land, and Micah came back to the house. Eliza feared he would soon be in the same shape as Joseph if he didn't get something to eat and lay down to rest. Mr. Samuel had decided to bring the general and his men from the attic, making them more comfortable on the second floor. Mamie and the other women continued to cook well into the evening to feed the additional Union troops.

Jessie had asked to go back to her cabin with the girls. Gunfire had long since ended, and the newly arrived soldiers had told Mr. Hawkins that their army had been routed. The Rebels were headed northward toward Louisville. Isaiah accompanied William as he took Jessie and the girls back home to Big John and their sons.

The following morning, two U.S. Army officers serving as scouts made their way to the Hawkins Plantation. They were in search of General William Bull Nelson. With four Union soldiers standing guard on the porch, Mr. Hawkins met the scouts in the front entryway. He quickly ushered them to his study where Micah was already waiting. Micah was feeling much better, having gone home with his wife and child for a full night's sleep.

Micah seated the two officers in front of the desk, then stood to the side while Samuel sat down in his chair across from them.

"Mr. Hawkins, the U.S. Army is grateful to you for taking care of General Nelson and his men. Are all of the troops able to travel?"

Samuel's head tilted. "All but two. The general and one other may need to stay here for a few days."

Micah knew he was referring to Joseph, trying to keep his son here as long as possible. But Eliza had come to check on Joseph early this morning. She had reported that his condition had improved greatly. He doubted the army would allow the young man to stay in his own home while the other soldiers moved out.

Dragging his attention back to the conversation at hand, Micah heard one of the officers tell Mr. Hawkins that they would order a hospital wagon for the general and the other soldier. It would be here by the afternoon.

Samuel's face blanched. He obviously wasn't expecting to gain his son, only to lose him within a day's time.

"May we see the general, sir?"

Mr. Hawkins cleared his throat. "Of course." He stood and went to the door. "Right this way, gentlemen."

Micah followed behind the trio, hoping there would be no conflict where Joseph was concerned. But when the men made it to the landing on the second floor, Joseph stepped out of his room, dressed in civilian clothing.

Samuel immediately moved between the officers and his son, ushering the men in the direction of the general's room. But when Joseph saluted the other soldiers, they both turned to face him. Micah could feel the tension rise.

"Who are you?" one of the men asked.

"Corporal Joseph Hawkins at your service, sir."

The officer now turned to Samuel. "Your son?"

Barely audible, Samuel answered, "Yes."

"Were you in the battle of Richmond?"

Joseph didn't hesitate. "Yes, sir."

"Where's your uniform?"

"I was just going to get it, sir."

The officer nodded, then turned back to Mr. Hawkins, indicating he was ready to see the general. Samuel looked as though he would be sick, although no one paid him notice, save for Micah.

Within the hour, all of the men in blue were ready for departure except for General Nelson. He would be left behind with his aid, Sergeant Rice, to await the hospital wagon later in the day.

The officers mounted up on the front drive and had already conscripted two mules from the barn and a wagon for the men who were unable to walk the long road to Lexington. Joseph turned to his father with a determined gaze. "Don't worry about me, Papa. I can handle myself."

A humorless laugh escaped Samuel's throat. "I have no doubt about that. But I can't promise not to worry about you, Son." He choked on his next words while pulling Joseph into a secure hug. "You'll never be out of my thoughts or prayers. I love you, Son."

Joseph squeezed his dad, then stepped back. "I love you too, Papa." Then, with a tip of his chin and a wave to his brother and sister, he squared his shoulders and headed out with the other men.

Later that afternoon, Eliza made sure General Nelson was being properly taken care of as he was loaded onto the U.S. Army hospital wagon. While the general was still pale and weak, he assured those within range that he would be back on the battlefield within the month. Everyone humored him by nodding in agreement.

When his commanding officer was settled, Sergeant Rice came to Samuel with an outstretched hand. "Mr. Hawkins, I wanted to properly thank you for your service to the United States Army." He nodded toward Eliza. "Your slave here saved the general's life."

For the first time, Samuel seemed to realize what these soldiers must've been thinking all along. "Sergeant Rice, our healer is a free woman, as are all the other workers on my plantation. They've been free for over two years."

The man's jaw dropped. For a long moment, the sergeant seemed to weigh the information he'd been given. Then, stepping toward Eliza, he turned his hand upward, extending it to her. She smiled and laid her hand into his while he humbly bowed and kissed it. "Thank you, madam, for your brave service."

Holding back an onslaught of emotion, Eliza nodded. "It was my honor."

Then, turning to Mr. Hawkins one last time, the sergeant said, "Sir, you're blessed to have seen your son. I've been informed that General Nelson's army suffered over eight hundred casualties in the battle of Richmond. We believe at least four thousand others were captured."

Samuel swallowed hard at the shocking news. It was all he could do to say, "I'm sorry."

"Well," Sergeant Rice said, "thank you all again for saving the general's life." His chin firmed. "This was only a setback. We're going to win this war soon."

With those final words, the sergeant stepped up beside General Nelson, and the wagon jerked forward.

Only Eliza remained in the drive until it was completely out of sight.

May 1865

W hy are you being so stubborn, Catherine?"
Beatrice Gray drilled her ten-year-old pupil with steely eyes, which perfectly matched her surname. While the tutor was a young woman, her sternness belied her age, making her seem much older than she really was. Even her tightly wound bun and drab clothing would cause anyone to believe she was a good decade or more beyond her actual years.

"You could easily learn French if you would put forth as much effort as Rachel here…whom I might add, is three and a half years your younger." The tutor's voice ended on a high-pitched note, which only brought mirth to Catherine's blue eyes. The girl glanced at her only classmate, causing Rachel to quickly lower her gaze.

At that very moment, loud voices and hurried footsteps echoed through the hall from downstairs, drawing the two girls' attention away from their French lesson. When Samuel Hawkins' voice could be heard above the din calling out a *welcome home*, Catherine leapt to her feet, tumbling her wooden chair onto the floor. "I think Joseph is home from the war!" she cried excitedly.

Miss Gray abruptly rose to her feet. "You will sit back down immediately, young lady!"

"But, Miss Gray, I haven't seen my brother in three—"

"I said, sit back down at once. I will gladly allow you to join the welcome if you'll but ask my permission in French."

By the look on Catherine's face, it almost seemed as if she'd been asked to launder her own clothing or butcher a hog for dinner. The phrase was already running unhindered through Rachel's mind, but she knew Catherine would never be able to come up with more than a couple of correct words.

When Miss Gray pointed a stubby finger toward the chair on the floor, Catherine slowly set it upright and took her place beside Rachel once more. "S'il vous plaît. . . ."

Impatient fingers tapping on the other side of the table did very little to help Catherine come up with the rest of the phrase. Finally, the girl turned imploring eyes upon her companion. Rachel opened her mouth, but Miss Gray slapped her hand loudly onto the table, capturing Rachel with a harsh glare. "You will *not* speak nor will you help." Then, turning her eyes back to Catherine, the tutor continued her admonishment. "We have been at this for years! You will seek permission in French, or you will stay right here and continue with your lessons."

It was obvious that Catherine's earlier amusement had twisted into hopeless disappointment. Her hands turned red as she wrung them tightly in her lap while searching for the correct words.

A loud sigh escaped the girl's throat as she tried again. "S'il vous plaît . . . je. . . ."

The silence that followed was thick—Catherine's angst so terribly obvious Rachel could feel it herself. "S'il vous plaît, puis-je être renvoyé?" Rachel blurted out, not caring if she would be punished.

"S'il vous plaît . . . puis-je être renvoyé?" Although her inflection was lacking, Catherine mimicked Rachel word for word, then swallowed hard, waiting for a response from Miss Gray.

Watching their tutor's lips press so firmly they turned white, Rachel wondered if the woman would give in. There was a noticeable battle going on inside of her. "Oh, all right. Go on then." Miss Gray flapped a frustrated hand toward the door.

Catherine didn't give the tutor a chance to change her mind. She was already out of her chair, running across the room for the door, pausing only long enough to say, "Thank…I mean, merci, Miss Gray." Her feet could be heard clattering down the hall and thudding on the stairs to the floor below.

Rachel didn't move nor did she dare make eye contact with Miss Gray. In the entire year that she had been joining Catherine in the nursery, now converted into a schoolroom for the girls, she had never so much as stepped out of line. That was certainly not the case with Catherine. Almost on a weekly basis, Miss Gray was sharing a less than glowing report with Mr. Hawkins concerning his daughter Catherine. Sometimes Rachel felt guilty over the compliments she would receive right in front of her schoolmate. Catherine never seemed to be bothered by it, usually making fun of their tutor during their lunch breaks when Miss Gray wasn't around. Rachel held back a smile just thinking about how Catherine could do an almost perfect imitation of Miss Gray.

"Well…there's no need to go on with our lessons without the other half of our class. You may join them downstairs."

Rachel dipped her head. "Merci, mademoiselle."

Although Rachel was relieved to part company with Miss Gray, she felt uncomfortable about joining in on Mr. Joseph's homecoming. While her mammy had let her know that Mr. Samuel was her real father, she felt almost no connection with the man. Many times, she observed him watching her, but he rarely seemed to care enough to engage her in conversation. As far as she was concerned, her only brothers and sisters were the ones she lived with—her mammy and pappy lived in the cabin over a mile from the big house.

Still, Rachel was curious to see Mr. Joseph. And knowing she couldn't leave until her sister Julia came to walk her home some two hours from now, Rachel quietly descended the main staircase. Following the direction of the animated conversation, she slid into the corner of the main parlor to watch the happy homecoming. No one even glanced her way.

"What are these medals?" Catherine asked, fingering them on her brother's dark blue uniform jacket. Joseph had pulled his sister onto his lap while Mr. Samuel and Mr. William sat in nearby chairs. All of the household staff, along with Micah, had gathered to welcome home the eldest son and to hear what news he brought.

Joseph gave his sister a dry smile. "Aww, they're just decorations, that's all." He tweaked her chin, then slid her off his leg onto the sofa beside him.

"We've all been so thankful that the war is over, yet saddened by the death of our President Lincoln in such a short span of time," Samuel told his son. But Joseph gave no response to his father's statement. "Of course, we don't need to be talking about such sad news. You're home now, and we all thank God!" Everyone in the parlor added their assent.

Samuel looked over his shoulder. "Is Mamie in the room?"

"I's right here, Mr. Samuel," she said, moving closer to her employer.

"What do you say we have a special meal tonight for our returning hero?"

"Oh, sir, I's already got in mind a roast beef dinner just for the occasion." She gave the young man a generous smile. "Welcome home, Mr. Joseph."

Joseph nodded his head and murmured, "Thanks."

Curious to get a look at the medals on his jacket, Rachel crept a little closer. When she moved into Mr. Samuel's view, he gave her a warm smile. But when Joseph noticed Rachel, his glare upon her was distinctly cold. She knew beyond all doubt that she wasn't welcome in his presence.

Backing away, Rachel slipped into the hallway completely unnoticed as the conversation in the parlor took a lighter turn. Tiptoeing down the hall, she let herself out the back door of the upper kitchen. Her stomach was in knots. It was difficult to erase the look of contempt she'd seen in Joseph's eyes.

Sitting down in the shade on the back porch steps, Rachel racked her brain. What had she done to make Joseph hate her so? Folding her hands on her knees, she bent over, resting her forehead on her hands. Whatever it was, she must've done it a long time ago, because he'd been gone for most of her life. Maybe she could ask Catherine next time they were alone.

Something tickled the side of her neck, and Rachel instantly sat up, swiping at it. Seeing what had touched her, she let out a much-needed laugh. "Liberty Ann, where's your mama?"

The wiry three year old leaned her elbows onto Rachel's lap and giggled.

"Did you get away again?" Rachel instantly clasped her little hand and stood up, knowing Eliza would be worried sick if she realized the child had snuck out of the house. Liberty Ann was living up to her name. If she wasn't being watched, the girl escaped to the outdoors every chance she got.

"Come on. We better get you home," Rachel said.

Just as they walked into the Simmons' front yard, Eliza came barreling out of the house to meet them. One of the women from the plantation followed her onto the porch.

"Baby, I can't turn my back on you for even one second." When Eliza got to the girls, she laid a gentle hand on the side of Rachel's face. "Bless you, child. Where'd you find her?"

"I was just sitting on the back porch of the big house, and she found *me.*"

Eliza's tongue tsked. She reached down and picked up her daughter, then turned back to her patient who had descended the porch steps. "Darcy, I'm so sorry I ran out on ya like that. Did you have any questions about the treatment?"

Darcy held up the tin of ointment. "No, I understands everythin' ya told me."

Reaching out and squeezing the woman's arm, Eliza told her, "Be sure to come back next week. I want to see how you're gettin' along."

The other woman nodded and said goodbye.

"Rachel, aren't you supposed to be in class right now?"

Rachel looked up at Eliza and shrugged. "Mr. Joseph came home, so Miss Gray let us out of class."

"What! Joseph's back from the war?" Eliza immediately started walking toward the big house with Liberty Ann wrapped snuggly in her arms. After a few strides, she glanced over her shoulder at Rachel. "Well, aren't you comin'?"

"No thank you," she said in a hushed tone.

Eliza's eyes grew soft. "Somethin' happened to you, child." It came out as a statement, not a question.

If something had happened to her, Rachel didn't know what it was. She only knew she had to stay away from Mr. Joseph.

Eliza came back to Rachel and reached for her hand. "Come on, let's sit down on my porch. I can welcome Mr. Joseph later."

Rachel gladly sat down beside Eliza on her porch steps.

Getting Liberty Ann situated on her lap, the healer reached over and laid a gentle hand on top of Rachel's thigh. They sat that way for a short moment before Eliza said, "Don't you worry, precious child. It'll be all right."

Looking into Eliza's deep brown eyes, Rachel felt the knot loosen in her stomach.

"Can you tell me why you're out here instead of in there?"

Rachel's eyes trailed over to the big house, and she stared at it for a while. Finally, she turned her face back to Eliza. "I don't belong there."

"Did someone tell you that?"

All Rachel did was shake her head.

"This doesn't have anything to do with your lessons, does it?"

"No," she said quietly.

"Then, sweet girl, why did you leave the house?"

Unable to put her notions into words, Rachel shrugged her little shoulders.

Eliza wrapped her hand around the inside of Rachel's leg and drew it next to hers. "You are so much like your mother. When you get older, I'll tell you some more about her, but for now, would you like me to tell you a few things I know?"

Rachel's brow pinched. "But I have a mammy."

Slowly nodding, Eliza said, "Yes, that's true. Jessie is your mammy, and I know she's told you that your real mother passed on the day after you were born. But for those few precious hours that your mother got to hold you, I don't know if I've ever seen a woman love her child more."

Eliza kissed the top of Liberty Ann's head as if to let her know how precious the child was to *her*. "You know, your mother was probably the most beautiful creature on this plantation. Wherever she went, people's eyes couldn't help but go to her. But she wasn't vain—she didn't see her beauty as somethin' to use for her own purpose. Your mother was thoughtful and gentle. I never heard her say one unkind word about another human bein'."

Rachel leaned into Eliza as she listened. Just the sound of the healer's voice brought her blessed comfort.

"You may be too young to understand this, child, but your mother, Naomi, is one of the reasons why all the people on this plantation were set free three years before President Lincoln proclaimed us so and even before this terrible war got started." She looked down at the girl up against her. "And one other thing I want you to know…her very last word was *free*. I've thought about that for a long time." Eliza's eyes took on a faraway look. "I got the feelin' that she was tellin' your papa to free his slaves with her very last breath, 'cause when she said that sacred word, she had been starin' right at me."

While Rachel didn't quite understand it all, she felt a warmth flow through her at the thought of her real mother. For the first time, she longed to know the woman who had brought her into this world.

When Eliza fell silent, Rachel looked up and noticed tears on the healer's cheeks. And then she asked the question she'd never felt brave enough to ask before. "What color was my mother?"

Fall 1865

T hat's it, Son. You's got 'im right where you wants 'im." Isaiah kept his voice low, watching Franklin's interaction with Gypsy King, a young stallion from the Prince of Madagascar's line. The thoroughbred was a dark bay with black socks and a streak of black all the way down his muzzle. He had taken to Franklin from the very moment of birth. For the past two and a half years, Gypsy had followed Franklin loyally, without so much as a lead rein attached to his halter.

The thirteen-year-old boy ran a gentle hand down the beautiful animal's neck. "I's just gonna sit up on your back for a bit. It just be you 'n me, fella." He drew the horse's head to his chest and whispered in his ear. "It's always been you 'n me."

Gypsy let out a puff of air and nuzzled Franklin's chest. Franklin chuckled, then moved closer to the saddle. Slowly he put a foot in the stirrup and eased his body off the ground. Gypsy turned his head, but his eyes remained placid. "That's it, fella," Franklin said as he gradually swung his right leg over the top and sat astraddle.

The horse gave a gentle buck and then another, almost playful-like. Earnestly watching the two, Isaiah leaned his elbows on the top of the paddock fence. He couldn't help but grin at the connection between the horse and boy. While Prince's bloodline had produced many foals with a wild nature, it almost seemed like part of Franklin's ability to harness that nature had been bred into each one of them. His gift was uncanny.

Isaiah caught a movement out of the corner of his eye and turned to see Micah and Joseph Hawkins striding toward him. He moved several steps away from the paddock railing to greet them. He didn't want anything to disturb such a vital interaction between Franklin and Gypsy.

Noticing the look on Micah's face, Isaiah steeled himself for hard news. Something was obviously wrong. "Can I help ya?" Isaiah asked.

"Isaiah—" Micah started, but Joseph didn't give him a chance to continue.

"I've come to let you know that I'll be selling off several of the thoroughbreds in our stock. We'll only be keeping the ones that can be used for breeding." Joseph looked down at the leather notebook in his hand and turned a page. "These are the ones we'll be taking to auction in Lexington in October."

Isaiah glanced at Micah for help. Surely Mr. Joseph knew he couldn't read.

Micah cleared his throat and rattled off most of the names of the horses that he could remember.

Isaiah's brow wrinkled. "And Mr. Hawkins be fine with this?"

Joseph pierced Isaiah with an impertinent gaze. "Now that I'm home, I'll be taking over the operation of the stables. You'll answer to me from now on…and so will your boy."

Not wanting to reveal his shock, Isaiah merely dipped his chin. "Yessir."

Brushing past Isaiah's shoulder, Joseph headed for the open door of the stables. Micah told his boss, "I'll be right there," but the young man didn't bother to respond.

"I know what you're thinkin', Isaiah," Micah said, shaking his head. "This is gonna take some getting used to."

Isaiah removed his hat, letting out a long breath. "That young man ain't his papa, that's fer…." Halting in mid-sentence, Isaiah cringed. "I's sorry. I didn't mean to speak unkindly."

"No need to apologize. Eliza and I have been sayin' the same thing ever since Joseph came home." The overseer looked over his shoulder to make sure they were still alone. "He even tried to bump William out of his place with the mule operation, but thankfully, Mr. Samuel stood up to him on that one."

"Seems the war done took its toll on 'im. Maybe things'll settle down after a while," Isaiah said.

"We can only hope." Micah glanced over his shoulder again. "I guess I'd better get in there."

"'Fore ya go, can you tell me if Gypsy King be on that list?"

Micah swallowed hard, giving Isaiah an uneasy gaze. "Not yet," he said quietly, then turned away and strode for the stables.

❧❧❧

The next morning, Micah felt his chest pinch as he sat on the edge of the bed, pulling on his boots. He didn't like confrontation and usually did everything within his power to work out any differences he might have with someone, but it was much more challenging when the problem was with his boss. When he came into the front room, Liberty Ann was scrambling down the ladder from the loft, and he caught the little sprite around her waist when she was halfway down.

"G'mornin', baby child." He started kissing her belly, causing her to go into a fit of giggles. Then, releasing her to the floor, Micah sauntered over to his wife as she prepared breakfast. Kissing her on the back of her neck, he asked how she was feeling.

"A lot better this mornin', thank the Lord. At least I can stand the smell of bacon frying. That's somethin' positive."

Micah lowered himself into a chair at the table. "You still think this one's a boy?"

Letting out a soft laugh, Eliza turned around with a plate of eggs and bacon for her husband. "That's my feelin'."

He gave her a teasing grin. "And we all know about those feelin's of yours, don't we?"

Eliza set another plate on the table and called Liberty Ann to breakfast. The girl was standing on the top of the table beside Micah's reading chair. She quickly bounced onto the chair cushion and hopped to the floor.

"Baby, what'd I tell you about standin' on that table? That's not safe."

Liberty Ann pulled herself onto the high stool at the eating table, seemingly unfazed by her mama's rebuke. She picked up her cup of milk, gulping half of it down before digging her little fingers into the scrambled eggs.

"You not eating?" Micah asked his wife when she sat down beside their daughter.

"Maybe in a bit. I may need to take a walk in the fresh air before I can stomach somethin'."

Micah fell silent, concentrating on his breakfast. When he looked up, Eliza's eyes had a shimmer to them. "What are you not telling me?" she asked directly.

Letting out a snort, Micah shook his head. "I don't guess I'll ever be able to keep a secret from ya, will I?"

"Not as long as I've got eyes to see."

He picked up a strip of bacon and leaned back in his chair. "I found out somethin' yesterday that I'm gonna have to talk to Mr. Samuel about. I'm just not lookin' forward to it, that's all."

"Somethin' you wanna share with me? Maybe I can help you with it."

Chewing on the bacon, Micah contemplated her offer until he swallowed. "You know how I told you Mr. Joseph is selling off several thoroughbreds? Well, I found out that he's plannin' to sell Gypsy King. That horse and Franklin are practically glued to each other. The boy's gonna be devastated."

"Do you think you can get Mr. Samuel to listen to you?"

"That's the problem. I'm not actually supposed to know that information."

Eliza's brow pressed downward. "Then how'd you find out?"

Micah leaned in, resting both elbows on the table. "Joseph left his notebook in the stable office yesterday. It was open...."

"And you read it."

Micah nodded sheepishly.

"But you're gonna talk to Mr. Samuel instead of Joseph? Do you think there'll be trouble?"

Micah wiped his hand across his mouth and leaned back again. "I'm hopin' not. I know Joseph won't like me goin' over his head on this. Seems like...." He looked over at Liberty Ann and decided not to finish his sentence.

"Seems like what?"

Wrinkling his brow, Micah glanced back at his wife. He didn't like the way he was feeling about Joseph but wasn't sure he should actually put that opinion into words. "Well, it just seems like Joseph doesn't carry the same kind of respect for the workers on this plantation that Mr. Samuel does."

Eliza pressed her palms to her cheeks. Micah could see her thinking hard on what he'd said. "I feel it too," she said quietly. "I couldn't quite put my finger on it till just now. He makes me feel like I'm still a slave whenever I'm around him."

Micah shook his head and stood up. "If you're feelin' that way, I can only imagine how Isaiah and Franklin feel. They have to answer to the man every day in the stables."

Eliza got up from the table and went to him, sliding her arms around his waist. He surrounded her gently, not wanting to press too hard on her growing midsection. "I don't want you worryin' about all this, 'Liza. You just take care of our future." He slid his hand onto the place where their son lay safe and protected. Then, kissing her lips, he let go and kissed his daughter's cheek. "You be a good girl today. You hear me?"

Liberty Ann smiled capriciously, milk dribbling down her chin. Micah shook his head, knowing Eliza would probably have a harder time today keeping up with their daughter than he would taking care of the business at hand.

A few minutes later he found himself sitting in front of Samuel Hawkins' desk. After talking briefly about the final days of the cotton harvest, Micah cleared his throat. "Sir, I was wonderin' if I could speak to you about one of the thoroughbreds that's about to be sold."

At that moment a knock sounded on the door. "It's Abigail. May I bring your coffee in, sir?"

"Of course," Samuel said, rising from his desk. He pointed to the two comfortable chairs on the other side of his study.

Abigail entered and placed the tray with two coffee cups on the table. Samuel thanked her, and the two men sat facing one another. Although Micah had already had his morning coffee, he picked up the cup to have something to do with his hands.

"Sir, it's about Gypsy King. Have you ever noticed his attachment to Franklin?"

"I expect everyone on the plantation knows about that bond," Samuel said, smiling broadly. "Their relationship has been legendary for almost three years now." He brought the cup to his lips, blowing on the hot liquid before taking a sip. Suddenly his brow dipped, and he leaned forward, placing his cup back on the tray. "We're not selling Gypsy King if that's what you're implying."

Micah placed his cup on the tray as well. He was trying to figure out how to tell Mr. Hawkins about the information he'd read in Joseph's notebook. "Uh, sir, I'm pretty sure Gypsy King is on the list."

"I've already seen the list," Samuel said confidently, "and Gypsy King is not on it."

Micah rubbed his sweaty palms on the top of his legs. "I saw a different list yesterday, sir, and Gypsy King was definitely on it."

Samuel immediately stood up. "Have you talked to Joseph this morning?"

Rising to his feet as well, Micah quickly answered, "No, sir, I came here first."

"Come on, then. We'll get to the bottom of this right now."

Micah swallowed back the bile in his throat and followed Samuel out the side door.

⊰⋙⋘⊱

"Pappy?"

"Uh, huh?" Isaiah stretched his legs out from the chair on his porch, appreciating the soft September breeze at the end of a hard day.

"How's come you think Mr. Joseph be so mad at us?"

Isaiah looked down at the back of his son's head as he sat on the lowest porch step, whittling. Little shavings of hickory covered the tops of Franklin's boots and the ground around his feet. "Well, I reckon he's a might bit upset with his papa fer keepin' 'im from sellin' Gypsy."

"So he's takin' it out on us instead o' his papa?"

"Could be," Isaiah said softly, thinking back on the afternoon's events. Stretching his neck from side to side, he could already feel the muscles in his shoulders and back tightening up. After the confrontation with Mr. Hawkins and Micah this morning, Joseph had loaded down Isaiah and his son with work that several stable workers normally performed. He hadn't stacked feed sacks and carried water since his younger days. Isaiah reckoned hard work was good for his son, but it had been dispensed out of spite, not necessity. There was a difference.

For a long time, the pair sat in silence. Isaiah watched his kinfolk finish their visiting before heading into their cabins for the night. He waved and nodded to several of them. Just as he pulled his legs in to get up, Franklin broke the silence.

"Pappy?"

"Uh, huh?"

Turning slowly on the bottom step, Franklin looked earnestly into his pappy's eyes. "I's wonderin' if we could go live on our own land now?"

Franklin's words soared into Isaiah's heart like an arrow finding its mark. He'd thought about that very thing today while carrying heavy feed sacks on his back for Mr.

Joseph. It wasn't that he had been humiliated in front of the other stable workers—he hadn't been, but he'd felt his freedom slip away this afternoon. That realization had left him feeling like less than a man again. He couldn't afford to give up something so precious as his right to choose for himself. Today, he'd felt no choice, and it scared him.

"I tell ya what. Les pray on that tonight and see what the good Lawd tells us. I's perty sure when we wakes up in the mornin', we be knowin' the answer."

Isaiah stood up and headed through the cabin door. He lit the lamp, but Franklin didn't follow him inside. After a few minutes, Isaiah went back to the door, then stopped short. His son was still sitting on that bottom step, head bowed and palms turned upward toward heaven.

Isaiah felt a deep, emotional response. *Lawd,* he pleaded inwardly, *if'n you see fit to answer the boy's prayer, please be givin' me enough courage to act on it.*

Chapter 56

September 1870

Catherine finished her apple and threw the core against the trunk of a sprawling chestnut tree in the back of the garden. Laying down on her back in the soft grass, she hiked up her skirt and bent her knees, exposing both legs entirely. Rachel nervously sat beside her, knowing if they were late for their afternoon lessons again, Mr. Zachary would give them an extra assignment. Miss Gray had finally given up on ever getting anywhere with Catherine and had moved on to *greener pastures*, as she put it. She was now tutoring a young girl in Richmond, just up the road.

"Oh, come on, Rachel, live a little." Catherine yanked Rachel's skirt all the way up to her thighs. When Rachel quickly pulled it back over her legs, her companion laughed gleefully. "You don't know what you're missing. This feels heavenly."

Rachel seriously doubted it, but a giggle escaped her throat anyway. Catherine did have a way of making her laugh at the most inappropriate things. Instead of following her conscience, Rachel laid down beside her half-sister, making sure her legs remained fully covered.

"I do wish these next two years would fly," Catherine lamented. "I'm so sick of school." She turned her head to look at Rachel. "Aren't you?"

While it could be boring at times, Rachel loved learning and generally looked forward to her lessons. She merely shrugged.

Catherine smirked. "But of course, you love school because you're good at it." She flipped up Rachel's skirt again, uncovering both of her legs. This time, Rachel didn't fight it. She had to admit, the air on her legs made her feel lighter. And there was something about these chestnut trees that tugged at her heart. She felt a peace beneath them that didn't exist anywhere else.

"Can I ask you a question?"

This time Rachel turned her head to meet Catherine's gaze. "Sure."

"What are you? I mean, how do you think of yourself? Your father is my father… obviously. But your mother was a negro, and you live with her people. So…I was just wondering which one you are?"

Rachel didn't even have to think about that question. The instant Catherine had voiced it, she already knew the answer. "I'm my mother's people."

Catherine propped herself up on her elbows. "You mean you see yourself as a negro?"

Rachel nodded.

"What about when you look in the mirror? I mean, I don't get it."

"It's not that I don't see the color of my skin…I know it's like yours, but—"

Startled by someone loudly clearing their throat right behind them, both girls jumped to their feet, smoothing their skirts all the way to the ground. Rachel felt the heat rush into her cheeks as they stared into the face of Joseph Hawkins. His features were twisted by outrage. He pointed a finger in front of Rachel's face.

"I'm sure that's how the darkies act, but I'll not have you corrupting my sister." He reached for Catherine's arm and started hauling her toward the house.

Catherine immediately jerked her arm out of his grasp and turned back to Rachel. "Come on. We have to get back to class."

Joseph whirled around to face Rachel again. He pointed to the gate at the back of the garden. "Not today. Go on back to your black mammy where you belong." He grabbed Catherine's arm again, practically dragging her through the garden.

Rachel could hear Catherine trying to defend her, but Joseph wouldn't listen. He told her to hush her mouth and keep walking.

Offended and upset, Rachel headed to the back gate. As soon as she was free of the garden, she took off running, holding her skirt above her ankles to keep from tripping. After only a short distance she could feel hot tears forming, and she didn't bother to stop them. They flowed over her dark lashes completely unhindered. As her feet picked up speed, her tears turned into sobs.

Circumventing the cabins, Rachel sprinted a less-travelled road, hoping no one would see her. Eventually the road led straight to the gristmill. Seeing her pappy at work, a feeling of relief swept through her.

Big John never saw her coming. She ran right up behind him, throwing her arms around his waist. "Pappy!" she cried.

❦

Big John was thrown off balance in more ways than one. He was already upset by the damage done to the sluice gate earlier today. The water wheel hadn't been turning for the last five hours, and when corn wasn't being ground, money wasn't being made. The workers at the mill could scarcely afford to get behind. Time meant money, and money meant food in the mouths of their children. Although his eldest son, Job, had gotten married and moved away last year, John still had the most mouths to feed of all the gristmill workers.

Irritated beyond measure, he whipped his body around and shoved the child away. He hadn't known which one of his children it was, but if they knew what was good for them, they better hightail it home. When he saw it was Rachel, he couldn't explain it, his blood boiled.

"Pappy!" she cried again.

He completely lost his temper. Before he could stop himself, John slapped her face. "I ain't yer pappy!"

The look on Rachel's face was one of utter disbelief. She stood stock-still, mouth open, one cheek turning redder by the second. Then, without a word, she took off like a deer bounding through the forest.

John took several long breaths until his rage subsided. What had he done? He'd not only laid a hand on her, but after twelve years of raising the child, he'd probably said the most hurtful thing imaginable.

Turning back to the other workers, he realized most of them had witnessed his despicable act. He rubbed weary hands across his face, feeling the heat of shame. There was no excuse for what he'd done. No amount of words could make this right. Dropping his chin, he turned and headed for home.

ʔ☙ʕ

Rachel dashed helter-skelter through the woods—jumping over logs, brushing past trees, tripping on roots. She had no clue where her legs were taking her, only that she had to run. Letting out a scream of anguish, she plowed through thick undergrowth until vines and thorns caught her clothing and tore her skin. The girl had run headlong into a thicket, and now she was completely entangled. She could go no further, but to her dismay, she was unable to retreat. She was hopelessly trapped.

Standing still was Rachel's only option. Any movement brought sharp pain at points all over her body. If it had been winter, a heavy wool coat may have saved her. But her thin cotton blouse held no protection against the sharp thorns. They dug into her skin mercilessly.

Tears of agony now turned into cries for help. But it seemed her voice was only going as far as the trees around her. No one would ever find her. She was going to die here—she knew it.

Rachel stood in one position for so long, her legs began to shake, but she knew dropping into a sitting position would rip her skin to shreds. Not that she wasn't already torn and bleeding.

"H-help," she called weakly. "S-somebody, help."

Long minutes went by as the shadows shifted in the woods. How had she gotten herself in such a mess? Thinking back on her time with Catherine, she should've been more careful. While Catherine accepted her for who she was, it was obvious that her half-brother Joseph didn't even acknowledge her as his sister. He had blamed *her* for leading Catherine astray. Rachel chastised herself for not going back to the schoolroom on time. If she had done the right thing, none of this would've happened. She found herself wishing she didn't have to be so cautious in the big house, especially around Joseph.

Nevertheless, Rachel had always felt safe with her mammy and pappy…that is, until today. She could still feel the heat on her cheek where her pappy had slapped her. While that had been a shock, the sting of his words had done far greater damage. Rachel felt so utterly alone. There was nobody else on the plantation like her. Friends were hard to come by, although in many ways, Catherine and her Tillis siblings filled that void. Yet in just a couple of years, Catherine planned to find a man who would marry her and take her away from this place. Rachel knew when her half-sister was old enough, there would be no lack of suitors coming to call. The girl was beautiful and lively and wealthy.

Suddenly Rachel's knees buckled from fatigue. Thankfully she caught herself before going down. Somehow she had to free herself, but the slightest movement brought up a shriek from her throat.

"Rachel?" A voice came from somewhere far off. Someone was looking for her.

"HELP!" she screamed. "Over here!"

She continued to call out as the voice shouted her name over and over again. When the voice grew louder, she knew it was her pappy's. Rachel no longer cared if he was mad at her, she needed him to rescue her.

When the man came into view, Rachel's body shook with sobs. "Thank you… for…coming."

Big John's voice was low and thick with emotion. "Don'chu move, baby. I's comin' for ya."

Slowly and meticulously, John made his way into the thicket, pulling thorns out of his skin and stomping briars to the ground until he got in close to Rachel. "I's gonna get you outta here," he soothed.

Rachel scrunched her eyes tight as her pappy began to pull the tiny spears from her body, starting with her head and hair. The pain was sharp, but her relief at being rescued kept her from crying out. She would stand here and take her punishment for what she'd done today.

After several minutes, John reached his strong arms around her and lifted her close to his chest above the briars. When they cleared the thicket, he set her on her feet and dropped to one knee in front of her. Taking her gently by the shoulders, he said, "Child, I's so sorry for the way I treated ya today. There ain't no excuse for me doin' that to ya." He shook his head, and a tear slid down his dark cheek. "There's somethin' I need ya to know…." His breath hitched, and he took a moment to gain composure. "I's proud to be yer pappy…that is, if'n you still wants me."

The relief that washed over Rachel was indescribable. She threw her arms around his neck, squeezing tightly. The feel of his embrace brought a much-needed salve for her soul. "I want you, Pappy!"

When he loosened his grip, his eyes earnestly held hers. "I's thinkin' today we starts over, you 'n me. I wants ya to know, you's always gonna be my baby girl."

Rachel's arms went back around his neck, and John stood up with her. Her legs surrounded his waist, and he held her snug and secure all the way home.

"Oh, child." Jessie's love was thoroughly captured in those two words. "Come to your mammy."

John gently lowered the girl to the side of his and Jessie's bed—Rachel's bed being upstairs in the loft along with the others. Blood trickled in tiny lines all down her neck and arms. Her clothes were stained and ripped.

Clearing his throat, John said, "I's gonna fetch Eliza."

Jessie nodded. "That'd be a good idea." Then, turning to Jackson and Jenny, she said, "You two run on now. Les give Rachel some privacy."

When the room was clear, Jessie slowly helped the girl out of her tattered clothes. "Child, I don't even knows where to start." She took a cloth, dipped it in a water basin, and started gently dabbing the blood from her face and neck.

After several minutes, Eliza entered the cabin. She immediately knelt in front of Rachel, sliding the medical satchel off of her shoulder. Gently laying her hands on the top of Rachel's thighs, she quietly said, "Your pappy told me you got caught in a thicket. I need to make sure no thorns are still in your skin." Turning toward Jessie, she asked, "Can you bring over a lamp? I don't wanna miss anything."

Jessie quickly lit an oil lamp and held it close by so Eliza could do a thorough examination. The healer found several tiny briars embedded in Rachel's arms and legs. After a long and painful ordeal, she covered the worst of her wounds with a honey, garlic, and thyme mixture to keep infection away.

"There now, sweet girl," Eliza said, kissing her hand, "let's get you into a soft gown." Jessie was already standing there waiting to help her into it.

As soon as the light cotton gown was on, Jessie led Rachel to her rocking chair near the hearth. "You sit right here on yer mammy's lap…you's not too old. All's well, sweet child," she crooned. "All's well."

Rachel leaned back, feeling the sweet comfort of her mammy's arms and body. Although her legs reached to the floor, she felt like she was a small child again.

Eliza squatted down beside the pair, laying a tender hand on Rachel's arm. "I'll come back in the mornin' to check on you. I've got something I've been meanin' to give you."

Turning her head on Jessie's shoulder, Rachel gave the healer a curious gaze. "What is it?" she whispered.

"It's your mother Naomi's Bible. It should be yours, not mine." She raised up and kissed the girl's cheek. "I'll see you in the mornin'."

Eliza laid a hand on Jessie's shoulder, then headed outside.

For a long time, Rachel allowed herself to bask in the arms of the only mother she'd ever known. Jessie was her rock. Her security. The one who loved her for who she really was—even though she wasn't fully certain herself.

"Mammy?"

"Mm, baby?"

"Do you think anyone will ever love me?"

Jessie's brow wrinkled as she kissed the crown of her head. "Oh, child, I loves ya more than you could ever knows."

Rachel's head shook gently on her mammy's shoulder. "I know you love me, Mam…but I was wondering about a man. Will a man ever be able to love me?" Rachel felt quite certain no man would understand who she truly was. After today's misfortune, confusion had cracked open a tiny door and snuck inside.

"Oh, darlin', the Lawd above done already picked out a special man jus' fer you. He's out there a waitin' fer ya to grow up. And wherever he be, he's a growin' up too, just waitin' fer the right time."

Rachel was pretty sure she would never marry a white man. Between Joseph and Mr. Hawkins, she was none too comfortable around men like them. But the negro girls and boys didn't seem all that comfortable around her either. They were never quite sure what to do with her.

"Darlin', can I be askin' ya why ya run off from yer schoolin' today?"

Unable to approach that subject herself, Rachel felt relieved that her mammy had brought it up. She told her how she and Catherine had laid in the grass with their skirts pulled up and how Mr. Joseph had found them. "It wasn't my idea to have our legs showing like that, but Mr. Joseph acted like it was."

Jessie resettled Rachel in her lap so she could see her face. "You's gonna need to be real careful 'round Miss Catherine. That poor girl ain't had a momma ta help her through this life. She be left on her own, and she gots way too much spirit in her, if ya know what I mean. I don't want her gettin' ya into trouble with the men at the big house no more."

Rachel swallowed back the anxiety she was feeling and determined to be stronger around her half-sister. She didn't want any more trouble at the big house either—most especially where Mr. Joseph was concerned. But how would she ever be able to avoid him? It seemed as if he was watching her every move.

Chapter 57

June 1872

S tanding in the middle of Catherine's bedroom, Rachel felt her heart plunge. Watching her sister latch the third and final trunk made her want to weep.

Catherine lightly slapped her hand on the top of the trunk and stood to face her. "Ah, don't look so sad. It's not like we'll never see each other again."

"But what if we don't?" Rachel pined.

Catherine embraced her younger sister. "But we will. I promise." When she let go, her eyes sparkled with adventure. "I can't wait to be free of this place. I'm *so* thankful to be done with school and *le professeur*, Zachary!"

While Rachel found her sister's dramatic proclamation humorous, she couldn't bring herself to crack even the slightest smile. Catherine had been her saving grace in this house—even if she wasn't always the best influence. Without her, Rachel would be all alone in the schoolroom. Lonesome didn't even come close to describing how she would feel come September.

Grabbing Rachel's hand, Catherine pulled her down onto the side of the bed. "Did you know I asked Papa if you could come with me to Aunt Amelia's in Nashville?"

Surprised by her revelation, Rachel said, "No. Why didn't you tell me?"

"Well, I didn't want you to get your hopes up." She squeezed Rachel's hand. "I'll keep trying, and if he says no, then, when I get married, you can come live with me. I'll find you the perfect husband."

Something deep inside Rachel told her that would never happen. But she appreciated Catherine's determined gesture nonetheless.

When Catherine turned to her with a more somber gaze, Rachel felt her composure slip away. Both girls began to cry as their arms took each other in. For a long time, they desperately held on tight—their bond had been stronger than either had realized.

Finally, loosening her hold, Catherine kissed her. "I would've never made it without you." She cupped Rachel's cheek with one hand, wiping a stream of tears away with her thumb. "You'll be all right. Now that Joseph is married, he won't be so obsessed with you. Trust me, it's going to be fine."

Rachel nodded, trying to find courage in her sister's parting words. "Will you write to me?" she asked.

A capricious smile overtook Catherine's features. "I will. And when I find Mr. Wonderful, I want you standing beside me when I say, *I do*."

That brought a smidgen of delight to Rachel's grieving heart.

"Well," Catherine said, "I guess I should let Papa know I'm ready. Come down to see me off."

"Are you sure?"

With a snicker, Catherine grabbed her hand again, dragging Rachel toward the door. "Of course I'm sure, silly. You're my sister."

After Catherine's carriage disappeared around the curve in the drive, Samuel Hawkins and the rest of the family went back inside the house. Rachel continued her vigil until the sound of the wheels on the road and the clip-clop of horses' hooves could no longer be heard. Standing there alone, she breathed a prayer to her heavenly Father to watch over Catherine. And Rachel prayed for strength to endure this household without her companion.

Before walking back home, Rachel remembered that Catherine had left the novel *Autour de la Lune* on her bedside table. Mr. Zachary had given it to her as a parting gift. Afterwards, Catherine had rolled her eyes, telling Rachel she wasn't about to muddle through a book written entirely in French, and she wanted her to have it. Rachel was actually looking forward to reading Jules Verne's sequel to *From the Earth to the Moon*, which Catherine had grudgingly read in English.

When Rachel walked in the front door of the house, she was immediately met by Joseph and his wife, Marilee. Thankfully they turned away and headed toward the parlor. But as Rachel ascended the main staircase, she couldn't help but overhear Joseph's words to his wife.

"If it takes my dying breath, that girl will never inherit one penny from my father. Did you know she thinks she's a negro?"

Rachel heard Marilee gasp. "How could she?"

"Mark my words, I'll not let one of the blacks on this plantation have any part in our family's inheritance."

"I should hope not," Marilee trilled.

Running as fast as she could to Catherine's room, Rachel grabbed the novel, then headed down the back staircase, hoping to avoid seeing Joseph again. She was afraid he would accuse her of stealing Catherine's book. As she made her way down the hallway to the upper kitchen, Mr. Samuel stepped out of his study.

"Rachel, you're just the one I wanted to see. Come join me."

Quelling a strong urge to flee the house, Rachel nervously entered her father's study.

"Please, sit down. There's something I want to talk to you about."

Taking the chair beside the sofa, Rachel straightened her skirt and anxiously fingered the binding of the novel in her lap.

Mr. Samuel pointed to the book as he took the chair across from her. "What book do you have there?"

"*Autour de la Lune*, sir. Umm…it was Catherine's, but she left it for me."

Samuel laughed softly, putting Rachel at ease. "We both know what she thought about learning French."

Rachel found herself smiling at him.

"Well, I'm glad it won't be going to waste." Clearing his throat, he changed the subject. "I've been thinking about your schooling. I want you to know that I'm still resolute in providing a tutor for you for two more years, but seeing how you'll be turning fourteen in October, I would also like to offer you a job. I'm sure John and Jessie would appreciate a boost to their income."

"Yes, sir," Rachel said, fairly excited at the prospect of helping her family.

"Abigail has expressed an interest in having you help her maintain the front of the house. I'm not sure of all the particulars, but I've asked her to join us in a few minutes. How does that sound to you?"

Nodding, Rachel answered, "I'd like that. But if I'm in class, how would that work?"

"For the next two years, you would only work a couple of hours in the afternoon when your last class is over. You would also work during the summer. But the following year, when your schooling is complete, you would work full time in the house."

Daring to look into his eyes, Rachel could feel the warmth of his gaze. She sensed his longing for a relationship. Maybe with Catherine away, he felt more comfortable trying to get to know his other daughter.

Just then, a knock sounded on the door and Samuel stood. "Come in."

Abigail entered, and he offered her a seat on the sofa.

For the next several minutes, Abigail described to Rachel the details of the work she wanted her to perform. "I'm not gettin' any younger, you know. It would be a big help if you could do the cleanin' up front and even answer the door if visitors should come callin'."

"But you don't need to start right away," Samuel interjected. "We'll wait until you start school in September." Then, turning toward Abigail, he stood and thanked her for her time.

Rachel wasn't sure if she should also leave, but Samuel sat back down, not yet dismissing her. For the space of several breaths, her father merely gazed at her. She could feel the heat working its way up her neck and into her cheeks.

"Your mother would be so proud of you," he said quietly. "I wish she could be here to see you now."

Never once had Mr. Samuel discussed her mother with her. She wracked her brain for something to say, but it all seemed so awkward. Rachel was old enough to know what had gone on between her mother and the man that sat in front of her. She had heard that he'd loved her very much. Just by the fact that he had not taken a wife since her death somehow reiterated the fact that he might never be able to love another woman again.

Without any thought to her words, Rachel asked, "Am I to blame?"

Samuel's eyes narrowed. "For her death? Why would you think such a thing?"

"Maybe you would rather she was sitting here with you instead of me." Rachel was still reeling from the sting of Joseph's earlier words and finding it difficult to separate her father from her half-brother. When she saw his hesitation, she knew it was true. Somewhere deep inside, she'd always known that he thought of her mother every time he looked at her. It somehow kept a wedge between them.

He cleared his throat, eyes moistening. "I would hope that I have never given you any indication of such a thing, Rachel. Your mother taught me much about life and about God's providence. I now realize that God never promised that bad things wouldn't happen to us, but he has promised to be with us when the bad things come our way. He promises to work for our good." Samuel leaned forward in his chair. "Rachel, *you* are the good that God brought from your mother's tragic death. It was not your fault."

Letting out a pent-up breath, Rachel felt herself trusting his words. This man was not like his eldest son—not in the least. Although a relationship barely existed between them, she would have to remember that her father was not unkind or vindictive.

"I was just wondering," Samuel said, his voice full of emotion, "would you like to take Catherine's room and live here in the house?"

This was not at all what Rachel had expected him to say. She felt an emotion akin to panic rise up in her chest. The very last thing she wanted to do was live in the same house with Joseph and his new wife. If it were only William and her father, she might possibly consider the offer. But the very thought of it terrified her beyond words.

Noticing his face fall, Rachel realized her expression must've given away her answer. "I-I'm, sorry, I…." How was she supposed to tell her father that she was scared of her own brother? And more than that, how could she describe the love she felt for her *real* family. She was a Tillis in her heart, not a Hawkins.

Rachel's knuckles turned white as she pressed her fingers into the book on her lap. Suddenly rising to her feet, she blurted, "Thank you, sir, for…your kind invitation, but…." All she could do was shake her head. "I'm sorry," she said, as she stared into his red-rimmed eyes.

Then, abruptly turning, Rachel flew from the room, having no idea that her mother had made the same decision to leave this man for her own people some fourteen years prior.

October 1873

Isaiah stroked the muzzle of the long-legged colt as he waited for Franklin to emerge from the cave. His thoughts wandered back eight years to the day they'd left the Hawkins Plantation. While Samuel Hawkins had done his dead-level best to keep them from leaving, ultimately, he had wished Isaiah and Franklin all the best. To show his great appreciation for everything they'd done for him, he'd given them Gypsy King and a beautiful broodmare from his stock. Mr. Samuel had told him, "When the time is right, I want you to sell me the first foal from your herd." Isaiah had readily taken the man's hand on that deal.

When Isaiah and Franklin had come to their Winchester property in '65, they'd already decided to wait a year before starting a herd. Their first priority had been to construct a sturdy house. While living in the cave for that entire first year, the two worked diligently on erecting the house directly atop the hole in the ground. Franklin had even built the staircase that went from the house to the floor of the cave all by himself.

Letting out a shrill whistle, Isaiah thought it was high time for Franklin to be on the road.

"I's comin', Pappy," Franklin called, walking up from the cave with a small satchel strapped to his back and Gypsy trailing behind. "I's just checkin' on the herd 'fore takin' off."

"That be fine," Isaiah told him. "But I want ya gettin' there with plenty o' daylight, that's all."

Franklin swung his tall frame into the saddle, then reached for the foal's lead rope, wrapping it around his saddle horn. "I's gonna be there long before supper, Pappy. Don't you worry none."

Before Franklin could urge Gypsy forward, Isaiah took hold of the bridle. "You sells Mr. Samuel that horse, then get right back on the road first thing in the mornin'. You hear me?"

"Pappy, I's not a young'un no more. I's twenty-one."

"I ain't sayin' you's a young'un, but you's always gonna be my boy. So don't you be dawdlin'. There's lots o' things can happen 'long the way. Don'chu be on the road near ta dark."

Franklin leaned over, settling a hand on top of his pappy's shoulder. "I be seein' ya tomorrow afternoon."

Reaching up to pat his son's hand, Isaiah said, "Alrighty then, I be seein' ya."

Clicking his tongue, Franklin urged Gypsy to a comfortable trot. When he reached the edge of the pasture, he took off his hat, waving it toward his pappy, then disappeared down the steep pathway to the road.

Stopping near Richmond, Franklin was now regretting the fact that he would have to turn right around and make this trip again tomorrow. He wasn't used to four hours in the saddle—five after making it to the Hawkins Plantation. He was now wishing he'd told his pappy that he'd be staying two nights so he could catch up with his old friends in the stables. He was also looking forward to seeing Micah and Eliza before returning home.

After eating a boiled egg and some hardtack, Franklin took a swig from his canteen and led the two horses to a creek just off the main road. While Gypsy and the colt took their sweet time, Franklin thought about the amount of money he'd be carrying home tomorrow. He could still hear his pappy's words ringing in his ears. "Don'chu go fightin' with nobody over money. Ain't nothin' worth more than yer life, Son. You just gives 'em everythin' ya got, if'n ya have to."

Cramming his hat back on his head, Franklin threw the reins over Gypsy's neck and mounted up. His pappy worried too much. He'd already decided to stuff the money down in both of his boots and save a little bit for his pockets. That way, if anyone gave him trouble, he'd just empty his pockets without a fight.

The trees along the plantation drive had grown since Franklin had last been there. He deliberately rode along at a slower pace, feeling a rush of memories flood through his bones. A nostalgic sensation overwhelmed him, causing his chest to tighten. It was on this land that he'd been born. The most important women in his life had been here and held him affectionately as a little boy. While he'd long since lost the memory of their voices, he could still feel their love surging deep within him.

Dismounting, Franklin walked the rest of the way to the big house. When it came into view, he stood still for a moment, drinking in the sight. It still stood majestic and white among the trees. The well-kept grounds continued to hold their familiar beauty. Even though he'd been born a slave, he'd gained his freedom at the age of seven. He'd never really understood what it felt like to be owned—not until Mr. Joseph had come home from the war.

Franklin shook his head and moved toward the hitching post. Joseph Hawkins was one man he was hoping to avoid on this trip.

Looping his reins through the iron ring, Franklin climbed the steps of the porch with anticipation. He *was* looking forward to seeing Mr. Samuel. The man had been nothing but kind and generous to him and his pappy. He hoped the foal would bring him great satisfaction.

Hearing the approach of light footsteps in the front hallway, Franklin took a step back after knocking. Expecting Abigail to open the door, he was ready to swoop her into a hug, but his mouth dropped open instead. He was speechless.

A subtle smile played on the young woman's lips while she waited for him to speak. But Franklin couldn't seem to find any words at all.

"May I help you?" she finally asked.

"Uh…my name is…uh…."

She leaned in a bit, her smile lengthening, but in no hurry to help him.

"Franklin. That's it…my name's Franklin."

"I'm Rachel. Pleased to meet you."

"I know who you is," he said quickly. "You probly don't remember me, but—"

Looking past him at the horses, Rachel said, "I remember you worked in the stables."

"Yes'm, I's born here…but me 'n my pappy been gone fer…well, fer a few years now."

"Would you like to see Mr. Hawkins?"

"Oh, uh, yes'm. I's got a colt to sell to 'im."

When Rachel stepped back to usher him in, he quickly said, "Is you sure I should be comin' through like this?"

"Of course. It's fine."

Franklin stepped inside, nervously sliding his hat between his fingers. He couldn't take his eyes off of her. He remembered her as a little girl, but there was no doubt, Rachel was the most beautiful woman he'd ever laid eyes on. All he could do was stare at her as they walked through the main hall and toward the back of the house.

When his thighs hit the solid hall table with a loud thud, Franklin was utterly mortified. It didn't help that Rachel put her hand over her mouth, barely suppressing her giggle. He could feel the heat of embarrassment rush to his face as he backed away from the table and attempted to straighten it.

∾❦∿

Rachel thought she wouldn't be able to contain her amusement. It was all she could do to get to the door of the study without laughing out loud. Knocking on the door, she heard her father call— *Come in*—but when she opened the door, Rachel knew there was no way she would be able to introduce Franklin as his visitor. Any attempt to speak at this point would only come out as a burst of laughter. All she could do was step back and sweep her hand toward the room.

As soon as Franklin was inside, Rachel swiftly shut the door. Unable to control herself any longer, she let out the laughter that had been bubbling up inside. Even moving the table back into the right spot, she couldn't contain her giggles.

Rachel was still dusting the front parlor when the door to the study opened. She could hear the two men walk to the front door and head outside. Quickly running to the front window, Rachel watched her father smooth his hand along the colt's neck and muzzle. Franklin lifted a foreleg to show him his hoof. The animal was a beauty—no doubt her father would be pleased.

But Rachel found herself drawn to the young man who had brought him. Franklin stood tall and muscular, his big brown eyes and handsome face were hard to look away from. When he glanced up toward the window, Rachel quickly stepped back, hoping he hadn't seen her staring.

When she finally felt brave enough to look again, the men and the horses were gone. Her heart instantly fell. Checking the mantle clock, Rachel still had half an hour left before she could leave. She felt like nudging the hand on the clock to five. What if Franklin left without her seeing him again?

With ten minutes still to go, Rachel finally went in search of Abigail, finding her in the upper kitchen. "Miss Abigail, I was wondering if I might be able to leave a few minutes early today? I finished all my work." Seeing the look on Abigail's face caused her a bit of angst. "Of course, if there's something else you'd like for me to do before I leave…."

Letting out a low sigh, Abigail seemed to relent. "Oh, all right, head on then. But don't be makin' this a habit."

"I won't," Rachel chirped. "Thank you!"

Trying not to seem like she was in a hurry, Rachel ambled across the kitchen. Once outside, she walked a more deliberate pace. She found her feet leading her down the road to the stables. It would definitely take her longer to get home that way, but if there was any chance of seeing Franklin again, it would be worth the extra steps.

Glancing over at the stable door, Rachel slowed down. There was no sign of Franklin or his horse. She didn't have the nerve to actually go inside—she couldn't even make herself stand still and wait to see if he came out. Passing by the stables altogether, she felt the disappointment settle inside her chest. It just wasn't meant to be.

Heading around the first set of cabins, Rachel dropped her chin, kicking at an occasional pinecone or rock. Halfway home, she began to feel as though she wasn't alone. Raising her head, she saw movement out of the corner of her eye, but instinct told her not to look. Someone was walking in the same direction several yards away. When she slowed, he slowed. When she sped up, he sped up.

Eventually finding her nerve, Rachel turned her head just the slightest bit and felt her heart flip-flop against her ribs. Franklin was keeping stride with her, his path gradually bringing him closer and closer. Rachel shyly watched him through the trees. She noticed how careful he was not to run into one of them.

As soon as Franklin sauntered onto the road, Rachel stood still, and he came up beside her. She didn't want to go home yet if it meant she could spend some time alone with him. His grin nearly took her breath away.

They both started talking at the same time. Franklin let out a low chuckle and nodded to her. "Go ahead."

Releasing a soft breath, Rachel started again. "I was just curious if I'd get to see you again before you left."

His eyes didn't leave hers. "I's wonderin' the same thing."

"How long are you staying?"

Franklin shuffled his feet and rubbed the back of his neck. "I's sposed to leave in the mornin', but if you think you could spend a little time with me on the morrow… well, I's thinkin' 'bout stayin' an extra night."

"And go home on Sunday?"

"Yes'm," he said, eyes narrowing as he contemplated the plan. "Would you wanna spend the day with me?"

Rachel didn't know when she'd ever wanted anything more. "I would," she told him. "I don't have to work on Saturdays."

Franklin's grin widened. "Where can I meet ya?"

Not wanting to part company with him yet, Rachel asked, "Would you like to come home with me for supper? That way you'll know where I live."

Shifting his weight, he said, "I already knows where you live. Unlessen yer family done moved."

"We haven't moved. Come on," she said excitedly, turning toward home. "I'm sure Mammy's already wondering where I am."

Chapter 59

J ackson, quit yer showin' out," Jessie chastised. "Yer makin' a fool o' yerself in front of our visitor."

Jackson laughed with a mouthful of milk toast and ham. "I's just playin' around."

Big John gave his son a stern gaze. "You heard yer mammy. Sit up and eat the way you's 'pose to." Then, turning back to Franklin, he said, "Goodness, you's just a pup last time you's in this house. Seems to me Jackson and Rachel just be little uns."

"Rachel was a newborn and Jackson not more 'n a few months," Jessie chimed in. "Lands sakes, I can still see you a strokin' them two babies in the cradle. They wouldn't cry so long as you's with 'em."

Franklin smiled, vaguely remembering the few times he'd been in this cabin. He couldn't have been more than six or seven. "How's work at the gristmill, sir?"

"Aw, it be fine. But we's thinkin' 'bout movin' us all up north sometime soon. Job, our oldest, done gots a good job in a factory up in Cincinnati, Ohio. He's married and gots a young'un and another one on the way. We hears there be lots o' jobs waitin' fer workers up there."

Rachel made a small choking sound that drew Franklin's attention from across the table. Her face had grown pale. He wanted to ask her what was wrong, but she was working hard not to draw attention to herself. He decided to ask her about it later if he got the chance.

Big John didn't seem to notice and kept right on talking. "We's probly gonna wait till Julia here ties the knot with her mister."

Jackson hopped right in on that one. "But he's a draggin' his big feet. Probly ain't sure if he can stands to live with…"

"Alright, that's enough, Jackson!" Jessie pointed to the door. "You's done eatin', so head on outta here."

"Yeah!" Julia emphasized, giving her brother an angry scowl.

Scooting his chair back, Jackson did as he was told, but not before finishing his sentence. "Her temper." He pinched Julia's neck, passing by her chair, then headed out the front door with all haste.

Jessie shook her head. "No amount o' work can make that boy grow up. He be fifteen goin' on six, if'n ya ask me."

"The real world's 'bout ta get a hold o' that boy right quick. Jus give it time," John said.

When Jessie stood up to clear the table, Franklin stood as well. "Thank ya kindly for the supper, Miss Jessie. It be real good."

"Havin' you here after all these years is a mighty nice treat, Franklin. Now, why don't you'ins head out on the porch and catch up whilst us girls do the cleanin'."

Rachel gave Franklin a look that begged him not to leave before she could come outside. She needn't worry. He would stay up all night just to be near her again.

As soon as Rachel finally made it out on the porch, Big John stood up and said, "C'mon Jackson. Les you 'n me check on the mill."

"Pappy, we just left there an hour—"

"Now!"

Jackson shook his head and jumped off the porch. "See ya later, Franklin," he called.

Franklin nodded to the boy. "I be seein' ya, Jackson."

Moving out of his chair, Franklin walked over to the bench along the wall of the house. "Would ya like to come sit with me?"

Looking a bit shy, Rachel glanced over her shoulder toward the door. Her mammy and two sisters must've decided to stay in the house. She nodded and he waited until she was seated before sitting down beside her, careful to keep some room between them.

For a little while, they watched the Tillis kinfolk mill about, visiting with one another before the sun set. Franklin finally broke the silence. "I specs you never know'd how much yer mama meant to me."

Rachel looked up at him. "Jessie?"

He slowly shook his head. "Naomi." Just saying her name after all these years brought a lump into Franklin's throat. He cleared it away and went on. "I lost my mammy when I's four, 'long with my sister and the missus and her daughter all at once. You knows about that, don't ya?"

Rachel nodded. "I do."

Letting out a long breath, Franklin said, "If it hadn't been for yer mama, Naomi, I don't know what I'd done. She be the only one I wanted or needed for a long time. She stepped right in to be my mama. Only...." His voice trailed out into the dusk.

"Only, you lost her too," Rachel finished softly.

He nodded, feeling the pain all over again. "I didn't understand it much, I's just a boy, but...it hurt all the same."

When Rachel laid a tender hand on his arm, Franklin felt his pulse quicken. Looking down into her gorgeous brown eyes, he felt a sudden possessiveness. He wanted her all to himself. But she was too young—she was only fifteen. Realizing his desire for her, he moved his arm away and stood up. "I reckon I better head to the stables 'fore it gets too dark."

Rachel stood too. "So that's where you're staying?"

"Yes'm. They gots a cot set out for me." He stepped down off the porch, then turned back. "Can I be comin' for ya in the mornin'?"

"Yes," she said eagerly. "I'll be waiting."

He momentarily moved his gaze from her eyes to her mouth, then, capturing a deep breath, he dipped his chin. "Sleep well, Rachel." Slipping the hat on his head, he strode out into the half-darkness.

❧❦❧

The next morning, Jessie took Rachel by the shoulders and held her eyes with a steady gaze. "Rachel, darlin', you be careful today. Do ya know what I's sayin' to ya?"

"Mammy, we're probably just going for a walk. That doesn't sound too dangerous to me."

"Darlin', you know what I's talkin' 'bout."

Rachel let out a soft laugh and kissed her mammy's cheek. "You don't have anything to worry about with me. It's Julia you should be talking to," she teased.

Julia cast her a surly expression. "Very funny."

Jessie slipped her arm through Rachel's and walked with her onto the front porch. "Franklin's quite a bit older than you. He's a fully grow'd man and…well, I could see the way he was a lookin' at ya last night."

Rachel scanned the landscape, wondering if Franklin was on his way. But the sun hadn't been up long, and she figured he would wait until a more appropriate hour. She decided to keep the conversation going while she waited. "How old were you and pappy when you got married?"

The look on Jessie's face turned uneasy. "We was both nineteen when we know'd it was time."

"How did you know?"

Jessie briefly closed her eyes and let go of Rachel's arm. She sat down in one of the straight-back chairs on the porch. "You just knows when it's right."

Rachel sat down beside her, waiting for more of an explanation.

Jessie rubbed the palms of her hands together, then brought them to her cheeks before placing them back in her lap. "Gal, you's growin' up too fast on me. I's waitin' a bit longer 'fore talkin' to ya 'bout all this."

Rachel's brow furrowed, and she turned sideways in her chair. Her knees pressed up against her mammy's legs.

Jessie leaned her head back on the chair. "Oh, Lawd, girl, I don't even knows where to start. I reckon you know yer mama was a slave."

Rachel nodded and Jessie raised her head off the chair, turning to face her.

"There's lots o' folks that thought Mr. Samuel done took Naomi 'cause he was her massa, but I seen the love that was between 'em…I seen it firsthand. Rachel, your mama loved Mr. Samuel. Eliza done told me that Naomi went to 'im of her own free will."

"Mammy," Rachel interrupted, "you're not telling me anything I don't already know." She let out a little snort. "Don't forget I spent all those years in the big house with Catherine. She could be loose with her talk sometimes."

Jessie let out a deep breath. "I figured such."

"Then why are you telling me all of this now?"

"I's just a little worried 'bout you with Franklin. I don't want ya givin' yerself away thinkin' yer in love. You's only know'd him a few hours."

"But I feel like I've known him all my life." Rachel turned away from her mammy, searching for him on the road. "How can that be?"

Taking hold of her hands, Jessie drew Rachel's attention back. "When he were just a boy, he had some kind o' connection with ya 'fore you's ever born. Ain't no one could explain it, but he was always drawn to ya somehow." Her voice grew quiet. "Rachel, we ain't seen him in lots o' years—we don't knows him like we used to. Will ya just be careful?"

Rachel finally understood what her mammy was trying to say. Jessie didn't want her jumping into deep water and getting in over her head. Maybe that's what her real mother had done, yet she was determined not to follow that same path. But, oh, how she was drawn to Franklin, there was no denying that fact. She'd felt it from the moment she opened the door to him yesterday.

As the sun began to glimmer brightly through the autumn leaves, Franklin melted into view. Rachel hadn't even seen him coming, although she'd been looking. She immediately came to her feet, Jessie with her.

When he got to the porch, Jessie was the first to speak. "Have you had breakfast?"

"Yes'm," he said, removing his hat. "Ike can make a mean breakfast over at the stables."

"That's real good," Jessie said. "Would ya like to come inside?"

Franklin's gaze slid over to Rachel, then back to Jessie. "I's just wonderin' if it be all right for me to take Rachel for a walk?"

Rachel didn't even wait for her mammy to reply. "I'll run get my sweater."

Jessie followed her in straight away, and when Rachel descended from the loft, she took her into her arms. "You remember what I told ya, darlin'. Just be extra careful."

"I will, Mammy. Please don't worry."

The look Jessie gave her offered little hope on that account.

ം◦ളം

Franklin walked with Rachel to the stables where Gypsy King stood in the paddock. He was already saddled, stomping his front hooves impatiently. "Yer not afraid to ride, are ya?"

Although her smile was timid, her words were bold. "Not at all. But where's my horse?"

"We's ridin' double, if that's all right."

He untied the reins and slipped them over Gypsy's head. Hopping into the saddle, Franklin told her to step up on the wooden stool. Then, reaching down for her wrist, he swung her up behind him. He loved the sound of her laughter as she grabbed hold of his waist with both hands.

"I put a longer saddle blanket on 'im to protect yer skirt."

He could feel her twisting around behind him, trying to get her skirt situated. Finally he looked back to make sure all was well. "You ready?"

"Yes," she said confidently. But when he pressed his heels into Gypsy's side, Franklin felt Rachel's grip tighten.

"Here," he said, bringing her arms all the way around him. "You hang on tight." He kept a hold on her clasped hands to help her feel secure. "I's only gonna walk 'im."

"Good," he heard her whisper.

After a while she asked, "Where are we going?"

"We's headed to the very back of the plantation...into the hills. I's wonderin' if you ever seen where your mama was buried?"

"No one has ever taken me there." Her words were softly spoken, and he felt her chin rest up against his back. He looked over his shoulder, meeting her eyes.

"Thank you," she said.

Franklin nodded, then turned his gaze forward, feeling an unexpected emotion. He hoped he was making the right decision. He wasn't sure what to do if she started to cry. But then again, maybe he was the one who needed to worry about crying.

Rachel was the one who ended up pointing out Naomi's grave. His pappy had showed him where she was buried, but it'd been a long time ago. Being here didn't seem to bring an overly emotional response, for which Franklin was glad.

Dropping to her knees in the grass, Rachel traced her finger along Naomi's inscription. "I wish...."

Franklin went down on one knee beside her. "You wish what?"

"That I could remember her in some way." She looked up into his face. "That I could see what she looked like."

Grinning, Franklin said, "Alls you need to do is look in a mirror. She was beautiful…like you."

Rachel looked away, hiding her response. He hoped he hadn't been too bold with her. On the other hand, he hoped she knew just how beautiful she was to him and not only on the outside. Her heart seemed so pure. He saw such goodness in her.

Instead of mounting up again, Franklin and Rachel walked over to the next hill and found a good spot that overlooked the plantation. Several workers were in the fields, treading behind a mule and plow, turning up the old crops, tilling the ground before the onset of winter.

Franklin found it easy to be with Rachel. They could talk or sit in silence, either way, it didn't matter. And while it was true, he'd known her since birth, he felt like she'd always been with him somehow. It would be hard to leave her tomorrow.

At noon, the two shared a meal with Micah and Eliza at their house. When Micah went back to work, Eliza had kept them for quite a bit of the afternoon. Finally, Rachel thought she'd better get back home before her mammy sent all the kinfolk out looking for her.

When Franklin pulled Gypsy to a halt at the outdoor paddock, Rachel clung to his arm while he lowered her to the ground. When he stepped down, she was standing so close, he opened both of his arms and she didn't hesitate to fill the space. The feel of her up against him sent his head spinning. He knew he needed to be extra careful with her.

Kissing the top of her head, he stepped back, and when he did, his attention was immediately drawn to the open stable door. Joseph Hawkins was standing there, staring right at them. It was hard to read the intent in the man's eyes, but Franklin knew it wasn't a look of goodwill—far from it. Maybe it was because of Gypsy King. After all, Joseph had been dead set on selling the thoroughbred several years ago. And now here he was, standing tall and majestic in front of the man's stables, belonging to one of his former slaves.

Or was it Rachel he was staring at? A chill went all the way up Franklin's spine. If he thought that look was meant for Rachel, then he feared for her safety. Instead of taking care of his horse, Franklin took hold of Gypsy's reins and turned him toward the road. "Come on," he said to Rachel. "Let me walk ya home."

Rachel was unusually quiet on the way to her cabin. Franklin didn't know if she'd seen her brother or not. He'd tried to step in front of her to block him from view. But judging by her demeanor, he may not have succeeded. Quietly he asked, "Is you all right, Rach?"

She looked up at him with a gleam in her eye. "Rach?"

"Sorry 'bout that. I didn't mean ta sound too familiar with ya."

"No, it's all right. I like it."

She looked away—her delight short-lived.

Finally, she said, "Did you see my brother at the stables?"

Franklin nodded. "I did."

Rachel walked a few more steps before speaking again. She definitely seemed worried, and, after her next statement, he knew why. "If Pappy decides to pull up roots and move to Ohio, I'm sure I won't be allowed to go with them."

"Why not?" Franklin asked.

She stopped in the road, first glancing back toward the stables, then piercing Franklin with an anxious gaze. "I know for a fact my father would never let me move away with them. He'd keep me here, but that would be horrible."

"Because of Joseph?"

She nodded. "He hates me."

Franklin felt a protective spirit rise up within him. He would do anything to make sure Rachel was safe. But his hands were tied. She was too young for him to take her as his wife. Besides, she barely knew him. What if she didn't want him?

They started walking again, but this time in silence all the way to the Tillis' cabin.

The next morning, against his better judgement, Franklin stayed for the church service. It was held in one of the older barns. Mr. Hawkins had built a new barn and given this one to the plantation workers to use. Rudimentary benches, stools, and crates filled the open space, but for most of the service, everyone was on their feet. Franklin couldn't help but watch Rachel as she worshipped. She not only had a sweet, melodious voice, but she had no qualms about using her body as an instrument of worship. He had to ask the Lord to forgive him a couple of times for being so distracted.

Before the sermon started, Franklin knew he had to get on the road. His pappy would be more than worried about him by now. He started feeling guilty for staying the extra day. Leaning down, Franklin whispered to Rachel that he was going to leave for home. When he slipped out of the gathering, Rachel followed.

Gypsy King was saddled and tethered to a tree limb near the barn. He let out a sharp whinny when Franklin appeared. But instead of going straight to his horse, he grabbed Rachel's hand and pulled her around the side of the barn. Pinning her up against the outer wall, he bent and covered her mouth with his own. She seemed shy at first, he knew he'd caught her completely off guard. But when her arms came up around his neck and her body pressed into him, he deepened the kiss. Feeling his passions rise uncontrolled, he stepped back, breathing hard.

"I's so sorry, Rach. I-I...."

She laid a gentle hand on his chest. Her face was flushed. "I'm not."

"Yer not what?"

She laughed. "I'm not sorry." Then she raised her mouth back to his for a gentler kiss.

When Franklin stepped back the second time, it was all he could do not to throw her up behind him on the back of Gypsy and take her to his farm. Tears pooled in her eyes—he was finding it hard to hold back his own.

Clearing his throat, he said, "I's gonna come back for ya someday. Will ya wait for me?"

Rachel didn't hesitate. "I will." Then more urgently she whispered, "Please hurry."

April 1874

The link between Jessie and Rachel's hands was ripped asunder when the mules began to pick up speed. Rachel felt her heart tearing open as the connection was lost, and she sobbed hysterically. It didn't help that her mammy was wailing loudly from her seat on the wagon. None of the family could speak—tears streaked the faces of Big John and four of his other children.

"Mammy!"

Rachel cried out for the only mother she'd ever known, repeating her name over and over again. She'd walked beside the wagon all the way to the road. John had waited patiently in the gray light of dawn after Jessie jumped to the ground to hold Rachel one last time. They had clung so tightly to one another, it was hard for either to catch their breath.

Standing in the middle of the road, Rachel now watched until the wagon, loaded down with most of the Tillis' possessions, disappeared from sight. Instead of walking to the big house where she would be expected for lessons, Rachel slowly made her way back to her family's empty cabin and climbed the ladder to the loft. Pressing her body into the deepest corner, she spent every last ounce of her emotion in sobs of despair.

If only her father had allowed her to go with the family to Ohio. Rachel laid down on the floor, cushioning her head with her hands, remembering how hard Pappy had fought for her. She'd never seen the man defend her so passionately. But in the end, his efforts had been in vain. Mr. Samuel had made it clear that his daughter would remain on the plantation, living in the big house henceforward.

Rachel shuddered at the very thought of sharing the same home with Joseph. It wouldn't be hard to avoid her half-brother during the day—he would be working and she would be in class—but a dread sat heavily upon her chest concerning the evening meals. How would she ever be able to survive his hatred and not-so-subtle aggression toward her?

Sitting up, Rachel drew her knees to her chest. "Oh, Franklin, where are you?" she breathed.

It had been six long months since he'd come and gone. What if he'd changed his mind about her? Or what if something had happened to him on the way back to Winchester? With every passing day, her heart grew more and more anxious.

"Lord, please...." She couldn't even finish her petition. It began to sound futile to her own ears. What must her heavenly Father think?

Rachel laid back down on the floor, exhausted from little sleep the night before and the morning's emotional outpouring. When she awoke, a sunbeam shone brightly on her face from the small loft window. The cabin was filled with light. What's more, a horse's nicker from outside drew her attention.

"Rachel? Are you in here?" It was her father. She could detect the worry in his voice.

Sitting up, she leaned her head against the wall and closed her eyes. "I'm up here," she called softly.

Samuel wasted no time climbing the ladder to the loft. His features were so compassionate, merely glancing at him brought warm tears to her eyes. Unexpectedly, he crossed the room and sat down beside her, pulling her gently into his arms. Resting her head against his chest, Rachel released another swell of emotion. The side of his face rested on the top of her head. His breaths came unevenly.

When she grew silent, he tipped her chin upward with his forefinger. "I'm so sorry for this terrible loss."

Thankfully, her father didn't make any excuses for the decision he'd made. It was his right to keep her here. But if Franklin never came back for her, she determined to leave for Ohio on the day she turned eighteen. For now, however, she would have to keep her wits about her to ward off Joseph's animosity. Telling her father wasn't an option. She feared that would only make the situation worse.

"I don't want you to have to work in the house any longer," he said quietly.

Rachel straightened. "Why not?"

Letting out a deep breath, he said, "I only allowed it so your family would be helped. Jessie refused to take money for raising you years ago. She said it made her feel guilty because she loved you so. But now...." He allowed the rest of his words to drift away.

Thinking about the prospect of nothing to do after classes, Rachel could feel the uneasy rhythm of her heart. "What am I to do then?"

A half-smile turned his lips. "Whatever you want, I suppose."

Moving out of his arms, Rachel wiped the drying tears from her cheeks. "Then could I still live *here*?"

A soft laugh escaped his mouth. "All by yourself?"

She nodded earnestly.

"Rachel, I've already rented this house to another family. Besides, you belong with us at home."

The thought that another family would be living in this cabin added an extra layer of anxiety to Rachel's tender feelings. She had wanted to remain here where her lifelong memories had been collected. Memories of being raised by godly parents and loving siblings.

With that statement, Samuel stood and offered his hand to Rachel. Hesitantly, she put her hand in his and stood beside him. "Come back to the house with me. I've already dismissed Mr. Zachary for the day. You can get settled into your new room."

She looked over at all of her belongings scattered atop the only bed left in the loft—hers. "I need to pack up my things."

Samuel nodded and headed for the ladder. "I'll help you. I brought a trunk from the house."

Together, the two packed away Rachel's meager possessions, and her father easily carried the trunk out to the waiting buggy. When he helped her step up into the buggy and climbed up beside her, a feeling of déjà vu swept over her. It was a vague memory of her father protecting her from an encroaching battle during the war. She had felt fear on that day so long ago, but nothing compared to that which she carried inside of her now.

When the buggy passed the overseer's house, Eliza was standing on her porch. Both women held each other's gaze. The healer drew her hand to her chest, and even from a distance, Rachel could feel the strong presence around her. Though the day was warm, chills covered her arms. Rachel knew in that moment Eliza would be her deliverer.

After only being in Catherine's old room for a few minutes, Rachel answered a quiet knock on her door. It was a girl named Trudy, daughter to one of the wash ladies. "Miss Rachel," she drawled, "you's got a visitor."

Rachel stepped out of her room and walked beside Trudy down the hall. "Are you helping Abigail now?"

Trudy nodded sheepishly. "She says I's takin' yer place. Ya don't mind, do ya?"

Letting out a soft laugh, Rachel told her it was perfectly fine.

When they made it to the bottom of the main staircase, Trudy said, "The healer's waitin' fer ya in the kitchen." She nodded down the hallway.

Thanking the girl, Rachel quickly made her way to the back of the house. As soon as she caught sight of Eliza, she rushed into her arms. Eliza held her tenderly, stroking her hair and filling her with hope.

Stepping back slightly, Eliza took Rachel's face in her hands. "Sweet girl, the Spirit told me to come to you today. He's tellin' me we need each other." She kissed Rachel's forehead, then led her out back into the yard, keeping a possessive arm around her waist.

When they came out into the sunshine, Eliza turned to face her. "I need you," she simply said.

Rachel threw herself back into Eliza's arms. "I need you too."

"I know. So listen up, this is how it's gonna work." Eliza held her at arm's length. "When you're done with schoolin' every day, I need you to come to my house and take care of our young'uns. Liberty Ann got herself a job in the orchards." Eliza laughed heartily. "That girl can shinny up any tree and loves doin' it. So that means I need help with my other three. It's way too hard on me tryin' to care for all the women on this plantation while keeping an eye on the little ones."

"I'll do it!" Rachel said eagerly.

"Well, that's not all. I need you on Saturdays and Sundays too, all the way up till we get the rascals in bed. That means you'll need to be takin' the evenin' meal at our house, 'cause sometimes Micah has to be away at the same time. Can you do that?"

Rachel felt relief wash all the way through her. It seemed that God had found a way to rescue her before she even got the chance to ask.

Eliza smiled at her impassioned response. "Good, I can see you're agreed." She took hold of Rachel's arm and led her back to the house. "Now we need to get your papa to agree."

Samuel was just heading into his study when Eliza and Rachel stopped him. "May we talk to you for a minute, sir?" Eliza asked.

His smile was immediate. "Of course." He stepped back and allowed the two to enter the room. They both took a seat on the sofa, and Samuel sat down in an adjacent chair. "What can I do for you?"

For the next few minutes, Eliza laid out her plan. Rachel tried to gauge her father's reaction, but so far, he was listening without censure.

"As you may know," Eliza went on, "Liberty Ann has gotten herself a job. But our other ones are nine, five, and two. The help Rachel could give me would lift a tremendous burden from our family."

Samuel stroked his beard. "I assume there are others who could perform the same task for you."

"Oh, none that I've found, sir, and—"

"I want to do it!" Rachel interjected. Then bravely she added, "You told me I could do whatever I like."

Samuel's eyes crinkled at the corners and his chin lifted. "I did, didn't I?"

Rachel decided not to push the issue any further, so she sat quietly waiting for her father's answer. Finally, nodding his head, he said, "I have no reason to say no. Rachel, you're free to work with the Simmons children."

"Thank you," she said and started to rise.

But Samuel's hand came up, causing her to settle back onto the sofa. "You can start tomorrow. This evening Mamie is cooking a special meal to welcome you into the house." And with that statement, he stood, leading Eliza and an apprehensive daughter to the doorway.

That evening, Rachel dressed in her Sunday best before making her way to the dining room. Samuel was the only one there so far, and he leaned down, kissing her on the cheek. She found herself wondering if he'd been as affectionate with Catherine. Oddly, she didn't think so. She was certain her mother, Naomi, was the reason for his warmth toward her.

Seconds later, Joseph and Marilee entered with William right on their heels. Rachel found herself staring at Marilee's expensive dress, wondering what they must think of her brown skirt and cream-colored blouse. Self-consciously, she turned her gaze toward her father. She needed to know where to sit. Samuel pulled out a chair on the other side of William, and she quickly sat down.

Once her father was seated at the head of the table, he bowed his head and asked the blessing over the food that had been prepared. When Rachel looked up, she felt Joseph's stare directly on her, but she didn't dare make eye contact. As a matter of fact, she totally avoided looking his way the entire dinner. While Samuel and William engaged her in bits of conversation, Joseph and Marilee didn't even acknowledge her presence at the table. That had been just fine by her.

The following night, Micah walked Rachel back to the big house after her first afternoon and evening with their children. She had thoroughly enjoyed every moment with them. Not to mention, it kept her away from dinner with Joseph. As they approached the back door, Rachel noticed lights in the upstairs windows, but the kitchen was dark. She silently thanked the Lord for that blessing.

Micah pressed a gentle hand on her shoulder. "Thank you, Rachel. You're gonna be a huge help to our family."

Smiling brightly, she nodded. "I'm glad to do it. Tell Eliza I'll be there after class tomorrow."

Making her way through the kitchen, Rachel headed down the darkened hall toward the front staircase. A tingle began working its way up her spine. She was not alone. Coming to a halt, she wasn't sure whether to call out for help or run back toward the kitchen. But it was already too late. Joseph rose up off the bench by the wall. When she backed into the opposite wall, he swiftly placed his hands on either side of her shoulders, trapping her there.

Joseph brought his face down close to hers—she could feel the heat of his breath on her face. Fright held her firmly in place.

"You're a whore just like your mother," he seethed.

Rachel turned her head away from him, unable to stomach his words or his breath.

He grabbed her chin in a vice-like grip and yanked her face back to his. "Look at me, you little tramp. I know what you did with that n----r back in October. You disgust me."

"Leave me alone!" she said, none too quietly.

Joseph's hand covered her mouth, and he pressed his weight against her. She fought to get away from him, but he easily overpowered her.

His hand pressed so tightly upon her mouth Rachel could taste the blood. His other hand moved to her throat. "Just one word to Papa and he'll find out what you did with Franklin," he hissed. "And we both know who he'll believe."

Rachel brought her knee up hard.

A rush of air left him, and he shoved her away as he doubled over. Without faltering, she ran back down the hall toward the kitchen. Fearing he would follow, Rachel rushed into a dark corner, taking hold of the back of one of the chairs at the table. She wouldn't hesitate to hit him with it.

Just then a voice called out from the top of the stairs. "Joseph, are you coming to bed?"

Joseph cleared his throat, then said in a strained voice, "Yes...sweetheart. I'll be right there."

"Well, hurry," Marilee said in a pouty voice. "I'm lonely."

When Rachel heard Joseph slowly ascending the staircase, her knees buckled, and she went to the floor. What would've happened if Marilee hadn't called out to him? Bending over at the waist, she had to willfully hold back the urge to vomit. She could still smell the stink of Joseph's words on his breath.

After several minutes, Rachel gained her composure and tiptoed to the back staircase. She could get to her room that way without passing by Joseph and Marilee's. When she got to Catherine's old room, she silently closed the door and locked it. Although Joseph probably had a key, she felt certain he wouldn't come after her again tonight—not if he knew what was good for him.

October 1874

It had been raining all morning and for the better part of this Friday afternoon. Eliza had been called away, so Rachel put two-year-old Trinity down for a nap in the back room. She had just finished reading a story to Noah and Angel, and now the two children were quietly playing on their own. Rachel peered out the front window to see if the rain had stopped. She hoped to get the children outside so they could run and play. Someone was striding toward the side door of the big house wearing a rain slicker. His movements caused Rachel's stomach to tighten. It was Joseph. She quickly turned away from the window.

Thankfully, her brother hadn't laid a hand on her since that horrible night back in April. She had often wondered why he'd left her alone after that. Maybe using her knee in a strategic manner had made him realize she wouldn't so easily play the victim. Whatever the reason, she was relieved that she only had to endure his nasty remarks when their paths occasionally crossed in the house. He was very careful not to be overheard by anyone but her.

She'd often thought about the name he had called her during his physical attack. While she was innocent in that regard, what about her real mother? Had she been so loose with her morals? Her mammy and Eliza had always defended Naomi, even calling her one of the most righteous women they'd ever known. It troubled Rachel's heart that she was missing something. Something she felt was important for her to know about her mother.

A knock on the front door brought her out of her reverie, and she immediately went to answer it. Rachel stood frozen in the open doorway. She was completely stunned.

"I's awful wet, so's a hug is probly out of—"

She nearly knocked the air out of him. Franklin had to take a step back to keep from toppling over on the porch.

"I's gettin' ya soaked," he said. But he didn't loosen his hold—not in the least.

"I don't care." Rachel's arms tightened around his neck, and he picked her clear up off the ground.

When he finally set her feet back onto the porch, Rachel stared up at Franklin's giddy expression. She wanted to kiss him. She could feel an entire year of worry and anxiety fly away, and it was nothing short of glorious. Throwing caution to the wind, she rose up and pressed her mouth to his. He instantly sifted his hand into her hair at the back of her neck and took her kiss to a whole new level.

Someone cleared their throat behind them, and Rachel quickly stepped back. She could feel the heat rushing all the way through her. It made her a bit woozy. Thank the Lord it was Eliza. She was standing next to the porch in the rain.

Climbing the two steps to get out of the weather, she threw back the hood of her cloak. "Franklin?" Eliza said with a sly grin. "I was hopin' that was you."

Franklin turned from Rachel and gathered Eliza into a strong hug. "So good to see ya, Eliza."

"I'm sure not as good as seein' Rachel, but I'll take that." She clasped his arm. "Come on in and sit by the fire."

Franklin shook his head. "I can't be comin' in till I take care of the mules and wagon." He turned a hopeful gaze toward Rachel. "Will ya be here when I get back?"

She didn't want to let him out of her sight. "I'll go with you."

"You's already wet enough. I be right back, I promise."

Eliza laid a restraining hand on Rachel's arm, but her words were for Franklin. "She'll be here waitin' for you. We'll get some supper started while you're gone."

When Eliza let go and went inside, Rachel stepped close to Franklin again. "Why did you bring a mule wagon?" she asked.

He winked at her before leaping off the porch, then called over his shoulder, "Why do ya think?"

❧ ❧ ❧

That evening, it felt like one big happy family around their supper table. Eliza couldn't help but smile. Franklin and Rachel were scarcely able to keep their eyes from one another. She wondered if either one of them had heard a word she and Micah had spoken.

Micah sat back, wiping a hand across his mouth. "How long can you stay?" he asked Franklin.

Tearing his attention away from Rachel, Franklin leaned his elbows on the table. "I got till Monday mornin', then I has to get back home."

Eliza could literally feel Rachel's anxious spirit return. She prayed the dear girl wouldn't be hurt by Franklin leaving so soon.

When Franklin looked across the table at Rachel, he said, "I got in serious trouble last time I's here."

"After staying an extra day?" she asked, raising one brow.

Franklin nodded. "Pappy done let me have it good." He chuckled. "Practically forbid me ta ever leave the farm again."

"What did you tell him?" Rachel asked softly.

"I told 'im that this time next year, I's comin' home with a wife."

For a long moment, no one moved. Not even the children wiggled in their chairs. It seemed everyone around the table understood what Franklin was talking about except Rachel. Micah let out a loud laugh and slapped Franklin on the back. Eliza reached over, covering Rachel's hand with hers, but Rachel just stared across the table.

Franklin's grin grew wider by the second. "I's thinkin' this ain't the way I wanted ta do this, but now seems right. Would ya like ta marry me, Rachel?"

Eliza squeezed her hand when Rachel didn't respond. "Honey, the man just asked you to be his wife."

When Rachel was finally able to speak, only one word came out. "Tonight?"

Everyone started laughing, and Franklin scooted away from the table. He came to Rachel, drawing her out of the chair. With a low chuckle, he pulled her into a hug, whispering, "Soon."

Liberty Ann started clapping and whistling, causing the other children to do the same. Franklin stepped back to look at Rachel. "Was that a yes?"

Throwing her arms back around his neck, she gleefully cried, "Oh, yes!"

❦

Micah came back into the house and hung his jacket on a peg by the door. "Mr. Hawkins is ready for you in his study," he told Franklin. "Do you want me to go over with ya?"

Franklin released Rachel's hand and stood up from his chair by the fire. "No, I be just fine."

Rachel's face pinched. "Maybe I should go with you…so he knows how I feel."

Franklin was already shaking his head. "I reckon if he says no, then you can come with me t'morrow. But I needs to do this man-to-man."

She stood up and walked with him outside onto the darkened porch. A cool breeze was blowing—the rain had ended. Franklin gathered her to himself, wishing he could marry her tonight and whisk her away. But he would never do such a thing. He respected Mr. Hawkins and wanted to do this the right way for Rachel's sake and for the sake of her father.

"Will ya be here when I get back?"

Rachel slapped her hand lightly on his chest and giggled. "If it takes all night."

"Good," he said before leaning down to kiss her.

When he pulled back, Rachel cupped his smooth cheek in one hand. "I'm praying for you."

Letting out a deep breath, he nodded. "That's just what I's needin'."

With one more soft kiss, he leapt from the porch and strode into the night. Although Rachel could no longer see him, she waited until the beam of light shown across the gravel path at the side door before it closed into darkness.

❦

Franklin whistled a happy tune as he checked on the mules in the barn the next morning. He hadn't been a bit nervous, sitting across from Mr. Hawkins last night, asking for permission to marry his daughter. While it had been a long conversation, the man said he would wait on giving his final word until he talked to Rachel. When Franklin had gone back over to Micah's house to tell her, Rachel had flown out the door to the big house. Franklin followed her and waited beside Mr. Hawkins' door to be there when she came out.

Placing some alfalfa in the mule's feed trough, Franklin's heart was overwhelmed with love for Rachel. He felt as though he'd loved her all his life. Last night, when she came out of her papa's study, she had grabbed his arm and pulled him back inside with her. Mr. Samuel had not only given his consent, but he had drawn Franklin into a fatherly hug. While the man expressed his desire to call in the minister from Richmond, Rachel wouldn't hear of it. "I'm not getting married in the house," she'd told her papa. "We'll get married Sunday morning in the barn after church."

It had taken a bit of convincing, but it was clear Mr. Samuel wanted to make his daughter happy. He said he'd be attending the Sunday service in the barn too.

Satisfied that the mules were taken care of with food and water, Franklin stepped out of their stall. Someone was already standing there, waiting for him. When Franklin recognized him, he swallowed back an uneasy feeling.

Franklin acknowledged the man by dipping his chin. "Mr. Joseph."

Joseph's eyes narrowed, and he wasted no time getting to his point. "I always knew that girl would end up with a n----r."

Not breaking eye contact with him, Franklin stood completely still. While his blood boiled, he concentrated all of his energy into keeping his eyes calm. But as sure as the Lord was on his throne in heaven, he wouldn't stand here and let the man insult Rachel.

When Franklin gave him no satisfaction, Joseph stepped a little closer, shaking his head. "I don't know how she can stand the smell of you."

No reaction came from Franklin.

"I suppose she couldn't do any better than this." He flipped the lapel of Franklin's jacket. "She gets what she deserves." He swirled his mouth and spit. It landed squarely on the top of Franklin's boot.

Not a muscle twitched on Franklin.

Joseph looked around, then reached into his coat pocket, pulling out an envelope. Unfolding the paper within, he held it in front of Franklin's face. "Read this."

When Franklin didn't respond, Joseph lowered it and snickered. "Oh, right, pigs can't read. I guess I'll have to tell you myself. This document says that the half-breed you're about to marry will have no inheritance from the Hawkins Plantation." He folded it back up and returned it to the envelope. "Lucky for you there's nothing to sign. And this money is a payment of sorts. We're compensating you to take her off our hands."

Fanning out the bills, Franklin was horrified that it wasn't anywhere near the payment he'd received for the colt he'd brought here last year. It sickened him. There was no way he'd be taking that money. He'd burn it before he'd ever think about using it.

Putting the bills back in the envelope, Joseph flicked it down to the ground at his feet. A sudden memory flashed through Franklin's mind. It was the time Joseph had come and gotten him from Mammy Lou's to take him to the big horserace. Franklin's head slowly shook thinking about what must've happened to this man to change him so.

"Are you shaking your head at me? This isn't something you can refuse. Pick it up!"

Franklin didn't move.

Joseph came one step closer until his face was mere inches away. He leaned his mouth close to Franklin's ear and hissed, "I said…Pick. It. Up."

Taking a slow step backwards, Franklin reached down and picked up the envelope, holding it down at his side. A slow grin turned Joseph's lips. Letting out a string of epithets, the man finally turned and strode away.

Franklin released a long, shuddering breath. He didn't know if he could wait here until tomorrow to marry Rachel. Maybe he should run get her and take her away as fast as possible. But he knew in his heart he couldn't do it. Rachel and Eliza were back at the house excitedly planning what Rachel would wear. How could he take a wedding ceremony away from her in front of her whole congregation of people? That wouldn't be fair.

Stepping back inside the stall with the mules, Franklin leaned his forehead into the rough wood. "Lawd," he breathed quietly, "help me be the man you want me ta be, the kind o' man Rachel deserves." He paused for a few breaths. "And Lawd, please bring healin' ta Mr. Joseph's tortured spirit."

For a long time, Franklin stood there, pouring out his heart to God. Then, reaching into the envelope, he took out the small amount of money and placed it in the bottom of the feed trough. He didn't care if the mules ate it or not.

⋅⋘⋙⋅

Mamie had prepared a delicious buffet at the big house in honor of the bride and groom. When Rachel and Franklin entered the dining room, a round of applause arose. Rachel looked around the room at the people she loved. Micah and Eliza with all of their children, Abigail and the household staff, William and her father all stood there with congratulatory smiles on their faces. Joseph and Marilee were notably missing, for which Rachel thanked the Lord above.

All of the guests had no qualms about stuffing themselves with Mamie's amazing luncheon, but Rachel's stomach was in knots, she could barely touch her food. Even all of the sweets could barely tempt her into eating.

Micah stood and offered a toast to the newlyweds, and though it was Mamie's famous lemonade concoction, a hearty, "Here, here!" rang out through the dining room.

Franklin looked down at his wife in all of the hubbub. "You about ready?"

She timidly stared into his eyes. "I am," she simply said.

When the couple came to their feet, everyone else stood to offer them another round of hugs and handshakes.

Eliza pulled Rachel aside. "You and Franklin can have our house as long as you like." She pointed toward the back of the plantation house. "Our family will be just fine in these rooms by the kitchen." She lightly elbowed Rachel's side. "You should sleep in tomorrow before you leave."

Rachel glanced at Franklin, still talking to her father on the other side of the dining room. "We'll probably get on the road fairly early. Franklin doesn't want to worry his pappy."

Drawing Rachel into a maternal hug, Eliza whispered, "Just relax and enjoy each other."

Rachel didn't readily let go. She discreetly asked, "What if I don't know what to do?"

The wise healer let out a soft laugh and stepped back, her eyes dancing with delight. "Trust me, gal, you've got the rest of your lives to figure it out."

Epilogue

I saiah sat on the front porch—a long piece of bluegrass pressed between his lips. If Franklin didn't come home today like he'd promised, he was going to tan his hide. Never once had his son given him a bit of trouble—not in all of his growing-up years. But last October, that young man had willfully stayed at the Hawkins Plantation two full nights. Isaiah still held a remnant of fear deep down inside from that incident. He'd stayed awake all night long, praying that no one had snatched his son or killed him.

Pushing his tall frame out of the chair, Isaiah wandered out into the pasture toward the great oak. It was standing tall and majestic, showing off its orange and yellow leaves. They frolicked brightly in the gentle breeze, and he walked beneath them, reaching his hand out to the lowest ones. Straining his ears, he hoped to hear the clunk of the mule wagon making its way up the trail from the road, but all he heard was the rustle of leaves.

Before he could even sit down, the herd began to meander toward the tree. Normally, Franklin met them here, drawing them in with a whistle. But they must've decided to keep Isaiah company while waiting for the man who understood their hearts like no other.

When the five thoroughbreds gathered around the tree, Isaiah sat down with his back against the trunk. "He be here any time now," Isaiah soothed. "He's a comin'." Isaiah reckoned there was a good three hours of sunlight left. He determined not to allow worry to cross the threshold of his heart lest it permeate the herd.

After a while, Isaiah stood and worked his way among the thoroughbreds, rubbing their muzzles and speaking gentle words. He chuckled, running a slow hand down the neck of their newest filly. "Ya know what that boy done told me? He done said he's a bringin' a wife back with 'im." He took hold of the filly's chin and brought her head up to his. "I reckon he's messin' with ya, gal."

The filly inhaled and let out a puff of air, snorting in response. That's when Isaiah heard the sound of the wagon. "Oh, thank ya, Lawd," he breathed. He moved slowly through the middle of the small herd to get a better view of the trailhead on the other side of the pasture.

When the wagon came into view, Isaiah's heart leapt inside his chest. There was indeed a woman sitting beside Franklin on the wagon seat. She was pressed into his side, her arm intimately wrapped around his. Isaiah's breath hitched. This wasn't just some woman from the plantation—it was Rachel.

Franklin brought the wagon to a halt as soon as it emerged from the woods. They had yet to see him standing under the tree with the herd. Franklin's hand pointed toward the house, and by the way he gestured, Isaiah knew he was telling her about the cave. He reckoned that was where he needed to sleep tonight—maybe several nights.

When Franklin and Rachel turned their heads toward the oak, Isaiah felt an emotion rise up from deep inside. Here were the offspring of the two women that he'd loved with all his heart. Ruth had borne him Franklin, a son of great significance. The only one of six children that was left to him. And how could he have ever imagined that Naomi would've borne Rachel to become his son's wife? Rachel would be his beloved daughter.

Leaving the herd, he took purposeful strides across the pasture toward the pair. When he was several yards away, Rachel stepped down from the wagon and started toward him. In just a few steps she was running. Isaiah opened his arms wide to her, and she poured herself into them. Tears streamed down both of their cheeks. Kissing the top of her head, he whispered, "Welcome home, child. Welcome home."

That night, Franklin sat with his pappy on the front porch admiring the big orange moon just above the tree line. They were giving Rachel her privacy while she bathed.

"Pappy, Mr. Samuel gave me somethin' today I ain't sure what ta do with."

Isaiah looked over at his son with a wrinkled brow. "What's it be?"

"Well, sir, he gave me lots o' gold coins."

"What for?"

Franklin let out a long breath. "He be sayin' it would take care o' Rachel for the rest of her days. But I's thinkin' they's payin' me ta take 'er away from the plantation. Joseph made me take this paper." He pulled the envelope from his jacket pocket, hating the feel of it in his hands.

Isaiah sat forward, pressing his elbows onto his knees. "Why would ya think they's payin' ya for 'er?"

"'Cause that's what Joseph told me. Acted like they's glad to be rid of 'er."

Slowly shaking his head, Isaiah spoke softly. "That don't sound like Mr. Samuel ta me. Is you sure 'bout that?"

"Well, truth be told, I's not sure Mr. Samuel know'd about this, 'cause it already had some money in it." He held up the envelope. "But I don't want nothin' to do with them coins if'n he did."

"Where'r they now?"

"I hid 'em on the wagon."

For a long time, both men sat in silence. Franklin worried that Rachel would find out about the agreement. But at the same time, he was afraid to destroy it. What if it was something important that he should've kept?

Suddenly coming to his feet, he said, "I know what I's gonna do. You got a jar in the house?"

Isaiah nodded. "I gots a big fruit jar sittin' on the counter all cleaned out. Gots a lid and everything. You can have it."

Franklin disappeared inside and was back out in a few seconds. He jumped off the porch and ran to the wagon beside the shed. He'd crammed the bag of coins beneath the bench seat, all the way into the back corner. Then, running to the shed, he grabbed a shovel and hurried back to the porch.

"Here," he told his pappy. "Put the coins and envelope in the jar whilst I dig a hole."

"Where's ya gonna dig it?"

Hearing Rachel move about in the house, Franklin shoved his foot down on the edge of the shovel. "Right here, in front o' the porch."

Both men worked hurriedly, Isaiah sliding the coins quietly into the jar one by one. "Son," he whispered, "you sure 'bout this?"

"Yessir. Get that lid on nice 'n tight."

Isaiah turned it with all his might and handed it down to his son. Franklin pressed the jar into the hole and started shoveling the dirt back in. That's when Rachel walked outside.

For a moment, Franklin froze, wondering if her eyes had adjusted to the dark. Maybe she couldn't even see what he was doing. But she walked over to the edge of the porch right in front of him.

"What are you doing?"

Franklin immediately kicked the rest of the dirt over the top and stomped it down with his boot. Then he threw the shovel to the side of the porch. "Aww, just somethin' needed ta be buried, that's all."

He could literally feel her curiosity. "A dead animal?"

Franklin shook his head. "No, ma'am."

She descended the steps and walked right up to him. Franklin knew he had to think of something right quick. He wasn't about to start his marriage off with a lie. On a whim, he reached out and pulled her up to his chest, receiving just the response he was hoping for.

"Mister, I've already had a bath. I don't need your sweat all over me." She pushed him away, giggling. But then, surprisingly, Rachel drew close to him again, taking his hand. "On second thought, come with me. That bathwater's not going to waste."

Isaiah cleared his throat loudly and immediately stepped down from the porch. "I best be headin' 'round to the cave. See ya tomorrow."

He took a few strides away from the house but turned to look over his shoulder after receiving no response.

There in the orangey glow of the moon, he saw his two beloveds locked in a passionate kiss. Rachel broke away and pulled Franklin by the hand into the house, closing the door softly behind them.

Smiling broadly, Isaiah moved his gaze toward the magnificent moon. "I thank ya, Lawd. Yessir, I do."

Then, turning toward the cave, he chuckled all the way there.

Author's Note

We humans travel so many varied paths in the course of a lifetime. Some are joyful, filled with delight, while others are wrought with sadness. This work has been a journey producing both pleasure and sorrow in heaps. I am immensely honored that you have chosen to walk it with me. I have prayed that in no small way, this book would be a source of healing and redemption and peace.

A ledger, dating back to 1839, has been passed down in my family now for nearly two centuries. Along with that ledger, I possess quartermaster papers from the Civil War, documents from WWI, and numerous letters from the late 19th and early 20th centuries. I feel blessed to have an extensive family history written on paper. But for the Africans who were stolen from their homelands to be bought and sold in our country, their family histories have often been lost or fragmented through time and generations. Unless the stories were told accurately from generation to generation, experts say that their family history would have been totally lost by the fourth generation. You will find this to be the case in moving from *Blind Faith* to *Blinders,* and, finally, *Blind Hope.* The characters have not been able to relay an accurate account of the generation before them. A source of regret in telling Rachel's story was the fact that all of her life she believed that she had been born a slave. Rachel was never told that her mother, Naomi, was a free woman nor that she had been married to her father, Samuel Hawkins. None of the three people who could've told her the truth ever broke their silence. As a result, Rachel never learned of her mother's great significance on the Hawkins Plantation.

While the story you have read is purely fictional, it has been written with as much historical accuracy as possible. It is also a narrative told strictly from the perspective of the slaves and freed men and women. At no time was the reader privy to what was going on in the minds of the master and mistress. This was done purposely. This was not the master's story to tell. It was my desire to give voices to the slaves and allow the reader to consider their perspectives on life. After all, it is by the sweat and toil of so many of our African-American brothers and sisters that our country was built. Lonnie G. Bunch III, secretary of the Smithsonian Institution, says, "The story of the African-American is not only the quintessential American story but it's really the story that continues to shape who we are today."

And finally, in my extensive research, I found many stories of kind-hearted masters and mistresses, yet their benevolence never once excused the fact that owning another human being was cruel. Period. My ultimate purpose for writing this story was not for one of pure entertainment, but for contemplation, education, and hopefully introspection.

May God bless each of us with more of His Spirit!
Kristy Shelton

Mum Bett, an African slave, lost her husband in the Revolutionary War. Not long afterwards, she sued Massachusetts for her freedom and won on the basis of their newly formed constitution. Changing her name to Elizabeth Freeman, she said, "If one minute's freedom had been offered to me, and I had been told I must die at the end of that minute, I would have taken it."

Acknowledgments

To Catrina White and Darcy Huber, I can't thank you enough for walking another journey with me. I'm especially amazed that you were able to give *Blind Faith* any attention at all during such a difficult year of teaching school through a global pandemic. Both of you provided me with such incredible encouragement to keep going—Darcy with your pragmatic observations, and Catrina with your many wonderings. Your fingerprints are all over this story, dear ones. I am in your debt. You have my heartfelt love and gratitude. Now…what's next?

Darya Crockett, I am deeply thankful to you for reading this manuscript, not as my editor this time, but for your honest view as a Black woman. It was vital to me to get your reaction to this story. Thank you for your openness and blatant honesty and for keeping me historically correct. It is your words that have given me courage and peace.

Much gratitude goes to Dr. Bart Dahmer of Innovo Publishing, who continually gives me the opportunity to publish my writing adventures. While this particular book was a more difficult undertaking, I appreciate the way you have encouraged me as an author and continue to take a chance on my manuscripts. I'm thankful for our long history of partnership in publishing. I also want to thank my Innovo editor, Rachael Carrington, for all that you've done to bring this work to fruition. You are such a positive light.

Well-known Christian fiction writer Karen Kingsbury writes in a poem about the power an author holds in bringing hope and healing to someone's soul. "Now, Spirit, lead us every page; through our words, be center stage." That has been my deepest desire, that the words on these pages would not be my own but the words of God's Spirit living within me. My deepest gratitude goes to my heavenly Father for the inspiration that He provided over and over again in such a challenging work. On many occasions, I finished an afternoon of writing with the distinct impression that the words I had just written were not my own. For that reason, all glory goes to Him forever and always.

OTHER BOOKS IN THIS SERIES

BLINDERS

The Blinders Trilogy, Volume 1

Blinders, a novel by Kristy Shelton, portrays a beautiful relationship between a former slave couple, their love for a boy who wanders onto their farm, and the redeeming forgiveness of the heavenly Father. In this inspirational novel, Eugene, an eleven-year-old boy growing up in Kentucky in 1912, is drawn to a light in the distance that compels him to run away from his abusive stepfather. He is led to the farm of Franklin and Rachel Hawkins who live in a rundown house built on top of a cave yet have magnificent thoroughbred horses grazing in their bluegrass pasture. Eugene is adopted into the family, and as he grows up, gradually discovers secrets from the past that keep Franklin and Rachel isolated on their remote farm. Eugene is severely tested when he is seized from the farm at the age of sixteen and forced into the Great War now raging in France. He embarks on a dangerous journey that will put his life and faith to the test. When he returns two years later as a man, his only hope is to give his incredible burden of guilt to the One who can save him, and allow a mother's unconditional love to help him fulfill his destiny.

BLIND HOPE

The Blinders Trilogy, Volume 2

The words love, hope, and dreams are synonymous with family—at least that's what Eugene and Annie Wyatt believe. As they raise two sons on their horse and cattle farm outside of Louisville, Kentucky, life has a way of testing that love, crushing hope, and shattering dreams. In the face of the Ku Klux Klan, a thousand-year flood, and a wayward son, the family's strength is strained to its limit and yet able to weather each storm. But when their faith is put to an unimaginable test with the world engulfed in war for a second time, all hope appears to be lost. Sometimes God plants a seed of hope so strong within a mother's heart that nothing on earth can snatch it away. Not even death itself.

MORE HISTORICAL FICTION BOOKS
FROM INNOVO PUBLISHING

BURNT TREE JUNCTION HISTORICAL FICTION SERIES

Set in the fictional Arkansas community of Burnt Tree Junction, along a fifteen-mile stretch of country road between Berryville and Eureka Springs, the series depicts the people, relationships, and culture of this captivating early 1900s southern community—amidst the sweeping backdrop of industrialization, opportunity, and the pursuit of the American Dream. This *six-book anthology*, written by Joann Klusmeyer, whose parents lived this lifestyle, is instantly recognizable as authentic to the time, place, and culture. Taking this family-friendly journey to the rural south, with its delightfully entertaining twists and turns, will make you smile and will bless your heart.

THE OZARK MOUNTAINS HISTORICAL FICTION SERIES

This wonderfully written *seven-book historical fiction series* captures the unforgettable struggles, dreams, failures, and triumphs of settler life in the Ozark mountains at the dawn of the 20th century. Life there was rugged and almost always unforgiving. The people and families who called these mountains and River's Bend home were of hardy stock. They experienced great hardships and suffering, but they were gritty, tough, and stubborn (and faithful) too—and they persevered against even the bleakest of odds. Their inspiring lives and stories remind us that suffering builds perseverance, and perseverance builds character, and character builds hope—and hope, blessed hope, never disappoints.

TAMING THE WILDERNESS HISTORICAL FICTION SERIES

At high noon on April 22, 1889, fifty-thousand settlers camped on all sides of the Oklahoma territory began a fever-pitched race to claim their 160 acres of land and a new life. Most started at the sound of a cannon or gunshot on horseback, wagon, or foot at the appointed time around the territory. Land was claimed and sizable towns sprung in in a single day. More followed. But trouble was afoot too as the hopes, dreams, and even survival of the competing settlers collided with each other and the harsh realities of life in wild "unassigned" lands. The opportunity was great, but not everyone played by the rules, and the free land sometimes came at a very high price. This wonderfully researched, *four-volume historical fiction series*, Taming the Wilderness, captures the unforgettable struggles, dreams, failures, and triumphs of the settlers of the great Oklahoma Land Rush of 1889. Each volume presents two complete novellas with well-crafted characters and life-stories not soon forgotten.

THE SHELTERING STONES HISTORICAL FICTION SERIES

This *five-book series* begins when a privileged, well-educated teenage girl from New York and her seven-year-old little brother were made orphans by an unforgiving Christmas Eve house fire, and they found themselves shipped off to an aunt in the teacher-poor parcel of the Oklahoma territory where families were scratching for survival. Amidst the upheaval, the young girl realized that she was the only hope her little brother had for an education. Soon, neighbors begged for the privilege of letting their children just listen as she taught her little brother. As attendance grew, classes were moved to a virtual cave, made by an overhanging ledge. A room was constructed beneath that ledge with a rough flagstone floor and a strong, field-stone outer wall. How wonderfully strange that those who entered this shelter of stones would emerge with a gift that would stand the test of time, the Great War, and generations to come.

THE TRILOGY OF WISHBONE HOLLOW HISTORICAL FICTION SERIES

The Trilogy of Wishbone Hollow is an inspiring story of an unlikely heroine from a small rural community in Arkansas. The American Red Cross was preparing for war in 1916 and 1917 when America and England were trying to make it go away, and Germany was forging ahead. In the midst of this uncertainty, a young and determined Arkansas girl, smitten with the desire to be a certified nurse—and bolstered by a praying grandpa, unusual (and unconventional) bravery, and almost certainly an overworked angelic guardian—begins a journey that shapes the future for her, the folk of Wishbone Hollow, and many souls across the Atlantic.

BOOK CLUB GUIDE

Blind Faith

Kristy Shelton

This book club guide for *Blind Faith* includes an introduction, discussion questions, and ideas for enhancing your book club. The suggested questions are intended to help your reading group find new and interesting angles and topics for your discussion. We hope that these ideas will enrich your conversation and increase your enjoyment of the book.

INTRODUCTION

It's 1855 and the prosperous Hawkins plantation of Kentucky is not only home to Samuel, his wife, Elizabeth, and their four children, but to over two hundred enslaved souls. Born into slavery on the Hawkins plantation, Naomi makes quite an impression as Elizabeth's talented seamstress. Her beauty is unrivaled. Wherever she goes, everyone's eyes can't help but follow her. But Naomi is torn between a life of secrets and an extraordinary purpose far greater than herself. Through unimaginable tragedy, one woman becomes the means of a monumental shift to the Hawkins' way of life by which all souls on the plantation will forever be changed. And the faith that burns within her heart will become the very fabric that unites them all through the ensuing storm.

TOPICS & QUESTIONS FOR DISCUSSION

1. What was your favorite scene in the book? Your favorite quote?

2. What surprised you most about this book?

3. If you could have a face-to-face conversation with one of the characters, which one would you choose? What would you talk about?

4. At the end of chapter 2, Ruth has a powerful experience at her prayer log that leaves her weak and nauseous. Then on her first morning of working at the big house she has the distinct feeling that she will not be Elizabeth's companion for long. Have you ever had a premonition? How did it make you feel at the time? Did your premonition come to pass?

5. In chapter 12, Ruth finds herself dealing with gossip among her kinfolk concerning the attack on Naomi. She had no qualms about asking the other women, "What are you'ins talkin' about that you need to stop when I get here?" What do you think about the way she handled this situation with her friends? Could the way Ruth spoke to the other women during this section of dialog be helpful to you when you encounter gossip? Gossip could be defined as saying something negative about someone who is

not present. I've often challenged small groups of teenagers to go a full week without gossip. When coming back together and reporting on their week, I've found that they came up with some ingenious ways to refrain from gossiping. Maybe you too would be willing to take the challenge.

6. Someone who is privileged has an advantage or opportunity that most other people do not have, often because of their wealth or connections with powerful people. Sarah had lived in the big house since the age of nine as Isabella's companion. In chapter 15, Ruth tells her, "Lately, you been actin' like you's privileged." Was it possible for a slave to be privileged? Compare Sarah's privileges to a field slave. Compare her privileges to those of Isabella's.

7. In chapter 23, Samuel tells Naomi what a chestnut tree symbolizes: chastity, honesty, and justice. What ironies do you see playing out in the story involving the symbol of the chestnut trees?

8. The way people handle tragic loss is varied and often depends on how deeply spiritual one is grounded. Why do you think Samuel is struggling so horribly to deal with the loss of his wife and daughter? If you could say one thing to Samuel in his grief, what would it be? What was the difference in the way Samuel and Isaiah handled their grief?

9. What do you think Naomi and Samuel's marriage would've been like if she had survived childbirth? Do you think they would've been able to live as a true family in the latter half of the 19th century?

10. Grace is the underserved love and favor of God. Where did you see the grace of God in *Blind Faith*?

11. Before the emancipation of American slaves during the Civil War, many secured their own freedom through escape, self-purchase, or being freed by the slaveholder. What emotions do you think a former slave would feel after gaining their freedom? What obstacles do you think they would have to overcome to make a life for themselves as a freedman?

12. Why do you think the Tillis family, who raised Rachel to the age of 15, wanted to leave the Hawkins plantation to live in Ohio? How do you imagine their lives turned out?

13. What do you imagine life would've been like for the African-Americans still working on the Hawkins plantation once Samuel's son Joseph was in charge?

14. When Joseph comes home from the war, he shows his obvious disdain for Rachel. In chapter 54, Rachel tells Eliza that she doesn't belong in the big house. What obstacles did Rachel have to overcome growing up as a white girl, yet identifying as an African-American?

15. In chapter 61, Joseph confronts Franklin in the mule barn. How do you think Franklin's response is similar to Martin Luther King, Jr.'s approach to nonviolence?

16. Are there lingering questions from the book you're still thinking about? Are there questions you would like to ask the author?

17. Just for fun: If you could make *Blind Faith* into a movie, what actors would you want to portray the main characters?

Thank you for joining in this journey with me! If your book club would be interested in a Zoom call with the author or your church is looking for a ladies' day speaker, please feel free to contact me by e-mail: *ksheltonauthor@gmail.com.*

www.ingramcontent.com/pod-product-compliance
Lightning Source LLC
Chambersburg PA
CBHW080952020726
47505CB00009B/2173